DEEP IN LOVE

NICOLE CUBBA

Developmental Editing by Kara Merideth (Kat's Literary Services)

Line and Copy Editing by Brazen Hearts Authors Services

Cover Art by Summer Grove Illustrations

Interior Illustrations by Sydney Bell, SLB Art Co.

ISBN: 979-8-9991118-1-4

CONTENTS

Epigraph	VIII
Dedication	IX
Chapter 1	1
Chapter 2	11
Chapter 3	25
Chapter 4	35
Chapter 5	43
Chapter 6	49
Chapter 7	61
Chapter 8	69
Chapter 9	77
Chapter 10	83

Chapter 11   91

Chapter 12   103

Chapter 13   111

Chapter 14   121

Chapter 15   131

Chapter 16   137

Chapter 17   149

Chapter 18   157

Chapter 19   169

Chapter 20   179

Chapter 21   187

Chapter 22   197

Chapter 23   205

Chapter 24   215

Chapter 25   227

Chapter 26   237

Chapter 27   247

Chapter 28   259

Chapter 29   269

Chapter 30   277

Chapter 31   287

Chapter 32   297

Chapter 33   307

Chapter 34   315

Chapter 35   323

Chapter 36   331

Epilogue   338

Acknowledgements   347

About the author   351

DEEP-SEA CREATURES

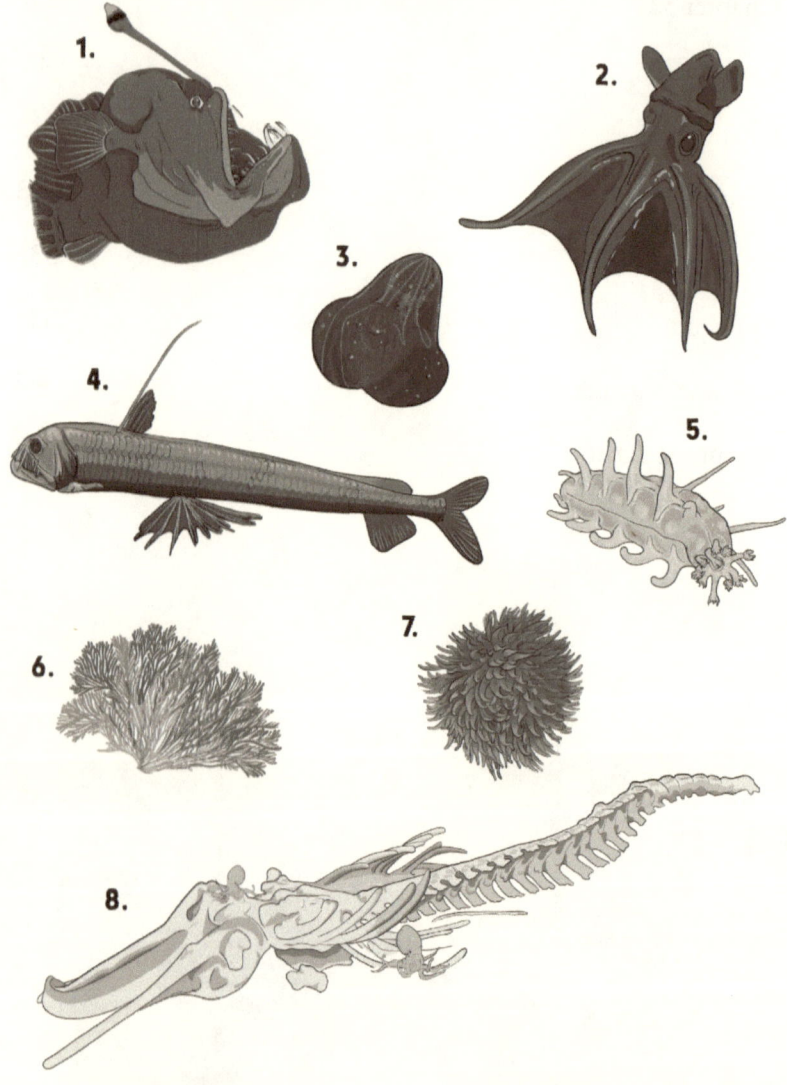

1. Anglerfish
2. Vampire Squid
3. Bloody-Belly Comb Jelly
4. Pacific Viperfish

5. Sea Pig
6. Bamboo Coral
7. Pom Pom Anemone
8. Whale Fall

"Nothing is easier than to admit in words the truth of the universal struggle for life, or more difficult—at least I have found it so—than constantly to bear this conclusion in mind."
—**Charles Darwin**

For everyone who works in STEM and continues to fight the good fight.

CHAPTER 1

CHARLIE

A cold sweat breaks out across my brow as I stare at a sea of apathetic faces, each student counting down the minutes until the break between summer courses begins. A solitary hand rises, and my mouth turns chalky.

"Yes?"

Oh, Neptune. Please *ask a simple question.*

"So, like, evolution happens because we have sex?"

I glance at the clock hanging on the back wall of the sprawling lecture hall. Two measly minutes before nine a.m., the time I am no longer obligated to fill in for my advisor's course.

One additional slide about selective mating could have prevented this question, thus saving my sanity, but I didn't want to drag the eight a.m. class out any longer than necessary.

Take the teaching position, they said. *Mentoring the next generation of scientists will be fulfilling,* they said.

Poor decision on my part because now I have to explicate that evolution is not parallel to Pokémon, and we, as humans, do not level up when we jump into bed with someone.

If that were the case, most people would *devolve* after a hookup.

"I-I'm sorry, could you clarify your question?"

Several heads turn to the student in the last row, with his baseball cap hung low on his forehead. He repeats the question.

His misinformed idea of evolution would almost be funny if I wasn't caffeine deprived and squirming beneath the attention of two hundred undergraduate students.

I don't teach large lectures—not my circus—but my PhD advisor, Cheryl, asked me to fill in at the last moment, and my lack of work-life boundaries means I agreed, even though I'm dying inside.

"Yeah, so when *people*"—he means himself—"have sex, they evolve?"

Is there a polite way to say "What a stupid question to ask" without facing the wrath of my advisor? She knows who she asked to fill in for her, but I don't anticipate the response would be well received, regardless of if it was justifiable.

I'm already in choppy waters after receiving a few negative reviews from students who cheated in the biology lab I teach. They couldn't fathom why I wouldn't budge on my grade of a big, fat zero.

If you're going to cheat, the least you can do is remove the AI chat prompt you copied and pasted. Instead of taking the zero, moving on, and accepting the option of makeup points in the form of cleaning out the lab, they complained to Cheryl and called me a "horrible TA with an attitude problem" and a "nasty hag who needs to pull the stick from my ass."

I fiddle with the small smoky quartz hanging around my neck, hoping the patience the stone claims to bring will wash over me like a lapping wave along a sandy shoreline.

"Not quite," I counter, and the kid frowns. "Evolution revolves around the idea of natural selection, where select individuals in a population possess traits better suited for survival. Those individuals pass advantageous traits to their offspring, who are now better adapted to survive until the trait becomes common among the population and they evolve. Does that help?"

He nods, but his disappointment is evident in the down curl of his mouth. He wanted to power up like a Pokémon, and I single-handedly crushed his every hope and dream.

"Midterms will be graded by the end of the week. I'll see you all after summer recess."

I slap my laptop closed and shove it into my tote bag, then race to the coffee shop directly off campus before I'm asked anymore questions that could send me to an early grave, right beside Charles Darwin.

Charlie Bowen: Death by stupid question.

I can see the words etched into my tombstone.

The University of Rhode Island is quiet as I hurry across the main lawn. A few students are scattered beneath trees, lounging on blankets, but the majority are gone for the summer. Only university staff, postgraduate students, and undergrads taking intensive courses—like Cheryl's Fundamentals of Evolutionary Biology—are still on the quaint campus.

Bright-yellow paneling and the cobalt-blue door of the coffee shop come into view, and I sigh with relief as the air-conditioning hits my skin and the aroma of roasted coffee beans fills my nostrils. *Home sweet home.* The worn-down wooden tables and colorful metal chairs are uncharacteristically empty, except for the economics professor who should have retired three years ago but refuses to leave.

I respect him. *The man* told him to retire, and he told *the man* to buzz off. He lifts his newspaper in greeting, then returns to the daily crossword. He's the type of person I want to be in fifty years: stubborn to my core but so intelligent that I can do what I want, and no one can say jack shit.

"Oh, Charles! Hello," Amy sings, leaning over the glass display full of mouthwatering pastries. Her curly bright-pink hair defies gravity as she slides a latte toward me.

Fondness settles beneath my diaphragm for my favorite barista, roommate, and platonic soulmate. We've been inseparable from the day we met in the women's bathroom in the biology building, and I wouldn't have it any other way. She was a much-needed light when there was only darkness in my life.

"God, Ames, I could marry you," I moan, sipping on the latte, which is exactly how I like it: four shots of espresso, very little milk. "It's been a long day."

Amy arches a brow, the fuchsia stone in her eyebrow jiggling with the movement. "Charles, it's only nine a.m."

I roll my eyes.

Two years of friendship, and I haven't been able to shake the silly nickname. My mild (see also: massive) obsession with Charles Darwin—world-renowned naturalist and all-around badass scientist—and my full name, Charlotte, gave her the fodder she needed to cultivate the *highly creative* nickname. My ensuing annoyance only added fuel to her fire, and now I will forevermore be her *Charles*.

My beloved Charles, she says when she wants something to go her way.

It works nearly every time.

"And the three hours I've been awake have felt like a million years." I drop my voice. "A student asked me if we evolve after having sex like we're Pokémon."

Amy gasps, then releases a booming laugh. She slaps the countertop a few times before she composes herself and pulls a lemon poppyseed muffin from the display. Dr. Yu—the economics professor—gives us an odd look before returning to his paper.

"You need this. You have grumpy face this morning."

She mimics a frown, her lips pursed cartoonishly and a deep V etched between her brows. Her interpretation elicits my own frown.

That is not how I look.

I steal a glance at my reflection in the display case. Okay, fine. Maybe it's an accurate impersonation.

"It's rude to call customers grumpy," I say, but snatch the muffin away. She grins broadly, my glare sliding off her shoulders. If I'm a storm cloud, Amy is my ray of sunshine.

"You got free coffee *and* a muffin, so I can call you whatever I want. You're my grumpy Charles." Her fingers hit my cheeks, tugging my lips into a forced smile. "I love you just the way you are."

Her words strike a chord, and I bite back the tears that spring to the surface. I don't want to cry, not here—or anywhere else, for that matter—so I mumble "I love you, too" before claiming a table in the back.

I drop the stack of midterms I need to grade onto the table, allowing them to act as an escape from the eddy of insecurity Amy conjured by telling me she loves me. She offers the words so freely, untethered by the weight of uncertainty.

I don't say it to hear it back. I say it because I mean it, she told me once, which promptly brought on an onslaught of unwelcome feelings and thoughts.

She has the emotional freedom I envy.

I'm midway through the ninth exam when my phone dings and I'm greeted by every PhD student's worst nightmare: a cryptic email from their advisor.

Are you free to meet at 3 on Wednesday? My office. -Cheryl.

It's a question, but nothing about its brevity suggests it's optional.

My fingers tingle as I respond, confirming I can meet with her, before I descend into a death spiral.

"Fucking hell," I whisper. My to-do list is ten miles long; I have lab work I've been pushing off for weeks, I'm far from addressing Cheryl's last comments on my thesis, and I still have forty exams I need to grade before Friday. Meeting with Cheryl in two days does not give me time to complete my list so she doesn't believe I'm lazy or inept.

Anxiety settles in nicely, right beside her old friend, self-doubt. The two of them are a deadly duo.

"What's going on over there?" Amy's gentle voice slices through the fog, and she bounds over, slipping into the seat across from me. Her eyes soften with concern as I pick at my nail polish, the once sparkly purple now chipped and littering the pile of exams.

Gah. I hate that look.

"Cheryl emailed me."

"So? She does that all the time."

While that's true, and Cheryl is notorious for sending too many emails, they're often lengthy and full of detail. This one is brief, and that's what sets me on edge.

I flip my phone so she can decipher the tone for herself.

"Oh."

One syllable with a thousand meanings.

The bell above the door chimes before Amy can add more, and she darts back to the counter.

My head lifts on instinct as two young girls, no older than thirteen, enter the coffee shop, but they falter a step when we make eye contact.

And just like that, the lemon poppy seed muffin I ate churns in my gut.

They each steal an uncomfortable peek at the brutal scar slashing across my forehead and down along my right eye socket, where it ends below my cheekbone. It's raised where the uneven edges meet unmarked skin, and even years later, it's still a deep mauve. The people close to me—Amy, my family, Cheryl—make it easy to forget about the scars that mark my skin, but strangers gawk without shame or remorse.

People believe they're subtle with their glances, but each one burns like acid.

I dip my head to hide my trembling chin, but it's futile, so I pack my things and disappear out the door. I've tried every remedy available to improve my appearance. Steroid injections. High-end makeup. Hell, I even cut my own bangs on a particularly bad night.

It didn't conceal the scar, but at least for six months, people fixated on my horrifying bangs instead.

Some aspects of the accident's aftermath have been easier to accept than others. I can handle aching joints before a treacherous rain and the uncomfortable pat down from TSA after I set off the metal detector. I've learned to manage my arthritis and banished my fear of driving, but I haven't overcome the hurdle of my image. The scars are a soft spot—an insecurity so raw, even a look or comment causes an ache in my chest.

A balmy morning breeze rustles my hair as I head toward the biology building. Large glass windows and brick-red eco-conscious paneling—a juxtaposition to the older stone buildings surrounding it—come into view, and I pick up speed, rushing to my desk to see if Willy Wonka left a surprise for me.

Every morning, there's a single dark-chocolate square, filled with gooey caramel, sitting on my desk.

I don't know who leaves them, or why, but I refuse to look a gift horse in the mouth, especially when it's a bright moment in my day. On particularly bad days, when the universe has cursed me, an afternoon treat will appear. I try not to think about how the mystery person knows I'm having a rough day, but rather just appreciate the kindness.

The chocolate, wrapped in blue foil, sits on my desk above a pile of strewn papers and crinkled sticky notes. I scarf it down in one bite.

Sometimes I wish I knew the secret identity of my Willy Wonka, because on days like today, when the world is heavy and every task feels impossible, the kind gesture reminds me there are slivers of light in every rainstorm.

A soft hum cuts through the fog of my sugar-addled mind.

Peeking around my monitor, I'm greeted by an all-too-familiar, cocky smile from Mateo Alvarez—fellow PhD candidate, thorn in my side, and, clearly, the universe's favorite.

He's been gifted every trait required to survive *and* thrive in our world. His scientific work is inspired—even if it gives me an ulcer to admit it to myself—and he skates through life with a level of confidence I could never achieve. Charles Darwin would take one look at Mateo and scribble down "marvelous specimen of a man" in his notebook.

Pisses me off.

On the flip side, I defy his idea of evolution. I was not adapted to survive, and yet, here I am, alive and kicking.

Not by choice.

I can't be an evolutionary biologist and disregard the idea of natural selection. That would be parallel to an assassin saying they don't believe in murder. The juxtaposition is otherworldly. But thanks to modern medicine, my mother's iron will, and a dozen pins and plates keeping me in one piece, I'm here to disappoint Charles, right beside tea sachets and unnatural rates of extinction.

When we meet one day, I'll apologize profusely.

I'm not the only one defying his work, though. The other sycophant blatantly ignoring well-established theories?

None other than Mateo: the most arrogant man on the planet and a fossil fuel supporter (not confirmed, but I have a hunch). He's six feet, two inches of *I'm smarter than you,* with an infuriatingly attractive Spanish accent.

What theory has he thrown in the trash? That Satan doesn't exist. He does, and Mateo is his chosen corporeal form.

His deep laugh skitters down my spine, leaving goose bumps in its wake.

"Something funny, Mateo?"

He sets down his coffee mug, an ostentatious vessel with "world's best scientist" etched on the front. Whatever chump gifted it to him never met Charles or me, because he wouldn't even be the world's first- or second-best scientist.

His arms rise over his head, and the crisp hem of his linen shirt rises, offering a glimpse of his lower stomach and the dusting of dark hair that trails down his toned stomach. My heart races as I follow the path down to his waistband.

Do not look at his zipper.

I look at his zipper.

My breath hitches as I lose control of my thoughts, my imagination running around like a wild animal, creating images of him without *any* clothing.

Ripping my gaze north, I find Mateo watching me, watching him. His lips tug up in a lazy, knowing grin.

Heat floods my cheeks—from anger, naturally.

He is exasperatingly sexy, emphasis on the first part. Worse, he knows he's attractive, and he flirts with me like it's a game to him. A way to establish his academic dominance. Fluster me into making a mistake.

I see right through his malarkey.

When we first met, I was foolish enough to believe we could be friends, but that dream died a brutal death after he won an award for best poster presentation at our first marine genomics conference. I was awarded *second* place, and his smarmy smile when they handed him the certificate hammered the final nail in our friendship coffin.

That day, he became my academic enemy.

"Just you, bruja," he purrs. His tone is low and raspy and makes me want to throw something against the wall.

I hate the nickname and how he mocks the crystals and essential oils by calling me a witch. They offer me a sense of peace, and every time he belittles them, it grates my nerves a bit more.

Besides, Amy and I tried to curse him with bad hair forever after a night of drinking wine coolers, but our spell failed, which means I am not a witch.

Who the hell even has hair that always looks that good?

I tap my Charles Darwin bobblehead, intent on ignoring Mr. Perfect Hair for the rest of the day, but he moves around my computer to wink at me. It only happens for one second, maybe two, but I get lost in the flecks of gold in his irises.

When I return to the real world, Mateo's grin is shit-eating.

"Do you think I'm pretty, Charlie?" he croons, batting his eyelashes.

I scoff, clamping down on my lip to fight the awkward blush that's creeping up my neck. Finding Mateo pretty and *liking* Mateo are two entirely different things. I wish my vagina understood what my brain does. Instead, she is a cavewoman.

"I think you're maddening," I grumble, but by the way his head tips back in laughter, my words don't land how I want them to.

Annoying asshole.

Chapter 2

CHARLIE

"Have you seen my top? The purple one that makes my boobs *pop?*"

Amy darts in and out of view, lifting throw pillows and seat cushions to find her favorite shirt. Midterms cover our thrifted rug on the living room floor, and she bends down to check beneath the papers.

"Hanging above the washer."

Amy and I live in a perfect, harmonious ecosystem; she misplaces something, and I tell her where she left it. She zips back and forth between the living room and the full-length mirror in my bedroom.

"Whatcha doin', Ames?" I ask, tossing another paper into the completed pile and treating myself with a piece of chocolate.

Complete a midterm. Eat chocolate.

It's how I keep my brain from rotting.

"It's trivia night at Bongos." She peeks around the corner. "You're going to come, right?"

The to-do list I wrote after Cheryl's email sits by my laptop, none of the items crossed off. Rather, I continue to add tasks in fear they will be the topic of her cryptic meeting.

There's no space in my schedule to pencil in "annihilating middle-aged men in trivia." My silence is answer enough, and Amy flops onto the floor and steals my grading pen—the perfect shade of blue—and taps it against my forehead.

"We've talked about this," she begins, winding up to start the same lecture she gives me every time I decline an invite. "There's a life waiting for you outside of the lab."

She sighs deeply like she always does when we have this uncomfortable chat; the one where she tells me my achievements do not define my worth and I ignore how her words strike a chord.

It's easy to get lost in my work. There's almost a rush of oxytocin when I achieve something great. It's the one aspect of my life I'm proud of.

I scramble for a rebuttal, but Amy has heard every excuse under the sun and has every counter argument locked and loaded, so instead, she shoves a piece of chocolate into my mouth.

"Wait here. I bought you something to wear." She pops up from the floor and sprints into her bedroom, while I chew the treat I was force-fed. Amy returns with a small bag.

"I don't want to go."

"No, you don't want to be seen."

Fuck, I hate how her words peel back every hardened layer I've created to protect myself.

When I first left the hospital, I hid away. Didn't leave my house until I moved from Philadelphia to Rhode Island for graduate school. In lectures, I would sit at the back of the class and avoid conversation. My groceries were ordered online and left outside my door. Every invitation to birthday parties or game nights was met with excuses and refusals. I was a hermit.

The only event I mustered up the courage to attend was the new student mixer, and I went partially to assuage my parents' concern. It's where I met Amy.

She found me in the bathroom, tears streaking my cheeks and wine covering my dress. One look at my mess and she leaped to action, dabbing away the wine with her stain stick and chatting away about the horrible date she had left.

She appeared when, more than anything else, I needed a friend.

Three weeks later, she moved into my two-bedroom apartment and brought life and love into the space when it was barren and cold.

It *has* gotten easier to exist in the public eye, but I'm not choosing to do so voluntarily.

Amy sees all, including the way my lip curls into a snarl at her statement. But she ignores my disdain and pulls a white linen long-sleeved top from the bag.

"It covers most of your scars, but it's thin enough that you won't get hot," she explains as she offers the shirt. The fabric is soft beneath my fingertips, and emotion clogs my throat. "Go put it on."

I'm halfway to my room when Amy adds, "And those cute jeans that make your butt look good!"

I change into the outfit she demanded, and for the first time in ages, I can hear it: the small, nearly silent voice in my mind saying I'm pretty. It's been ages since I heard her voice. The thought alone is enough for tears to form, but I sniff them away and smooth the wrinkles from the fabric. I spin left, then right, examining the outfit in the mirror.

It's fragile, but the foreign excitement of going out takes root. I'm running my fingers over the sleeves for the third time when Amy appears in my doorway and wolf whistles.

"Hottie on aisle four," she yells, before launching to wrap her arms around me in an odd hug. Once again, I'm left without words, unable to express my thoughts.

I've never been great at sharing how I feel or unpacking my emotions. With Amy, I don't need words. She understands everything I'm unable to say.

Her head falls onto my shoulder.

"Do you want to talk about it?" she whispers.

"Maybe tomorrow."

It's the same response I offer every time she asks. I don't want to burden her with my thoughts. She'll take on my emotions, try to carry my baggage, and she doesn't deserve the weight on her shoulders.

I don't miss the disappointment that flickers in her eyes.

Maybe one day I'll work up the courage to tell her what rattles in my mind, but today is not that day.

Tugging on a loose strand of my hair, she allows the moment to fizzle away.

"How about I help you grade a few papers before we destroy people in trivia?"

It would save me loads of time, but something stops me from accepting her help. Maybe it's the excited gleam in her eye or my sliver of self-confidence in this outfit, but I slide my to-do list into the cavern of my mind.

It can give me debilitating anxiety tomorrow.

"Why don't we go now and get a good table?"

Her brows rise in shock. "I know you're stressed. We don't have to go early."

"I want to spend time with my best friend."

A coral blush spreads across her cheeks, but she sprints to put on her shoes and grab her purse. She corrals me out the door like a border collie, afraid I might change my mind, but for the first time in forever, I want to go out.

"Charles, you're staring."

"I'm trying to melt him with my laser eyes," I amend, swirling my tongue through the air to find my straw. If my focus falters, the lasers won't disintegrate him.

Amy and I are hidden by dim lighting, perched at a high-top table in the back of Bongos, a local college bar.

Cheap tropical decor and signed dollar bills plaster the walls, and too-loud Jimmy Buffett filtering from old speakers drowns out the sound of chatter and shouted drink orders. Several groups settle in for trivia night and half-off drinks, but I cannot waste away in Margaritaville while my enemy encroaches on my territory.

Amy follows my line of sight until she's also watching Mateo from across the bar, laughing with his friend. "I'll never understand why you don't like him. He's kind and his accent is sexy."

It is *not* sexy. It makes my skin tingle—not in a seductive way, but rather like there are a million tiny venomous spiders roaming along my skin, poised to attack. His accent aside, Bongos is *my* bar. This is my kingdom, where I rule over all my other plebeians and show them who the queen of trivia is: Charlotte Louise Bowen.

"Do I need to pull out my list?"

"Have you added any new insane reasons?"

I shake my head. It's still the same.

Ruined my dress with red wine and ran away rather than apologize.

Has more publications than me.

Mocks my hobbies.

Rules over hell.

Has annoyingly perfect hair.

"That's what I thought. Maybe you see what you want to instead of what you're meant to," Amy says, fiddling with her flamingo earring. I pause my laser attack to school my best friend on why Mateo is, for a lack of better words, the most exacerbating human ever.

"We've been over this, Ames. The accent is to distract you from his true occupation as overlord of the underworld."

His coffee-hued hair, just long enough to run your fingers through, and deep emerald eyes, bright like a rainforest, are a mask. Behind it is a teasing, cocky know-it-all who finds joy in one-upping me at every turn.

Mateo may have been appealing once, long, long ago, but that was before two years of sharing an office space, teasing comments, and his total annihilation of my favorite sundress.

A ruckus at the front of the room drags my attention away from reciting my list.

"We have an incredible turnout tonight," the announcer booms into the microphone, "but not enough tables, so if you're at a table with empty seats, please raise your hand."

Amy waves hers high in the air like she's on a deserted island and spotted a plane. It's all I can do to stay in my chair while I yank her arm back to earth.

"Put your hand down," I hiss. I don't want to share a table with random people who might steal our answers. While I'm proud I left the apartment, and there have been zero crippling thoughts since we arrived, I am still here to win.

"Too late," Amy sings, waving at whoever she summoned. My heart skips as Mateo and his friend walk toward our table.

"What have you done?"

"We know them. It's better than strangers."

That's not true, not in the slightest.

I cling to the black tourmaline crystal hanging on my neck. *Protect me,* I plead to the stone, *guard me against Mateo and his charming smile.*

"Tired of staring from across the bar?" Mateo's raspy voice travels along my spine, and the blood drains from my face. I flounder for a response, which is exactly what he wants if the tilt of his lips is any indication. "I've told you before, bruja, you can stare all you want."

In a moment of sheer insanity, I take him up on his offer, drinking him in.

Keep your enemies close, right?

Starting at his worn brown leather boots, I leisurely drag my focus north, over the perfectly pressed chinos and cornflower-blue button-down with the top two buttons loose, revealing his sun-bronzed skin and a splatter of chest hair. I pause on the corded muscles of his forearms before moving to his soft cheekbones and supple lips hiding behind a five-o'clock shadow. When I meet his emerald gaze, it's smoldering, and the intensity nearly knocks me from my barstool.

He's so attractive it pisses me off, irrationally so.

"Like what you see?" he questions, but his teasing demeanor has vanished, and I don't know what to do with that, so I bite my lip. I'm not a liar, but I am *not* going to admit to Mateo that his appearance does some odd, medically concerning things to my nether regions.

His smile slips, only for a second, but I catch it before he plasters on another—a different one—for my best friend.

"Hi, Amy." He pauses, surveying her hair. "New color?"

"Stained the bathtub pink," she admits, twirling a curl around her finger.

No matter how many chemicals we threw at the stain, the acrylic is permanently stained a soft shade of pink. I say it's an upgrade from the melancholy beige, but I'm not sure our landlord will agree.

"This is Oliver. We were roommates in undergrad. He's visiting from London."

Mateo gestures to the man beside him, a tall blond with blue-gray irises framed by round metal-rimmed glasses. Amy glances at me, imperceptible to the men standing before us, but it conveys one clear message: she's fallen in love.

"I'm also the reason he's made it this far in life," Oliver says with a crisp British accent.

Consider my interest piqued. "What do you mean?"

"It's not really—" Mateo starts, but I cut him off. He will not ruin my opportunity to dig up dirt on him.

"Don't be rude. Let Oliver tell his story."

Oliver laughs and raises a brow, and Mateo sighs but gestures for him to continue. "First weekend of classes, there was a pool party off campus, where I met Mateo. Only, he was piss drunk, lost his initial roommate, and had switched to exclusively speaking Spanish." Amy giggles, but my focus is locked on Mateo, who's shaking his head. "I babysat him while he stumbled into a McDonald's and inhaled twenty chicken nuggets, and then made sure he got home. He moved into my dorm room a week later, and I've taken care of him ever since."

Huh. That story is more endearing than embarrassing.

"That's not how I remember it," Mateo grumbles.

"You don't remember *any* of it." Oliver turns to Amy and me. "It's lovely to meet you both."

"Amy Callagan." She extends her hand, clasping Oliver's and shaking aggressively. "So nice to meet you. I'm Amy."

"So you've said." He slides onto the barstool beside her. "Oliver Beauford-Taylor."

The two get lost in conversation, and I swirl my straw, focused on the ice cubes in my cup rather than the awkward silence between Mateo and me.

He mimics my action, batting his straw back and forth, when a droplet flies out of the glass.

"Be careful with that drink, Mateo. I would hate to lose *another* outfit."

He twirls the paper umbrella in his fruity cocktail, then stabs a cherry and pulls it between his teeth.

Neptune, save me.

The bar spikes twenty degrees, and I kick my feet beneath the table to create a breeze to my flushed skin.

His throat bobs in my periphery as he gulps down the liquid, but I study a dollar bill on the wall to prevent myself from fixating on the concerningly erotic action.

"Better?" he asks, swiping a rogue drop of liquid from the corner of his mouth with his tongue.

It's possible I track the way it darts out, how it drags along the seam of his lips. It's also possible someone put crazy juice in my glass, because under no circumstances should I be admiring Mateo's lips.

"I like the top," he murmurs, low and deep, before reaching out his hand, hovering it over my wrist. When I make no protest—how could I when my throat is dry and his gaze is heavy on my skin?—he gently runs his fingers along the fabric, his thumb grazing the bare skin on my inner wrist.

I snatch my hand away, the spot where he touched me ablaze.

Why the fuck am I flustered?

The remainder of my drink slides easily down my throat, and I scurry away to the bar to get another margarita before the competition begins. I'm going to have to get plastered in Margaritaville to get through this night.

Our answer sheet lies on the chipped wooden high-top when I return. Amy is in full flirtation mode, and based on how Oliver leans into her, they're both a lost cause to help.

Mateo glances in their direction before he makes a face, and I have to hide a small laugh behind a cough. Amy stole my spot to sit closer to Oliver, so I slide onto the barstool beside Mateo and pretend my head doesn't dizzy from his cologne.

He scribbles on the top of the answer sheet.

Charles Darwin's Bitches.

This time, I can't stop the laugh that bubbles from my chest or ignore how my heart skips when Mateo responds with his own.

"Looks like it's just the two of us," he says, bumping my shoulder. "Think you can survive without falling in love with my intellect?"

"Neptune on a cracker, you are full of yourself," I mumble, snatching the paper away. "They don't call me the queen of trivia for nothing, Mateo."

"Queen of trivia, huh? Do you need a king by any chance?"

I roll my eyes, ignoring his teasing, and the first question is called out.

"Who is the 'king of football'? Or soccer, for us Americans."

The blood drains from my face. Not a great start. I know very little about sports. I tap the pen against the table, scouring the corners of my mind for an answer.

"Well?" Mateo asks, drawing his lower lip between his teeth. "Got the answer?"

"You know I don't."

"Good thing we're a team." Mateo pulls the pen from my hand and writes in the answer. "It's Pelé."

I click my tongue, pretending I know who that is, but I make a mental note to search him tonight at home, because there is no way I am asking Mateo to enlighten me.

The questions fly, and we find a rhythm, competing to answer the question before the other. Occasionally, only Mateo knows the answer, but glee floods my system when the question is about the greatest boy band to ever exist.

"What are the names of the five members of One Direction?" the announcer asks, and Mateo's face falls how mine did earlier.

I seize my opportunity.

"It's time to woo me with your intellect," I say, offering the pen.

"Bruja."

"Mateo."

We face off in an epic stare down before he sighs in defeat.

"If you're going to be the king of trivia, you have to know the five members of the greatest boy band to ever grace the human species."

Mateo huffs. "Just write it down."

"I need to bask in this moment." I lean back, throwing my arms wide and pretending the warmth of the sun's rays are hitting my skin. When I rise, Mateo wears a goofy smile. "What?"

He shakes his head. "Nothing."

It didn't feel like *nothing*, but I let it go and list out the names. "Harry, Niall, Louis, Zayn, and Liam."

He scribbles them down while I wonder if the rare smile he offered me will reappear.

The last question is called out, which Mateo and I both know, and we impatiently wait as the announcer tallies the score. The silence between us isn't awkward like earlier, rather anticipatory for our impending victory.

He reaches our table and offers the second-place prize: a twenty-five-dollar gift card.

"Congrats. You came in second!"

His cheeriness to our devastating loss rubs me the wrong way. Second place is just first loser.

That's not right. From the huffing, puffing, and groaning I heard around the bar, this was a tough night for others, meaning Mateo and I should have won.

"What do you mean we placed second?" Mateo asks, full of disbelief.

The announcer gives us a dumb look. "Someone answered correctly more than you."

"Who?"

As much as it pains me to admit, Mateo and I absolutely killed it. The only questions we missed were obscure, pre-1975 pop-culture facts, and neither Mateo nor I were alive in that era.

No one here should have been able to beat us.

The announcer scans his sheet. "Charlie and Mateo's worst nightmare. Odd name."

"*Excuse me?*" My voice raises two octaves.

I glance to where Amy and Oliver traveled after complaining that Mateo and I were too competitive. We both scoffed, proving their point, and they've been there ever since. They're both lost in conversation and unlikely to be our enemies.

"What the..." Mateo trails off. "Can you point them out?"

We follow the announcer's hand, which points at a couple on the opposite side of the room, hidden in the shadows. They peek out of the booth, and that's when I spot my advisor, Cheryl, and her husband, Dan, who is Mateo's advisor.

They wave, shit-eating grins on their faces. Cheryl winks and wiggles her eyebrows, and for the first time in two years, I agree with something Mateo says.

"Those two need to pay for this," he mutters as Cheryl mouths, *Better luck next time.*

I'm ready to confront our advisors when a body slams into mine from behind and Amy's distinct vanilla-cupcake scent fills the air.

"Did you win?" she yells, before leaning in close to whisper, "I think I'm in love with Oliver."

I offer her a fond, bemused smile. Amy falls in love with every-one she meets—a trait I envy. Oliver stands close to her, his palm splayed on the small of her back, as if he can't help but touch her.

He steals a peek at her ass when he thinks no one is watching, then *blushes*.

Go, Ames.

"Our advisors beat us," Mateo grumbles, an uncharacteristically annoyed tone in his voice. I can't help the cackle that tumbles out. His face freezes at the sound, like he can't believe what he's hearing, before he responds with one of his own.

"It's late," I say, unsure how to react, and throw a hand over my shoulder. "Time to go home."

"It was great to meet you, Charlie," Oliver says, before ensuring he has Amy's number. They hug, and it lingers long enough that Mateo makes another face—his nose scrunched and tongue pok-ing the inside of his cheek.

"See you later, bruja," he purrs as we weave through the crowd toward the exit.

Amy links her arm with mine. "Sorry I left you alone with Mateo."

The guilt in her voice is unmistakable, but as we walk back to our apartment, I admit something I'm not quite ready to accept. "I had fun. With Mateo, I mean. He's still aggravating, but he made a good partner."

She squeals, then throws her fist in the air.

"I fell in love, and you're learning to tolerate Mateo. That's a successful night."

"How was talking with Oliver?"

I listen to Amy recount their conversations, how he's a history buff and likes to run marathons. It's not until we're halfway home that it dawns on me. I spent the whole night without a single thought about people staring, and Mateo was likely the cause.

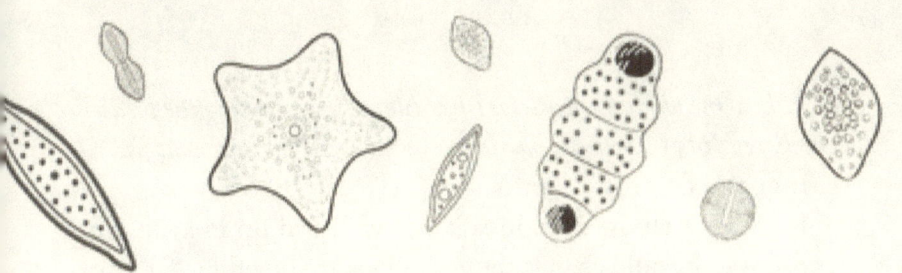

CHAPTER 3

MATEO

"It was only a matter of time before Elora fell for the charming pirate. Behind his hard exterior was a man desperate for someone to hold him close. She knew it in her heart."

What Elora should be concerned about is sexually transmitted diseases and her vitamin D intake. And I don't mean vitamin dick.

The historical romance drones on in my ear as I scrape soil from a tube and onto a weigh plate. Dump. Weigh. Put it in the dryer. Repeat.

I've been going through the motions for the last hour, completing each mundane protocol step while begrudgingly listening to Elora and her adventures with the rogue pirate who stole her away.

I'm seven chapters into the audiobook, and frankly, this feels like my abuela's version of payback for the last book I chose in our little two-person audiobook club. I found the nonfiction about Earth's history through fossils fascinating. She said it made her ears bleed.

Well, mine are suffering the same fate thanks to Elora's poor decisions.

"'Show me what the world is like,' Elora said, stroking the pirate's cheek, reveling in how his hardened skin grazed her innocent flesh."

Innocent flesh? Is she serious?

If I wasn't elbow deep in soil and wrapped up in a lab coat and gloves, I would change the audiobook to something far more stimulating, like the new one I bought about fungi communities.

Instead, I listen as Elora *explores* all the world can offer—on a boat in the middle of the sea in the 1800s, where she has no access to a shower, proper nutrition, or contraception. I doubt Elora and Dominic—the rogue pirate who *stole* her—are having any conversation about consent, prior partners, or pregnancy prevention.

I scribble down a note in my lab notebook to call my abuela and tell her this is by far the worst thing I've ever listened to, and I'm adding "morally questionable historical romances" to our list of banned genres, right beside "boring nonfiction."

We've listened to historical romance before, but those were outstanding, highlighting characters with complex backstories based on the era they were from. This book is a pile of trash, and my gut tells me she knows and it's why she chose it.

I release an exasperated sigh when Elora comments that she's experiencing new emotions around the pirate, but since I wasted twelve dollars on the audiobook, I'm going to listen to every second to get my money's worth.

It's impossible to hear anything over Elora's oblivious internal dialogue. *He doesn't want to show you the world, he wants under your petticoat. Get it together, girl.*

Her concerning choices make it easy for a pipette thief to enter the lab, sneak around, and steal the tool used to repeatedly measure small amounts of liquid. Unfortunately for her, her distinctive scent gives her away—cinnamon, clove, and something I can't quite place. I catch her reflection in the glass cabinet above me as she tiptoes toward the far bench where the repeat pipettor resides.

It's not the first time it's been stolen, disappearing for a day, then magically reappearing before a department-wide memo could be sent out.

As she scoots closer, her head swings like she's a meerkat wary of predators. I focus on my task like I'm unaware Charlie has slipped into the lab and is moments away from committing a scientific crime.

When her hand is inches from claiming her prize, I purr, "Hi, bruja."

She squeaks, her shoulders bunching to her ears as she rips her hand away from the pipette rack to glower at me.

"What are you doing?" I ask, innocence and faux confusion lacing my voice as I pause my audiobook.

Charlie sputters for a response, red creeping up her cheeks all the way to the tips of her ears. Her hands fly around before she glues them to her side.

"I was..." She trails off, searching the lab, looking anywhere but at the pipette. I lean back in my chair, pulling off my gloves to watch her flounder for an excuse like a fish out of water.

The skin beneath her right eye twitches, pulling on her scar, as she continues to scramble before her focus lands on a shelf of preserved specimens. She sticks out a finger, swiping it against the glass jar housing a juvenile giant Pacific octopus.

"Dust," she declares. "I'm checking for dust. And this place is riddled with it."

Her nose wrinkles before wiping her hand on her overalls.

"You came into my lab to check for dust?"

Dios, she is pretty.

Her legs stretch beneath her jean overalls, which are covered in a mosaic of quirky patches stitched into the fabric. She tugs at the frayed edges of her navy URI sweatshirt, covering the abundance of bracelets on her wrists, each a different color of the rainbow.

Piercings filled with colorful stones line her earlobes, framed by wild honey-blond hair.

But it's her eyes, the brightest shade of Caribbean blue, that captivate.

We engage in an epic stare down, like if we're locked in some weird tension, I won't notice her hand wiggling behind her back, blindly searching for her target. She draws her lower lip between her teeth, and my attention dips. Right as I shake the urge to pull her lip between *my* teeth, the pipette disappears.

"You know what," she says airily, "you're *right*. It's not my place to check the dust in your lab. If you want to keep an unclean space full of points of contamination, it's not on my conscience to stop you."

She crab walks toward the door, glowering at me like I'm an error her coding software spit out. Her steps are methodical and slow-moving to prevent her stolen goods from falling out of her back pocket, allowing me time to block the exit.

Charlie glares, crossing her arms over her chest, and my dick twitches.

I've been pining over Charlie Bowen since the day we met, and all she accomplishes with her razor-sharp looks is giving me a raging hard-on that I have to banish by reciting mundane lab protocols.

"Where are you going?" I force away a smile and press against the door. Her hand snakes behind her back and jiggles the doorknob.

She sniffles and fakes a sneeze. "Away from all the dust particles." Another sniffle. "Let me go."

"And if I were to ask you to...empty your pockets, would you be able to do that?"

Her face pales, but she doubles down.

"Absolutely not." She peels my hand away from the door, and my skin tingles as she shoves it to my side. Her touch lingers for a second too long, and then she rips her hand away like I've burned her. Clearing her throat, she says, "Now, if you're finished holding me hostage, I have tubes I need to fill and no undergrad to pawn the task off on."

Instead of letting her sneak past with her stolen treasure, I block the exit again and drop my voice to nothing more than a whisper.

"I've always had a thing for thieves," I tease, tugging at a loose strand of hair, which rewards me with one of her iconic glares—sharp, but intoxicatingly sexy.

"Good thing I follow the letter of the law," she says, her pitch an octave higher than normal.

Liar.

"Does that law condone the theft of lab equipment?"

I raise a brow, and Charlie sighs in defeat. "Six. Hundred. Tubes," she groans. "Some noob broke ours, which means I would have to pipette ethanol *six hundred times*." She raises the tool into the air like a scepter. "This bad boy will save me hours of work."

My chest aches as I suppress the urge to laugh, not because she's attempting to be humorous, but because she's naturally funny. Though maybe finding her hilarious is a by-product of a two-year-long crush, which grows daily. Regardless, when Charlie's around, it's difficult to do anything but smile.

She often frowns in response.

Charlie may be my favorite person, but I am not hers. I don't even crack the top ten, let alone get close to Sir Charles Darwin. Trying to bump him from the top spot is futile, but I've been aiming for a close second since we met.

I reach out a hand to bracket the doorframe, and Charlie slips below my outstretched arm, whooping in victory as she runs down the hall to her lab space, three doors away.

"I'll bring it back later," she yells.

I'm hot on her heels when a head of wild, spindly gray hair pops out of an office and stops me in my tracks.

"I thought I heard you. Do you have a minute?" Dan asks, his head tilting as I stand in the hallway, torn between chasing after my little criminal and engaging in conversation with my PhD advisor.

Unfortunately, the unexpected chat with Dan outweighs seeing Charlie's triumphant smirk.

"Sure."

I slide into his office, an untidy space cluttered with binders, old books, and half-broken machines he's convinced he can piece together into one semi-working machine. Last month, he patched together a fluorometer for cell counting, but its efficacy is questionable, and you have to caress the side of the machine and whisper sweet nothings for it to function.

It's temperamental but thrives on praise.

Kind of like Charlie, now that I think about it.

The thought pulls a small chuckle as I fall into the sunken armchair in the corner of the office.

"Do you have plans for the break?" he asks, shuffling through a stack of papers on his massive oak desk.

"Just catching up on lesson plans for the laboratory course and completing the extractions on the sediment samples taken from the hydrothermal vent systems."

"Quite right. It's going to have to wait." He extends a piece of paper, but it hangs in the air between us.

Dan's always been eccentric, as is his wife, Cheryl, and I admire that trait about him. It was one reason I chose to complete my PhD with him. He's laid back in his mentorship, allowing me the space to build my own schedule, and respects work-life boundaries, which I've worked hard to establish, otherwise it would take over my life.

The good outweighs the odd, so at times—like now—I look past his unconventional behavior.

With extreme trepidation, I take the proffered paper and scan the words at the top. The first sentence registers, and I reel back in shock. Air lodges in my throat as I read the rest of the printed email. My interest piques with a particular name—one that lights firecrackers in my chest.

"Is this real?"

Dan nods, brimming with excitement. "Do you want to go?"

"Is that a serious question?"

He laughs, but I elaborate, just to ensure there's zero confusion. "Of course I want to go."

"Great," he cheers, handing me a stack of papers and the lab credit card. "Book everything you need. Cheryl is going to meet with Charlie, and if she chooses to go after we discuss details, we can add her to the bookings."

"It's on her bucket list. She's going to say yes." I tap the logo on the top of the paper—a gray research vessel with the portholes shaped like starfish. It's the same logo drawn on the scientific bucket list Charlie has tacked on the wall beside her desk. "But it should be a surprise."

He nods in agreement. "I'll remind Cheryl to keep quiet until their meeting on Wednesday. She can be a blabbermouth when she's excited."

The papers are heavy in my hands as I leave his office and pack up my things at my desk. I'll have to hide from Charlie before her meeting, or else I may become the blabbermouth.

I'll watch her rustle through the papers on her desk, then I'll cave and tell her a secret she didn't even know I was hiding.

My resolve is weak around her, which is why the lab is always unlocked for her to steal the pipette whenever she needs.

"I need you to water Fergus while I'm gone," I say, tapping my fingers against the cold beer bottle as laid-back music plays in the background of Bongos.

"I visit you for a month after you *assured me* your schedule was lighter thanks to the summer break, and a week in, you're asking me to water your finicky fern while you're on a boat in the middle of the Pacific Ocean?"

"Fergus is not finicky," I chide, defending my baby. He's particular, and he has every right. He's had a difficult life, and I brought him back from the brink of death after I bought him for fifty cents at the hardware store.

Now Fergus is living his best plant life by the window in my apartment.

"Oliver, I—" I begin to apologize, but he cuts me off.

"I'll protect your plant with my life," he mocks, his snappy English accent adding to the comment. "And find ways to occupy my time now that you're ditching me for a fancy boat and unlimited time with your girl."

"She's not my girl," I grumble, taking a deep swig of my beer.

The words burn like hydrochloric acid.

Oliver squeezes my shoulder. "That could change. Three weeks at sea is a long time."

"It's been two years."

"And you haven't given up or moved on," he counters, like it sounds impressive rather than pathetic.

But he's right.

Two years of flirting with zero reciprocity, and yet, like a fool, I haven't given up. I've harbored the delusion that one day, Charlie will see me as more than her competitor or the guy who annoys her. Half the reason I still live in my world of ignorant bliss is I've never seen her with someone else.

Never heard her speak of a boyfriend or date. No photos on her desk. No one dropping by, except for Amy.

"Maybe it's time you tell her how you feel," he suggests, signaling to the bartender for another round. "Take the time to get to know each other."

"I know her."

"But does she know you?"

I pause long enough for him to know he struck a chord.

"Wow her with your personality," he says with a shit-eating grin, "because you're not going to win her over on looks alone." He slides a beer across the bar as he laughs at my frown.

"Very funny."

"I thought so." He stares down at his drink, before adding, "If you want to be seen, Mateo, then you need to stand in the spotlight, even if the light may burn your eyes."

"Is that your way of saying I need to buck up or shut up?"

He beams. "Precisely. Either tell Charlie you're into her—and have been for a *long* time—or chuck those feelings overboard and move on."

I sigh, picking at the label.

If only it were that simple.

Telling Charlie how I feel is easy on paper. But to stand in front of her and slice my chest open for her to root through my emotions and decide if they're up to par? Well, I don't know if I'm strong enough.

Because if I show her who I am, and she deems me unworthy, I don't think I could look her in the eye for the remainder of our long program.

CHAPTER 4

CHARLIE

There are *two* pieces of chocolate on my desk Wednesday morning, as if my mysterious Willy Wonka knew today was going to be a testament to my strength. I devour one and set the other aside for later when I'm nearing a bitch fit and need the sugar to calm my anxiety.

The last twenty-four hours have been a scramble to complete as many tasks as possible, and I need every minute until three p.m. to finish the last of the list.

I want to be as prepared as possible for my meeting with Cheryl, especially after trivia night. The last thing I want is for her to believe I neglect my work to go out to bars.

Falling into my chair, I filter through Cheryl's comments on our manuscript. I ignore the ones that require changing graphs—I do not have it in me today to battle with data analysis software—and make grammar and structural edits.

I'm halfway through the introduction, checking citations, when the silence hits me. It's never silent in the office, mostly because

Mateo hums while he works, much to my chagrin. But right now, it's too quiet.

I peek around my monitor, which I strategically placed to avoid looking at Mateo, to find his chair empty. His laptop is missing and there's no coffee mug on his drink coaster, meaning he hasn't arrived yet.

Mateo *always* arrives before I do, greeting me every morning with a cocky smile and a "Hi, bruja." It's become routine, which I thrive on, and now that I'm aware it's been broken, it's not settling well.

Ignoring my many tasks, I search for him so we can perform our song and dance, and I can move on with my life and stop thinking about where he could be or why he hasn't shown up this morning.

He's not in the lab, though I scare a poor undergrad. I search the common areas on the first floor, but there's no sign of his perfect, wavy hair. Midway through typing a panicked text message, I pause when his distinct humming filters from the kitchenette down the hall from our office.

I round the corner with the speed of a racecar at the Indy 500, and there he is, leaning against the counter, his strong fingers wrapped around his diatom coffee mug as he lifts it to his lips.

"Hi, bruja," Mateo says, and relief washes over me like a cool ocean wave, the odd riot in my stomach settling.

He's exactly how he always is. Loose linen button-down, rolled up to display the strong, sinewy flesh of his forearms. Perfectly pressed chinos, tight on his thighs. Rainforest-green eyes that glitter beneath the fluorescent light, and wavy, deep-brown hair, not a strand out of place.

I stand like an idiot in the small kitchen's entryway, staring at him. Why am I relieved to see him? That's not right. The unsettled feeling returns, but for a different reason.

"You're not at your desk."

Mateo's brow arches high on his forehead.

"Astute observation." He takes a languid sip of coffee. "Why have you been stomping around the building?"

I bite my lip so forcefully the metallic tang of blood hits my tongue. How could he have possibly known I was running around the building? I didn't see him anywhere, so how the hell did he see me?

"I don't stomp," I deflect. Let's hope this turns into an argument and he forgets about why I was stomping in the first place.

I'm not explaining to Mateo that I was looking for him because a small, irrational voice in my mind was worried that he was hurt or sick, and the thought unsettled me, so I had to search for him. I'm not unpacking that. Not with him, and especially not with myself. We'll consider it a reaction to my own trauma.

"You do."

That smug grin appears, and annoyance—a more familiar emotion—washes away my concern.

He assesses me as I linger in the doorway with no logical explanation for being in the kitchenette, so I feign nonchalance and stroll over to the fridge.

A thief has been stealing people's lunches, and if they took my—

"How are you feeling about your meeting with Cheryl?" Mateo asks, his voice holding an edge of excitement.

I slam the door shut. "What do you know?"

His lip quirks upward on the right side, which is his tell that he knows something. Anxiety churns in my gut.

Normally, I would write off Mateo's bizarre behavior and go about my business, but one thought has haunted me since her email Monday: I've disappointed her by not doing enough, or worse, doing everything poorly.

Did I fuck up and everyone knows but me? Did Cheryl mention my inadequacy to Dan, and now Mateo knows, too?

"Nothing." He says it with neutrality, but his lip twitches again. "Dan mentioned your meeting with her this morning, that's all."

I'm ready to hurl something at his perfectly symmetrical face. I've hit my threshold of overstimulation, and this might be the tipping point.

"Fine. Don't tell me."

The response is petulant, and so is my stomping as I exit the kitchenette, but I'm overwhelmed by the wave of self-doubt, the uncertainty of my meeting with Cheryl, and my unwanted concern for Mateo's well-being.

I'm halfway to my office when thick fingers curl around my bicep, halting my getaway.

"Charlie, are you all right?"

I stare down at his brown leather boots, weathered and wrinkled from continual wear.

What a loaded question.

Am I all right?

No.

I can't escape the swirling in my gut, the anxiety and trepidation. I want to be great—no, remarkable—and the pressure, the stakes I place on myself, threaten to consume me today.

Some days, I can meet the expectations head-on and tackle them, but on others, they pummel me until I'm ragged and defeated.

Today, I am being pummeled.

Mateo still has a hold on my bicep, and I gently release myself from his grip.

"I'll be fine."

"That's not the same as *being fine*," he retorts, and I don't know why, but that pulls a smile from my lips. Maybe it's because he didn't ask what's bothering me, or why, but instead pointed out a flaw in my logic.

I escape into the office and fall into my desk chair to hide from him and his suspicious behavior this morning.

Of course, he follows me and settles into his desk.

He hums while he works, flipping through papers and tapping against his laptop keys.

Settled in the normalcy, I find a steady rhythm and power through my tasks, checking them off one by one until I'm on the last of my list: my meeting with Cheryl.

I collect my things—laptop, notebook, water bottle—one by one to delay the inevitable, and Mateo pauses his work, rises from his seat, and bolts to the door.

As he disappears from view, he calls out, "Have fun in your meeting!"

It will be a miracle if I make it out without throwing up.

My foot taps beneath the oak desk in the middle of Cheryl's office. Towering bookcases span the back wall, overflowing with dusty textbooks and long-forgotten novels. Soft light filters through the window, cranking the heat in the room and worsening my anxiety sweats.

I glance down at my smartwatch. *3:04 p.m.*

The last four minutes have been my personal hell. I've watched in silence as Cheryl searches for her glasses, then her special pen, followed by her notebook.

If I didn't know any better, I would say she's stalling.

"I finished grading the midterms for BIO 201," I say to fill the quiet.

"That's great," she replies, laser-focused on the door.

A claw clip pulls back her salt-and-pepper hair, and though it's eighty degrees outside, she's wearing a purple turtleneck, paired with a chunky teal statement necklace. Matching orchid-purple glasses perch on the bridge of her nose as she reads something on her phone, huffs, then sets it down.

"And I addressed some of the comments on the manuscript. I'm still working on the statistics, but the introduction is done."

"Wonderful."

She isn't focused on me, but rather, continues to watch the door, like Bill Nye the Science Guy will spontaneously appear in the threshold.

Each passing second adds to the discomfort beating in my chest until I'm squirming in my seat.

Her phone dings, and she snatches it, reads a message, peers at me, and then responds on her phone.

Sweat dribbles down my back, and her manic smile aimed in my direction sends a tremor through my body. *Why is she looking at me like a villain in an action movie?*

The skin around my thumb stings as I scratch at my cuticle.

"Did you have fun at trivia with Mateo?" she asks, returning her phone to the table beside a small sign that reads "How can I kelp you today?"

"Huh?"

The muscles in my face defy my brain, and my jaw falls slack in bewilderment.

"It's great that you and Mateo are learning to get along."

The only response I can offer is a grunt, because I wouldn't say that we "get along." Trivia was a one-off where the need to crush the rest of the participants outweighed any animosity between us.

I pull out my notebook with flair, hoping it will inspire Cheryl to start the meeting.

"Was there a specific reason you wanted to meet?" I ask, flipping to a clean page. "Is it the manuscript? Lab work? The BIO 201 course?"

Am I spiraling?

Maybe.

"No. No. None of those things." She waves me off. "I'm just waiting for—" A knock rattles the door, and joy blooms on Cheryl's face as she calls out, "Come in!"

I'm ready to jump out of my skin, confused as hell, when I hear the two words that send me into a tizzy.

"Hi, bruja."

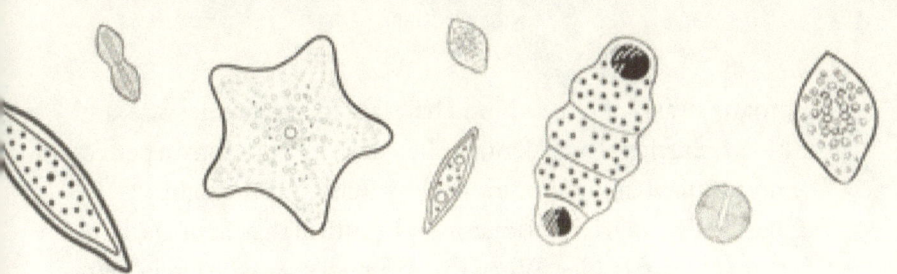

CHAPTER 5

MATEO

Charlie is super fucking confused. Mouth agape, rapid blinking, deer-in-the-headlights confused, and I want to kiss the befuddled look off her face.

Her notebook slips from her grip and tumbles to the floor, and she scrambles to retrieve it.

"Sorry we're late. The coffee shop was slammed."

Dan slips into the office and plants a wet, nauseating kiss to Cheryl's lips.

I drop an iced latte in front of Charlie, who still wears the adorable stunned look. She rubs an eyeball, blinks at the drink, then glares so forcefully the skin around her scar pulls taut as her eyebrows scrunch together.

"What are you doing here?" she hisses under her breath.

I ignore her. "I made sure Amy made your coffee so the ratio of espresso to milk was right."

She examines the to-go cup like it's a bomb, and I slide into the chair beside her. She tentatively lifts the drink to her lips. The caffeine hits her tongue, and the tension in her shoulders falls away.

A rogue strand of honey-blond hair falls in front of her face, and she blows, shifting the piece out of her view. Her lips form a perfect O, and I squirm in my seat, my cock twitching at the sight.

Charlotte Bowen is so distractingly beautiful that, at times, I lose function of my faculties. When she cornered me in the kitchenette this morning, I nearly spilled scalding coffee on myself from the shock of seeing her.

Cheryl and Dan whisper on the other side of the desk, and with every furtive look, Charlie descends deeper into a whirlpool of negative thoughts.

It happens often, and when it does, her hands begin to shake and her skin pales, darkening the pink of her scar.

"Mateo, what is happening?" Her question is accusatory, and I'm unable to hide my smile.

I spent my time at the library this morning, avoiding her so I wouldn't spill this secret, until her stomping around finally caught up to me. But I still managed to hold my tongue then, so I refuse to ruin the surprise now.

She pulls her lip between her teeth, and I avert my gaze. Thankfully, Dan clears his throat and draws her attention before I do something truly stupid—like kiss her.

"We're so glad you could make it," Cheryl starts, buzzing with enthusiasm.

"You said this was mandatory," Charlie grumbles under her breath.

Cheryl lifts a brow but is undeterred by Charlie's grumpy attitude.

"Dan and I have a very exciting, *very exclusive* proposal for you."

My knee bounces beneath the desk, excitement for Charlie coursing through my veins. This is on her scientist bucket list—number two, to be precise—and when she finds out, she's going to freak.

She glances in my direction, nerves radiating off her, and I offer a smile.

You know she's off-kilter if she's looking to *me* for reassurance.

My instinct is to take her hand in mine and offer her comfort, but it's not my place. The lines defining our relationship are odd. I could tell her that I'm into her—have been since the moment I saw her at the new student mixer—but the confession would catalyze a series of events I'm not sure I'm emotionally prepared to face.

I've perpetually flirted with her, hopeful that she would walk into our shared office space one day and flirt back, but she never has.

On a few rare occasions, I've caught her admiring me—at least, that's how it felt. But she's never expressed interest in *me*, and it continues to hold me back.

The limbo state is growing old, if I'm being honest.

"Okay?"

She picks at the sparkly purple nail polish on her finger, chips of paint decorating her jeans.

"We've been contacted by RogueWave Productions. Have you heard of them?" Dan asks. "They're well known for documentaries."

Dan and I had this conversation yesterday after I finalized the plane tickets and hotel bookings, but Charlie is still in the dark. It may have been a poor choice, given she looks like she may vomit.

"No..." Charlie trails off.

"You're going to be on TV," Cheryl blurts out, and dread settles in my stomach. We were supposed to sprinkle in the TV part but lead with the research vessel. There's also the small issue that the cabin only has one bed, but I am *not* poking that beast until I have to.

Hopefully someone will break the news to her, because I can't do it without conjuring dirty images of Charlie splayed out in the bed, naked and writhing beneath me, my name on her tongue.

"Hell no."

The words rip me back to reality, where Charlie's twirling a white-and-gray bracelet around her wrist, her nail polish completely demolished.

Dan's brow furrows, and I snake my hand beneath the desk to squeeze Charlie's thigh. I don't touch her often, because she despises me, and based on the look she's offering right now, she might hate me even more after today. Which is problematic because we're about to spend three weeks at sea together.

"Hear them out, bruja," I say, giving her muscles another squeeze. Her eyeballs bulge from her skull. Thin, dainty fingers grip mine with shocking strength and pry my hand off her thigh.

I cough to disguise my laughter.

"Jett Parks is funding the production of a documentary in the Monterey Bay National Marine Sanctuary. Cheryl and I were invited to collaborate as research advisors; however, we have a nonrefundable all-inclusive vacation in Bermuda," Dan says. "We suggested sending Mateo and you in our stead, and the production crew and Jett agreed. You're set to spend the next three weeks upon the SeaStar research vessel."

The room is silent, and Charlie spins in my direction, utter shock marking those pretty features. Disbelief shifts her irises to a stunning shade of bright blue.

"W-what?" She slides her shaky hands beneath her thighs. "I-I—SeaStar?" she stutters, and I offer her a moment to compose her thoughts.

"We have full access to the research lab and the sampling apparatuses on board, meaning we can collect soil and water samples." *Pause for dramatic effect.* "All for free."

It may be the most exciting aspect of the voyage, at least for a PhD student with a tight research budget.

"Free?" she croaks.

"Free," I confirm.

"If you agree—and we hope you do since Mateo already booked flights and accommodation—you'll spend the next three weeks identifying species and offering commentary on biological processes," Dan says.

Cheryl adds, "The documentary is called *Aliens of the Deep,* so your focus will be on deep-sea species."

I wish I could film Charlie's reaction, her expressions jumping between confusion, disbelief, concern, and my favorite, sheer joy.

"Who is Jett Parks?" she asks, stringing together her first full sentence.

"He's a tok-tiker instafluencer, I think," Cheryl says, and Charlie's lips quirk as she flips to a clean page in her notebook.

"He has a popular YouTube channel," I amend. "It started with pranks but now focuses on explaining odd or *alien* things about Earth." Charlie's eyebrow raises. "I googled him yesterday."

We all exchange a sly glance as we wait for her to say something. It was my suggestion to surprise her, given how badly she wants to go on the SeaStar vessel. Only one thing beats it on her scientist bucket list: meeting Charles Darwin. Unfortunately, it's incredibly unrealistic unless necromancy is real.

Charlie fans herself before grabbing her latte and sucking down the liquid in one gulp.

"What's the catch?" she asks.

"No catch," I respond, but Cheryl and Dan share a look of mischief. Charlie doesn't notice it, and I choose to ignore it.

They're the quirky married professors on campus, but they're also incredible advisors and brilliant researchers. Sometimes you have to ignore the weird looks for peace of mind, which is what I'm doing now.

"Sofía Martinez is part of the production crew and has been working with Mateo to ensure everything is set. They only agreed on Monday, so it's been a bit hectic," Cheryl explains. "Your flights leave Friday, and you board the ship Saturday morning."

Charlie scribbles down notes on the logistics, then grimaces as she asks, "Do we *have* to be on camera?"

"For the documentary, no, but for Jett's personal YouTube channel, it's a possibility. You could ask for him to exclude you, but from my understanding, it's supposed to be a behind-the-scenes thing," Dan says, and Charlie swirls her bracelet again.

A nervous tic.

Her eyes dart around like a cornered animal, so I deflect, throwing my arm over her shoulder and pulling her toward me.

"Just you and me, bruja."

She peels my hand from her shoulder, holding my wrist like it's a soiled diaper. God, she's funny, especially when she's not trying.

"We are going to be thick as thieves."

"Keep dreaming, Mateo."

Oh, I am.

Have been for two years, and this trip could be my opportunity.

It's time for Charlie and me to evolve. I'm tired of where we're at. The back-and-forth is fun, but I want more, or to know it's never going to happen.

Oliver's words bang around in my head. *You need to stand in the spotlight.*

I'm not sure I'm ready for a full confession, but maybe we can test the waters, get to know each other outside the daily stress of graduate school.

Despite her love for evolution and Charles Darwin, she despises change. Runs from it when necessary, and when she can't, she rages against it. But her beloved Charles said it best: *It is not the strongest species that survives, nor the most intelligent, but the one more responsive to change.*

Time will tell if Charlie is responsive or not, and if she is, well, then maybe this odd relationship will evolve into something more.

Something magnificent.

CHAPTER 6

CHARLIE

"What do I pack?" I scream over the early-2000s music blasting from the kitchen, where Amy is cooking dinner.

In reality, she's transferring frozen food from the baking sheet to a plate, but I don't comment on her idea of cooking as long as she shares.

The song's bass rattles the wall, and I'm sure we'll have a passive-aggressive note on our door for the sound, but the walls are thin. If I have to listen to my neighbors rock the bed every night, then they can listen to our perfectly curated playlist of pump-up jams.

"At least forty pairs of underwear," Amy yells, and I rush to my dresser and dump my bucket of granny panties into the large duffel bag on my floor. "What if you shit yourself a bunch?"

Fuck, so true.

The possibility that I become incontinent and soil myself isn't zero, thus all the underwear is coming with me.

It took two hours to recover from the shock of my meeting with Cheryl, Dan, and Mateo. I'm not sure I'm fully convinced any of this is happening. If it weren't for the contracts I signed and the plane ticket on my phone, I wouldn't believe it at all.

Three weeks on the SeaStar vessel is a dream come true. State-of-the-art research facilities, two remotely operated vehicles, submarines, and complete access to their labs. The only downside to the whole thing is that Mateo's involved, but even that disappointing fact isn't enough to squander my joy.

The last forty-eight hours since the meeting have zipped by in a blur, and now I'm panic packing only an hour before Mateo picks me up to head to the airport.

I shove a few pairs of pajamas into a packing cube, followed by a handful of tops and long pants for the days we're in the lab. With one swoop, I slide the crystals off my dresser and into a small pouch, then toss it into the duffel bag.

Amy bounds into the room, a platter of taquitos and chicken nuggets in her grasp.

"Eat," she demands, dropping the plate between us. "Airport food is expensive."

I snatch a T-Rex dinosaur nugget and pop it into my mouth as I continue to shove what I need into the duffel. Deciding to pack the morning I leave was a poor choice. I have no idea what I need to survive as an ocean explorer.

"Are you excited?" Amy asks, chomping on a taquito.

"If I think about it for too long, I get light-headed."

What I'm *not* thrilled about is the flight to get to California. I've never enjoyed flying, and after my accident, I've avoided it at all costs. Instead of flying home for the holidays, I take the train from Rhode Island to Philadelphia, even though it takes hours longer.

Airports teem with people, and people love to stare, and no matter how many times someone tells me turbulence isn't a big deal, I still get nervous.

I'm packing up the last of my toiletries, including my trusty vibrator—three weeks at sea is a long time for manual mode—when Amy extends a tote bag.

"This is for you."

I dump the contents onto the bed, and tears threaten to fall. A box of lemon sugar protein bars. Chocolate. The balm that helps when my joints ache. Another pouch full of crystals. Three different alien romances that Amy swears are the best books ever written.

"It's an at-sea survival kit. It has everything you could ever need."

I crawl beside her and throw my arms around her neck, forcing back my tears. If I cry, I'll flush, which is the last thing I need when I'm seeing Mateo so soon.

"I'm going to miss you," I admit.

This is the longest time we'll have spent apart since I went home for Christmas last year. Even though I love my parents—and wouldn't be here without them—it was the most boring two weeks of my life, and I learned that Amy and I have separation anxiety from each other.

"You're gonna have the experience of a lifetime, and I'll be right here when you get back, ready to hear all about it." Tears brim on her bottom lashes. "Don't kill Mateo while you're there. Orange is *not* your color."

Flight attendants pass along the aisles, checking seat belts and chatting with passengers to prepare for take-off. My knee bounces as I buckle up, pulling the strap as tight as possible while I can still breathe.

I'm not a great flier, preferring to keep my feet on solid ground, and sitting in a tin can in the sky is a torturous form of immersion therapy. Sitting in any moving vehicle for prolonged periods sets me on edge, but airplanes are the worst.

I figured cars would be my big issue, considering I was nearly smashed while driving, but when I was released from the hospital, my father forced me into the passenger seat of his car. It took us an hour to drive five miles. He drove slowly, and my mom fed me chocolate the whole time while asking obscure questions about the ocean to keep my brain occupied.

If it weren't for them, it might have taken months to get into a car, let alone drive one.

Planes are a different beast, and the sky adds a greater terror: the plummet back to earth.

The aircraft jerks forward, beginning to taxi, and my nails dig into the plastic armrest. Shallow, uneven breaths fill my lungs as I focus on the safety briefing and catalog the emergency exits.

Flight attendants find their seats for take-off, and the plane rattles as it picks up speed. Mateo sits quietly beside me, unfazed by the concerning sounds. We lurch from the ground and into the sky, and my arms flail outward, swatting him in the chest, before I scramble to find his hand and clutch it.

The need for human contact—for comfort I rarely ask for—outweighs every reason to ignore Mateo, which was my original plan when we arrived at the airport.

My fingers tremble as I squeeze his hand like I'm making orange juice.

He pulls out his phone, pausing whatever he's listening to, and clasps my hand between both of his.

"Are you okay?"

It's probably a rhetorical question, given the nervous sweat dotting my brow and the impending anxiety attack looming, but I shake my head. We gain altitude and my ears pop, adding to my discomfort.

"I-I don't like flying," I admit, the confession sour on my tongue.

"It's completely safe," he assures me, "even if there's turbulence—" He pauses when he clocks my terror. "You're right. Not helping."

Nausea rolls in my gut as Mateo peels his hand out of my death grip. I can add embarrassment to the slew of emotions banging around my chest, right beside undiluted fear, and my stomach swirls with physical and emotional discomfort.

I'm not a fan of others witnessing my weaker moments, and this one right here, while occurring thirty thousand feet in the air, is very close to rock bottom.

He's supposed to view me as the one woman he can never seem to beat. The incredible, witty scientist with a brilliant mind. Not a fully grown woman who is terrified of flying.

Somewhere toward the back of the plane, a child screams—a loud, sharp pleading sound. *I'm right there with you, buddy.* The heat from Mateo's touch lingers against my palm, and although it's horrifying to admit, I miss the fit of his fingers between mine. It's not his job to offer me comfort. We are not that person for each other.

The barrier between us vanishes as he lifts the armrest and, without warning, pulls me against his side. His skin is warm, a balm to my anxiety, and it wards away the chill of the aircraft. If I weren't mortified, I might admit how nice it feels to accept the comfort offered by another person.

In one smooth movement, Mateo interlaces our fingers and rests our hands on the hard muscle of his thigh. My pulse beats erratically as I study the sharp bridge of his nose, the soft flush of his cheekbones, the subtle smirk perpetually curving his lips, and the barely there dimples on each cheek.

He's a complicated mathematical equation I can't solve. For every teasing comment or sharp retort, he offers a moment of unexpected gentleness. Right when I believe I've solved the problem, the equation changes—our relationship morphs—and I'm back to staring at the chalkboard.

Though he calls me "bruja" and teases me for my messy desk and collection of bobbles, he continually checks in on me with a concern that feels genuine. He has no obligation to ask how I'm doing or offer his help, yet he does so freely.

And I don't know how to answer the simple question: *why?*

"Here." He offers an earbud, and I slide it in, ready to drown out my muddled thoughts with whatever music Mateo listens to, but instead, I'm greeted by a woman with a crisp English accent describing a...ship?

"What is this?" I ask, trying to concentrate on the words for context. The narrator of what I assume is an audiobook describes the linens of a bed and how rough they feel against the supple flesh of her thighs.

What the hell is Mateo listening to, and why the fuck is my stomach tingling?

"Historical romance," he says, his voice rough around the edges.

The answer surprises me, but it's outdone by the words spoken in my ear.

"Dominic's member twitched beneath his britches, and though Elora was inexperienced in lovemaking, he made her feel alive, offering a deep pulsing between her thighs she'd never felt before."

The earbud is ripped from my ear as Elora dives into how his velvety member feels between her thin fingers.

"I didn't know it was *explicit*," Mateo shrieks, his cheeks flushed and palm sweaty against mine.

His flustered appearance helps dissipate my anxiety, and a small laugh tumbles out when he swats at my hand as I try to snatch the earbud.

"Give it back," I demand, stretching over him to reach his far hand. "It was getting good."

"The book is horrible."

"One man's trash is this woman's treasure. I need to know how Elora feels about his throbbing velvety member."

The woman in the row across from us chokes, and Mateo's face deepens to a shade of lobster red.

Before I can further convince him I'll riot if I can't listen to the audio, the plane jostles, jerking through turbulence, and I yelp while my heart skips a beat. The seat belt sign sings the tune to our impending demise, and the flight attendants scatter to their seats.

We're going to die.

Maybe it's the anxiety or the sudden consciousness of my mortality, but my panic increases tenfold. I can't die; I've accomplished *nothing*. No first author publications. No whale falls. No PhD. Loveless. No money to my name. Celibate.

The last one washes over me like arctic water.

I cannot die without one more decent romp in the sheets.

My last hookup was a dud, and I decided it wasn't worth spending weeks vetting someone new when he would only last thirty seconds.

"Breathe," Mateo whispers, pausing a beat before reaching out and tucking a stray hair behind my ear. "It's going to be fine."

He slides the earbud back into my ear, but instead of the audiobook, the beginning notes of "Bohemian Rhapsody" play.

A goofy smile blossoms as he softly sings the beginning lines of the song. He wiggles his eyebrows, and the corner of my lips twitches.

The plane shakes, and his grip around my fingers tightens—a solid shield against an invisible enemy. His shoulders shimmy while he hovers our connected hands in front of my mouth.

I sing a single line on a shaky breath before the aircraft dips again and the air is ripped from my lungs.

Mateo takes over, singing every word of the seven-minute song until the turbulence ends and the seat belt sign flickers off. When I regain function of my legs, I fly to the bathroom, desperate for space from him—at least as much as I can manage in this soaring metal deathtrap.

I grip the sides of the tiny basin, horrified by my reflection. I'm a fucking wreck. My hair is out of sorts, my skin pale and clammy, and the scar crossing my brow is a deep, angry red.

The skin is puffy against the pad of my finger, the edges ragged all the way down to my cheekbone. Crude suturing work performed by a resident rather than a plastic surgeon left a lasting impact, and I'm reminded of one doctor's choice every time I pass a mirror. Had it been a plastic surgeon, maybe it wouldn't be so ugly.

I force a tilt of my lips, but it falls flat.

After smoothing out my hair and adjusting my top, I return to my seat but falter at the tender smile Mateo offers. The crinkles at the corners of his eyes haunt me—a ghost I both want to exorcise and demand to torment me forever.

Attraction barrels into my chest with unexpected force as I slump into my seat, and my heart flutters when he picks up my hand without a word and places it in his lap, nestled between each of his palms.

It's the hand-holding, I tell myself to justify the weird flipping sensation in my chest. *You're touch-starved and anxiety-ridden. This is a response to that.*

"Feeling better?" he asks, swiping his thumb against the back of my hand. I nod, unable to form a coherent response, because, surprisingly, I do feel better knowing he's sitting beside me. "Good."

He squeezes my hand, and for the remainder of the flight, I try to banish the tingles left by his touch.

I drag my duffle bag onto the ground, huffing from the exertion, when a hand wraps around the handle and lifts it with ease. I know it's heavy because I had to bargain with the airline workers to avoid the overweight fee.

"I am entirely capable of carrying that myself."

"No one said you weren't." Mateo slings his bag over one shoulder and mine over the other. My jaw may drop at the sheer strength required to carry both bags.

I nearly threw my back out carrying my own.

"Hand it over," I demand.

The last thing I need is for him to believe I am some damsel in distress or incapable of completing tasks on my own. I may have pins and rods in my body, and my knees may creak when I walk up a flight of stairs, but I can still carry my bag.

"Just because you *can* carry it, doesn't mean you have to."

"It's my bag."

He can't do this for me, not when my emotions are out of whack and he comforted me through an anxiety attack without a single teasing remark. I need solid ground, so I tug on the handles, trying to wrestle it away from him.

He doesn't let go. Instead, he tightens his grip, and I careen into his body, the air escaping my lungs when I ricochet into him.

"Fine!" I throw my hands up as I find my center of gravity. I asked for solid ground, but I'm annoyed that he's about as solid as it gets. "If you insist on being a pack mule, I'm not going to argue with an ass."

His laughter follows me out the doors and into the hot, dry California air.

I whip around to flee into the airport, where air-conditioning reigns, when I make contact with the wall of muscle that is Mateo's chest.

The two hits have rattled my brain.

"It's not that hot." Mateo chuckles when my face twists, but he's not wearing leggings and a sweatshirt. A droplet of sweat forms at the base of my neck and glides down my back. My skin crawls.

"That's because you're Satan," I grumble, pulling my crewneck in and out to create a breeze. I try to slip around his frame, but he easily slides to block me.

Who the hell has this much muscle, anyway?

Mateo's laughter is deep and throaty before he chokes out, "Satan?"

"The fiery pits of hell don't bother him. This horrid heat isn't bothering you. Considering I've never seen you and Satan in a room together, I can't rule out the hypothesis."

His laughter worsens, a duffle bag slipping from his shoulder as he doubles over. I stand like a pole in the middle of the road, awkwardly and out of place, as people pass by.

We begin to draw attention before he finally rises.

"You're funny, bruja," he declares, stepping up to the taxi.

Something rotten, almost like pride, blossoms in my chest, which is crazy because I shouldn't care if Mateo finds me funny. *I shouldn't.*

Shifting my head to disguise my burning cheeks, I slip into the back seat, thankful for a small reprieve from sitting beside Mateo and having to suffer his intoxicating, subtle citrus scent.

Not only does he have perfect hair, but he smells like a cool summer breeze, and I want to huff the scent until I can identify every note. He drives me fucking insane.

Right as the tension in my shoulders washes away, he slides into the seat beside me with a goofy smile.

"Ready for an adventure?" he asks, winking.

Neptune, have mercy on my soul. I don't know how I am going to survive this trip.

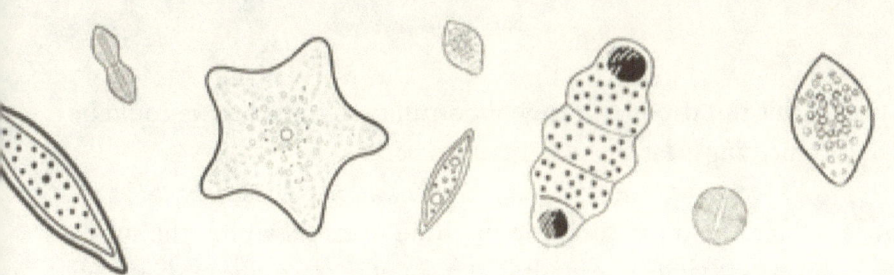

CHAPTER 7

MATEO

The skin on my palm burns where Charlie's hand clutched mine like a lifeline thrown in a raging sea. The cinnamon and mint aroma of her perfume lingers in my nostrils on every inhale.

She leads us into the outdoor bar connected to our hotel, and I allow myself three seconds to admire how her hips sway back and forth beneath her leggings.

We find the table reserved for the crew, and Charlie avoids my gaze as we order drinks. She's been doing it since we slid into the taxi.

I'm not foolish; I know she's not my biggest fan. Do I know what I did to get on her bad side? No, but since we met at the beginning of our PhD program, she's remained closed off from everyone but Amy.

I've tried to scale those walls, flirt with her to show her I'm interested, and offer her an ear when she's having a bad day, but my efforts have failed. Dozens of times, I've nearly worked up the courage to ask her on a date, only to change my mind at the last moment.

But this trip may be my opportunity to show her we could be something great, if she wants us to be.

If you want to be seen, you need to stand in the spotlight.

Her blond hair sits atop her head in a messy bun, the subtle breeze swaying loose tendrils in front of her face. She pushes them away as she scans the crowd, and I watch as her finger catches on her scar. She passes along the edge, and the shift in her demeanor is instantaneous.

Charlie's beauty is raw and uncut, but her smile, the way every feature joins in on her joy, is like reaching a mountain peak and looking out in the great expanse while wondering how lucky you are to lay witness to something so spectacular.

My knee bounces beneath the table as I search for potential topics of conversation to pull her away from whatever thought rattles in her mind.

Did you have a good flight? Poor choice, considering her panic attack.

Are you excited to embark tomorrow? Lame.

How's your drink? Boring.

I land on the world's dumbest question and fight the urge to drop my head in my hands.

"Do you like the weather?"

Dios mío, Mateo.

Charlie pouts. "It's *so* hot," she whines as she fans herself and pats the condensation from her glass against her forehead.

The urge to kiss Charlotte Bowen when she's grumpy is overwhelming. That urge is present at all times, but when the corners of her mouth pull downward and her bottom lip sticks out, it screams "kiss me silly."

I reach out and tug on the string of her sweatshirt.

"You could take this off," I say, twirling the cord around my finger. "It's eighty degrees."

"No." The response is quick and sharp. She chugs the remainder of her drink. "I'm fine."

"I'm watching a droplet of sweat fall down your cheek. Why won't you take the sweatshirt off?"

She gasps like I've caught her sneaking chocolate in the lab, and she whispers, "I-I only have a tank top under this."

"I have seen arms before, bruja. I think I can handle it."

Bright, irritated blue eyes snap to mine.

"That is *not* what I meant, and you know it."

I lift a brow, and after a moment of hesitation, Charlie pulls the hem over her head and wraps the sleeves around her waist.

The strength of her sigh could fill the sails of a schooner, and it's obvious she was dying in the thick material. I may have said I could handle the sight of Charlie's shoulders, but I'm a liar and already losing brain function, so I focus on the soft dimples of her cheek.

"Was that so hard?"

She purses her lips, her features blank. "No comment?"

I reel back from her defensive tone, shocked by the under layer of anger in it. "Comment about what? It was obvious you were sweating to death. Mentioning it again would be overkill."

"No, about my scars."

I peek at the expanse of her skin, and it's all I can do to contain my gasp. A mosaic of scars—large and small, some ragged and deep, others only with the precision a surgeon could have—pepper her arms and chest.

For two years, I've studied Charlie like she's a foreign language I'm desperate to understand, but I never knew about these scars, the ones that hide under clothing. Something twists deep in my chest at the recognition of the pain she must have endured to receive them.

Bile rises in my throat at the distrust and hesitation written all over her face.

"Beautiful," I murmur, allowing truth to sink into my words.

While the marks cover a majority of her skin, there is something shockingly stunning about each and every one, about *her*; how resilient and powerful she is to have endured what she has.

"W-what?" Her voice cracks and she slumps inward, crossing her arms to hug herself.

I reach out, tracing the small scar below her collarbone, and her skin pebbles beneath my touch.

"Each one of these scars," I start, trailing a finger along a larger one on her upper arm, "tells a story. They tell me you are brave, resilient, *increíble*."

Her throat bobs as she surveys the empty bar. Charlie rises, snatching her sweatshirt. "I need some air," she says, before running back into the hotel.

I bite back the urge to tell her we're sitting outside and instead watch as she disappears deeper into the hotel lobby. The longer I sit alone at the table, watching the condensation collect on our glasses, the more my concern for her grows.

Charlie's never run from a fight with me, but what I just witnessed was her fleeing. Disappointment riots in my chest. I told myself this trip was my chance, but if her reaction to me calling her beautiful is to run away, then maybe this was a bad idea.

Did I misinterpret her lingering glances as something more?

Do I have it all wrong?

I always thought our relationship needed a push, an extinction-level event to force evolution, but I may have been wrong, and it's a sour feeling.

After twenty minutes of sitting alone with my depressing thoughts, I rise to find her, when her laughter fills the air. My chest bubbles with warmth at the sweet sound. She walks beside a petite woman with wavy brown hair and a massive bag that screams "I mean business."

Charlie's wearing her sweatshirt again when she sits down, and I bite back the frown pulling at my lips. Do my words mean nothing to her?

"Mateo, this is Sofía. She's the project coordinator for Rogue-Wave."

Sofía reaches out a hand, and begrudgingly, I shift my attention away from Charlie and her bewilderment.

"Mateo," I say, and as my name rolls off my tongue, Sofía's head tilts.

"¿Hablas español?" she asks.

Does my abuela make the world's best tamales? Of course she does. The ratio of masa to filling is crucial, and she nails it every time.

I nod but answer in English for Charlie's benefit. "I moved from Mexico City when I was ten."

I was terrified to move, to leave Mexico and my friends, but my dad got a promotion as chief engineer for the automotive company he worked for, and they sent him to Detroit.

"My family is from Monterrey." She's cut off by a loud ruckus at the front. "Jett is here."

Sofía exhales a shuddered breath as a small pack of people closes in on our table. Jett leads the group, and he is exactly how he appears in his videos. Slightly scruffy appearance, complete with a faded graphic t-shirt, cargo shorts, and scuffed-up checkered Vans.

I would bet the entirety of my savings account he played or still plays Hacky Sack.

A backward hat sits atop his head, covering his shoulder-length hair, and Charlie giggles as he extends a fist, and she fist-bumps him.

"Dudes and dudettes," he yells. "You two must be my super geniuses. Gotta say, I thought you two were a bit older."

Charlie giggles—again. That's two giggles for Jett in two minutes, when I have yet to receive a single giggle in the two years of knowing her.

"Our advisors had previous commitments," she says, "but we are *way* cooler."

"Right on." Jett pumps a fist into the air. "What do we think? Shirley Temples for the table?"

"Extra cherries?" Charlie asks, fanning herself with a menu.

Jett grins, and I track the interaction, jealousy raging in my chest. I want Charlie's smile and giggles, but instead, I have to witness her offer them to someone else.

"I'm Mateo," I say, shifting Jett's attention. "Really looking forward to the trip."

"Dude, it's going to be *amazeballs*. I did a whole segment on my YouTube about real-life aliens, and it was *killer*."

Moments later, he's back to chatting with Charlie, and I'm left to watch them, her laughter infectious as they joke back and forth. There's an energy about Charlie—one I'm not sure she knows she possesses—where people gravitate toward her. Quick-witted and funny, she has an orbit that's easy to fall into, and it's clear the others agree.

I only wish she would fall into my orbit, too.

The sun sets in the sky, basking Charlie's silhouette in hues of soft pinks and purples. The air has cooled, and a soft, salty summer breeze cuts the heat. An acoustic band sits in the back of the bar, preceded by a small dance floor full of couples swaying to the slow '70s songs.

Charlie chats with Sofía, the two of them speaking in low whispers. Every few minutes, they glance in my direction, or Jett's, and giggle. It's infuriating but also adorable to watch Charlie act like a schoolgirl on the playground.

On one occasion, I wink, curious to witness her reaction, and it could have been the sunset or fairy lights hanging above us, but I could have sworn her cheeks were rosy.

Moments like that lead me to believe we could have a shot. She's attracted to me, at least physically, if her lingering stares are any indication, but that's a long shot from seeing me as a partner.

The song ends and the beginning notes of "Dancing Queen" by ABBA ring out. Charlie's head jerks toward the band, and she bobs her head to the energetic beat.

She loves this song.

Her soft smile, and the blush earlier, is what drags me from my seat to stand in front of her, palm outstretched.

"Dance with me, bruja," I demand, my words holding a silent plea.

Take my hand. Show me I have a shot.

"I can't dance." Her gaze holds a million questions as it darts between my face and palm. It's not a denial, so I grab her hand and drag her onto the dance floor. "Mateo, what are you doing?" She squeals, "Let me *go*."

"Not until you're having fun," I yell over the music, spinning her around twice until her marvelous giggle fills the air.

When she's facing me again, I place a hand on her hip, guiding us through a rough salsa. She steps on my toes and stumbles, trying to pull away, but I draw her closer, quickening the pace until she finds a rhythm.

I shimmy my shoulders before launching her into another spin, hoping I get a smile this time, a real one where the joy overtakes her. Bafflement flashes across Charlie's face before it's replaced by the version I crave.

"Having fun yet?"

"Yes," she responds like she's shocked by her answer. "Now spin me again."

I heed her demand a dozen times by the end of the night, her delightful giggles replaying in my mind until the moment I fall asleep.

CHAPTER 8

CHARLIE

My fists bang against Mateo's hotel door, my bags thrown at my feet. We are going to be late if he spends any more time on his hair and doesn't move his ass toward the exit.

"We need to go," I yell through the wooden barrier. "Mateo!"

My patience is not thin, it's gone, eaten away by a poor night's sleep, all because of Mateo and the uncomfortable sensation he left lodged in my throat when he called my scars beautiful.

No one should be awake at five thirty in the morning with no access to caffeine, and Mr. My-Hair-Needs-To-Be-Perfect is making it worse by adding to my baseline level of anxiety.

It's already elevated compared to the average person, but it's at an all-time high right now.

Everything is changing, including my relationship with Mateo, and I'm off-kilter and unsteady. I had to escape to the lobby yesterday to settle my racing heart, to digest the gentleness of his touch and the sincerity in his declaration. Jett distracted me with his antics and long-winded stories for most of the evening, but when Mateo pulled me onto the dance floor, my heart raced again, thumping in my chest in time with the music.

Spun round and round, I replayed his words in my mind: beautiful, brave, resilient, incredible. I almost wanted to believe him.

"Are you trying to wake the entire hotel?"

Spinning, I find Mateo leaning against the wall with coffee in both hands. "Do the little stomp again. It's adorable."

A cocky grin teases his lips, and my knees almost buckle from the strength of it.

Murder is illegal.

I do not look good in orange.

There are no iced lattes in prison.

The third reason reverberates deep within my soul, and I snatch my duffel bag, bypassing Mateo to the elevator.

"Look everyone, Charlie is stomping."

That's it. I cannot deal with Mateo's snarky bullshit before the sun rises, especially when his smile sends me into a tizzy and his words bobble around my mind. I turn around, ready to...I don't know, yell at him, I guess, when Mateo shoves the to-go cup into my hand, peels the duffel bag from my grip, and saunters into the open elevator in three swift moves.

I stand, dumbfounded, with an iced latte in my grip.

Mateo watches triumphantly in the elevator. "C'mon, bruja. We're going to be late."

"No, no, no, no, *no*," I chant, hoping the more I say it, the less real this nightmare becomes. "No."

When Sofía handed us our room keys, Mateo disappeared, but I stayed behind to talk to her. I needed space from Mateo and the wild emotions racing around my mind, and I needed to establish a BSF: Best Sea Friend.

Sofía reminds me of Amy: soft, kind, outgoing, confident in herself.

She was easy to talk to last night at the bar, offering small details about everyone at the table. In return, I told her about our advisors and our unorthodox dynamic.

Solidifying her as my BSF went splendidly. Sometimes you just know when you click with someone, the same way you know you hate something with your whole soul.

I redirect my attention to the very thing I currently hate with every fiber of my being: Mateo lounging on *my* bed. The *only* bed. In the center of the cabin. The one meant for me and my body. Alone.

He is sprawled out over the maroon sheets, his arms thrown behind his head. "Maybe try saying it in Spanish." Mateo raises a brow. "*No.*"

I blink.

Asshole.

"What are you doing?"

"Relaxing in my room. What are you doing? Here to finally admit you're madly in love with me?"

I choke on any coherent response, and my face flames a thousand degrees when he raises a brow. He's stunned me into silence, and he knows it.

My duffel bag slumps to the ground.

This is my worst nightmare realized. We cannot share this tiny room, and we definitely cannot share the bed. There's only a sliver of space on each side of the queen-sized mattress, and a small nightstand hangs off the wall on the right side beneath an ornate gold sconce.

A faux-marble desk and an upholstered chair sit against the left wall, paired with a large mirror mounted against swirling tan wallpaper. There's a closet across from the bathroom and a cubby with two shelves. It's smaller than Cheryl's office.

I need more space from Mateo, not less, to squash the odd feelings in my chest.

Whipping the door open, I storm from the room. Mateo's laughter chases me down the hallway as I search for Sofía to fix this minor mishap and assign me my own quarters, free of tall, charming, attractive men whom I want to throttle with the full force of my body.

Terror is the wind beneath my wings as I try to navigate the vessel, my dread-filled body blindly guiding me down empty hallways and into storage rooms. Fall in love with him? Please. He'll be lucky if he makes it through the trip without me flinging him overboard.

Sofía is in the galley, speaking with the chef, when I find her.

"Can I speak with you for a moment?" I try to prevent the panic from creeping into the question, but it's bubbling closer to the surface by the second.

"What's up?"

"There's been a mistake with Mateo's room and mine."

Her brow furrows as she flips through her paperwork. "Room 209?" At my nod, she says, "No mistake. That's your room."

"Yeah..." Annoyance creeps into my tone. "So why is Mateo claiming it as his room also?"

"Because it is?" Sofía's face morphs from confusion to shock, then disbelief. "Your advisors didn't tell you that you had to share a room?"

Oh, I am going to kill Cheryl and Dan. In my mind. I could never tell Cheryl I was upset with her; it would give me an ulcer.

"No," I bite out, "they did not."

"I'm so sorry. We told them when they asked for the switch that we didn't have any single beds with the extra film crew. They told me not to worry about it."

She apologizes again, but I wave her off. It's not her fault my advisor forgot to mention I would have to share a bed with *him*.

This is going to be a big fucking problem. My plan was to avoid Mateo as much as possible by hiding in my cabin and only interacting with him when we had to advise. It's what I concocted last night when I couldn't sleep because I was too busy thinking about how he spun me around on the dance floor and how easy it was to escape the swirling thoughts often clouding my mind.

Getting out of my head doesn't happen often, but twice with Mateo, the voices have grown quiet, and for a few precious minutes, I could live in the moment, untethered from my thoughts.

I hope Mateo has a good back, because he's about to become quite cozy with the floor. Three weeks at sea with him was going to test my patience, but three weeks commingling in a queen bed on a rocking vessel with no windows will end in bloodshed.

"Well?" he presses, his arms flexing as he sits up when I return to the cabin.

I ignore him and the smug look on his face, and aggressively unpack. My poor duffel takes the brunt of my anger, but it's either the bag or Mateo's face. He huffs, the sound uncomfortably intimate, and I stumble, kicking my luggage before disappearing into the bathroom to unpack.

Rogue strands stick out around my face, and my right eye twitches—a telltale sign I'm teetering on the edge of a conniption. I smooth out my hair and wipe the sweat from my brow, then haphazardly store my toiletries, monopolizing the little storage space the bathroom offers.

"Uh...Charlie?" Mateo trails off, the deep timbre of his voice traveling through the cabin and dancing along my spine. "I think your bag is buzzing."

My toothpaste tumbles from my grip, crashing into the sink as his words register. *Oh, fuck.*

"Close your ears and plug your eyes," I scream, diving for my bag.

This cannot be happening.

"Close my...what?"

"Look *away*, Mateo," I screech, digging through my clothes so I can end this nightmare. "If you choose one moment in your life to listen to me, *please* choose right now."

I could vomit from the embarrassment creeping up my throat as I pull out my blue vibrator and shut it off.

"Is that..." His husky accent puffs against my ear as he pops my personal-space bubble. The crisp, summery scent of his cologne assaults my nostrils in a tantalizing way.

"Get away," I yell, spinning to block his view, the bright-blue vibrator tight in my grip. My body collides with his chest and the toy whirls, swatting him on the cheek.

Mateo recoils, staring down at my hand with horror.

Oh, Neptune, I just whacked Mateo with my sex toy.

I gasp. Mateo responds with his own. Time creeps to a stop as he examines the sex weapon in my hand.

"Did you just slap me with your alien dick?" he asks, each word slow and full of disbelief.

My jaw slackens.

"This is not an *alien dick*," I say, whacking him in the chest with the vibrator. "It is a normal fake penis. Thank. You. Very. Much."

Each word is punctuated with a good ole dick slap between his pectoral muscles.

"Stop hitting me with it!" He rips the blue silicone out of my hand and waves it in the air. It jiggles back and forth, and I don't know what's worse: that the toy looks small in Mateo's grip or the way my core bottoms out as he waves it through the air.

"Mateo." I hold up a hand, creeping toward him like he's a viper poised to strike. "Hand me the *item*, and we can forget this ever happened."

His smile is mischievous as he takes a step back.

There is no crystal found on earth that could save me from this predicament, and the small round fire opal dangling around my neck mocks me.

You asked for fiery passion, it whispers, *well here you go. I'll serve you up sexual tension on a silver platter.*

"Were you going to use this?" he asks, his question low and intimate. The raspiness of his accent cranks the sexual tension dial to ten, and my knees wobble.

What the fuck *is happening to me?*

We don't knee wobble for Mateo. I need to deflect, fast, to save myself from this situation.

"Are you shaming me for using a toy, Mateo? How very *archaic* of you. This is the twenty-first century." Smug satisfaction floods my veins when he gulps. "Women enjoy sex as much, if not more, than men."

His cocky grin falters, and I seize my opportunity, stealing the toy and returning it to my duffel bag.

"Now that you've groped my pleasure device," I scold, and his face pales further, "I am going to the lab to see what they have for sample processing."

He stands mute and baffled in the middle of the cramped cabin.

"*Adios, Mateo,*" I purr, squaring my shoulders and sauntering out the door to exude the idea I was unfazed by that interaction.

The door clicks shut, and I slump against the hallway, a shuddered breath escaping. I use the wall for stability while I take deep breaths to cool down my racing heartbeat.

I'm not going to survive in this small cabin—not with the mental image of Mateo holding my vibrator burned into my retinas.

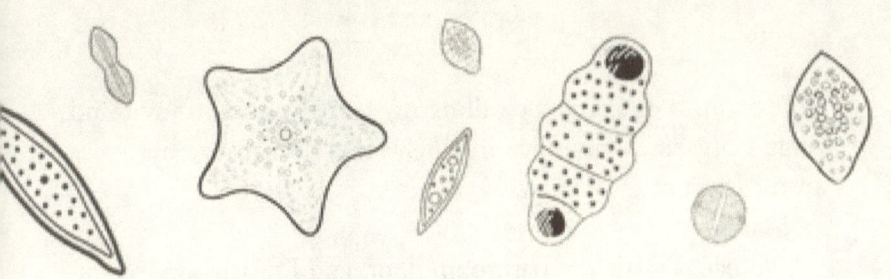

CHAPTER 9

MATEO

I am a weak man consumed by thoughts of honey-blond hair splayed against maroon bed sheets.

A steady stream of frigid water batters my skin but does nothing to extinguish the fire coursing through my veins.

I brace my palm against the shower wall, slowly pumping the other up and down my shaft, bawdy thoughts of Charlie consuming every corner of my mind. A groan tumbles out as I imagine her legs falling open, her hand trailing down her stomach until she finds the apex of her thighs. I nearly crumble at the idea of watching that vibrator dipping in and out of her.

Weak, wanton man.

The pressure at the base of my spine compounds as I stroke myself, every titillating fantasy of Charlie beneath me, on top of me, writhing beneath my tongue, flashing across my mind.

My head drops against the beige plastic shower wall as I barrel closer to completion. Those Caribbean-blue eyes, a window into her thoughts, fill my vision, and I combust.

The sound of her voice calling my name echoes in my mind while I orgasm. Only once the high fades do I realize her voice wasn't a part of my fantasy.

"Mateo!"

Two bangs rattle the bathroom door, and I nearly slip, scrambling to right myself before I land on my ass.

"One minute," I yell, my voice hoarse. At lightning speed, I dry myself off and get dressed. I steal a few seconds to hype myself up in the mirror before returning to the room, where Charlie perches on the end of the bed, her foot tapping impatiently. "¿Qué pasa, bruja?"

I dawdle about the cramped room, and she tracks my movements.

"We have a safety briefing." Her lips purse in dissatisfaction.

"Thank you for the reminder."

She clicks her tongue. "We're going to be late." She doesn't add *because of you*, but I hear it in her silence.

What I don't understand is why she's still here if she's so anxious about it. She could have left, but instead, she's stewing in her anxiety to wait for me.

It should mean nothing that Charlie waited so we could walk to the lounge together, but I am working on very little with her, so the likely meaningless action means something to me.

"I'm sorry, bruja. Let's go." I'm halfway out the door before I notice she hasn't moved from the bed. Her face is scrunched in confusion in the most adorable way. "Charlie?"

She shakes from the stupor and pops off the mattress.

"Uh...yeah." She looks at me oddly, like I'm a dilution series she can't get right. She flies past me in the doorway.

We walk down an industrial hallway, the walls covered in journal covers and newspaper clippings that mention SeaStar. Bright golden sconces line the walls of the ship's lounge, illuminating the area meant to relax after a long day. Several large wooden tables are scattered throughout the space, and a sofa and television are nestled in a back corner.

The decor mimics that of the stateroom. Dark wooden furniture with maroon and gold accents. Crew members and personnel from RogueWave fill the space, and Sofía stands at the front of the room.

We arrived with two minutes to spare, but Charlie pauses, her head swinging between the seats and me.

What's going on in that pretty little head?

I slide into an empty seat at a table in the back, and she tentatively sits in the seat beside mine.

Our thighs are flush, and it requires every ounce of self-restraint I possess to turn away from where we touch and listen to Sofía explain safety procedures and where to muster in an emergency.

Charlie squirms in her seat.

"Don't worry, I'll save you if we sink," I whisper beneath my breath.

She sticks out her tongue.

"There are cameras stationed throughout the common areas for Jett's personal filming. In addition, Doug may film you while you work or ask you to answer questions. Please accommodate him."

Doug stands—a man in his late forties with a long peppered beard—gives a wave, then plops back into his seat.

"You all signed a release form," Sofía says, "but this is a reminder—do *not* do anything illegal or explicit. I don't want to have any awkward conversations."

With that *friendly* reminder, Sofía jumps into the boat's amenities and walks us through the map, pointing out the lab, control room, and mess area where we'll eat. A few photos pop onto the screen behind her, and Charlie barely muffles her excited squeal.

"It's a cool ship," I mumble, finding any reason to talk to her.

"*A cool ship?*" she asks, incredulously. "The only way this boat could be any cooler was if it was the HMS *Beagle*, we were exploring the Galapagos, and I had unfettered access to Charles Darwin and his magnificent brain."

I choke on my laughter, and a few heads swing in our direction.

Before I can formulate any verbal response—I have a physical one, which is to kiss the shit out of her—Sofía steps aside, and a woman with a sandy-blond pixie cut takes her place, a no-bullshit look on her face.

"My name is Vivian," she says. "I am the head pilot for *Poseidon* and *Neptune*, our two remotely operated vehicles, or ROVs. Our first descent will occur tomorrow at eight a.m. Lucas is the copilot but will focus on operating the cameras for the documentary."

"Right on," Jett hollers, and Vivian quirks a brow.

"Most of the SeaStar crew are familiar with the expedition process and what we expect to find in Monterey Canyon, but in addition, we have two researchers to provide insight and identify species. Charlie, Mateo, can you stand?" Vivian asks, and the entire room turns to us.

I rise, focused on Charlie as she pulls down the cuff of her sweatshirt.

"If you have questions about what we see or are curious about deep-sea ecosystems, we are more than happy to chat."

Sofía returns to the front, announcing dinner will be ready soon, and as I sit, Charlie leans in close enough that her perfume lingers in the air.

"Thank you."

Only two words, but they hold so much more meaning. There's no contempt or annoyance, and it allows irrational hope to form in my chest. Maybe we're moving somewhere new, a place where I could tell her how I feel and not face immediate rejection.

Charlie spends the rest of the evening laughing with Sofía and Vivian, and like a creep, I watch her, enraptured by how she twirls a strand of hair around her finger. I bask in the comfortable warmth her laughter offers, settling beneath my navel.

Jett clears his throat, dropping into the seat beside me with a knowing look. I shut my laptop, though I haven't written a single word of my protocol in an hour. Charlie laughs again, and subconsciously, I look over. Her head is tipped back, her hands flying out to cover her face.

Sofía offers a laugh of her own, and Jett's head swings.

Hmm. Seems like I'm not the only one interested in an occupant at that table.

"What are you hoping to see?" I ask to banish thoughts of the stunning blonde who does wicked things to my insides with a simple smile.

"A viperfish," Jett blurts out. "Their teeth are insane, man. Imagine eating corn with those chompers."

A surprised laugh escapes me, and Charlie's head jerks, our eyes connecting from across the room. All else fades away as something soft, something foreign, flashes across her gaze. It's gone as quickly as it appeared, and she returns to her conversation.

"I'll never get that image out of my mind." I chuckle, but my focus remains fixed on Charlie.

I would give up everything for a peek into her mind. She's brilliant, precise, but an enigma. Does she truly dislike me, or is there room for change? Are her subtle perusals something more, or am I projecting?

Charlie rises from her table, and I give her a thirty-second head start before ditching Jett like a bad habit. Anticipation and trepidation overwhelm me as I slip into the room right behind her.

Sharing a bed with Charlie may kill me, but at least it will be a glorious death.

CHAPTER 10

CHARLIE

"We need to establish some ground rules," I say, discarding my clothes into a corner and slipping on a sweatshirt and sweatpants while Mateo uses the bathroom. The pajamas I brought are *far* too revealing, and I would rather sweat to death than wear those around him, especially after what happened at the bar.

His words were so authentic, so genuine, and my skin tingles at the memory of his touch, the way his fingers danced across my skin, caressing the scars.

They felt like something beautiful, something to be revered, rather than the ugly reminder of the lowest points of my life. For a split second, it was as though my scars didn't subtract from my value but made me remarkable.

I haven't been able to compartmentalize how badly I want to believe in that feeling, to take Mateo's words as truth, and allow myself to believe he might find me desirable.

"Ground rules?" Mateo's voice is muffled by the bathroom door, but I hear his confusion.

"Yeah. You sleep on the ground. I sleep on the bed. Those are the rules."

The bathroom door flies open, a toothbrush hanging out of Mateo's mouth and minty foam dribbling down his chin as he shakes his head.

"No," he mumbles, and I lean back in the small desk chair, waiting while he frantically finishes brushing his teeth. "I have a bad back."

"And I don't sleep beside men I'm not having sex with."

The words escape before I can stop them, and the silence in the room is a living thing.

Mateo gulps, his Adam's apple bobbing, and my eyelids fall shut as I take a deep, calming breath.

Why do I say the things that I do? What part of my brain believes that mentioning the word *sex* after dildo-gate is a good idea?

It's not even the truth.

When I do sleep with someone, which hasn't occurred in a painfully long time—my vagina has cobwebs—I force them to leave immediately after. It's one of my rules. No lights. No sleep-overs. No missionary.

All three of those things allow emotions to creep into the action, and that's not what I want. I want the release, not someone to see the scars covering my body or how uncomfortable I am in my own skin.

"Charlie, I can't sleep on the floor for three weeks."

His voice is dangerously close, and my eyes snap open to find him hovering over me, a pair of sleep pants hanging dangerously low on his hips.

When the *fuck* did he lose his shirt?

He needs to find it, stat.

The expanse of bronze skin, and the way his muscles ripple as he leans down to grab his glasses from the table, consumes my sight. His crisp citrus-and-salt scent fills my nostrils, and I can't breathe.

I *cannot* fucking breathe with him this close to me, shirtless and putting on tortoise shell glasses.

Someone get this man a freaking shirt before I combust.

He moves around the room, comfy and ready for bed, and this image, this moment right here, should be illegal for all others to witness. His perfect hair is now unruly, and his beard is growing in, adding to the scruffiness of his appearance.

Not once since I met Mateo have I denied how handsome he is; I would be a liar if I did. But I was never affected by it. I was too busy with serious things—like establishing my academic dominance over him and hunting for my Willy Wonka.

But now, as Mateo tugs a shirt over his head and his back muscles undulate, I am wildly affected by him. I need a cold shower. My thighs tighten in a desperate attempt to release the pressure building at my core.

This would be a perfect time to use my vibrator if he wasn't in the room.

I'm reciting the protocol for DNA extractions to cool myself down when Mateo crouches, his back facing me, to slide a small briefcase from his duffel bag.

Utter disbelief replaces my overwhelming horniness at the sight of slate-gray cotton and stripes of blue. I creep closer to Mateo until I'm hovering over him, a demented smile on my face. This is akin to Darwin discovering his finches.

Fucking groundbreaking.

"Mateo?"

He hums, focused on his task.

"Is that a CPAP machine?" A giggle bubbles out past my lips. "Oh, Neptune, this may be the greatest day of my life."

This totally tops the dildo debacle.

Mateo's glare could slice glass, but the exuberance thrumming in my body counteracts his scowl. He has a flaw. It's a victory until I realize the small thing makes Mateo more desirable. Since I met him, he's always been put together, but knowing he's not flawless, that maybe he dislikes this part of himself...oh, shit.

No.

A thread weaves around my heart, squeezing, until I'm fighting for breath.

"The right side has a nightstand," I grumble, disappearing into the bathroom.

I'm not fond of the tightness in my chest at the idea of sharing a bed with someone else. Everything is morphing, shifting into new, dangerous territory, and I don't know what to do with myself.

I splash cold water over my face before reentering the cabin.

Mateo perches off the side of the bed, placing his glasses on the nightstand and popping a retainer into his mouth.

"There *will* be a wall," I declare, shoving each ornate cushion to the middle of the bed, fluffing them to increase their surface area. "Consider it impenetrable."

I'm nearly through building the Great Wall of Pillow when I hear Mateo's muffled laughter and realize my mistake. So many words in the English language and I chose the one word that contains *penetrate*. How I survived this long is a wonder to us all.

"Impenetrable, huh?"

Mateo's eyebrows waggle, and I chuck a pillow at his face.

"Shut it, Darth Vader."

"Are you crying?" Mateo's voice is muffled by the CPAP mask, and a small click echoes through the room, followed by the whooshing sound of air before he turns off the machine.

"No."

I sniffle again, giving away my lie. Amy sent me precisely forty-seven videos, and I've been diligently working through each one, offering my reaction. I didn't expect to watch a dog adoption video.

"Look at me," Mateo demands.

"No."

"Why not?"

"Because it's going to look like I've been crying, and I don't know how to spin the lie."

Mateo laughs, shifting on the bed and destroying the fortress I worked hard to build. The space between us shrinks, and the air crackles with an energy I can't identify. It sets me on edge.

"Why were you crying?"

Instead of trying to explain that watching the dog morph from distrustful to a happy-go-lucky canine pulled at my heartstrings, I pull out my earbuds and hold my phone up for him to watch.

The small dog sits in a kennel, cowering as someone offers him a treat. A melancholy tune plays in the background, before the song and video switches to the dog running through a park, its tongue out as it chases a ball.

Its tail wags aggressively, and like the first time, I completely lose it, tears trailing down my cheeks. There's only so much one girl can handle, and I draw the line at receiving comments on my manuscript and videos about dogs. If either happens, I'm a mess.

The video ends, and sniffling fills the room, only it's not my own.

"Are *you* crying?"

"Yes. That was very sad." He scoots closer, the light from my phone illuminating his features. "Do you have more of these videos?"

His head leans closer on the pillow, and if I shifted my position, our mouths would be inches apart. My attention falls to his lips and the soft, supple shape of them. The perfect slope of the upper one and the thickness of the bottom.

Objectively speaking, his features are very kissable.

His brow furrows, so I explain, "It's TikTok." *Neptune, why is my voice like gravel?* "Amy sent me these videos."

"I don't have one of those."

Of course he doesn't. Mateo is an old man at heart. He wears an analog watch and prefers paper and pen to record his lab work instead of the electronic software other PhD students use.

I watched from my desk as he cursed the "cloud" for deleting his downloaded papers and witnessed him googling "how to post a story on Instagram."

He is an *old* twenty-six.

We watch the videos Amy sent in silence, and after about ten, my favorite true-crime page pops up, and the woman jumps into explaining a murder, leaving no gory stone left unturned.

She's midway through a detailed breakdown of a beheading when a large finger flies in front of the screen, swiping the video away.

"Nunca más," Mateo declares, his shoulders twisting as a shiver slithers down his spine. "I'll never sleep."

"Not a fan of true crime?"

I laugh at the horrified look on his face but switch it to my For You page, and we lie, side by side, watching videos.

Periodically, he laughs or huffs, and right now, in the comfortable darkness of the small cabin, there's something different between us. Here, I'm just Charlie and he's just Mateo—two overworked, underpaid, chronically tired PhD students.

Mateo readjusts, and I steal the opportunity to catalog his features. Stray pieces of thick brown hair fall in front of his viridescent irises before he drags his fingers through the strands, pushing them away.

I'm not sure I've ever looked at him for no reason other than to admire him, but right now, beneath the glow of my phone, I find myself wanting to map every freckle on his face.

I don't know what to do with the urge, so instead, I flick to another video and pour my focus into the ten-minute date recap.

Mateo and I are seven minutes in when Amy's name pops onto the top of my screen, followed by:

> Amy: How's it going on the ship? See anything cool yet?

I release a shuddered breath. She could have said anything, and she isn't known for her filter. I let my guard down, but then she messages again.

> Amy: Perhaps discovered what hides inside Mateo's pants?

I choke, the air in my lungs seizing as her words register. Mateo makes an odd sound, and I stare up at the ceiling.

Telling Amy we have to share a room was a colossal mistake. The world pauses on its axis and the tides cease their push and pull when another message appears, this one far worse than the last.

> Amy: May I suggest an exploratory mission to the southern hemisphere of Mateo's body with your tongue?

Undiluted panic takes over the function of my limbs, and I pitch my phone across the bed. It bounces at the edge of the mattress and lands with a thud on the floor.

"I am going to kill her," I whisper.

Why the hell is she awake? It's two a.m. on the East Coast. Doesn't she have better things to do than suggest I give Mateo a blowjob?

This is a work trip. Amy should exude some semblance of class. There will be no blowjobs. Zero. Zilch. *Nada,* as Mateo would say.

The man himself slides out of bed, a wry grin on his face as he retrieves my phone.

"You dropped this," he says, then pulls his bottom lip between his teeth. He extends the phone, and his shoulders quiver from suppressed laughter.

"Don't."

He holds up his palms in surrender, and the hem of his shirt lifts, offering a sliver of golden skin and taut muscle. My cheeks flame, and thank Neptune and his big blue sea that it's dark in here, or Mateo would witness the effect the fragment of skin has on my nervous system.

The bed dips as he gets comfortable, strapping the CPAP mask back onto his face. As the machine turns on, I hear him mumble, "Don't forget to text Amy. She's patiently waiting to hear about your scientific exploration."

I whack him with one of the throw pillows.

Cocky asshole.

Chapter 11

CHARLIE

Can he move any fucking slower?

The muscles in my lower back ache from maintaining my uncomfortable position, and my joints scream in protest from the pressure on my hips and angles of my knees. A girl can only pretend to be asleep for so long, and my arthritis is telling me I'm reaching my tipping point.

A pillow beside me rustles, and I hold my breath, peeking over the covers. Mateo moves around the room, humming to himself as he shuffles through his shirts in the closet.

He turns, and I slam my eyelids shut.

Don't move. Don't breathe. Don't think.

As long as he believes I'm asleep, we don't have to have a conversation about last night or any of the other tension-filled moments since we embarked. The bathroom door clicks shut, and once the water turns on, I fly out of bed to escape before he exits. I'll greet the rest of the crew with horrifying morning breath before I face what may be happening between us.

If there's no interaction between us, I don't have to address Amy's messages or how, when I woke up this morning, I was closer to Mateo than when I fell asleep. The pillow wall was still intact but barely holding itself up.

I slip on a pair of pants and a top, not bothering with matching, when a shiny blue wrapper glistens in my periphery.

I know the distinct color and can imagine the sweet caramel on my tongue, followed by the smooth dark chocolate. It's placed on the vanity, my crystals and trinkets moved to surround it in a circle, with a note folded and tucked beneath a heart-shaped amethyst.

Have to keep up the tradition.

It's scribbled in Mateo's distinctive handwriting—messy and scrunched together, like his brain moves more quickly than his hand.

The tradition? What tradition?

It takes a beat to understand his meaning, but when it lands—when it becomes clear who's been leaving these on my desk—it becomes difficult to stand.

My legs buckle, and I fall onto the edge of the bed, the sweet treat clutched in my grip and an uneasy sensation burrowing in my chest.

It's a piece of chocolate, yes, but it's so much more. It's the daily kindness from Mateo I've never acknowledged. It's the fact he leaves a *second* one on bad days. Hell, it's the notion he knows when I have bad days.

The piece of candy shakes in my grip.

It's even my favorite kind. Not the store-brand version I buy to save money, even though they're half as good as the original.

Mateo exits the bathroom, steam pouring into the room as he dries his hair with a towel.

I'm momentarily stunned by how attractive he looks back-dropped against steam, but quickly remember why my heart is racing in my chest.

"You're my Willy Wonka?"

"What?" A confused smile brightens his features, as if I said something endearing and didn't ask the question that's rocking my world. He glances down at the blue wrapper in my palm. "Oh, good. You found the chocolate. I tried to get Darwin the Bobblehead to hold it, but it wouldn't stay up."

He shuffles his clothes in the closet, pulls out a sage-green button-down, removes the t-shirt he's wearing, and then buttons the shirt, all while I sit on the bed and stare at him, dumbfounded.

"You've been leaving these every day?" I hate the way my voice quivers.

A chocolate every day for two years means something, doesn't it? This is more than a kind gesture on a bad day. Leaving one daily is a conscious choice, one that requires effort. But why?

It's shocking how a single piece of candy can uncover layers upon layers of suppressed emotions. Guilt swirls in my chest alongside something far more unsettling: yearning.

I've always been afraid to be noticed or perceived, but as I stare down at the wrapper, I'm painfully aware Mateo has seen me all along.

Memories flood my brain, a tsunami of small moments I overlooked. Iced coffee at joint meetings with our advisors. Chocolate every day. Knowing things about me I've never told him. What kind of person am I for treating him as a rival all this time?

A pretty shitty one.

My breathing quickens as I stand at the precipice of a life-altering discovery: Mateo's never been the cocky asshole. I have.

I need Amy to pull me out of the spiral I'm descending into and bring me back to the real world. I need her kind yet wise words about how to move forward, because right now, simply looking at Mateo rots my insides with guilt.

His smile is tender, and something in my chest cracks.

"Every day since I first saw you eat one." He laughs, and the sound dances along my skin. "You scarfed it down in one bite and did this little pitter-patter." He pushes up on his tiptoes, hopping back and forth to mock the movement. "I decided I wanted to see that every day."

I frown at the accuracy of the reenactment.

"You're scowling because you know that's exactly what you do every time," he says, and this—the back-and-forth—is what's comfortable, not the quiet moments in bed or the way his fingers dance along my scars.

Those intimate moments leave me vulnerable.

And right now, I feel like a snail without a shell. Entirely exposed.

I hum, switching between observing Mateo and my favorite treat, like together, they hold the key to solving climate change. Right now, uncovering that may be easier than unraveling my muddled feelings.

"You never said anything," I whisper.

"I thought you knew."

Silence hangs heavily between us, but I'm unable to form a response. I struggle to meet his gaze, and when I do, there's surprise in those verdant irises. A surge of understanding flickers over his features, and his lips pop open like he wants to say something.

Instead, he changes the conversation.

"Jett wants to film the sample collection prep for the ROV. I'll be in the lab, if you need me," he says.

He's halfway out the door when I call out, "Thank you, Mateo."

He peers over his shoulder, surveying me, before saying, "You're welcome, bruja."

And with that, he's gone, leaving me with my thoughts and a piece of chocolate.

Monitors mounted to the wall bathe the space in artificial light, and gauges and buttons flash and shift as the crew members on the main deck release the ROV into the choppy waves. The glacial descent beneath the surface begins, and the camera technician, Lucas, confirms the video is functional. As it moves down the water column, Mateo explains to Vivian how many soil and water samples to take.

"We're going to about a thousand meters today," Vivian announces.

Mateo, Jett, and I stand behind the control system that resembles a spaceship, and Lucas twists the camera with a joystick, searching the water column as *Poseidon* continues down through the photic zone.

"There are five main zones of the ocean," I explain to Jett, who watches the video feed with rapt attention, "epipelagic, mesopelagic, bathypelagic, abyssopelagic, and hadalpelagic. Right now, we're in the epipelagic zone—or photic zone—the area of the ocean where sunlight can penetrate."

Mateo winks when the *word* tumbles from my lips. My cheeks flame, and I lose my train of thought.

Darkness creeps in as *Poseidon* drops into the aphotic zone and the temperature decreases on the monitor.

"Wow..." Jett trails off as pitch black consumes the camera before the floodlights flash on, illuminating the deep abyss.

"We're entering the mesopelagic zone, also referred to as the twilight zone," Mateo says, "where species begin to utilize bioluminescence."

There's little more than darkness and debris for over an hour, and as the minutes continue to tick by, a blanket of boredom falls over the room. Jett whispers to Sofía, and Doug sits across from them, making faces each time one giggles.

Mateo scribbles down notes about the environment and some of the small cnidarians, and I pretend not to stare at him like an idiot.

It's hard work.

Finally, Vivian calls out, "I think I see something," and everyone in the room scrambles toward the screen, surrounding her and Lucas.

We all hold our breaths, leaning in, and Lucas zooms the camera while Vivian adjusts course. Small iridescent columns of light pulse and shimmer in the darkness like a beacon.

As Vivian moves the ROV closer, the floodlights illuminate the organism, allowing the dark, blood-red hue of its body to luminesce as it floats in the water column. Lucas zooms in further, and the bright red of its stomach comes into view.

"That's a bloody-belly comb jelly," Mateo says, awe lacing his voice. "Most light can't reach this depth, and red light is the first to go, making the jelly invisible to its prey."

"This is absolutely bonkers!" Jett smacks my back in jest, and I catapult forward, directly into Mateo's chest. "Holy shit, my bad."

Jett scrambles to help me, but Mateo's strong grip holds my bicep, keeping me standing. His finger dips beneath the hem of the sleeve, swiping against a small scar. I felt brazen this morning when picking out my outfit. Whether it was Mateo's emboldened words at the bar or the softness he offered me this morning, I left the long-sleeve cardigan in my duffel bag.

And when he returned from the lab to tell me Vivian was deploying the ROV, and registered the bare skin—saw the scars I've spent years hiding—he nodded approvingly and uttered words I immediately googled and will never forget.

Te ves deslumbrante.

You look stunning.

And the shocking part, the one I've struggled to accept, is that I *believe* him.

"I am so, so sorry," Jett says, his arms flailing for emphasis. "I've been hitting the gym, and now I don't know my own strength..."

His arm darts out, and I narrowly avoid getting whacked again.

"Maybe we keep our limbs at our sides," I say, stepping out of the danger zone.

Jett nods emphatically, focusing back on the screen. Mateo hovers nearby, not close enough to touch, but with so little space that my skin is lit aflame, a thousand firecrackers dancing along my arms. He shifts, leaning to grab his water bottle, and the overwhelming, intoxicating scent of his cologne permeates the air.

Doug films the room, focused on Vivian and Jett, who chirps a mile a minute, hands waving enthusiastically in the air.

I have made it my mission to avoid Doug and his camera at all costs. I start to slink back, but he swings around, focusing on Mateo and me. My heartbeat quickens, thudding faster and faster, but I'm paralyzed by fear.

The short-sleeve top was a horrible idea.

I'm sure I look like I've seen a ghost because the camera falls and Doug offers a quizzical look. "Are you okay?" he asks.

"Mm-hmm." Freaking out at the mere idea of millions of people viewing me online. No big deal.

Doug shrugs and moves on, and I creep to the back of the control room, out of the camera's aim. The screen is visible if I squint and stand on my tiptoes, so I can do my job just fine in the back corner.

I make it three steps before I slam into a wall of concrete, also known as Mateo's chest.

"Where are you going?"

He peers down at me with mirth.

By the minute, it becomes more difficult to deny my physical response to him. The way my pulse quickens when he walks into a room, or how, when he rolls his sleeves up to display his forearms, my core clenches and my internal temperature spikes.

"Hiding from the cameras," I whisper conspiratorially. He doesn't need to know why I'm hiding, only that I am evading Doug and his recording device. Mateo's tall; maybe he'll let me use his body as a human shield.

"Why?" he whispers back, but the single word is full of understanding as he shifts to distance us from the group.

This is too much. This trip. His kindness. The cameras. My scars. It's all too overwhelming. If we were at home, or hell, even just on land, I would run away. Hide until I could shove my emotions deep into the abyss and pretend they don't exist.

Here I have nowhere to run, and Mateo continues to shine a light on all the emotions I've tried to hide away.

Mateo clears his throat, and I realize I've been staring. "Bruja, why are you hiding?"

It's a question and a demand, and I fight the urge to curl in on myself, but still subtly cover the scars on my forearms. This morning I was daring, but right now I want *safe*.

Frowning, he moves so closely I can spot the speckles of gold in his irises. He blocks the rest of the room from view before whispering, "Do you want to go change?"

One question, asked with softness and understanding, and I nearly crack, the flood of emotion threatening to consume me. I've never grown comfortable with the scars. I wish I could say I wear them as a badge of honor, as a reminder that I fought and survived, but I can't.

Every scar is a reminder of the weeks spent in a hospital. They represent whispered conversations between my parents about overdue medical bills. And though they've told me hundreds of times not to worry about the cost of my recovery, I know they had to cut into their retirement savings to support me. The scar crossing my brow is a brutal reminder of the sacrifice and loss, one I'm forced to face every time I look in a mirror.

I shake my head, lifting my chin with more confidence than I feel, and if I were insane, I would say pride flickers across Mateo's gaze. I cling to that asinine thought, moving to the center of the room to watch the video feed.

The ROV reaches the seabed, and Mateo and I work together to identify any organisms or points of interest while documenting the time stamp. We collaborate for the first half of the day, before taking shifts to complete the remainder of the time.

I'm on a solo shift, documenting sea pigs and, sadly, plastic debris, but whenever there's a lull in the video feed, my mind wanders to Mateo, to the way he shielded me, saw my discomfort, and offered a solution.

He returns to the control center with Jett, sitting on the opposite side of the room at the small table and chairs. Every time he laughs or huffs, my concentration shifts from the video. I want to know why he's laughing.

The jealousy strikes unbidden, and I physically recoil from its strength, knocking my phone and notebook onto the floor. It lands with a loud thud, and Mateo spins, concerned. My stomach flips and I nearly vomit.

What the fuck *is happening to me?*

"Charlie, are you all right?"

My name rolling off his tongue does wild, concerning things to my insides. I need to go somewhere far away, void of the sensual way he says it. Maybe I'll plunge myself into the ocean to cool off.

"Going to the bathroom." My voice squeaks at the end, and I increase the space between me and Mateo's cologne, at least as much as possible on the boat.

If he was less attractive, mean, and inconsiderate, I would not have this issue. All he had to do was prove my theory that he was the mighty ruler of hell. Instead, he threw my theory in the trash and revealed himself as endearingly sweet and mind-bogglingly hot.

This is Mateo's fault.

By the time Mateo lies down on the bed, I've moved my arms into a dozen different positions. At my sides. Behind my head. Across my body like a corpse. I'm nervous and don't know what to do with my limbs.

The pillow wall jostles as he settles beneath the covers. He's so close I can barely breathe, afraid that a rogue puff will give away what thoughts are swimming around in my mind.

An arm flies over the barricade and I yelp, arms flailing. Mateo's laughter is a deep rumble that caresses my skin.

Fuck.

I turn to peer over the pillows, and time slows. In the dim light, his irises resemble moss, illuminated by rays of sun peeking through the canopy. His lips tug upward, one side lifting higher than the other. The shadows of a beard have grown after the long day, and his hair, the color of rich, freshly brewed coffee, is messy.

It's unlikely that many get to witness Mateo this way, unkept and mussed, worn down by the day. It's special, I'd assume, that someone gets this version of him, and for some insane reason, I'm absorbed with the thought that *I'm* that person.

A sharp cough breaks my trance, and the tips of my ears burn.

"Uh...what?"

A slow, knowing smile glides across his face, and the dimples in his cheeks hypnotize me.

"I was asking if we could watch more of the TikToks."

"Sure." I spin away, hoping to conceal my blush in the darkness, but Mateo removes the pillows dividing us, and I'm confident he could see the red of my cheeks all the way at the bottom of the ocean.

My breath hitches in the quiet room, and I conceal it with a cough.

While we scroll through videos, he leans his head on his bicep, his gaze fixed over my shoulder. Every soft chuckle causes goosebumps along my skin.

Eventually, my heartbeat finds a steady rhythm the longer we watch, but after a story time video, a heavy weight falls onto my shoulder. Affection lodges in my throat when I turn my head and find Mateo's cheek resting on my arm.

A pang of longing strikes my chest, and it's like a douse of frigid water, dragging me back to reality. This is not meant for me. I am not the found safety needed to fall asleep on someone's shoulder. I am not soft or vulnerable in the way men desire.

My body is not a divine shrine, but a battlefield, full of emotional wounds and physical flaws.

These moments—the ones hidden in the fold of silence where people fall in love—they don't belong to me, but perhaps for the first time in my life, I desperately want them to.

It terrifies me, the deep-rooted yearning that burrows in my chest.

I pack it away with every other emotion I've buried over the years, locking it into a cage. It's easier to pretend those feelings don't exist than allow them to consume what's left of me.

"Mateo," I murmur, and he rustles, his body inching closer. My heart sinks. "You need to put your mask on."

His sleepy eyes crack open, and so, so slowly, he rolls to the other side of the bed and slides the mask over his face. The area where he touched me cools, and a small voice whispers for him to come back, but I throw it into the cage where it can't grow and hurt me.

I plug our phones in and turn off the light, and as I fall asleep, I feel like a fool for missing how his body felt against mine.

CHAPTER 12

CHARLIE

"There you are!"

The sudden noise surprises me, and my ears meet my shoulders as I drop the pipette onto the bench. It bounces and slams against a microscope. Sofía bounds into the lab, searching the space before running to the back bay and falling into a rolling chair.

She plays with the preserved specimen on the benchtop in front of her, lining the jars of fish and invertebrates in a neat row.

"Uh...here I am?" I pause my music and rerack the pipette. "Did I miss a meeting or something?"

I've sequestered myself in the lab all morning, taking advantage of the quiet space to process samples and avoid Mateo.

So far, things have been going *spectacularly*. I'm halfway done with my protocol to extract DNA from water samples, and I haven't seen him since breakfast, where he offered me an iced coffee and I nearly melted into a puddle on the floor.

I need space to unravel what's going on with my mind, body, and spirit, and why each has decided Mateo is the object of its desire.

Frankly, it's concerning, and I haven't been able to disentangle each thread to discover where the foreign emotions originate.

"I'm hiding from Jett," Sofía says, spinning in the lab chair, her long brown hair flying around.

"Why?"

"He keeps asking me random questions, and when I asked why, he said, 'I'm trying to understand you,' which freaked me out. Then he said he thought I was pretty, and running felt like the best plan of action."

Right on.

I'm all for running when you don't know what to do in a situation. I've never been a fighter, but I'm damn good at fleeing an uncomfortable situation.

"Oh, so he has a *crush*," I tease. "Fourth day on the boat and you've found yourself a fling."

"There is no *fling*," she yells in a shrill voice. She pauses her spinning to glare at me. "It's unprofessional to tell me I smell like candy."

I take a sniff; her perfume is very sweet, like cotton candy. It's fitting for her—an extension of her kind, welcoming personality.

"You do smell like candy. It's sweet." I giggle at my pun, but Sofía does not find it nearly as amusing. "He's *sweet* on you."

Damn, I'm on a roll.

This is much more fun than thinking about my own love life, or lack thereof. All I have is weird tingling when Mateo touches me, and I'd much rather tease Sofía than unpack that novelty.

I have a hypothesis, but it's not one I'm ready to accept.

"He's nice, I guess." She hums as she stacks tube racks on top of each other, creating a small pyramid. "It's just weird."

"That he's flirting with you?" I ask, the question laced with amusement.

She groans, then whispers, "That he's flirting with me and *I kinda like it.*"

Her hands fly to cover the blush on her cheeks, and my laughter echoes around the room.

"Flirt back."

"I can't!"

"Why not?"

"I-I don't know."

Her brow furrows, and she busies herself with random items on the bench. It's a contemplative silence as I resume my work, and my mind wanders to Mateo. His mussed hair in the morning and how adorable he looks with his CPAP mask on, like he's cosplaying as a fighter-jet pilot. How he argues with his abuela about audiobooks but continues to listen to the one she picked out, even though he hates every second.

He's grumbled about Elora and her lack of critical thinking skills since we've been on the boat. She's had quite the impact on him.

I've learned more about him in the last four days than I have in the two years since we met, and it's jarring because what I've learned doesn't feel like enough. It's an age of discovery where every stone turned leads to something new, something exciting.

It's a peaceful half hour before she bulldozes into my happy bubble with a highly unprofessional question—ironic, given the reason she's hiding from Jett.

"So are you and Mateo hate fucking? What's going on there?" She doesn't lift her head from opening and closing an Eppendorf tube. "*Lots* of tension between you two."

My first response is to choke on my saliva and hope it sends me to an early grave. When that doesn't work, I pretend I didn't hear her probing question and continue my work like she didn't just send me into a state of disarray.

It doesn't work, and she asks again.

Hearing it a second time is no less jarring than the first.

My pulse races and my hands sweat profusely beneath the nitrile gloves.

Why would she ask such an insane question? Mateo and I sleeping together is...when did it get so hot in here?

"No."

My voice jumps an octave from shock.

Yes, that's what this is—the insane thumping in my chest.

"But you want to," she says smugly, like she's caught me with my hand in the cookie jar.

"I never said that."

"Oh, you didn't need to." She waves a hand around in a circle near my head. "Your face did all the talking. And it's saying 'I want to sleep with Mateo.'"

I huff, cleaning up my bench space and ignoring her laughter.

We are *not* hate fucking. We are barely even friends.

Even if I have thought about it—which I would not admit to Sofía—thinking about him is far different from actually seeing him naked, which based on the way my pits are sweating, I don't know how I would handle myself if it actually happened.

Faint, maybe.

I saw a sliver of abdomen yesterday when he stretched, and I had to tear my gaze away before my jaw fell open.

This has to be some sort of sickness.

Sofía spins in her chair again, and I'm nearly done cleaning when the door bursts open and she drops to the floor like there's a fire.

"Who is it?" she whispers, crawling under the bench, knees to her chest.

"You're insane," I whisper back, but also crouch, peeking my head around to identify our visitor.

My heartbeat thrashes when a very manly arm comes into view. "It's a man."

"Which one? There are so many."

"I don't know." I try for another angle, and my stomach drops when Shaun appears.

I ignore the mild disappointment and wave at him from our hiding spot. I have no idea why I'm still down here or why we hid in the first place, but I'm following Sofía's lead, so if she says hide, I'm not going to question her.

"There you are," Shaun, an ROV technician, says, glancing around the rolling chair I placed to block us. "I've been looking for you."

Why is everyone *but* Mateo looking for me today?

"Yup. That's me. Right here."

I give him a thumbs-up, and Sofía hides a laugh with a cough. My hand darts out to whack her.

Shaun stares at me oddly, probably because I'm crouched beneath a lab bench beside Sofía, who is giggling like she's drunk.

"I wanted to check what collection equipment you needed deployed with the next ROV dive."

"Just a Niskin for the water samples and a grab for the soil."

He nods and gives me another peculiar look, one I can't decipher, when I make no move to get up from the floor. "Will I see you at dinner tonight?"

His voice is low, his attention focused entirely on me, and I have to suppress the urge to squirm.

"Uh, yes? I mean, probably. Will there be food?"

Sofía cackles again, which morphs into a grunt when my fist connects with her stomach.

"I'll see you tonight, then."

My brow furrows at the bizarre tone, but before I can think about it any more, he disappears and we fall into a fit of giggles.

"Boys are so weird," she says between breaths.

"I don't understand how their brains work. Freaks me out," I admit.

I never know what Mateo is thinking or how he's feeling. He teases me, but does he like me? Do I annoy him? Does he find me abrasive or hypercompetitive?

We've spent the last few days on top of each other—metaphorically speaking. The room is small, the bed isn't much bigger, and most of our day-to-day tasks are the same. It's the most time I've ever spent with someone besides Amy, and I haven't spontaneously combusted yet.

I don't know what to do with the knowledge.

"My last boyfriend was really into drinking chlorophyll water," Sofía says.

"That seems like a scam."

"It was! Made his pee green. Maybe it makes me a bad person, but it freaked me out and I broke up with him."

My stomach cramps from laughter, tears beading on my lower lash as she giggles along. We're still on the floor, and I want this moment to last. It's been so long since I've had this much fun with anyone other than Amy.

"I haven't been on a date in a long time."

The confession falls from my tongue, and I immediately want to shove it back into my mouth.

It's difficult to explain that I no longer go on dates because I grew exhausted of how they made me feel: inadequate, undesirable, unfulfilled.

Very few made it past a first date, and I only slept with a handful and never spoke to them again after. None of them were fond of getting kicked out immediately after they came, but I have rules, and I wasn't breaking them.

I don't need to add the anxiety of a relationship to the shit show that is my mind, so I deleted the dating apps.

"They're overrated," she says, missing my obvious surprise at her lack of probing.

The urge to word vomit an explanation strikes like a lightning bolt, but before I can embarrass myself, a deep voice booms through the lab.

"Charlie?"

I scramble off the floor, smooth away the dust on my pants, and readjust my top.

Mateo leans against the bench, one leg folded over the other, thinly veiled amusement on his face. My heartbeat skips when a full smile blooms.

"Hi."

"Hi," he responds, and the air grows thick.

Sofía kills the tension, popping her head from our hiding spot. "Hi, Mateo!" His head jerks, startled as she crawls out. "I've got...work. Yes. Things to do!"

She scurries away, pausing at the door to waggle her eyebrows behind his back. Before I can make a face, she's gone, and it's just him and me, standing in the lab.

What do I do with my hands?

They flail before landing on the bench with a thud.

"How are you doing?" he asks, his attention roaming my body like he's checking for injuries.

"I'm...good."

Often, I'm far from "okay" or "fine," but I follow the societal obligation of answering the question with one of those two answers when, usually, I'm neither of those things.

But today, I *am* good.

And there's something thrilling in that.

I'm wearing an outfit I typically wouldn't—my arms on full display—and I admitted something uncomfortable to Sofía and didn't allow it to eat me up inside.

"Good," he confirms. "I came to get you for lunch."

"You did?"

Why in Neptune's big blue sea does that make my chest explode with warmth?

He nods, his cheeks flushing a soft pink. "You hate soggy french fries, so I wanted to make sure you didn't miss the fresh ones."

"There are french fries for lunch?" My voice rises as I scramble to collect my things, and Mateo's laughter follows me as I rush out the door.

I'm halfway down the hall when it hits me he knows I hate soggy fries, even though I've never told him.

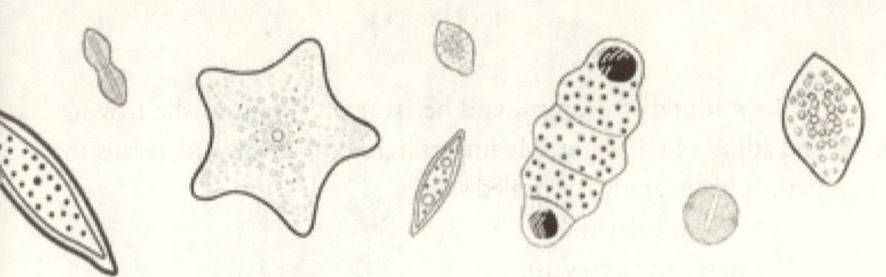

CHAPTER 13

MATEO

"C'mon, Charlie."

I wrap my hand around the ankle sticking out beneath the covers and drag her to the end of the bed. Her limbs flail, legs kicking and arms swatting the empty bed around her.

"No," she groans, throwing the covers over her head. "Snooze."

I bite back a chuckle, moving to crouch beside her.

"We have work to do. Your manuscript isn't going to edit itself."

Her head bobbles beneath the sheets while she mumbles into the pillow. "I've hired goblins to help me. They work before nine a.m., and I work after."

She glowers at me as I lift the blanket off her head. Her irises are gray in this light, like an incoming hurricane moving toward land.

"It's time to join the living, bruja."

Charlie's nose twitches in disdain, and fuck me, she's cute in the morning. Golden hair mats against the side of her head, and her features are still sleepy, even if they're full of annoyance.

She's adorably grumpy, and her scar pulls taut as she frowns and adjusts to the light. My fingers itch to trace the pink tissue, to pepper kisses along the healed skin.

"I have chocolate..."

"Really?" She perks up.

"A whole bag waiting for you."

With a groan and a few concerning popping sounds, Charlie rolls off the side and falls into the crack between the bed and the wall. I move to help her when a quiet "I'm okay" fills the air. She presses up, and I stand perfectly still as if I've spotted a rare creature in the wild and am afraid to scare it away.

This is the most skin Charlie has ever shown, and every nerve in my body vibrates. She was careful to change into her pajamas after I turned out the light and took my glasses off, but the early-morning light filters in from the small porthole and illuminates her skin and every single scar on her chest, of which there are many.

I busy myself with her knickknacks on the desk, the ones she unpacked and lined up with precision. Her beloved Darwin bob-blehead. A collection of rocks. A framed photo of her and Amy. I don't want her to hide, to assume I'm staring at her scars, when really I'm staring at *her*.

Charlie moves past, and air lodges in my throat at the sight of her pajama shorts wedged between her butt cheeks. She saunters around the room, entirely unaware of the predicament. We barely survived the ordeal with her vibrator. If she realizes I can see the whole globe of her left ass cheek as she rummages through her bag, things will go south.

I squirm, arousal zapping down my spine, and focus my energy on preventing a boner. I shouldn't stare at her, *I shouldn't*, but every sound she makes is a test of my strength. She mumbles some-thing to herself, and I snatch my laptop and bag, beelining for the door.

A glimpse of ass cheek, and I'm on my knees for her.

"I'm gonna find a table and some coffee," I yell, halfway out the door and refusing to look back. If I do, I know I'll never leave.

"Extra espresso, Mateo," Charlie calls out as the door falls shut.

Charlie releases a deep, slightly arousing sigh after she takes a sip of the iced coffee I made for her. Rogue strands of hair fall out of her braid as she sits across from me at a table in the main lounge.

The ornate room is empty besides the two of us, the rest of the crew working hard to prepare for another dive before the ship arrives at our next destination. It's much-needed time to catch up on the tasks I've neglected since we embarked nearly a week ago.

The faded Charles Darwin sticker judges me from the front of her laptop. Surrounded by decals of deep-sea creatures and science puns, Darwin watches the effect Charlie has on me.

I've always found her little obsession adorable. When I pointed out the fallacy in her dream to meet him, Charlie scribbled an asterisk beside the point to clarify that visiting his grave would also suffice.

She treats her bobblehead of him like a shrine, and in times of confusion or frustration, I've heard her whisper "What would Darwin do?" beneath her breath.

"When do I get my chocolate?" Charlie asks, eyeing the bag hanging off my chair.

"When you earn it, bruja."

Bowing her head, she focuses on the table before saying, "I don't like it when you call me that." Her voice is nothing more than a whisper. "I'm not some crazy witch because I believe in astrology and crystals. I only cursed you *one time.*"

"You what?" I ask, a disbelieving laugh leaving my lips.

She's cursed me?

Why is that incredibly arousing?

"It didn't work," she mutters with a deep scowl. "You still have perfect hair."

"Perfect hair, huh?"

"It's not stupid to believe in that stuff..."

She twirls a bracelet, one of many on her wrists, the deep blue a contrast to her light skin. The vulnerability she expresses stings like a shallow cut. She plays it off with eye rolls, but it's right there, so overwhelming that I have to fight the urge to rub away the discomfort in my chest.

I never knew the nickname bothered her this deeply.

"I don't think that, Charlie," I insist. I don't call her bruja because she likes crystals or finds comfort in the cryptic words of a constellation. Reaching out, I pluck a bracelet from her wrist, sliding the pink stones onto my own. "Now we both believe."

Her jaw slackens, her focus fixed on my wrist.

"What crystal is this, anyway?" The stones are warm, heated from her skin. The knowledge causes a buzz along my spine.

"Uh...rose quartz."

"What does it mean?" I ask, and she hacks for air, her face flushing a deep strawberry hue.

What did I say?

She wheezes, then gulps down the remainder of her iced coffee and says, "Love, compassion, and emotional healing."

Oh. *Oh.*

Of all the bracelets on her wrist, I chose the one symbolizing love. The universe wasn't aiming for subtlety. Having lost the use of any rational part of my brain, and void of any response to her love crystal, I dig a piece of chocolate out of my bag.

An offering to both her and whatever love god is willing to listen.

Let the bracelet be a sign.

She gets the same goofy look every time she spots the blue foil, like it's the greatest thing she's ever tasted. Her shoulders wiggle and she tears apart the wrapper, a woman on a mission, before devouring the chocolate in two impressive bites.

"How many more do you have?" she asks longingly.

"Enough for the trip if we ration."

"*Ration*?" She sounds like I told her to cut off a toe, not limit her sugar consumption. "What kind of restrictions are we talking about? One a day? I won't survive that. We're not at war, so why do we need to cut back?" She hums, her fingers flying across her keyboard while she talks to herself. "If we have eighteen days left...Amy gave me two bags." She glances up. "How many pieces do you have?"

"One hundred and twenty."

I packed two Costco-sized bags. It felt wrong to not leave a piece for her in the morning.

"Oh." She jerks backward. "You came very prepared..." She trails off, and I can see the gears turning in her mind. Does she realize I have feelings for her? Could she feel the same?

"I didn't want you to go three weeks without your favorite treat," I admit, though the confession feels silly on my tongue.

Her throat bobs. "Thank you, Mateo."

My heart does twisted things when she says my name like that, with intent and purpose, each of the syllables sharp and full of inflection. I want to hear it more often.

I focus on my computer, responding to emails from undergrads and grading reports from the BIO 301 lab course I run. The timer I set rings out, and I offer Charlie the candy.

Every hour, the alarm goes off, and each time, she beams at me and firecrackers explode in my chest.

As the fourth ring goes off, Shaun stops at the table, turning his body to face Charlie.

"Hey."

He greets her but ignores my presence entirely, leaning a hip against the table. I've noticed his lingering looks at her, the way he searches for her at dinner and engages her in conversation.

She blinks at his proximity, and I brutally bite down on my lip. Her brows dip in confusion.

"Oh, hi, Shaun."

"Some of the crew are playing board games tonight after dinner if you want to join."

The suggestion in his voice is disgustingly obvious, and it requires every ounce of professionalism I possess to control the rage simmering in my chest.

I've been flirting with Charlie for two years, so if he wants his turn, he needs to get his ass in line.

"Sounds fun!" Her cheery response fans the flames of jealousy, and only after a long stretch of silence do I realize they're watching me. Charlie's brows scrunch, her head tilting before she asks, "Are you going to play, Mateo?"

Shaun cuts in. "If you're busy with work, I can keep Charlie company."

Her lip pulls between her teeth, her focus shifting between Shaun and me.

"Sounds fun," I grit out. If he's going to flirt with her, he's going to do so under my watchful eye, where I can curse him the way Charlie tried to curse me.

Shaun nods, but his disappointment is evident, and the urge to stick out my tongue is almost overwhelming. Charlie's rubbing off on me.

Since we've met, I've wanted her to see me as anything more than a rival. But since we've started this adventure, something has changed. The tectonic plates our relationship is built upon have begun to shift, only I can't decipher if they're moving closer or further apart.

I've fought the same battle in my mind—to tell her how I feel or silently let go and move on. Buck up or shut up, as Oliver so eloquently put it. But watching her build something with anyone else might kill me, which means I'm at a crossroads.

"There are too many people to play," Shaun says, and I cut him a glare. I know where this is going. "But if we have partners, it could work."

And there it is. Hook, line, and sinker. All he has to do is wait for Charlie to take the bait.

He's been this way all evening. Sitting beside her, stealing her air and attention. Offering her a drink after dinner, leaning in close to speak into her ear, touching her bicep after she says something amusing.

And I've had to watch it all. Witness her respond to the subtle touches and whispered words. It's a tough pill to swallow, watching from the outside looking in. Has she ever reacted to me like that?

Have I harbored these feelings for two years with no chance of reciprocity?

The pasta I had for dinner sours in my stomach. The slight sway of the vessel doesn't help matters.

Here it comes, the question he's set up. Three...two...one...

"Charlie, do you want to be my partner?"

So predictable.

Her gaze slides to mine from across the table, and there's something hesitant in it.

Say no.

Her lip twitches, then morphs into a smile. It's becoming difficult to sit here, to watch as she offers her warmth to someone new. In Rhode Island, I had the benefit of ignorance. If I didn't hear about her dating life or see her with anyone, I could live in wonderful, unenlightened bliss with the belief that she harbors intense feelings for me.

Watching her with Shaun makes me want to throw him overboard and feed him to sharks.

"Uh, sure," Charlie says. "As long as we can be blue."

I want to be a petty asshole and steal those pieces, then crush him with my Catan skills.

"I already chose blue," Jett admits, laying them on the table in front of him.

If his chaotic energy, outrageous sayings, and perpetual good mood weren't already growing on me, this moment would be the tipping point from acquaintances to an unbreakable lifetime bond.

"We can be partners," I declare, moving seats to sit beside him while keeping track of Shaun and his smarmy face, afraid if I turn my back he will whisk Charlie away.

"Mateo and I are going to crush you all like little bugs!" Jett points around the room but pauses when Sofía lifts a brow.

"And if Vivian and I beat you?" she asks.

"Not gonna happen, dudette," he boasts, before leaning over and whispering, "How do you play Catan?"

Oh, this is wonderful. I can mold him to do my bidding. I rise, signaling for Jett to follow. "We're going to strategize."

"You can't do that," Charlie yells as we huddle in the corner. "Not fair!"

"You have a partner, *Charlie*," I say pointedly. "Strategize with him."

Her eye twitches, the telltale sign she's pissed off but trying to mask it. Makes two of us.

Leaning in, I tell Jett the plan. "I don't care about winning. I only care about sabotaging Shaun."

Jett's head tilts before a roguish grin appears. "Ah...This is about Blondie, isn't it?"

Blondie laughs across the room, and the sound skitters along my spine.

"She's wicked cool, man."

I know she's wicked cool. So does Shaun, which is why he's trying to flirt her right out of her panties, and I hate him with every fiber of my being, because it might be working.

Five days on the boat and he might accomplish what I never have: earning Charlie's attention.

It's embarrassing how badly I want her to notice me, to see me, but my inner demons whisper that if she did see me, something would have happened these last two years.

I've never been subtle in my flirting, but maybe she's never seen me in that light, and every effort has been futile.

Crippling fear of rejection is not a phobia easily shed, especially not when it played a pivotal role in my developmental years. I blame Karla Jergens and her brutal annihilation of my self-confidence at thirteen when I asked her to the winter ball and she laughed at me like it was some kind of prank.

I didn't ask another woman out until college, and even then, she essentially told me to ask her out because she was tired of waiting. What I felt for Karla pales in comparison to how I feel about Charlie. Karla's rejection crushed me, but if Charlie tells me she has no interest in me, it will result in a Permian-level extinction of my ability to put myself out there.

"So, like, you love her, right?"

My head jerks to Jett, who wears a lopsided grin. I frantically search around to make sure no one else heard him, and he throws up his hands in peace. "No dramas, man. She's dope, but like, I'm right, *right*? You're totally in love with her. I can see it."

"I am not *totally in love*."

Jett laughs, and the sound grates on the last of my nerves.

"Sure," he drawls, "you just watch her all the time in a creepy, stalker kind of way and have been trying to murder Shaun with your eyes."

He pats me on the shoulder, like an elderly man, and walks away.

Creepy, stalker kind of way?

"I do not stare at her like that," I hiss, stomping after him. Have I denied his claim? No, but I'm not sure I can, at least not fully.

Could I love Charlie Bowen?

With every fiber of my being, if she would let me.

The thought settles deep in my chest, that kernel burrowing into the marrow of my bones. When I return to the table, she is watching me, nibbling at her lip.

Her mouth opens as if she's going to say something, but Shaun steals her attention, solidifying my resolve.

I have to annihilate him in Catan.

CHAPTER 14

CHARLIE

Mateo is brooding, and I'm so turned on by it I might burst into flames.

The man is pissed off about something, his brow furrowed and arms crossed over his chest, and fuck me, it's hotter than hell.

He's been this way all afternoon.

"I'll trade you three lumber for one ore," Shaun offers, and like every other time, Jett and Mateo turn down his trade.

They'll trade with Sofía and Vivian, but if Shaun asks, the answer is always no.

"That's more than a fair trade," Vivian says, her head bouncing between Mateo and Shaun.

Jett flicks through their cards and hums. "Look, dude"—he shrugs—"we don't need any lumber."

Mateo stretches his arms over his head, leans back in his chair, and glares at Shaun like he's the singular cause of climate change.

What the fuck is his problem, and why am I physically responding to his pissy behavior?

Shaun sighs, then rolls the dice.

"I didn't expect such harsh competition." He chuckles. "I was hoping to impress you by winning."

Impress me?

Oh my god…is he flirting with me?

My brain flies through past events. The offer to play board games but excluding Mateo. Sitting close to me at dinner. Offering me a drink and demanding I be his partner.

Shaun fixates on my lips, and my jaw slackens.

Holy shit, he *is* flirting with me.

The realization forces my attention to Mateo, whose scowl deepens, and I jerk away from Shaun, increasing the space between us. A tingle ripples along my arm from the intense glare on Mateo's face.

No man has any business looking this sexy with a scowl. The fabric of his ivory button-down pulls taut against his broad chest and his fists flex open and closed as he surveys the board.

I squirm in my seat.

Mateo's once-infuriating competitive nature is now doing absurd things to my brain chemistry, creating the impulse to maul him with my mouth.

It's a highly concerning urge.

The game ends, and to no one's surprise, Jett and Mateo win by a landslide.

"Catan Kings," Jett yells. "Get this on film, Doug."

Doug moves around the table, recording the board and Jett's celebration, before returning to his laptop. The gloating winners clean up the board as Vivian shakes her head in amusement.

"I knew that goober was going to win," she says, leaning back and running her fingers through her short pixie cut. "My girlfriend, Amber, loves his channel. She's jealous that I get to spend three weeks with him."

A shadow falls over me, and I peer up at Shaun, who hovers beside my chair. "I was going to watch the sunset on the deck, if you want to join."

The words are a suggestive whisper, an invitation to spend time alone, but my stomach roils as I clock Mateo with an incorrigible frown. With a shake of his head, he disappears, and I want to chase him down.

I can't shake the feeling I'm the cause of his anger, only I don't know what I did. There's been no teasing today, no back-and-forth. The morning was productive, the two of us working in a comfortable silence until I earned a piece of chocolate. But something shifted this evening, and while it was hot, now I'm in my head. What did I do to upset him?

I shake my head. "I'm going to head to bed, but thank you for the offer."

"Next time," he says, his hand brushing my shoulder, and I wiggle off his touch when he's out of sight. I wait with bated breath for Mateo's return, but when it's clear he's not coming back, my anxiety takes over.

With a quick goodbye to Sofía and Vivian, I search for Mateo, hoping his mood has nothing to do with me.

My fingers stiffen as my anxiety rages while I wait for Mateo to exit the bathroom. The minutes tick by, and my rogue emotion stake over, tears pressing against my eyelids.

When it all becomes too much, my body short-circuits and I cry. It's horrifying.

The door finally creaks open and Mateo appears, his shorts slung low on his waist, revealing the sculpted expanse of his chest and a soft peppering of chest hair between his pecs.

When he notices me sitting on the edge of the bed, his jaw clenches.

I ignore the pang beneath my diaphragm.

"I thought you'd be with Shaun," he mumbles, moving around the room with a storm cloud over his head.

"Why would I be with Shaun?"

Mateo lets out a disbelieving, bitter laugh. "I thought you liked him."

"He's nice." I shrug, then blurt out, "Are you mad at me?"

I never thought I cared about his opinion of me, but maybe it's the opposite, because as Mateo silently moves around the room, I'm embarrassed by how deeply I want him to like me.

"No."

So, yes.

The tears I tried to banish spring back as I choke out, "I-I thought we were...changing."

I don't have another word to explain the shift between us or to describe how I feel around him. When he's around, my chest bangs with a sensation similar to the anticipatory fall of a roller coaster. It's terrifying, the power he holds over me, and I want to hide from it and chase it simultaneously.

"Do you see me, Charlie?"

When the silence stretches and morphs, anguish flares in his eyes, but I don't understand—the question *or* why he's looking at me with despair and resignation.

"I—I don't know what you mean."

He nods, clicking his tongue. "I didn't think so."

My heart squeezes as the room falls quiet.

"I'm tired," he says, fluffing the pillow wall and sliding into bed. My body is rigid and disconnected from my brain as I mindlessly shuffle around the room. Mateo clicks the light off, and I slip into my pajamas, emotion clogging my throat.

"Do you want to watch TikToks?" I ask in the darkness, feeling bold enough to speak.

We've watched them together every night since we arrived, and right now, when my emotions are volatile, I need a sense of normalcy.

"Not tonight." He pushes against the pillows, securing them, and then rolls to face his back to me. His breathing evens out while I stare up at the ceiling.

The blatant dismissal strikes like a barb to the heart.

The darkness consumes me, letting every awful, self-deprecating thought creep in until I'm swimming in reasons why he hates me. Why I'm not good enough and never will be. Why I'm unlovable.

Tears track down my cheeks, soaking the pillow. And on soft feet, I slip out of bed, snagging a sweatshirt and heading to one of the private office spaces. The FaceTime ringtone fills the air while I swipe away the tears, the only evidence I'm impacted by Mateo's behavior, that I'm *hurt*.

I know what's happening, why I feel this way, but I can't say the words out loud and make it real.

It's one a.m. on the East Coast, but I pray Amy is awake, because right now I need my best friend. I need to hear her voice, and I wish I didn't depend on her so much, but I need her to help me work through my muddled thoughts.

I've always put too much of my emotional baggage on Amy's shoulders, but I can't always work through it on my own without shutting down.

Amy's face pops onto the screen, her pink hair fanned out on a pillow. "What's up, Charles?"

A sob rips from my chest at her familiar smile, and the signal between my brain and mouth disconnects as everything I'm feeling bubbles to the surface.

"I think—and Mateo. Well, the thing is—he's upset, but I don't know why, and now my brain is scrambled eggs because I don't know how I feel or how he feels..."

The words are a string of incoherent nonsense.

I have no idea how to arrange my thoughts. Everything between Mateo and me before this trip was black and white. He was the annoying thorn in my side, put into a definable box, but now everything is gray.

Uncovering this new side of him—the version that leaves chocolate and touches my scars like they're special to him—is a discovery akin to people in the 1600s learning Earth is neither flat nor the center of the universe.

Life-altering.

"Are you high?" Amy sits up, a blanket falling off her chest until I'm eye to eye with her pierced nipples. "I didn't understand a single word you just said."

I'm unfazed by her nudity. After a night of pounding back wine coolers and watching true-crime documentaries, we decided we needed to know what the other's boobs looked like in case it was the only way to identify our bodies after a gruesome murder.

A large hand moves into view of the camera, covering both of her breasts, and a smug smile blooms on her face.

"Ames...are you with a man right now?"

A deep, very British accent says, "As nice as it is to see you again, Charlie, please get to the point so she can get back to the man lying in her bed."

For a split second, my predicament fades away as I squeal, "*Oliver?*"

Amy nods, her eyebrows wiggling, before shifting to Oliver, who, after a moment of silence, releases a groan not meant for my ears.

Gross.

"Mateo isn't the person I thought he was, and now my brain is freaking out because he is actually kind and thoughtful and attractive, and for years, I thought he was this big, cocky asshole, but he's not the asshole." I pause before admitting what is an incredibly difficult pill to swallow. "I am."

The words whoosh out on a breath, and the admission loosens a kernel of guilt in my chest.

"Oh, wow. It's finally happening."

"What's happening?"

"*The reckoning*," she whispers. "I've been waiting for this day. Oliver, will you grab that binder?"

A worn-down t-shirt replaces his arm, and Amy smirks, focused on whatever's happening in her room.

"Binder?"

"Hold on." She flips to the first page and begins reading. "Today, we have witnessed a miracle," she starts in a monotone voice. "Our beloved Charles has blossomed from a girl in hate into a woman in love."

My jaw flies to the floor.

What the fuck is this?

"On this glorious day," she continues, "Charlotte Louise Bowen has conceded that Mateo Alvarez is, in fact, not a 'pain in her ass' but the object of her skewed affection."

"Amy, what is this?"

"I wrote this three weeks after we started living together, and I have patiently waited to be right. I played the long game." She flicks through the pages. "It has become clear that Charles's intense, self-proclaimed rivalry is truly a shield for the feelings she harbors for a certain tall PhD student."

Oliver snickers in the background as I sit stunned, listening to Amy's speech.

My first instinct is to deny her words, to bury any feelings I have until they fade away, but there's no point in lying to her or myself.

I *am* harboring feelings for Mateo, and I was hurt today, enough to call my best friend.

"Say hypothetically, I agreed with your hypothesis, and perhaps have potentially developed a smidge of feeling for Mateo." Amy beams a victorious smile, and I hiss, "This is all hypothetical!"

"Sure it is," Oliver chimes in.

I ignore the truth in his annoying British accent. "And let's say Mateo and I were exploring new territory in our relationship, but now he's suddenly upset, and I can't shake the feeling I did something to cause it."

"All hypothetical?" Amy cocks a brow.

"Yup." I pop the *p*, and she gives me a knowing look.

"Did you say anything?"

"I-I don't think so. We were fine. He's Willy Wonka, Amy." I drop the truth bomb, letting it explode between us.

How many times have I jokingly said I would marry whoever was my chocolate fairy?

"*Oh.*"

"He brought the chocolate on the boat for me," I whisper. "He's being so fucking kind that I don't know how to act anymore! But now he's turned into this...this different person, and he barely spoke to me after board games, and we didn't watch TikToks."

That stings the most. It became a nightly routine for us and the best part of my day, when Mateo is mussed and ready for bed. I like when it's the two of us.

"So you've been watching TikToks, and now...?"

"Nothing," I say. "And when I asked him if he was upset with me, he said, 'Do you see me, Charlie?' What the fuck is that supposed to mean?"

"Oh. That is not good." Amy shakes her head.

"What do you mean, it's *not good*?"

"Do you see him, Charlie?" Oliver asks.

"I don't know what that means," I scream.

"Who do you look for first in a room?" he asks, and it all clicks. Oh, shit. "I think she sees him," Oliver says, and the walls close in on me. My lungs constrict, and the beginning stages of a massive spiral begin. Sweaty hands. Shallow breaths. Racing thoughts.

"Uh...Charles, don't get weird when I ask you this—"

"I won't get weird. I'm not weird."

My head does an odd jerking motion, which does not validate my declaration.

Do you see me? Do you see me? Do you see me?

His words replay on a loop in my mind. He's all I see, and it's infuriating and terrifying, and I've never felt so utterly consumed by someone before.

"Do you have a crush on Mateo?"

"*What*? No!" I don't know why my first reaction is to deny my feelings, but the words are shrill and unbelievable.

"I'm just asking because you've spoken about him every day since we've met, and your eye is doing that twitching thing when you're upset and bottling it up."

She shrugs, her pink hair bobbing. I hate when she does that annoying best-friend thing where she sees straight through my bullshit.

"Ugh. Fine. Maybe I do. But it doesn't matter because he will barely speak to me. I've finally begun to like him, and now he *hates* me."

"Maybe apologize," she offers. I open my mouth, and she lifts a hand. "Even if you don't know what you did wrong. It could help."

"You're right."

"I know," she preens. "Now, if you'll excuse me, there is a very hot man lying naked in my bed."

"You think I'm hot?" Oliver teases.

Bleh.

"Go."

129

At least one of us is going to have a good time tonight, because I sure as hell am not going to while I practice my apology speech.

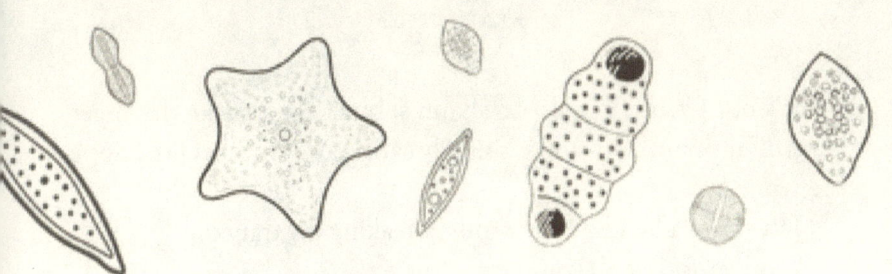

CHAPTER 15

MATEO

"Wanna share your feelings?"

I leap, nearly spilling my scalding coffee as Jett's hot breath hits the back of my neck.

"It's not healthy, man," he continues, flopping into the chair across from me in the mess area. "Your insides will rot."

"I'm fine," I say, using one of Charlie's favorite phrases.

"You're not a great liar."

I huff a laugh, but it's bitter and empty.

How do I explain to him that when I woke up this morning and turned over, Charlie was right there within arm's reach, but she felt miles away?

Or how watching her sit beside Shaun made me sick with jealousy?

And everything I feel is a product of my own choices, so I have no one to blame but myself. Frustration bubbles to the surface, with nowhere to release the tension.

It's not Charlie's fault, or Shaun's, but I can't shake the anger and disappointment, and it's slowly eating away at what little hope remained.

Jett waves a hand over my mug, breaking my trance.

"You've gotta spill your beans," he says.

"It's not that simple."

"You like a girl. You tell the girl. Easy peasy." Jett's smile is bright and toothy, and I wish I could live in his world where it's black and white.

But I'm in the real world, where actions have consequences, and telling Charlie how I feel has real repercussions. What if she rejects me? How do we navigate the remainder of the voyage if she's uncomfortable? How do I look at her for the next three years of our PhD program and not relive the heartbreak?

It's never as easy as it seems, and Charlie is a complex being built like a Jenga tower. With a gentle touch, she's strong enough to stand, but with a heavy hand or poor decision, she'll crumble.

I've studied her—documented every new discovery until I became an expert.

"I won't survive the rejection," I admit, my breakfast souring in my stomach.

"Who says she'll reject you?"

Occam's razor states when considering multiple explanations for an event, it's usually the simplest one that's most likely to be true. Charlie will reject me. It's the simplest explanation for what will happen if I tell her. It uses the fewest assumptions, and by the law of parsimony, it's the obvious choice.

My phone rings before I can put together a logical explanation, and my abuela's photo fills the screen.

"My abuela is calling," I say, hoping he takes the hint and leaves.

Instead, he snatches the phone and answers the call, adjusting his beanie and wiping his face as the call connects.

"Hi, Mateo's abuela," he yells, waving enthusiastically at the camera. "I'm Jett."

"Uh...Hello. Have you seen my grandson?" she asks, and I slide my head into the frame. "Did you finish the audiobook?"

Her grin is enormous, bordering on insane, and my hunch is confirmed. She picked the book *knowing* I would hate it, and now she wants me to admit it.

"Not yet. It's been busy getting settled."

And I never want to listen to another minute ever again.

"What audiobook?" Jett asks. "Maybe I'd like it."

"Probably not," I grumble.

I don't need Elora's poor choices to add to the storm of thoughts whirling in my brain. My own thoughts are company enough.

"It's a historical romance," my abuela explains, "with rogue pirates, high stakes, and a main character exploring the high seas."

"She's much more focused on exploring what's happening beneath Dominic's britches."

"She's doing that, too." My abuela winks, and a laugh bubbles from Jett's chest.

"Righteous! Send me the link," he says, looking in my direction.

My mind flies to Amy's text—her comment about Charlie's exploration beneath my waistband—and discomfort and confusion settles beneath my diaphragm.

Was it a silly joke, or was there merit behind the comment? Has she thought about me in a not-so-friendly way? Did I misinterpret her response? Was the flush from discomfort rather than schoolgirl embarrassment?

This is the problem and why I haven't told Charlie how I feel.

I descend into a spiral of questions and concerns until I've convinced myself it's easier to keep my thoughts to myself and flirt in hopes she'll pick up on the cues and drop some of her own.

Only she hasn't flirted back, nor has she said anything that suggests my advances would be welcome.

My smile slips, and my abuela catches it. "What's wrong? Are you not eating enough?"

I shake my head, ready to reassure her I'm eating plenty, but Jett beats me to it and spills my dirty secret to her.

This feels like a direct violation of the sacred rules beheld by the Brotherhood of Catan.

"He's super bummed Blondie is not digging his vibe."

She blinks, head cocking, as she translates his nonsense into a digestible sentence. When it clicks, she sighs.

"Mateo."

"Abuela."

"Don't *Abuela* me. She is a fool for not seeing you."

"She's not," I whisper, though my words are firm.

I haven't stepped into the spotlight.

Flirt with Charlie? Easy. Tell her how I feel? Yeah, I would rather not without hard evidence I won't get Karla Jergensed.

"If Charlie's a fool, then so is Mateo," Jett says plainly, and my abuela cackles. "Charlie is silly for not seeing how *awesome* Mateo is, and Mateo is a goober for not telling Charlie how he feels."

"Quite right," my abuela hums in agreement. "She is *not* Karla Jergens," she admonishes, but moves on. "I called to remind you to send me pictures of your trip, and that I've picked the next book."

"Don't worry, Abuela," Jett says, "I'm recording everything, and Doug, my videographer, is creating killer content, so I'll shoot it your way when it's done."

"Is the next book like this one?" I ask with trepidation.

"Oh, no." She winks. "It's much better."

I'm smiling, shaking my head, when Charlie walks into the galley, drowning in the fabric of an oversized sweatshirt, the hem falling to her mid-thigh.

She scans the room before landing on me, tugging at her sleeves. A million words left unsaid stand between us.

I heard her sneak out last night, only to return an hour later, tiptoeing around the room to keep quiet. Only I was awake the whole time, imagining every scenario of her with Shaun. What they could be doing, speaking about, sharing with each other.

"You could cut the tension between you two with a knife." Jett picks up his butter knife and waves it through the air. "Your abuela hung up, by the way."

I don't know what to say to her.

Something in my chest pinches when she takes her coffee and plate of food and sits at a table alone, her head hung low.

This is not what I want. I don't want her to distance herself, or for us to walk on eggshells around each other.

"You could tell her now," Jett says. "She's looking at you like you mean something to her."

My head lifts, first to Jett in surprise, then to Charlie, who's staring across the room. Her eyebrows are furrowed in concentration and the scar on her brow is crinkled.

Even now, in the early hours of the day, she's breathtakingly beautiful.

It hurts to behold her, but it's even more painful to look away.

"Listen, man," Jett starts. "You just gotta muster up some courage, walk over there, and tell her how you feel."

He rises from his seat and, without warning, shoves me out of mine. I scramble for footing, and Charlie watches on with confusion and concern.

Nerves rattling around my chest, I smooth out my shirt and take the first step toward her table. Then another.

I'm halfway there when someone slides into the seat across from her. She glances up briefly, a hidden message in the look, one I can't decipher.

The voice grows louder, and the hairs on the back of my neck rise. Shaun laughs, reaching out to squeeze her forearm.

My fist clenches as I move closer, and I'm a step away from the table when I hear the end of his sentence.

"...last night."

It's like someone dumped ice water over my head, and I'm frozen as Charlie offers him a hesitant expression.

She did leave last night to meet him.

I never had a shot.

The food I ate churns in my stomach and bitter resignation falls like thick snow, suffocating me until I have to spin on my heels and leave. Escape the soft laughter and playful smiles she offers so freely to Shaun.

I make it to the room—our room—and the first breath is freeing until the scent of *her* fills my nostrils. Cinnamon and mint. Intoxicating and poisonous.

There's no escape. She's in every nook and cranny. Her scent in the air. Her trinkets on the desk. Piles of clothing on the bathroom floor.

She's consumed every inch of the space and every cavern of my mind, and I don't know how to banish her. How to stop thinking about her or caring. How to get rid of the pain in my chest knowing she slipped away to spend time with *him*.

Jealousy is a bitter, ugly thing, and I'm its victim.

The silence is suffocating, but when it becomes easier to breathe, I slip in an earbud and allow Elora's poor decisions to drown out my own.

Maybe one of us will get a happy ending.

CHAPTER 16

CHARLIE

Mateo silently labels sampling tubes on the bench space across from me, his head down with his earbuds in. As he moves a tube from one rack to another, I jerk to look around the centrifuge, hoping we'll make eye contact.

When I woke this morning, he was gone and the sheets on his side of the bed were cold. There was no chocolate sitting on the desk, no morning smile upon exiting the bathroom, no companionable walk for coffee.

I found him sitting at a table with Jett, halfway through his meal, laughing, but when he spotted me, his demeanor shifted. Too afraid to sit with him, I sat alone, nibbling on my toast, watching him like a lunatic until Shaun joined me. When I was finally able to check for Mateo again, he was gone.

He's evaded me all morning, as much as he can in the small lab space. If we're walking at the same time, he slides as faraway as possible. Every glimpse of him worsens the deep ache in the center of my chest.

Am I so horrible that he's tired of dealing with me? Did I cross a line, take something too far, and now he wants nothing to do with me?

He rises from his bench, and I steel my nerves, spinning to intercept him.

"Mateo, can we—" My words are slow and unsure, but he bull-dozes past me and into the reagent room.

You've got to be fucking kidding me.

I slam a pipette back onto the rack with brutal force.

"Hey, asshole, I was talking to you," I yell, stomping into the small room, Mateo's back facing me when I grip his arm.

"Agh!" He leaps a foot into the air and rips out an earbud. Oh, shit. I'm glad he didn't hear me call him an asshole. Probably wouldn't have helped with clearing the air. "What, Charlie?"

I don't know if it's his tone, harsh and direct, or the use of my name instead of bruja. My name sounds wrong on his tongue. I want to be bruja again.

"Oh...I—" The practiced apology fizzles off my tongue as he stares. His irises have always been a comforting green, a verdant shade that pulls me in, but right now they're guarded. "Did you want some help?"

I refrain from smacking myself upside the head. *Just apologize, you big doofus.*

"I'm bleaching Nalgene bottles. I'm more than capable of han-dling it on my own."

His lips purse, and I physically recoil, stumbling into the door. A single look and it's like I've been shallowly sliced a hundred times.

I'm paralyzed by the glare, rooted in front of the door, desperate to understand what I did. A tear slips out, trailing down my cheek, and then I run out of the lab, escaping the way he looks at me like I'm dirt on his shoe, which is how I feel.

Tears falling freely, I slip into our room and lock myself in the bathroom, dropping to the floor. Mateo has never looked at me like that before, like I am the root of every issue in his life, and all would be right if I disappeared.

And I hate it, the way one glance cuts like a knife and how his opinion of me matters so deeply I'm crying on the bathroom floor. I hate this version of myself, the one so desperate to be valued that it's become my driving point for existence.

I spend every spare hour working on side projects for Cheryl because I'm terrified to say no and disappoint her. I made Mateo nothing more than someone to beat, all to feel a sense of accomplishment. But now I see Mateo—he consumes my vision—and he refuses to look at me.

I'm deep within a space of uncomfortable self-reflection when the door to the cabin unlatches. Mateo rustles around, and after wiping my tears and taming my hair, I find a morsel of courage to step out of the bathroom.

Mateo's facing away, midway through disrobing, and maybe it's the sight of his back muscles—okay, it's definitely the rippling muscles—but I stumble and face-plant on the floor with a loud, unattractive yelp.

He spins around, a wild look on his face, but I pop off the ground in an embarrassed frenzy. I grab my water bottle and a book Amy gave me and sprint to the door.

He takes a step forward. "Are you okay?"

They're the first words he's said to me today that hold no undercurrent of anger or disdain, and I don't know how to handle that, so instead, I offer him a mute thumbs-up and walk backward to reach the hallway.

"I'm going to the top deck for a while, if you want to join," I say before I spin on my heel and run away.

139

The blazing sun beats against my back as I devour my book. It's captivating, the world-building so immersive that, for the last few hours, I've been able to forget everything that haunts me—Mateo, my thoughts, massive metal cyber trucks.

I understand what Amy means when she says books are her escape, a way for her to leave the real world behind, if only for a short time.

The human woman is discovering that her new planet is host to ten times the number of men than women, and she's the mate of a chief, when laughter fills the deck, dragging me back to reality.

Lifting my head, I forget the book entirely at the sight of Mateo walking beside Jett, carrying a towel and...is that a fucking thigh tattoo?

The book slips from my hand and falls to the ground as he moves closer, displaying the artwork above his kneecap. Thin lines intersect thick, bold ones to create a stunning depiction of a monarch butterfly, wings stretched as he moves.

My heart pounds in my ears as I scramble to recover my novel while the guys sit on chairs across from me. I'm eye level with Mateo's tattoo, and as he twists, more ink peeks out from beneath his shorts. I'm nearly salivating at the idea of discovering what other ink he hides.

Neptune, why is his thigh so hot?

Why am I so hot?

Words blur on the cream-colored pages, and the ocean breeze does nothing to cool my skin while I eavesdrop on Mateo and Jett's conversation.

"They're amazing," Mateo says, and I peer over the pages to see what he's referring to. "I've been addicted since I was a kid. Wanna try one?"

"Hell ya, man. Hit me with it!" Jett snags the lollipop from Mateo's hand and pops it into his mouth. "These are *mad* delicious."

Wind whips my hair, and I duck my head backdown to hide the emotions evident on my face. I don't need Mateo to like me. Who cares what he thinks about me?

The thought falls embarrassingly short. At least I can retreat into the fantasy world where the alien man dotes on his mate. The big blue guy is making his mate breakfast, when the sunlight disappears.

I peer up, hoping it's Mateo, but my stomach falls as Shaun's cheeks pull up in greeting. He's been nothing but kind to me, but the one person I'm interested in is avoiding me like I'm the cause of the contamination in his experiment.

"I was hoping to find you here," Shaun says, perched on the edge of the seat beside Mateo.

"Here I am." My laugh is stiff and uncomfortable as Mateo's scrutiny pierces my soul, a lollipop sticking out of his mouth. "Just reading."

I hold up the book, and Shaun's eyebrows crinkle. "Is that an alien on the cover?"

"Yep. A big blue one." The words slip out of my mouth, and dildo-gate appears front and center in my mind. The way Mateo swung the vibrator in the air, his hand engulfing the toy.

My core clenches and the sun scorches my skin. I make the mistake of meeting his gaze, and it's smoldering. He pulls the lollipop out of his mouth, twirling it around his tongue, and I almost fall off the side of my chair.

For fuck's sake, someone take the candy away from the man.

"Can I read it after you're done?" Jett asks.

"It's a romance," I say, quirking a brow.

He shrugs. "I don't care. I like aliens."

"Sure. As long as you're okay with alien sex."

Mateo chokes, and the lollipop launches from his mouth and onto the deck. He rises and leans down to retrieve the candy, and when he returns from throwing it away, he grabs the hem of his top and pulls it over his head.

My mouth dries as he drapes the shirt over the back of the deck chair, a grand expanse of golden skin illuminated from the sun. He spins, muscles pulling and twisting, and I'm faced with his chest, broad and strong, with a soft smattering of hair trailing past his belly button and disappearing beneath his waistband.

Holy mother of pearl.

I offhandedly notice that Jett and Shaun have also lost their shirts, but a mermaid could surface off the side of the boat and I still wouldn't be able to drag my gaze away from Mateo.

He crosses one leg over the other, and I've never considered myself turned on by the sight of a man's thigh, but as he leans back and I get another peek of his tattoo, it might be the hottest thing I've ever witnessed.

Mateo refuses to look in my direction, and bitter disappointment swirls with the unquenchable lust in my lower stomach. He chats with Jett, and I hang off his every word, desperate to decipher them like the code to uncover the root of his behavior lies within them.

I'll have to corner him tonight and clear the air. This energy isn't good for us. I've already cried today, and one time is one too many. Will it be hard to sleep beside him with a brain full of thigh tattoos and tanned skin? Undoubtedly, but if Charles Darwin survived for years at sea, then I can survive three weeks with Mateo.

The sun dips below the horizon, painting the sky in cotton candy hues, and I am no farther in my book than I was two hours ago. My skin is warm, both from the sun and the honeyed sound of Mateo's voice as he waxes poetic about the importance of ironing linen shirts. I've learned more about him through his conversation than I have in the years since I met him.

He loves Chupa Chups—the lollipop he gave Jett—and watches *Survivor* religiously. Each word is like uncovering a trait of a species newly discovered. I'm greedy for it all.

"Stay with me and watch the sunset?" Shaun asks, drawing my attention.

My stomach sours, and a bead of sweat drips down my temple. His interest in me is flattering and unexpected, and in a different world, maybe there would be the flutter of anticipation in my lower stomach, or the quickening of my pulse when he walks into a room. But those feelings, they belong to someone else.

"Can we talk for a second?"

I gesture to an empty area on the other side of the deck, out of earshot from the rest of the group. For a few moments, he stands beside me, leaning on the railing and looking out toward the horizon. Inhaling the salty air, I ready myself to explain, but he beats me to the punch.

"You're into Mateo, aren't you?"

"It's complicated."

"I get it." His hand lands on my shoulder, offering a friendly squeeze. "I hope things work out for you."

"Thanks." We stand side by side, watching the sunset for a moment before I leave to find Mateo to clear the air, until I catch him storming away. "Mateo, wait!"

Disregarding my plea, he speeds down the hallway toward our room, and I sprint to reach him, catching his wrist, but he rips his arm out of my grasp.

"What do you want, Charlie?" His words are venom, each word striking a lethal blow.

"C-can we talk?"

He ignores my question to unlock the door, and when he lets it fall behind him and nearly slam in my face, I have to contain the scream begging for escape. Embarrassment and anger are living beasts in my chest, converging until I'm consumed by them.

Since we stepped onto the gangway, he's unearthed emotions I've spent years burying beneath the surface. Does he think I *want* to spend every waking moment with him on my mind?

Pure, unbridled rage slams into me.

I don't deserve this. *I don't.*

"What's your problem?" I stomp toward him until there's nothing but a hair's breadth between us.

Mateo meets my gaze, and there's something dangerous emanating from his aura. A warning that if I push him too far, whatever's happening between us will change—evolve or devolve, I'm unsure.

"Let it go," he demands, dismissing me and opening the closet.

I push anyway.

"What the hell is your problem with me?" My voice is shrill, overwhelmed, pleading, as the anger washes away and my shoulders slump. "You've changed."

He lifts his chin. "I don't know what you're talking about."

"You've stopped teasing me! No more jokes or calling me bruja. No morning chocolates." My face contorts into an ugly snarl. "We were finally becoming friends," I whisper, "and now you won't look at me. Why?"

"Why do you think, Charlie?" My name is sinful on his tongue, and as his face flushes a bright strawberry, I regret every word I said. I wish I could shove them back into my mouth and run away.

"I-I don't know." The walls close in, the temperature spiking as he glares at me.

"I think you do." Mateo takes a step, then another, until he's inches away. "It's the reason watching Shaun touch you made me want to throw him overboard."

I instinctively step back, my knees hitting the mattress. I have nowhere to run, not from this conversation or the rapid beating beneath my ribcage. I clutch the crystal dangling around my neck, gripping it with godlike strength, as if it can prepare me for what Mateo's about to admit.

"It's why I can barely look at you," he continues, his voice lowering, "because you look at him in a way you have *never* looked at me." He laughs, but it's a hollow thing. "There's nowhere for me to go. I have to share this fucking room where it smells like you *all the time.* Sleep in the bed beside you and pretend you're not inches away."

"What are you saying?"

This conversation is so overwhelming my body shuts down and enters a state of hibernation so I don't have to process what he's insinuating.

Mateo shakes his head, resignation settling over his face.

"You consume my every thought," he admits, stealing the air from my lungs. "Every morning, I leave a chocolate at your desk with the hope I can see your smile when you take the first bite. I've read every paper you've ever written because your mind is brilliant and I want to explore every cavern of your brain to understand how you work."

His chest heaves, and his fist clenches tightly at his side. I've lost the feeling of my limbs, unable to do anything but stand rooted in place.

"I've flirted with you for two years, desperately hoping one day you would *see* me, but it's clear now you never will, so *please* spare me the discomfort and try to hide whatever you do with Shaun."

He searches my face before disappearing into the bathroom, leaving me alone with his massive, world-changing confession. I'm frozen as the shower turns on, my heart racing in my chest and a thousand unspoken words clogging my throat.

What would Darwin do?

I don't think he was ever the recipient of a confession of a magnitude close to Mateo's, but his words, his theory, flicker through my mind: adapt, change, *evolve.*

I storm into the bathroom, fueled by tentative hope. Steam fills the tiny space, suffocatingly humid as I march up to the curtain and jab my finger against the fabric until I hit flesh.

"Get out," Mateo screams, followed by the thud of a shampoo bottle hitting the floor.

Everything in my body short-circuits like someone spilled water on my mainframe. If I was of sound mind, I wouldn't be in the bathroom, ready to admit to Mateo I'm into him, but I left my critical thinking skills on land.

My only response is to scream right back at him, but louder so he knows I mean business.

"I was staring at you, asshole! I don't fucking care about Shaun." There are half a dozen emotions battling for control, but anger is winning, overwhelming the hopefulness and fear. "I can barely think when you're around, and it's *infuriating*. My thoughts are jumbled by your kindness and annoyingly perfect hair and the way you smell like a summer breeze. You've got me so screwed up, Mateo, I'm comparing your smell to a goddamn breeze like I write fucking poetry."

I poke the curtain a few times for good measure, jamming my nail into Mateo's body.

"I had to call Amy and admit I have a crush on you. Do you know how embarrassing that is? Twenty-six years old, and I had to call my best friend and tell her the boy I like won't talk to me and it's *hurting my feelings.*"

The words tumble out, the shower curtain a shield granting me the strength to spill every secret I couldn't say to his face. Behind the thin plastic, I'm fearless, but if he pulled it away, he would see what I really am: petrified.

"I don't know how you *think* I look at you," I murmur, the water nearly drowning out my words, "but when I look at you, it's hard to breathe."

I leave him with the uncomfortable truth, returning to the cabin to pack my belongings. I'll ask to bunk with Sofía, and if she says no, I'll beg Vivian, and if that doesn't work, I'll hunker down on a deck chair. There's no chance I can look Mateo in the eye after my angry, yet truthful, monologue.

And once I find a new place to sleep, I need to devise a plan to survive the rest of this voyage with Mateo.

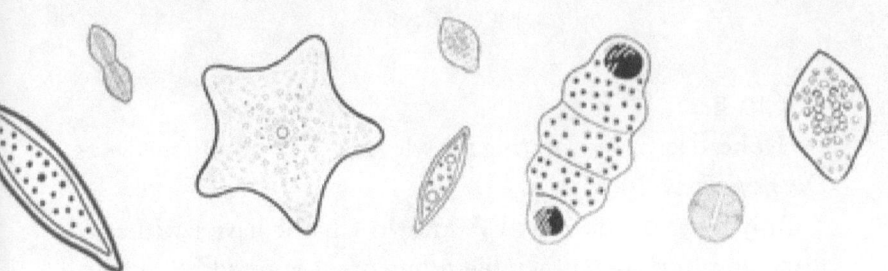

CHAPTER 17

MATEO

I fly out of the shower, nearly slipping on the wet tile, as Charlie's words ring in my ear.

Water drips down my spine as I wrap a towel around my waist, and my brain scrambles, frantically putting the pieces of Charlie's speech together.

Crush. Feelings. Hard to breathe.

Oh, Dios. I've been an asshole. A big, grumpy, jealous asshole.

Thoughts of her with Shaun tore apart my sanity—his hands on her skin, in her hair, tracing the scar on her cheek. Each one stoking the flame of jealousy in my chest until the fire consumed me wholly and burned her in the process.

I'm wrapping a towel around my waist, trying to convince myself this is real, that Charlie is telling me she *sees* me. The door to the bathroom slams open, and steam wafts around me as I scramble into the cabin.

She's shoving clothes into her duffle bag, gently laying her Darwin bobblehead on top.

Why is she packing?

"Charlie?"

Her head jerks up, spearing me with her wild, red-rimmed eyes. *Oh, fuck*. Fuck, fuck, *fuck*.

Only twice in the years I've known Charlie have I witnessed tears, and in those vulnerable moments, I ignored her flushed cheeks and soft sniffles. It's only ever happened after she had a meeting with Cheryl, and when she would disappear to the bathroom, I would leave her an extra chocolate. Something was going on in her head that she couldn't process without tears, and witnessing her discomfort led to my own.

I've seen her lose the war against her emotions, but I've never been the catalyst, and recognizing I'm the origin makes my stomach roil.

Two steps, and I'm standing in front of her, the cold cabin air causing goose bumps to form along my wet skin.

"Did you mean it?" I ask.

"I'm not a liar," she responds, her nose scrunching like my question is an insult to her character.

One more step, and I've closed the space between us. A single, barely perceptible move, and I could touch her, kiss her, claim her.

"You like me?"

I ask the question like a schoolyard boy and not a grown man, but none of it feels real, and I need to hear the words again to know I'm not hallucinating.

"Yes," she snaps, her patience fraying, "I like you and it's maddening—what are you doing?"

Her scar pulls taut as I palm her cheek and graze my thumb over the raised flesh. My focus darts to her lips, and I imagine what she would taste like on my tongue.

A thousand unspoken words hang between us as those mesmerizing blue irises stare into mine, so full of fear and hope. She pulls her head back, but I lift my other palm, keeping her close.

I trace her cheekbone with the pad of my thumb, the flesh soft and plush against my calloused skin. She's so beautiful it aches deep in my chest. The kind of ache you can only crave, demand more of, until you're consumed by the feeling.

"Charlie." Her name is a prayer and a plea, a new beginning and years of history.

"Mateo," she responds, peering up at me beneath long lashes.

Time slows, creeping to a halt, as I dip my head and brush my lips against hers. It's questioning, hesitant, before I pull away, only a few millimeters.

Barely a kiss, but my heart is pounding, and my brain riots for more.

Charlie pushes up on her toes and crashes into me, her palms splayed against my abdomen as she consumes me whole.

This kiss is nothing like the last. This is a wildfire consuming the last of the oxygen. A hurricane barreling toward shore. An earthquake rattling the ground. It's tongue and teeth, demanding and controlling as her breasts press against my chest.

My fingers tangle in her hair, the strands like silk while I wrap them around my fist, pulling as I take control, guiding the kiss into something slower, passionate. I've thought about this moment for years, and I plan to savor her like the finest tequila, get drunk on her.

Charlie moans when I trail my tongue across the seam of her lips, demanding entry. The space between us shrinks, the towel around my waist perilously close to falling.

A shudder racks down my spine as her hands roam along my skin, up my back, across my chest, down my shoulders. Each touch is more exploratory than the last, likes she's learning each curve and angle of my body. I groan when she deepens the kiss, nipping at my lower lip, and the pleasurable sting spreads through my limbs.

We slam against the cabin wall, and my knee rests between her thigh, holding her upright. Her hand trails along my jaw before she reaches out and flicks off the light. My heart skips at the sudden shift to darkness, then skips again when she presses a kiss beneath my ear and down my collarbone, each one softer than the last.

Stars burst along my vision as she kisses the column of my throat, then down to my pectoral muscles. She lingers above my heart, and I have no doubt she can feel my erratic heartbeat. Her finger grazes my skin above the towel, and my eyes snap open.

The darkness hides her mischievous smile, but I know it's there—as confidently as the earth is round. I cover her hand with my own.

"We should stop," I say, reaching out to turn on the light. I want to see her.

"I thought you were the smart one," she purrs, her fingernail dragging down the center of my chest, leaving a trail of sparks along my skin as she inches toward what the towel can no longer conceal. "What happens on the boat can stay on the boat."

The light snaps back on, and I pull away from her touch. "I want more than sex, Charlie."

How could she believe that all I want from her is sex?

A crinkle forms between her eyebrows, offering the world's cutest confused face, but a pit grows in my stomach from her words.

"What? Like cuddling after?" she asks. "I guess we could do that."

Her tone tells me she's not sold on the idea, but she waves a hand in dismissal like it's not a big deal. Wide, frightened pupils tell me it is a *massive* deal and she's doing all she can to exude nonchalance.

"No." I step back. "I want more. Date you. Get to know you."

"*Date me?*" She slams a finger against her chest. "Like boyfriend and girlfriend?"

"Potentially." I shrug. It's the end goal, but she's freaking out about cuddling, so I'm not going to jump the gun.

"I—Well...What?" she sputters. Maybe it was too bold to say, but then again, she was ready to drop my towel, so not *that* bold.

"It's this thing," I start, knowing it will get a rise out of her, "where two people get to know each other, and if they *like* each other"—I wiggle my eyebrows—"they become *exclusive.*"

"I know how dating works."

"Just wanted to make sure we're on the same page, because it's what I want, bruja. What happens on the boat won't stay on the boat for me."

The words I don't say hang in the air. *All or nothing.*

I don't want a silly fling with Charlie, and I've spent too long silently standing by. If I can't be honest with her about what I want, I have no right to pursue anything at all.

But I know what I want, and it's Charlie. Not for a night or a three-week trip, but tomorrow and every day after until our days run out. I'm sure about her, about us. Only took two years for me to workup the courage to admit it to her.

The adrenaline of her kiss fades, and I realize I'm standing in my towel, nearly naked, while she deliberates on my proposition. I slip on a pair of shorts while she flits her focus around the room, deep in thought.

This is her thinking face—her weighing-every-option face—and I hold my breath, hope vibrating in my chest.

"What are the rules?"

A surprised laugh tumbles out. "Rules? There are no rules, bruja."

"So we make the rules, then?" Her eyebrows scrunch, and I itch to reach out and smooth away the tension.

"Do you really think—"

Her eyes snap to mine, mildly panicked, so I amend my statement. "We can make rules."

Structure. Rules. Routine. Charlie relies on these things to make life less daunting. While she worships Charles Darwin and his work on evolution and change, she is not a fan of it in her own life. I've seen what happens when she's faced with abrupt change; she shuts down.

Our relationship has evolved at a glacial pace, and this trip is akin to rapid climate change.

I snag one of her pocket notebooks—the ones she carries with her everywhere—and flip to a clean page.

"Rule number one," I say, moving to sit beside her. "No more pillow wall." I want to sleep right beside her, hold her in my arms. "I am Arnold Schwarzenegger, and I am demanding the wall come down."

Charlie giggles and the sound strikes my solar plexus like a rogue lightning bolt. She steals the notebook.

"Rule number two: No rationing my chocolate intake."

She's scribbling it down with a victorious grin when I ask, "What does that have to do with...our situation?"

I don't know what to call this, don't know what word to use that won't freak Charlie out.

"Everything, Mateo." She clicks her tongue. "We'll never survive dating if you're rationing my treats."

She doesn't notice her verbiage, but the words stick, and I'm biting back a goofy, boyish grin.

Charlie and I are dating!

I can't wait to tell my abuela.

"Rule number three," she continues. "No displays of affection in public. No kissing. No touching."

"I object to that rule."

A lot. I object to rule number three emphatically.

"This is a work trip. I am overruling your objection."

I chuff, but she nervously meets my gaze. "We can kiss...if no one is around."

She says it like it's a question, rather than a fact, and I take the notebook from her hand and fling it across the room, stealing a kiss.

She yelps when I drag her against my chest.

"Sealed the deal with a kiss," I murmur, my grin so grand it could be seen from the International Space Station.

She peers at me, stunned, before she whispers, "Do it again."

I lean in, offering a quick kiss, nothing more than a peck, but she sighs, and it's the softest sound I've ever heard from Charlie. Lots of huffing and puffing, but nothing as intimate as the sigh she releases now.

"Again," she demands, and she receives another barely there kiss. Her voice lowers to a hesitant whisper while she asks, "Why were you mad at me?"

"I wasn't mad at you, bruja. I was jealous."

"Oh." She tries to school her features, but her nose twitches and the apples of her cheeks flush. It pleases her to know I was jealous, even if she's trying to hide it. She dips out of my hold, moving her half-packed bag back to its corner and returning her trinkets and bobbles to the desk, fiddling with the placement.

I lean back on my palms, content to watch her exist.

"Where were you going to go?" I ask.

"Sofía's room, and if she said no, I was going to claim a deck chair."

She gently places Sir Charles Darwin the Bobblehead on the desk, surrounded by all of her crystals, a shrine to her icon. I bit my tongue when she decorated the first time, pulling a trinket out, one by one, and finding the perfect spot on the small desk space.

"You would have rather slept on a deck chair than with me?"

I try to ignore the stabbing sensation in my gut.

"After I confessed I had a *crush* on you and said you smell like a breeze, I thought about throwing myself overboard to avoid the embarrassment of facing you."

My laugh is deep, worsening when she punches my shoulder and disappears into the bathroom.

"A summer breeze, huh?" I yell through the door, "Do I also smell like sunshi—"

The tease dries up on my tongue as Charlie steps out of the bathroom wearing a bubblegum-pink silk pajama set that leaves little for the imagination. Small strawberries decorate the fabric, and she shifts on her feet, wringing her hands. A long, straight scar starts at her mid-thigh, disappearing beneath her shorts.

I've lost function of my tongue and the beating of my heart, which races erratically in my chest.

Charlie scans the room as I stare, enraptured by her beauty. She coughs, and I shake away her siren grip, only then noticing her discomfort.

"Can we watch TikToks before bed?" She twirls a loose strand of hair, inching toward the bed. "I-I like when we watch them together."

I hear what she doesn't say. *She was upset we didn't watch them together last night.*

What's happening is foreign, odd. There's an air of nervousness, both Charlie's and my own, but the exhilaration of the opportunity and unknown flows through my veins.

"Sure, bruja," I say, my voice hoarse. "We can watch them every night, if you'd like."

"Deal." Charlie wets her lips, and pleasure trickles down my spine. So, so softly, she asks, "Seal it with a kiss?"

She asks as if she expects me to say no, when in reality, that question is an answer to one of my many wishes when it comes to her.

Leaning down, I graze the scar along her collarbone, and as she shivers beneath my touch, I seal the deal with a kiss.

CHAPTER 18

CHARLIE

> Mateo and I kissed.

I send the text and slip my phone into my back pocket, ignoring how my heart flutters like a kaleidoscope of butterflies have taken residence in my chest. The confession still rings in my ears, his words a caress against my skin.

Mateo wants to date me. Not fuck for a night or have a secret fling.

He wants more with *me*.

I've never had someone feel that way—confess they've thought about me for two years—and it terrifies me how deeply I hoard the knowledge, holding it close to my chest like it's precious.

For most of my life, I've put weight on other people's words and opinions, never learning how to separate their thoughts from my own, and those opinions have defined me, pushed me, helped me grow.

A teacher in middle school told me I was bright and had potential, and I've chased those words ever since. Cheryl returned a paper with comments suggesting I could do better, and I worked to prove her right. Mateo called me brave, and I wanted to show him that, though it frightens me to my core, I can be.

It's why I wore my pajamas out of the bathroom while the light was still on. I could be fearless if he looked at me like I was the only thing in the room. I could be courageous because *he believes I am*.

"Dude, the ocean is, like, the most peaceful place on the planet," Jett says, startling me so thoroughly I yelp and collide my fist with his stomach. "Ugh," he groans, doubled over, clutching the railing for support.

"Shit, I'm sorry." I pat his arm awkwardly as he rights himself.

Can't sneak up on a girl deep in self-contemplation.

The water is as smooth as glass, endless, as the first rays of sunlight peek over the horizon. I lean over the railing, gazing down into the blue abyss. I've always wondered what's below the surface, what lurks where the sun no longer shines.

"Do you ever wonder what's below us?" I ask.

He leans over to watch the water with me, deep blue swirling with the wake of the vessel. Crew members hustle, preparing *Neptune* to deploy at our next location, a thousand meters deeper than the last.

There was a brief period when I was ten that any body of water frightened me, but I blame my father, who let me watch *Anaconda*, which led to fear that snakes would leap out of the water to attack. I would rather face whatever lurks in the deep ocean than a massive, human-consuming snake.

"Scared of the ocean, Blondie?" Jett asks, half bent over the railing, and I seize my opportunity to mess with him. I leap toward him, grab his shoulders, and make a disconcerting sound.

"I'm scared of the creatures lurking in the deep, waiting for their moment to strike. The kraken. Megalodon. Mosasaurus."

"Those don't exist."

"They did," I respond with a shrug. "We know so little about the bottom of the ocean. Who's to say they aren't still down there?"

He steps back from the edge, watching the water like a kraken will appear to drag him down to Davy Jones's locker.

"Or what if there's something worse, and we have no idea?"

"There you are," a deep voice purrs, and my skin pebbles beneath the low timbre. My heartbeat quickens to a sickening pace as Mateo saunters toward Jett and me, two coffees in hand and a knowing smile on his lips.

"Is it true?" Jett asks, meeting Mateo halfway. "We are members of the Brotherhood of Catan, you have to tell me the truth."

Brotherhood of Catan?

"What am I supposed to tell you?" He stops inches away from me and extends a coffee. "Hi," he whispers, low and intimate, his free hand caressing my lower back in a possessive touch.

I jerk in surprise from the contact.

Last night I was bold, but this morning, I am a coward who snuck out of our room while the sky was a deep purple to avoid any awkward interactions.

It's the earliest I've woken up by choice in years, but I would rather rise before the crow caws than face Mateo. Last night was a dream—or a weird hallucination—and I was afraid morning would arrive and everything would change. He would take back his words or realize he made a mistake.

I'm not good at these things, understanding cues and subtle hints, evidenced by my ignorance of his feelings, but worse, I struggle to express my emotions in cohesive ways.

My face flushes when Mateo fixes his gaze on me, and the corner of his mouth lifts.

He dips his head to my ear, and his breath dances along my skin as he whispers, "Nervous, bruja?"

"What? N-no." My voice cracks as his hand slides down my back to palm the globe of my ass, his movements covert as Jett waits for his response.

"Could the kraken exist?" Jett asks impatiently, his voice harboring an undertone of panic. I didn't think he actually believed my comment.

"¿Qué?" Mateo peers down at me with his brow raised, and I shrug, feigning innocence.

"Blondie said it's possible since we know so little about the bottom of the ocean." He peers over the side of the boat. "I did see this documentary about the megalodon that seemed pretty real..."

Mateo's head tips back in laughter, his Adam's apple bobbing with mirth. "*Blondie*," the nickname rolls off his tongue, "is messing with you."

Jett whirls on me.

"You jumped to conclusions without the facts," I say in a saccharine tone.

"You're my fact machine!"

Shit. He's got me there. He knows it, too, and I can't help but laugh when Jett's toothy grin grows larger.

"They aren't real. But it would be super cool to ride a mosasaur with a saddle," I admit.

It was a weird dream I had after a late night.I was riding one like it was a horse, and my hair was windswept seaweed, decorated in opal shells and speaking starfish. Instead of scars, my skin was covered in blue-green iridescent scales.

"That would be baller," Jett exclaims. "I'm going to tell my followers!"

He's gone in a flash, leaving Mateo and me alone on the deck. He slides to stand in front of me, removing his palm from my ass and allowing a sliver of rational thought to return to my brain.

"You were gone this morning," he comments, crossing his legs as he leans against the railing.

"Wanted to get an early start."

My stomach flutters at the sight of his bemused perusal. Has he always seen through my bullshit?

"The words *early start* and *Charlie Bowen* have never once been used in a sentence together."

I gasp. "Not true."

I avoid his eye contact, but we both know it is. Early mornings are the worst, especially on nights when sleep evades me. The pink stones surrounding his wrist steal my attention. He's worn it since he stole it, since I *let* him steal it.

"Eyes up here," he commands, and mine snap to his, his lip pulled between his teeth. "Why did you leave early this morning?"

He waits patiently until I muster up enough courage to say, "I'm nervous."

My stomach revolts as the confession hangs in the air, but he closes the space between us, tipping my chin up.

"Now you know how I've felt every day for the last two years." His irises darken to a shade of deep evergreen as he swipes his thumb across the seam of my lips. I frantically search the deck, making sure no one is witnessing what feels like an incredibly intimate moment. "We make the rules, Charlie."

His words are casual, nonchalant, but nothing about this is easy or chill. I'm walking a razor's edge; one wrong move, and I'll slice myself open with no way to heal the wound.

Mateo drags me to a chair, and I protest, attempting to glue my feet to the ground. I'm afraid to face the impending conversation, especially in the daylight. I prefer to avoid the vulnerable chats entirely, but if I have to participate, it's much easier to admit my weaknesses and flaws in the dark.

My phone chirps, one message right after another, and I ignore it.

"Do you need to get that?"

He jerks his chin to my pocket, where Amy is blowing up my notifications.

"It's Amy," I say, and when his eyebrow lifts, I add, "I told her we kissed."

Now, I've seen a number of Mateo's smiles since we met at orientation. His soft morning version when he leans around his computer monitor. The smug tilt of his lips when he outsmarts or flusters me. His victorious grin yesterday after we kissed.

But I've never been offered this smile, one that makes my toes curl and stomach plummet ten stories with anticipation.

This one...it's intimate, selective, not meant for anybody. It begins small until it overtakes his features, illuminating him with joy.

"Is that so?"

I offer an odd choking sound in response.

"Well, let's see what she has to say."

He snakes his hand into my back pocket, stealing my phone, and like earlier, the contact sets my skin on fire. Mateo scrolls through the messages, and I peer around his bicep.

> Amy: Charles, what the fuck?

> I need more information!!!

> Was there tongue? I bet there was tongue.

> Was it a spiritual awakening?

> Did he do that thing where the guy cups your jaw? I need to know for SCIENCE.

> Oh my god. I'm sweating.

> CHARLES!

"I think she's excited for us," he says with a raw, throaty laugh, worsening the blush creeping onto my cheeks.

This is mortifying.

Time to run.

I jump off the deck chair, resigned to leave my phone and this horrifying situation, when Mateo's arms wrap around my shoulders, caging me within his embrace.

My legs flail as I attempt to escape, feet flying as his chest rumbles.

"Where are you going now?" he asks, whispering in my ear.

"To crawl into a hole and die," I mutter.

I have experienced one too many embarrassing moments in the past twenty-four hours. Mateo has witnessed enough for his lifetime.

He starts to say something, but footsteps fill the air, and he releases me from his grip. Sofía rounds the corner, a gentle, welcoming presence radiating from her in waves. Her brown hair falls in soft curls, and she effortlessly pulls off her business-casual outfit.

She's far more put together than I am.

I recoil from the thought, taking a step away from Mateo.

"The ROV is reaching three thousand meters," she says. "We need you in the command center."

"Coming!" I use her as an excuse to escape my thoughts, this situation with Mateo, and the uncomfortable tightness in my chest. Sofía disappears through the door before Mateo's hand grips my bicep, pausing my getaway.

"Later, bruja," he says, "you and I are going to talk about us and what all this means."

His words terrify the shit out of me, so I do what I do best: I frantically nod before running away to the command room.

If Mateo's arm brushes mine one more time, I might scream.

For the last seven hours, we have sat in close quarters, our skin brushing every time he or I move, and it's fucking torture. We've identified nothing but benthic organisms—creatures that live on the seafloor—and I've seen plenty of sea pigs and rocks for this lifetime.

Morale is low in the room. Jett lounges in a chair, half focused on his phone. Sofía types away on her computer, filling out paperwork, and Doug is asleep in the corner, snoring softly.

"Where are all the cool animals?" Jett whines as the ROV glides over the seafloor, little around except for spiny sea stars and worms. Don't get me wrong, I love all deep-sea creatures, but I would *love* to see something rare right now, like a barreleye fish or anglerfish, to distract me from Mateo's touch.

This time, his foot taps mine as he shifts, and I almost release a frustrated squeal.

Pulling out the small amethyst from my pocket, I weave it around my fingers, hoping the calming energy will permeate into my skin and ease my unsettled stomach. I *might* be freaking out about our impending conversation and what it means for our future.

"I think I see something," Vivian says, and we all leap to our feet, scrambling to the screen as she gets closer. I watch with bated breath, hopeful for something unique, but instead, I groan in disappointment.

"It's a freaking rock," Jett yells, defeat in his voice.

The room silently stares at the offending boulder, covered in encrusting tunicates, when Vivian declares we're going to end the dive and begin ascent. I return to my seat, covertly moving it farther from Mateo, but he thwarts my efforts and scoots his chair beside mine.

His fingers dip below the table, trailing along the outside of my thigh. I'm embarrassed by the small mewl that escapes my lips. Mateo is the picture of calm professionalism, his face focused as he watches the video, but a rogue dimple appears, and his hand inches upward to my hip before he moves south.

Back and forth.

Back and forth, until I'm squirming, unable to focus on anything but his lingering touch as he moves.

"Oh my god." Jett's voice, brimming with excitement, cuts through the fog, and I focus on the camera footage, which zooms in on a thin creature, its slim blue-silver body shining beneath the ROV's floodlights.

It hovers in the water column, no longer than the size of a ruler, but its teeth, abnormally long and protruding from its jaw, mark it as a predator. Without the lights, its ultra-black skin would make it nearly undetectable in the deeper sections of the ocean, where light can't penetrate.

My jaw is agape as the Pacific viperfish moves closer to the camera, shifting to display its razor-sharp teeth and large eyes.

Jett hyperventilates in the corner, fanning himself, before shrieking, "The camera, Doug! Record this on your camera!"

Doug jerks awake, startled, but hurries to follow Jett's command to film the momentous occasion. Until this moment, we've seen very little outside of the bloody-belly comb jelly and benthic invertebrates. I inch closer to the screen, reveling in this moment, in the rarity of witnessing the creature in its natural habitat.

"Diurnal vertical migration," I say, offering no context to the scientific term, too enthralled by the small creature.

Its features aren't flashy or beautiful; rather, the creature is built to survive in an environment designed against it. In a world where bright scales draw attraction, it's camouflaged itself. In a domain where it's kill or be killed, it's evolved teeth to attack and defend. It adapted to survive, its beauty secondary to its primary goal: to thrive in an inhospitable habitat.

Mateo's intoxicating cologne fills the air before the weight of his hand falls on my lower back, invading my personal space.

"It's beautiful," he says, and my chest tightens.

Is it beautiful?

I don't think so.

It's gnarly and dangerous, a perfectly designed predator, but I wouldn't describe it as beautiful. There's nothing inviting about a viperfish; it's ugly—alien.

"What's diurnal vertical migration?" Jett asks, hovering over Vivian while she works.

How the fuck did he get across the room so quickly?

"It's a migrational pattern where organisms will move to shallow waters at night, then return to deeper depths during the day. We likely caught the viperfish moving up the water column to feed," Mateo says, his hand still glued to the curve of my spine.

Jett nods enthusiastically, childlike joy overtaking his features, as he watches the viperfish disappear when the ROV breaks the surface.

"This is the best day ever," he says, throwing his arms around Vivian. "Thank you for finding him!"

Vivian chuckles but peels his arms off her to finish driving the ROV to the retrieval location.

I begin to collect my belongings—computer, notebook, colored pens—when Mateo returns to my side and takes my tote bag from my hands, sliding his own things into the bag before flinging it over his shoulder.

"We'll see you guys at dinner," he says to the room, before nodding toward the door. I'm rooted in place as he walks away, and when he realizes I'm not with him, he walks back to me, takes my hand, and intertwines our fingers.

Mateo pulls me out of the control room, and my skin tingles where our palms meet. My heartbeat is in my throat, stopping any words from forming.

Once we're alone, Mateo utters the words that strike fear, and buried anticipation, into my heart.

"It's time to talk, bruja."

CHAPTER 19

CHARLIE

"Talk?" I croak, nerves eating away what confidence I have left.

The sound of the door falling shut is deafening in the quiet space. Mateo places my bag on the desk and perches on the edge of the mattress, patiently waiting for me to move closer, but I can't.

Every moment on the boat has led to this moment—this one conversation—and it holds so much weight that I'm crushed by its intensity. Every emotion I've spent years suppressing now lingers at the surface, and I'm petrified he's going to see more of me than I'm ready for.

"Charlie." My name is a caress, spurring me to move, and I drop into the chair across from him. He lifts a brow but allows me the space. "I won't bite...unless you want me to."

It takes a moment for his joke to land, but when it does, I level him with a glare.

"There she is," he purrs, bracing his elbows on his knees as he leans forward. "I told you yesterday, but I'll say it again: I want to date you, Charlie. And I know this is an unorthodox situation, but I want the chance to get to know you outside of normal circumstances."

He's so calm, offering his truth like it's nothing more than the weather report, but my hands tremble.

The walls I've painstakingly built are crumbling, taking me with them, but I don't want to fall, so I pull the carnelian stone from the corner of the desk and grip it in my palm.

With a shaky voice, I say, "I want that, too."

A brilliant smile breaks across Mateo's face, and I offer him one of my own.

"Come here, bruja," he says, and my stomach flips with anticipation when he pats the bed beside him. It dips beneath my weight, and as soon as I land, his hands are on me, dragging me closer.

"I know you're nervous," he says, working his palm up and down my thigh, "but I'm nervous, too."

"You are?"

I don't know why I'm surprised—why his admission is so shocking. Maybe it's because he's always held this unwavering confidence in himself. His words are sure and decisive when our advisors ask questions. When he walks into a room, he holds his head high, his shoulders back.

It's hard to picture Mateo as anything other than confident—the opposite of who I am.

His laugh is soft, little more than a huff of air.

"Yes, bruja, I'm nervous." His touch stills. "I am going to be brutally honest for the next thirty seconds, even though it scares me." He pauses, and I gulp, unready for whatever truth he's going to offer me. "I have flirted with you every day for the past two years, hoping you would see me, and now that you do, I'm afraid it's going to end. I'm terrified that we're going to step off this boat, and you're going to brush me off like this all means nothing. Because for me, this means something—*you* mean something to me—but

I don't want my heart crushed if you're not all in. Because I am. I'm all in, Charlie."

He drags his fingers through his hair, a nervous tic I've learned he has, and I spot Darwin sitting in the corner, watching us explore the unknown territory in front of us. I've spent the day worried about the new terrain, afraid of what I may uncover, but maybe I'm going about it the wrong way.

It's unfamiliar, but instead of standing at the edge of the unexplored jungle, fearful of the creatures lurking behind the foliage, I could embrace the uncertainty and the potential to discover something incredible and life changing.

Darwin's head bobbles as if to say, *You're on the right path*, so I take the first step into the uncharted territory and offer him a truth of my own.

"I want to try with you."

I've always run from emotional connection, stuck to my rules to keep me safe and detached, but I don't know how to separate logic from what I feel for Mateo.

I won't lie; I'm scared shitless I'll fuck it up, or he'll realize I'm more effort than it's worth, but I'm realizing he's worth the risk. Mateo is kind in ways I'll never be, understanding and patient, and vulnerable with his heart.

"I've never really tried with anyone," I admit, timid and unsure, but I reach out a hand and lace our fingers together. It's better to be frightened, I think, than not try with him at all. "I don't know what I'm doing."

Nerves eat at my insides, but he squeezes my hand, and my throat dries from the tenderness. Mateo deserves far more credit than I've ever given him, because he hears every word I can't formulate, and he understands.

"We'll learn together," he says, shifting to face me. His free hand reaches out, and the pad of his index finger trails down my scar to cup my jaw. "Deal?"

"Deal," I respond, and my lashes flutter shut as he offers a gentle, probing kiss.

His hand slips to cradle the back of my head, his fingers tangling in the strands of my hair as the kiss deepens into something charged with raw energy. The air crackles as he grabs my hips and pulls me onto his lap, swiping his tongue against the seam of my lips.

I want to bottle the feeling banging around in my chest—capture it so I can experience it forever. It's the nerves of preparing to speak in front of a crowd. The anticipatory fall when you reach the peak of a roller coaster. The thrill of discovering something new.

He grips my waist, digging into my flesh to pull me into his chest. Mateo leans away, far enough to speak, but still so close I can identify the varying shades of green in his eyes. Moss. Seaweed. Evergreen.

Mateo's hand slips below my top, grazing against my bare skin, and I jerk from the contact—not from discomfort, but in anticipation. I'm distracted by the tiny freckles scattered along the bridge of his nose, but his hand pauses on my stomach.

"Do you want to stop?"

His lips are swollen, hair in disarray, and he's never been as attractive as he is right now. I lean in until our foreheads touch. He sucks in a breath, and I press a feather-soft kiss to the corner of his mouth, the stubble of his beard scraping against my flesh.

"No."

His thumb swipes across my torso and over the scar from my spleen removal. One, two, three times, he passes over the raised skin, and I hold steadfast, mustering up every inch of courage I possess.

Pounding fills my ears as my heart races.

I'm not used to people touching me how Mateo does—like I'm art, meant to be admired. It's not inherently sexual in its nature. Rather, it's appreciative, and I'm trying to believe the unspoken words in his actions.

I don't want to self-destruct and take him with me.

"Will you tell me if you do?" he asks. I nod, tugging at the hem of his shirt until his chest is bare, rising and falling. I lay my palm over his heart, and he moves to rest his hand atop mine. "It's always like this," he whispers, pushing my hand against his skin. "When I look at you, it always beats like this."

It's not a steady beat but an erratic pounding, identical to mine, thanks to his confession.

If his possessive touch wasn't proof enough of the truth lacing his words, the beating in his chest would give him away. My cheeks heat, this moment more intimate than any other I've ever experienced, and my nerves skyrocket as I move our palms to cover my own heart.

Words have never been my strong suit, but this I can offer him. He leans in, and this kiss differs from the prior as he takes control, nipping at my lower lip until I gasp.

Mateo's hands drop, playing with the bottom of my shirt.

"Can I take this off?" he asks, breaking the kiss and clearing the fog from my mind. He holds my top in his grip, and with one nod or a single word, I would be bare in front of him.

"Lights off," I demand, my voice cracking.

His features soften in understanding, and it's like a punch to the gut, but he refuses to surrender.

"I want to see you, Charlie. All of you."

He waits, chin raised, and I coil in on myself. To allow him to see everything...it's too exposing.

"I-I..." The words fizzle off my tongue.

Be brave, Charlie.

The thought is the only thing stopping me from denying him outright.

Mateo waits, leaning back on his palms as I rise to stand in the middle of the tiny cabin, at war with myself. I've been battling for so long, with myself, my body, how society perceives me. I've spent so much time hiding in the darkness, I don't know how to step back into the light.

"It's okay," he says, rising to pull me against his chest. "We won't do anything you're uncomfortable with."

I'm limp within his arms, fighting back the tears his reassurance brings to the surface. There's a sense of freedom in the safety he's creating. He told me what he wanted, but he's also respecting the boundary I'm struggling to verbalize, and the one small action speaks a thousand words.

All of them telling me if I show Mateo my scars, he's not going to disappoint me.

The sea-salt scent of his cologne envelops me, and I wrap my arms around his waist, sinking into the hug. My Charles Darwin bobblehead catches my eye, and I break from the embrace to turn him around to face the wall.

He's not allowed to witness what's about to happen.

"What would Darwin do?" I whisper, before responding to my question. "He would be courageous."

When I spin around, Mateo is watching me with a goofy grin and a raised brow. "What was that?"

Before I can lose my nerve, I take the hem of my top with my shaky hands and lift it over my head. It flutters out of my grip, and I fight the urge to fidget as Mateo's jaw slackens.

"I've never allowed anyone to see all my scars," I whisper. He'll never be able to see them all—the worst of them invisible—but the longer I stand, the greater my confidence builds. Not because he's looking at me like he might drop to his knees in worship, but because I'm facing something that's been holding me back.

This is not for him, but for me—the woman who has spent years in a body she's struggled to accept as her own. I still have to force my shoulders back and calm the tremor in my hand, but I'm standing, and tomorrow morning, I'm going to call Amy and tell her about this because I want her to be proud of me.

Because I'm proud of myself.

Mateo reaches me in a single step, and then I'm flying through the air, a surprised squeal escaping as I collide with the mattress.

"Mateo, what are you—"

"Estás regia, Charlie," he says, his palms splayed on both sides of my head.

"I really hope that's nicer than 'witch.'"

He steals my tease with a kiss, a grin blooming against my lips. Then his hands roam, exploring the planes of my skin, pausing when he reaches a scar. He never stops kissing me, but on every section of battered flesh, he makes a second pass.

Mateo stops on my surgical scar, the one that cuts down from my mid-abdomen to my belly button. He lifts to offer a questioning look.

"Spleen removal."

He's quiet, and it makes me nervous, until he says, "Useless organ anyway. Who needs it?"

The comment is unexpected, and my head tips back in laughter. I never thought about it that way. My hands fumble with my bra clasp, and when the tension releases, a relieved sigh escapes. The straps slide off my shoulders, and Mateo's laugh is deep and throaty.

"This thing is a torture device."

"You'll find no protest from me if you never wear one ever again," he says, the corner of his mouth ticking up.

"Is that so?"

He hums, lowering to take my breast into his mouth. He circles my nipple with his tongue, and I reel from the sensation, from how my head clouds with pleasure.

He moves lower, trailing down my abdomen, and I jerk when he reaches the band of my shorts and tugs on the tie. Reality crashes down, my muscles locking and my breath quickening.

No. No. No.

This is not supposed to happen. Not now. The tips of my fingers prick with tingles, my breasts heaving as I stare at Mateo with scared eyes, because that's what I am: utterly terrified.

The adrenaline pumping through my blood is gone. Discomfort knots beneath my diaphragm, and I scramble upright to cover myself. Every gulp of air feels like a knife tearing apart my vocal chords.

Mateo rises, alarmed, and I curl in on myself, pulling my knees tightly to my chest.

I was fine—excited, even—for what was about to happen. No apparent trigger to the panic attack, but my body trembles.

It's been months since the last one. Early spring brought a torrential downpour on my drive home from the lab. I managed to pull into a grocery store parking lot before the panic attack took over entirely, but I knew the rain was the trigger.

When I calmed down enough to call Amy, she rushed to pick me up. I never was able to tell her what happened.

"Charlie." Mateo stands at the end of the bed, a worried tone lacing my name.

I don't want the panic attacks and nightmares or the fear when my scars show. But most of all, I don't want him to see this side of who I am. The person who is broken and battered.

He reaches out, slowly enough for me to turn him away if I want, but I don't. I let his hand fall on the top of my knee, let the warmth of his skin sink into the bitter chill of mine. He grabs his discarded shirt and slips it over my head, guiding my arms into the holes.

I'm so fucking embarrassed, but my throat is too raw to speak, so I sit in silence as he dresses me. I wouldn't blame him if he broke this off tomorrow—decided this was more than he bargained for.

He's witnessing the invisible scars I pretend don't exist because it's easier to live my life pretending I'm okay. And if no one sees the low moments, then I can keep up the facade.

"What helps?" he asks, and a fissure forms in my chest from the gentle concern lacing the question.

"I don't know."

I don't know how to fix anything; I only know everything is broken.

Mateo reaches out, tipping my chin up. A flash of despair crosses his face, and for the life of me, I can't understand why.

Is it because he realized this won't work, or is the sadness actually pity for me?

The thought is sickening, but he holds my gaze and whispers, "Can I help?"

Three words. Simple, meaningless words on their own, but when he strings them together and whispers them with care, they mean *more*.

I nod, and Mateo crawls into bed, leans against the wall, and spreads his legs. He taps the mattress between his thighs in a silent command, and I will my limbs to loosen enough to move.

My back falls against his chest, and he wraps his arms tightly around my shoulders. He turns out the light, and darkness falls around us as he cocoons me within his embrace.

"I'm sorry," I whisper.

Sorry I ruined the moment.

Sorry I'm broken.

Sorry. Sorry. Sorry.

I wanted to grow—to evolve into someone new, someone I was proud of—but maybe it's a foolish dream to think I could be any of those things.

Mateo presses a soft kiss on the crown of my head, and the fissure deepens with the intimate act.

"Don't apologize to me. Not for this." He pulls me tighter. "Never for this."

I don't have a response, so I sit in his arms until the exhaustion makes my eyelids grow heavy and my heartbeat slows to time with his. Mateo's grip never loosens, even after his breathing deepens.

When I wake in the middle of the night, the hosing from his CPAP presses against my back as he clutches me in his arms. Rather than face the reality tomorrow may bring, I allow myself to fall back asleep in his arms, where things feel safer.

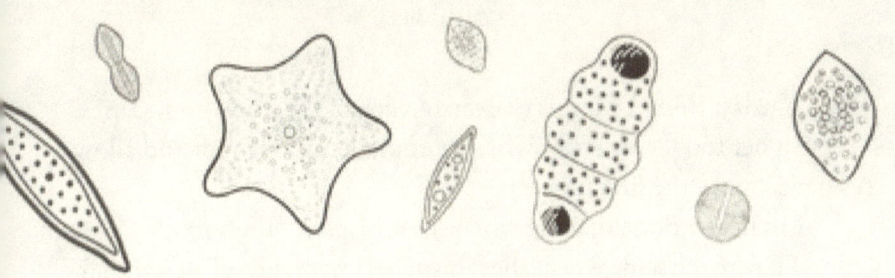

Chapter 20

MATEO

"Mateo?"

A soft knock echoes through the bathroom as I shave. I drop my razor on the side of the small sink and crack the door open to find Charlie drowning in the t-shirt I offered her last night.

She was still in bed when I slipped in here, and I wanted to give her some time to sleep, given last night's events.

I've seen a panic attack before. I know the signs, and when Charlie's features went blank and her hands began to tremble, I knew she was in the early stages of a major attack.

She shifts on her feet, playing with the hem of the shirt.

"I wasn't sure if you left for breakfast," she says, staring at the shaving cream covering my face. Red spreads across her cheeks, and she shifts her attention to the carpet. "Sorry, I'll let you finish."

"You can sit with me if you want."

She hesitates before slipping behind me to perch on the toilet seat. Wordlessly, I resume my task, dragging the razor along my skin. She watches me through the mirror, her blond hair frazzled from sleep.

The last thing I want is to overstep any of Charlie's boundaries, push her too far and ruin what we could have. So I wait and allow her to make the first move.

I'm nearly done shaving when she whispers, "I'm sorry."

They're the same words she whispered last night, full of so much self-hatred it was a punch to the gut. Her head hangs low while she picks at a loose thread on my shirt, like the guilt is too heavy to look up.

"For what? Letting me in?" Surprised by my question, she snaps her chin up and meets my stare. "There's no shame in leaning on someone." I spin to rest against the tiny basin, heart thudding in my chest as I face her. "Can I ask you something?"

"Sure."

"Do you want to call it? Put an end to whatever's happening and return to how we were before?"

My heart lodges in my throat, but I need to know. I don't want to give her any more of myself if she's going to break this off. She already holds so much of my heart. If I give her any more, it will become hers alone.

She doesn't understand. Doesn't know there's nothing she could do or say to scare me away.

"I don't want to burden you."

I barely hear the confession, the pained words she believes are true. But it's not a yes, and I lean into that.

"You don't get to make that decision." I take a step and lift Charlie's chin. "You don't get to decide what I want or don't want. What I consider burdensome or worth the effort. But, in case I haven't made myself clear, you are worth it. To me, you will *always* be worth it."

She doesn't say anything, but her pupils glass over like she's fighting to believe the words.

"I need to know if you think *I'm* worth it," I continue, "because I can't stand here and give you everything if you're not willing to try to do the same."

Does she see I'm as scared as her?

I have no idea what I'm doing, standing at the cliff's edge, teetering, and all it would take is one gust of wind before falling. She has no clue how deeply she's embedded in my chest.

Relationships require work—two people making a conscious decision to choose each other. It's not fate or destiny; it's a daily choice to see the other person, to acknowledge their flaws and fears, to cherish what makes them special, to champion their accomplishments, and pick them up when they stumble.

I've witnessed it in my own parents, who strive every single day to lift up the other. Even in their fights, they never forget the love they share. I hear it in the way my abuela talks about the forty years she shared with my abuelo before he died, how he would have stolen the moon for her if she had asked, and she would have done the same.

No relationship is perfect, but rather, it's a complex weaving of two people giving it their all—that's what I want with Charlie.

My stomach churns as she remains silent. One minute grows into two, and bitter disappointment sits heavily on my chest. Maybe I'm not worth it after all.

I spin to leave when she grabs my forearm, digging into my skin.

"I-I'm sorry," she sputters, and I pull my arm from her grip, exiting the bathroom. I need some air to escape the sickening feeling in my chest that's telling me I'm not enough for her. "Mateo, wait!" Charlie flies out of the bathroom. "I'm trying to say—"

"I hear you loud and clear." My throat tightens. "Let's go back to being—"

She launches herself, hurtling into me so forcefully I stumble back onto the bed. Her head collides with mine, and pain sears against my temple. Clutching my cheeks between her palms, she forces my head upward as she stands between my legs.

"I'm in. I don't know what it means, and I can't tell you I won't mess this all up, but you're worth facing the fear. I just need you to hold my hand while I face it."

Her thumb swipes against my cheek, and I lean into the touch, my lashes fluttering shut. The words she offers are a balm, soothing the hurt, and when my eyelids crack, she's watching me with an open expression, full of fear and admiration. It's a shock to the system, seeing her openly vulnerable.

"You have to let me in," I say. "No more running away."

She nods, dropping her forehead against mine and wrapping her arms around my neck.

Letting someone know how you're feeling, what you're thinking, is a form of intimacy. It's something that requires trust, and we're still building the foundation.

"Be patient with me, okay?" she murmurs against my skin.

"Always, bruja. Always."

Charlie stands, smooths out her hair, and draws her shoulders back. She nods, as if she's having an internal conversation with herself, then fiddles with her clothes.

"Breakfast and then to the lab?" she asks timidly.

"Sounds like a great plan," I respond, and before I can say anything more, she leans down, places a small kiss on my lips, and escapes into the bathroom—all with a creeping blush. I'm still sitting on the bed when the door creaks open and Charlie pops her head out.

"Oh, and Mateo?"

I hum.

"You look *hot* when you shave."

And with that, she slams the door shut, leaving me sitting on the bed with unshakable pride.

"Look, we got a worm!"

Charlie dangles it between her forceps before she places the creature into a specimen bag and labels it. We quietly process soil samples collected on yesterday's ROV dive, each of us enthralled in our task except to offer a brief break, like now, where one has an update.

Her discovery of a worm is much cooler than my previous update, which was to tell her the soil smells like farts. She gave me a disgusted look, unscrewed the cap to the sampling tube, and promptly gagged from the horrendous scent.

I tried to warn her. She should have listened.

She mutters to herself as she continues to subsample, and I pause my task to admire her beauty. As she digs through the soil, she tucks her lower lip between her teeth, the hair pulled out of her face. Her breath hitches when she finds a shell, and I'm an insect stuck in her web as she carefully cleans her treasure and sets it to the side.

Our conversation this morning was heavy, and Charlie was quiet at breakfast, but when she slipped her hand beneath the table and intertwined our fingers, my heart soared.

It gives me hope—hope that we can make this work if we both try.

"Good find."

I resume extracting DNA from the water samples, lost in my task. We work in silence for another hour before Charlie says, "You hum a lot."

"Huh?"

She begins to hum. It's unrecognizable at first—her humming skills need some work—but as she reaches the chorus, I recognize the song she's mimicking, the one my abuela loves to sing at the top of her lungs when she's in the kitchen. The song I've apparently adopted as my tune.

"It's always the same song. You hum it while you work. What is it?"

"'Tuyo.' It's the theme song of *Narcos*."

I never realized I hum—not to the point that she not only notices but can repeat the tune. Maybe she pays more attention to me than I give her credit for. I might be crazy, but the idea sends a tingle down my spine.

"Ah..." I draw out the word. "Correct me if I'm wrong, but what I'm hearing is that you're *so* obsessed with me, you can identify the song I hum."

A flurry of emotions flashes across her face. Confusion. Realization. Annoyance.

"That is not what I said."

"It's implied."

"No it's not."

"Admit it, you're obsessed with me." I tug a strand of her hair and raise the pitch of my voice. "*Mateo is so* dreamy. *He smells like a summer breeze and looks hot while shaving.*"

Her face scrunches like she ate something sour. "I am never going to live down my summer breeze comment, am I?"

"Not a chance, bruja. I will hold that compliment close to my chest until the day I die."

She huffs, pausing her digging through the soil to cut me a glare. God, I love that glare and the conviction that takes hold of her when she's ready to debate something. It does something wicked to my insides.

"Fine. But if you're going to keep calling me bruja," she grunts, "then it's only fair you have a bad Spanish nickname."

"It's only fair?"

"Isn't that the rule? If you're dating, you give the other person a nickname?" Her voice softens like she's shy. "I've never given anyone a nickname. How do you say 'annoying asshole' in Spanish?"

Her question hangs in the air before I keel over in laughter. I was anticipating a vulnerable moment where she asks if she can call me babe or honey, or hell, she finally asks why I gave her the nickname bruja, but instead, Charlie throws me a curveball, asking the question with the seriousness only she's capable of mustering.

She's fucking incredible.

I mull it over, pretending to hesitate offering her the answer. If I'm too quick with my response, she'll grow suspicious about the true meaning of the word I want to offer her, but if I act like I don't want to give it away, she may not ask any questions and take my word at face value.

"Well?" she presses.

I sigh, more deeply than I probably need to.

"Cariño."

She repeats the word, testing it on her tongue, and my cheeks twitch. If I want to pull this off, I need to protest—convince her I would rather keel over than have her call me the endearment.

"I don't really think we should—"

"It's perfect!"

Huh, that took less acting than I thought. Her smile is feral, pleased she's one-upped me, or so she thinks.

She returns to her work, and her energy remains for the rest of the day, all the way until we go to bed, when she whispers into the darkness, "Goodnight, cariño."

It's the perfect ending to a long day.

CHAPTER 21

CHARLIE

"You have to tell me everything," Amy says, her voice filling the cabin. "You ignored my messages—rude, by the way—so now you're obligated by the best-friend code to spare no detail."

I fall back onto the bed, laying the phone beside my head.

Amy called when Mateo and I were getting ready to head to one of the common areas to get some work done before the ROV deploys this afternoon. Vivian hopes we can catch species moving into shallower waters if we deploy around sunset, so the plan was to catch up on PhD work, until Amy called.

Now I'm being interrogated.

What does she want me to say? A lot has happened in the last ten days, and I don't know how to unpack it with myself, let alone with her.

"It's been...good," I offer.

"Charles," Amy groans, "I need you to give me more than that. Have you frolicked between the sheets? Are you having fun? Is your chest fluttering? This is what I want to know, not 'good.'"

"No. Yes. And yes."

"Ugh, you're giving me *nothing*!"

"I let him see my scars," I admit quietly. "I let him see, and…"

"And?" she presses. When I'm silent, she adds, "Let me guess, he proved you wrong because you thought he would turn away after he saw them." *Well, fuck.* She hit the fucking bullseye with that one. "You never did give Mateo enough credit."

"What?"

My stomach grows queasy at the accusation in her voice.

"It's just…" She sighs. "He asked me for your coffee order once so he could memorize it. And every time he orders at the shop, he asks about you. He's done it since the day he realized we were roommates. Mateo has always been kind to you, even if he teased you and called you that silly nickname. He's always cared for you."

"I never knew."

"Would it have made a difference if you did?"

An uncomfortable sense of guilt weighs heavily on my chest, because no, I don't think it would have made a difference, and the realization leaves me unsettled.

Ashamed with myself, really.

It wouldn't have made a difference because I didn't want to see Mateo any other way than a rival. It was easiest if that was the box I placed him in—the one that kept me safe because I didn't have to acknowledge how I felt differently around him.

A tear slips out.

"I'm a horrible person," I mutter.

"No, Charles, you're afraid. Have been since the day we met. You're terrified people are going to get too close and then decide they don't like what they discover."

Now I'm sobbing because she's right. She knows it, and I know it, too. I've allowed those thoughts so much control, I've hurt myself, and Mateo, too.

"I haven't run, and neither has he, so when are *you* going to stop running?"

Amy calls me out on my shit, always has, but right now, it's like she's saying everything she's been holding back, hoping I would figure it out for myself but haven't, so now she has to tell me herself.

I don't want to hate my skin or spend days avoiding my reflection. I don't want to waste hours wondering why someone was staring at me in the grocery store. I don't want the joint pain or the pins in my hip or the scar that cuts across my eyebrow. I don't want to hesitate every time Mateo compliments me, because my initial reaction is to brush off his words as a lie.

But I don't know how to function any other way.

"I don't know how to stop." Stop running. Stop hating myself. Stop pushing people away. "I'm scared, Ames. But I'm trying. He asked me if he was worth it."

And it broke my heart.

Witnessing him stand in front of me in the small bathroom, his uncertainty palpable, and ask if I thought him worthy enough, it fucking shattered my heart into a million pieces. Because for one moment, he and I were the same: two people terrified the other was going to throw them aside.

"But I think he might be," I continue. "I think he might be worth the risk."

Amy squeals. "Isn't that so exciting?"

"No, it's fucking terrifying!"

"It means you care for him—a lot—and I, for one, think that's fucking incredible. You deserve someone who makes you happy, and if that's Mateo, then chase that feeling, and when you catch it, don't let go."

"And if I get hurt?"

She releases a gust of air, rattling through the speaker. "Charlie."

"What?"

It's a valid question. What if when we get off this boat and return to reality, Mateo realizes this is a bubble? That what happens on the boat is not a reflection of real life? That he's choosing someone who has to pull over in a rainstorm and freaks out on airplanes? What happens when he realizes I have nightmares and wake up drenched in sweat?

What happens to me when I let him in and he realizes I'm broken?

"The only person who could potentially get hurt in this scenario is him."

"You think *I* would hurt him?"

Why does that feel like a fucking dagger straight to the heart?

"I think you have the power to, if you wanted."

My sniffles are the only sound between us.

"I'm not saying you're going to hurt him, I'm just saying that he's as vulnerable as you are. Falling in love is an act of blind faith. It's trusting another person so fully you give them everything that could hurt you—hand it to them on a silver platter—and believe they would never use any of it to cause you pain. It's letting them see every soul wound you possess and allowing them to help you heal."

Her words sink into my soul, settling and growing roots.

Falling in love is an act of blind faith.

I have to decide whether Mateo is worth the faith, if I trust him enough not to hurt me, the same way he would trust me.

If it wasn't for this trip—the way he has helped me step out of my comfort zone—I don't think I would have been ready to hear Amy's words and fully understand her meaning.

"Are you smiling?" she asks. "I have a best friend's intuition, and it's telling me you're smiling."

My fingers trail along the seam of my lips, where a tentative grin appears, nothing more than a tilt at the corner, but she's right. She always is.

"No," I say, but she can hear it in my voice, and she laughs in response. "How long have you been waiting to have this conversation?"

These weren't words in the moment, but a speech practiced and repeated, like she's been anticipating this moment.

"Since you called a few nights ago. Had a feeling you might be ready for a chat. I love you, Charlie. I hope you know that."

"I love you, too." More than she will ever know. I sniff away the tears threatening to fall.

"Now, tell me about all the cool shit you've seen before you have to go work."

"Do you have your to-do list?" Mateo asks, and I lift my notebook to show him my page filled with everything I need to complete before the ROV deploys at seven.

His dimples appear, and my chest does this odd constricting thing where it becomes momentarily difficult to breathe. I don't know if I hate it or if I want to feel it again and again.

Species identification guidebooks and notebooks cover our table in the lounge, and a condensation ring from my iced coffee stains a scientific paper about population genetics in green sea turtles. My fancy gel pens are lined up in a row, and my to-do list is color coded by priority and how much anxiety the task gives me.

"You know the rules," he says, displaying the massive bag of chocolate, then setting it off to the side. "When the timer goes off, you get a reward."

"You should give it to me now."

Do I believe sticking out my lower lip and batting my eyelashes will convince him? No, but when it comes to my treats, I've never been one to give up without a fight. He raises a brow, amused but undeterred, and my stomach flutters when his foot grazes the inside of my calf.

"Cute, but no. You've got to earn the chocolate, bruja. We've been over this."

"This is not helping disprove my 'ruler of hell' theory."

With a loud, exaggerated huff, I flip open my laptop. The keys clack as I bang against them. *If only I had some sugar. Then this email wouldn't make me want to gouge my eyes.* There's a deep chuckle, and then the blue foil interrupts my vision.

Thank you, Neptune! And Mateo, I guess.

The gooey caramel melts against my tongue, and I devour it with the grace of a bridge troll—that is, with none at all. This piece was smashed in the packaging, and I lick the wrapper to clean up the leftover crumbs. Only after every ounce of sugar is consumed do I realize I essentially just made out with a candy wrapper.

Warmth creeps up my neck, but before I can defend myself, Mateo searches the empty lounge, takes my face between his hands, and plants a searing, breath-snatching kiss on my lips.

Never have I been kissed like that, as if I'm the air he needs to breathe on a planet lacking oxygen.

There's little I can do to still my racing heart or the adrenaline-induced tremor in my hands, so I tuck my palms beneath my thighs.

"I've always wanted to kiss you after you eat a piece of chocolate. See if you would taste like the candy you devour," he admits in a gravelly voice.

"And did it?" I manage to croak.

The temperature in the lounge spikes ten degrees, and my throat dries as his tongue travels along the seam of his lips.

"Tasted even better than I could have imagined."

An ember of pleasure forms in my lower stomach, and Mateo stokes the flame when he touches my leg again.

"What tastes good?"

Jett's voice cuts through the air, and I screech, launching out of my chair and knocking my things off the table.

"How the *fuck* are you so quiet?" I yell, clutching my chest to press my heart back into its cavity, because surely, it just launched out of my ribcage. Mateo is laughing, doubled over, and Jett is staring at me like I've grown two heads.

This is not funny. I nearly soiled myself in fear.

"Sorry, Blondie. Didn't mean to frighten you."

"We need to get you a bell," I mutter, and Mateo snorts. Wildly, I swing my foot beneath the table until I hit his calf and he groans. *Serves him right.* I nearly shit myself, which is not a good look when you're in the early stages of whatever Mateo and I are doing.

Shitting yourself is for seasoned relationships.

Jett slides into a seat beside Mateo, whose cheeks are so red they resemble a fire hydrant, and asks, "What are you guys doing?"

"Catching up on some PhD work. Charlie is working on creating lesson plans for her lab course"—Mateo gives me a look, and I stick out my tongue—"and I'm grading reports for the invertebrate biology lab I run."

Jett looks unimpressed, so I add, "For every hour we work, we get a chocolate."

His demeanor shifts instantly. "Does finally responding to comments on all my social media pages count as work?"

"Does the idea of completing the task make you want to bang your head against a wall?" I ask. That's how I make my lists. Minor inconveniences at the top, and "this is going to lead to a meltdown" at the bottom. He mulls over my question, then nods. "Then, yes. It's work."

Mateo sets the timer on his phone, and we each work in silence. Jett snickers to himself every few minutes, and Mateo hums while he grades his papers.

The first alarm goes off right as I finish the lesson plans I've pushed aside for weeks, and I patiently wait as Mateo digs a chocolate out of the bag and places one in my hand, then one in Jett's awaiting palm.

He restarts the clock, and I accomplish another task. The hours fly by, and somehow, I'm deep into my to-do list, completing the duties I thought were a long shot to reach.

The chime rings through the air, and without looking away from my screen, I stick my hand out. Jett does the same, never glancing away from his phone.

I only look up when my palm remains empty and Mateo snorts. He peers down to our hovering hands, then to the timer, and finally to me. His face quivers as he attempts to restrain himself.

"What is so..."

I blink, stunned, as my brain catches up to his realization. *No fucking way.*

He's going to talk about this forever, and I will never live it down. The day Mateo Alvarez managed to Pavlov Charlotte Bowen will be marked in the history books as the worst day of my life.

It might be dramatic, but I think this is worse than my accident, if only because the cocky grin on Mateo's face makes my toes curl even if I want to throttle him for turning me into an experiment.

"I cannot believe you fucking 'Pavloved' us." I seethe as his laughter deepens, the sound smooth like honey. "We are not his dogs, salivating every time you ring a bell."

Except, maybe we are. But that's not the point. The point is, my...whatever Mateo is, has trained us both, and he thinks it's fucking hilarious.

"It wasn't intentional, I swear. But when you held out your palm as the timer went off, well...I connected the dots."

Leaning over the table, I steal the bag of candy, snatching a handful and splitting it between Jett and me. If we're going to be Mateo's lab rats, we're going to get paid. With chocolate, of course.

We're talking about this later, putting *No experiments on the other person* on our odd rule list.

"You will pay for this, cariño," I say, and his grin grows even brighter, amused I'm calling him by his shitty nickname.

He calls me a witch constantly, so it's only fair I call him an annoying asshole, even if using the endearment makes my cheeks heat and my stomach flutter. There's something intimate about giving another person a nickname, sharing the small inside secret with them.

I'm lost in the bright green of Mateo's irises, tracking the way they brighten when I call him cariño, when Jett asks, "Who's Pavlov, and why are we dogs?"

Oh, hell, I don't know how to explain this, so instead, I offer him another piece of chocolate.

"The less you know, the better," I say, patting his shoulder.

Mateo laughs again, and when Jett looks away, I mouth, *You will pay for this later.*

He winks.

The cocky asshole winks, and fuck me, my stomach flutters.

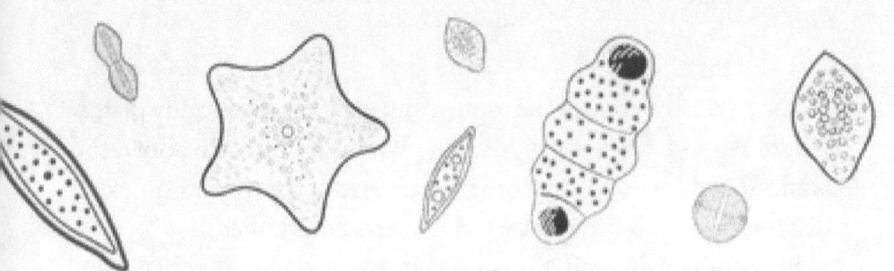

CHAPTER 22

MATEO

I draw another tally on my notepad when Jett yawns. Sixth time in ten minutes.

Vivian steers the ROV from the control panel at the front of the room, guiding the joystick to adjust camera angles and the path trajectory. The main lights are off, and the monitors and dashboard buttons illuminate the space in bright artificial light.

Steam rises from the coffee in my hand, filling the small room with the scent of ground beans, and the caffeine is all that's keeping me awake.

When I sent Charlie to bed, I didn't realize the sword I'd fall upon. My hope was to witness something incredible while she was sound asleep, but so far, the ROV dive has yielded nothing rare.

Vivian circles a seamount, the rocky, jagged slopes teeming with life. Mauve corals and tangerine feather stars dot its outer edges. Anemones, small and bright, sway in the current. She hovers by a small bubblegum-pink lumpfish, its sucker attached to free rock. It looks apathetically at the camera, like it's tired of the paparazzi.

She passes the edge of the mount and explores the muddy plains, where isopods and sea pigs reign. We hover directly above the seafloor for an hour, and other than one octopus, too quick to disappear, there's little to keep the others entertained.

Every organism excites me—not as much as the microbial communities within the sediment—but the small invertebrates have lost their sparkle for the rest of the crew, Jett and Doug included.

Jett went from barking orders at Doug to film every possible minute to slouched in the chair in the corner, fighting sleep—and losing. Doug is drooling, his beanie lowered to block the light. Vivian switches her music to early-2000s club hits and bobs her head as she works.

"You can go to bed," I whisper to Jett, who jolts upright in his chair, having dozed off after his last yawn.

"What is it?" He scrambles to the screen, leaning in close to view nothing but seafloor. Lots of sediment, very few living creatures he would find interesting.

In reality, the sediment is teeming with life, invisible to the naked eye. There's potentially thousands of species undiscovered at the seafloor—many of which could hold unique characteristics to improve science and healthcare.

"Dirt. More freaking dirt. Where are the cool-ass creatures with no eyes or clear heads!"

Uh-oh.

Jett is approximately ten seconds away from a toddler-style over-tired meltdown. Vivian meets my stare, and the fear in her expression pulls a chuckle from my chest.

Jett whirls on me, overwhelmed and too tired to process his emotions. Thankfully, Charlie has prepared me for this moment. The number of times I've had to steer her away from the edge of a mental breakdown is not incredibly high, but it's happened once or twice.

And those are the moments I feel closest to her—when she lets me see behind the mask she wears to keep herself safe. When she allows me to witness the rawest parts of her soul and doesn't pull away when I examine them.

For Charlie, showing vulnerability gives someone else control; power to hurt. It's a mindset rooted in the need to protect oneself from the world, from the harsh realities they've had to face. She simply needs someone to show her there's strength in offering the most vulnerable parts to someone else.

"It's late." I lower my voice into something soft. "Why don't you head up for the night?"

"I don't want to miss anything..."

"You won't. If we see anything, I'll come get you."

Jett contemplates the offer, unlike Doug, who's out the door and disappearing down the hallway without a goodnight or goodbye.

"All right." He moves to the door but pauses. "If *anything* has razor-sharp teeth, you have to run and get me."

I nod and shoo him out before he can change his mind. When I'm confident he's not going to return, I drop into the empty seat beside Vivian.

There's an amicable silence between the two of us until she brutally murders it by asking, "You and Charlie are getting your freak on, right?"

I sputter for a coherent response that doesn't incriminate us, but it's too late.

"I knew it!"

"I didn't say anything," I grumble, rubbing my jaw.

Unless having uncomfortable conversations where I have to ask her to put me out of my misery or give us a shot is considered "getting your freak on," then no. We have been getting our emotional freak on, I guess.

The emotional trust between Charlie and me is still growing, a small sapling I've been tending to on my own. It can grow into something sturdy, able to withstand time and storms, but only if she chooses to nurture it, too.

"I see all," Vivian says ominously, zooming in and out on the camera. "I am everywhere and nowhere, all at once."

"What does that even mean?"

"I saw you kiss her forehead after breakfast this morning."

"And?"

"You only kiss the forehead of someone you're fucking or in love with, so which is it?" She doesn't look away from the control board, focused on her task while she interrogates me. I should have kept Jett around as a buffer.

"No comment."

"Ugh, you're the worst."

"Some have referred to me as the mighty ruler of hell," I say offhandedly, my thoughts pulling to the blonde waiting for me in bed.

"Who? They seem like they know what they're talking about."

I pause, then say, "Charlie."

"Atta girl," she says, laughing as she begins the ascent back to the surface.

We're halfway there when her arm whips out and collides with my chest. She pulls back a few inches, only to hit me again.

The air whooshes from my lungs, from her attack and from the onyx-black fish hovering in the water column. Sharp teeth protrude from its lower jaw, and as we move closer, its flesh turns to a mottled brown. A light glows from the end of the lure extending from its head.

She snaps photos and adjusts camera angles as the ROV moves closer to the deep-sea anglerfish.

A small squeal escapes from me when a lump appears at its side.

"There's a male!" I point to the mass. "They attach to the female before mating."

We stare at the marvelous creature, and I snap a few photos to show Charlie in the morning. She's going to be pissed she missed the sighting. Shit, so will Jett.

It's too late to get him now. The creature moves on, passing the ROV, and Vivian radios to the main deck after shutting down the cameras.

I busy myself while she works, reading through text messages I've ignored while in the lab or identifying species.

> Oliver: I have to go back to England early.

> Family is having another meltdown. Apparently, it can only be solved with my presence.

> The tragic life of a duke.

> I hate the title. I would give it up if they would leave me alone.

> I mean, you have a castle. Pros and cons. How's Fergus? Is he alive?

> He's alive.

> Send proof of life.

> This isn't a hostage situation.

A photo pops up of my beautiful, not-finicky fern perched atop his plant stand, basking in the final rays of sun for the day. It's a beautiful photo, minus the large middle finger sticking up on its own.

> Rude.

Amy said she would take care of Fergus for you. Her exact words were "I'd love him like he was the offspring of my womb."

> That's the energy I expect every time I ask you to plant sit. Tell her thank you.

Will do. How's the boat? Tell Charlie you're head over heels for her?

> Actually, yes.

Wait, what?

Seriously?

> She told me I smell like a summer breeze.

What does that even mean?

> I don't know, but I love it.

*you love her.

> You and Amy have gotten close.

I see what you're doing.

I don't know what you're talking about.

Amy is making it difficult to leave.

So stay.

You know I can't.

Just wanted to let you know Fergus will be well cared for.

I expect a full update when you're off the boat.

Oh, and next time, you're visiting London.

Deal.

"Why are you smiling at your phone?" Vivian asks, "Did Charlie text you?"

Her question is teasing, but she's cut off from adding any more when Shaun radios that the ROV is being pulled from the water and she can release controls. She sighs in relief, shutting down different functions before disabling access and collecting her things.

"I'll see you tomorrow, Vivian," I say, ignoring her comment.

I'm ready to slip into bed beside Charlie and pull her against my chest to feel her heartbeat—a slow and steady rhythm singing me to sleep.

I'm halfway out the door when Vivian calls out, "Have you always known?"

"What?"

"About Charlie." She doesn't elaborate, but her meaning is weaved between words.

"She's far rarer than any species we'll see on this trip. So, to answer your question, yes. I've never had a doubt about Charlie."

It's hard to live your life by absolutes. The world is complicated—messy and ever-changing. But she is my one absolute; my heart begins and ends with her.

CHAPTER 23

CHARLIE

Light filters into the room, blinding me, before darkness quickly returns.

I've tried to sleep, but the bed is cold and empty without Mateo, who volunteered to watch the video with Vivian when I could barely lift my head after nine p.m. He sent me to the room, and I've been wide awake ever since, waiting for him to return.

I don't know what it says about me that it's harder to sleep without him beside me, but I'm choosing to ignore it.

Mateo tiptoes around the room, getting ready for bed, and I rustle so I don't scare him.

His five-o'clock shadow is growing into a small beard, and he yawns deeply before saying, "I thought you were asleep."

I shake my head, lifting the covers for him to slide in beside me.

There's no pillow wall tonight, hasn't been since he held me until I fell asleep, but we've kept to our sides of the bed.

Mateo wordlessly puts on his mask and burrows into the covers. When he rests his arm behind his head, leaving the side of his body open, I make the impulsive decision to scoot closer and lean my head on his chest below the crook of his arm.

He sighs, and my heart races with the small act of intimacy. I grow bolder, draping my arm over his chest so my body molds against his side. His free hand lifts to cover mine, to keep it firmly planted on his chest.

Sleep slowly drags me under until I hear the sound of his mask unclick and the pressurized air whoosh.

"Go on a date with me," he whispers.

"What?"

"Tomorrow night, will you go on a date with me?"

"Okay," I murmur against his skin, right before I fall into a deep slumber.

Vivian and Sofía chat in the lounge, paperwork spread out between them, and I creep toward the table, hoping I'm not interrupting.

"Hi."

Ugh. That came out way meeker than I wanted. I was aiming for cool and casual, not flustered and ready to flee.

"Charlie, hi!" Sofía smiles brightly, clearing the table. "Please, sit."

I slide into the seat, and I'm panicked again. Nerves eat at my confidence, and I pick at the cornflower-blue nail polish I put on this morning. Asking Vivian and Sofía for help means admitting there's something happening between Mateo and me, and that makes it real.

"Sofía and I were going over the plan for the remaining ROV dives. We've had pretty good luck at these sites previously." Vivian points to a handful of areas on a map. "Is there anything you hope to see? I can try to adjust them for you."

"A whale fall, but that's unlikely."

Vivian surveys the map, her brow furrowed in concentration.

"I can't make any promises, but this area"—she circles the map—"has had remains of whale falls on previous cruises. We can try."

"Thank you." I volley between Sofía and Vivian, then take a deep, calming breath. "I was hoping...well, I was thinking maybe..."

Fuck, I can't get a freaking sentence out without stumbling over myself.

I groan, dropping my head into my hands.

"Never mind, sorry."

I rise from the table to handle my embarrassment in private, but Sofía grabs my arm and drags me back into the seat.

"Does this have something to do with Mateo bribing me for a bottle of wine and a special meal from the chef?"

"What?"

A special meal?

He refused to tell me what he had planned this morning, only told me to meet him at seven on the top deck. Needless to say, I'm freaking the fuck out. I can't recall the last time I've had the anticipatory fluttering in my chest before a date.

"About half an hour ago, Mateo showed up with some requests," Vivian says, her eyebrows rising and falling suggestively.

"More like demands," Sofía mumbles. "Are you here about the same thing?"

"Uh...maybe?"

Sofía squeals, clapping her hands together, and Vivian cheers. My jaw falls as they celebrate before giving me their attention.

"I was telling Amber about the odd sexual tension between you two," Vivian admits. "We've been rooting for this. Sofía caved immediately and gave Mateo everything he wanted when he said he was trying to impress you."

I can't stop the heat creeping up my neck or the girlish smile tugging at my lips.

Another round of squeals echoes around the table, and they both discard the paperwork to lean in close.

"So what do you need?" Vivian asks.

"You want it, you got it," Sofía adds.

"Well, I was hoping maybe you guys could help with my hair...and maybe a little makeup?" I look at Vivian, whose eyelids are a bright pink, covered in iridescent sparkles.

The two exchange a look.

"My cabin. Five p.m.," Vivian says with a manic expression that sends a wave of apprehension through my body.

Tonight, I'm going on a date, and I'm really, really excited.

The cool sea breeze whips through the loose curls Sofía spent the last hour perfecting, then dousing in hair spray. Nerves eat at my stomach, but I refrain from touching my face in fear I'll mess up Vivian's makeup. I've never worn this much before, and when I looked in the mirror, I almost didn't recognize myself.

I smooth out the sundress Sofía let me borrow, cream with small pink flowers and a milkmaid cut. My chest and arms are bare, but with the pink shawl Vivian lent me, I'm able to ward off any chill.

Music filters from the top deck, and as I take the last stair, I stop in my tracks. A large blanket is laid out on the ground, covered with pillows. White wine and the bag of chocolate sits in the corner beside two covered plates.

Mateo stands in the center of it all; his linen button-down flows with the wind, and the khakis fit snugly against his thighs. The coffee-hued waves of his hair are in pristine condition, as usual, and his hand flexes at his side.

"Hi, bruja," he purrs, reaching out a hand. I place mine in his, and he pulls me against his chest. "You look beautiful."

I'm mute as he guides me to a spot, helps me sit with my dress, and drapes a blanket over my lap.

I've officially lost function of my tongue, and I fiddle with the fire opal dangling around my neck to dissipate a sliver of the nerves.

We're here, which means we're moving in a new direction, and I want that—I told him as much. But it still frightens me because there's an energy hanging in the air, one that suggests who I am tomorrow won't be the same person I am today.

He's smiling at me, and it's the goofy, lopsided grin that settles a bit of the riot in my chest.

"Hi."

Ah, good. I can still form words. Full sentences? Not quite, but I've got a greeting down.

He's still staring at me, radiating happiness, and warmth blooms in my chest right beneath my diaphragm.

"Your hair is perfect," I blurt out, overwhelmed by the depth of my affection for him, how wonderfully his shirt pulls against his broad shoulders, and the romantic energy buzzing in the air.

I slap my palm against my forehead. Neptune, I sound like a doofus.

Mateo laughs deeply. "Thank you."

"Don't let the compliment go to your head," I grumble, embarrassed by my awkwardness, but also blown away by *him.*

"How could I? If I did, it might ruin my *perfect hair.*"

"I'm gonna go." I throw a thumb over my shoulder. "If you need me, I'll be floating in the ocean."

I push to my knees, but Mateo rips me back down to the blanket, his chest rumbling with laughter.

"If you go overboard, I'd have to follow you, and our pasta would get cold."

"You'd follow me?" I ask, hung up on the statement.

"I'd follow you anywhere, Charlie."

Any response I have falls short, but he doesn't seem to notice as he uncovers the plates, placing one in front of me. The aroma of basil and parmesan fills the air, and a perfectly grilled cut of chicken sits atop a bed of cavatappi pasta.

It's my favorite meal. Down to the shape of the noodle.

He knows my favorite food, but I don't know his, and the lack of that knowledge settles like a rock in my gut.

"What's your favorite meal?"

"Pizza. Doesn't matter the toppings," he responds, "but if my abuela asks, it's her barbacoa."

I immediately store the fact, locking it away into a mental box.

He digs in, while I slowly pick at the noodles, too nauseous to enjoy them.

How much has he learned about me in the two years we've known each other? How little do I know about him?

"Is your food cold?"

It's fucking delicious, but my stomach is already doing somersaults, and if I eat all the food, I fear I may vomit.

"I'm too jittery to eat," I admit, smoothing out my dress. He lifts a brow, a silent demand for an explanation, and in the spirit of honesty and showing Mateo he's worth the effort, I offer him an uncomfortable truth. "I haven't been on a decent date since before my accident, and you know far more about me than I know about you, and I feel bad about that, and you look really good. I'm flustered."

My cheeks flame as his smile grows into something magnificent—as glorious as the final rays of a sunset.

He sets our plates to the side, patting the empty spot between his legs. I crawl over the blanket to settle into the space and lean back, using his chest as a pillow and burrowing into the warmth he offers.

"What do you want to know?" he asks, his breath hot against my shoulder.

"Everything," I admit.

I want to know every detail about Mateo, down to his sock preference. What he loves, what he hates, his fears and dreams. I want to know *everything*.

His fingers tangle in my hair, brushing through the loose curls, before pulling my head to the side and placing a tender kiss on my lips.

There's no rush to it; instead, it's an exploration, slow and unsure.

When we break apart, my head is spinning.

"All right, bruja. I'll tell you everything, as long as you offer me the same."

"Deal." I place my hand on his thigh, right where the butterfly tattoo hides beneath his pants. "How many tattoos do you have, and what do they all mean?"

The question is rushed. I've wanted to know since he revealed the ink, but there hasn't been a good time to ask.

Covering my hand with his, he huffs a laugh, and it skitters along my spine.

"My family is from a small town in Central Mexico. It's where my grandparents were born, and it's close to the area where the monarch butterflies congregate in the winter. My abuelo loved them and would spend hours talking about how they covered the trees and filled the air. I got the butterfly for him after he passed away."

I slip my hand out and move up his thigh to where I think the rest of his ink hides.

"And the one here? What about this one?"

My hand is inches away from his zipper, and I'm not oblivious to how he hardens, pressing against my back.

"Been checking me out?"

I swat his thigh, and his laughter worsens.

"It's a quote from a poem I love. Those are my only two."

"What are your favorite things?"

"You want to know them all?"

I nod, and he lists things he enjoys. Soccer. Crossword puzzles. Watermelon-flavored Chupa Chups. He talks and talks, and I listen, hanging off every word, memorizing every fact and story he shares. I'm greedy—a pirate hoarding its bounty.

He shares stories of his adventures with Oliver in Europe after they graduated from the University of Miami, and how he could live the rest of his life without ever stepping into another hostel.

"Oliver's your best friend?"

His arms tighten around my shoulders. "Wouldn't know what to do without him. He moved back to London right before I moved to Rhode Island. We don't see each other as much as I'd like."

"He and Amy are sleeping together," I admit, not sure if he knows our best friends are keeping each other company.

"I know." He sighs deeply, like the information hurts him. "He's fond of her, but his obligations are complicated, and his family's expectations are high."

"What?"

"Oliver will never be able to follow his heart, not the way Amy follows hers." His words linger between us, and a sadness washes over me for our friends. Mateo recognizes the energy shift and places a soft kiss on my temple. "They'll be okay," he assures me.

Bright white stars speckle the deep navy-blue sky. It's shocking how clear the view is at sea. No light pollution to block the constellations or dull the glow of the moon. Out here, the universe feels expansive, never-ending, infinite, compared to my tiny world in Rhode Island.

Mateo holds me in his arms as we look up at the endless sky.

It would be daunting—how irrelevant we are in the scheme of the universe—if it wasn't for the way he holds me, grounding me to earth.

"Is it a full moon tonight?" I ask.

"Why?" His breath is hot against my shoulder. "Did you want to try to curse me again?"

I smack his bicep. "I only did it that *one time*, but no, if it's a full moon I can charge my crystals."

"Did you want to go get them? You could show me how to do it."

"Really?" I perk up.

He chuckles, swiping my hair over one shoulder and placing a gentle kiss on the other.

"Teach me how to be a witch," he murmurs against my skin.

Before he can change his mind, I fly across the deck toward our room. "You would be a warlock," I correct, disappearing to gather my collection.

It's only when I return and his face brightens as I sit beside him do I realize the nerves are gone, replaced with giddy excitement.

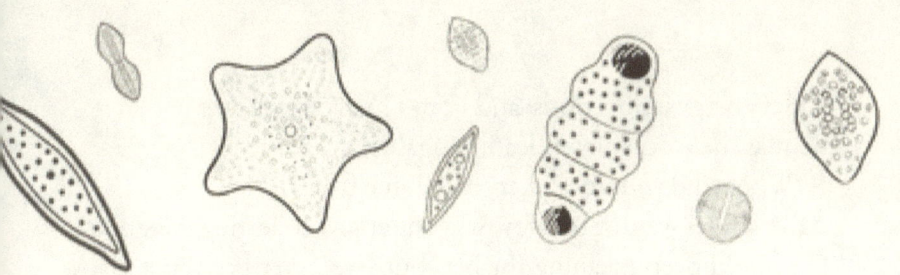

Chapter 24

MATEO

Charlie neatly lines up her crystals on the deck, ensuring each has full access to the powers of the moon.

Her blond hair shines beneath the moonlight, the strands like spun gold as she pushes loose curls away from her face. I've been breathless from the moment she appeared at the top of the steps, timid but with a tentative smile.

I'm staring at her like a lovestruck idiot as she fiddles with her impressive collection of rocks, treating each one with the utmost care.

"Okay," she mutters, sitting back on her knees. The dress billows out as she repositions, offering me a peek of what's beneath—or rather, what's *not*. Besides a thin strip of lace, it's nothing but bare skin.

My stomach drops, lust settling at the base of my spine.

"The moonlight cleanses the energy the crystal holds and recharges it with positive energy while reestablishing its natural properties," Charlie explains.

Her energy is infectious, and I can't help but fall into her excitement as she scoots closer, leaning against my arm.

"Where did your love of crystals come from?"

I've always wanted to know why she enjoys collecting the stones. They hold deep meaning for her, but I've never been in a place where I felt comfortable to ask. Until now.

"My parents bought me one of those gemstone dig sets, and once I unearthed the first one, I was intrigued. Then I learned each had meaning and intention, and they called to me. I don't know as much as others, but they offer me a sense of peace and direction when I feel lost." She trails off, unsure of herself. "It's silly."

"I don't think so. How old were you?"

"Nineteen," she admits, and I let out a small chuckle. She picks up a dark-green stone, marbled with lighter swirls, and places it in my palm. "You can have this one. It's moss agate. It's supposed to help with stress." The crystal is cool to the touch. "It reminds me of your eyes."

She offers the small confession with a bright blush, and I slip the stone into my pocket. My heart beats double time as I lean down to steal a kiss. When we break, her irises glitter with starlight.

"Now what do we do?" I whisper.

The crystals line up to form a star, the largest at the center, surrounded by the smaller stones—a small hole where she removed the moss agate. I know very little about crystals for healing energy, or the powers the moon holds, but there's power in Charlie's smile.

"This is it," she whispers back, her focus locked on the crystals.

Are they going to move? Or shine? Or do anything other than sit on the deck?

"You're not a very good witch," I joke, and she bites the inside of her cheek. I run my fingers through my hair. "No wonder your curse didn't work."

She groans, folding her arms.

"It wasn't my fault. It was the spell."

"Oh?"

"I needed a lock of your hair for the recipe, but I couldn't figure out how to cut a piece off without you noticing, so Amy and I left it out." She gives me a look. "That's obviously why it didn't work."

"Obviously," I assure her, grabbing her by the hips and pulling her onto my lap.

She squeals, the sound inciting a pounding in my chest as she giggles and melts in my arms.

This moment, right here, is what I've been waiting for. Everything seems so unimportant, so trivial, when I'm with her.

"Mi bruja," I whisper, placing a kiss on the crown of her head.

I've spent so long waiting, hoping, yearning for something to happen, it feels surreal, almost dreamlike now. It's foolish to admit I've spent so long desperate for Charlie to take a shot on me, but it's my truth. I've never had a doubt in my mind about her. It only took a few moments to know Charlie was meant to exist in my life forever.

People dedicate their lives to a cause—curing cancer, saving biodiversity, helping others—but I think...I think if Charlie let me, I would be content to dedicate my life to loving her.

"Why do you call me that?"

"Do you really want to know?"

She hesitates before nodding.

"When we first met, I couldn't stop thinking about you. I would hear your laugh in the hallway and chase the sound. I would try to convince Dan to host co-advisor meetings so I could spend time with you. You had cast a spell on me, so you became my witch. *Mi bruja.* Cursing me to fall for you all over again every time you would offer me a smile."

She's quiet in response to my confession, but her eyes have always been expressive, a window into her emotions, and right now, the surprise in them is unmistakable. They say everything she can't, and I don't need to hear the words to know my answer was the last thing she expected.

"Mi bruja," she parrots, trying to roll the *r* off her tongue. Once, twice, three times she repeats the endearment, whispering it to herself and growing more confident with each pass of the words.

A surprised laugh tumbles out of me as she darts in and steals a kiss.

"I like it. The nickname, I mean." She pauses. "Well, I used to hate it, but now...now I like it. You can keep using it," she declares.

"I'm glad you approve."

She leans into my chest, her head falling to rest on my shoulder. "It makes me feel a bit bad that I call you an annoying asshole."

Now would be a good time to fess up that her nickname doesn't mean what she thinks it does, but I can't do it. I fucking love how she calls me cariño with that shit-eating grin like it's the funniest thing she's ever said.

It will undoubtedly bite me in the ass when she figures it out, but fuck it, I'm not telling her.

I hum, ending the conversation before she gets bit by the inquisitive bug and asks a few too many questions. She's a scientist, after all. Curiosity runs in her veins.

We sit in a comfortable silence, listening to the waves crash against the vessel and staring up at the night sky, full of twinkling stars. I snake my arm around her shoulder, tugging her tighter toward off the creeping chill. Her bare skin is cool, and I lay a palm down on the bare flesh to warm her up.

Half a dozen scars press against my hand, and my thumb swipes over a raised one beneath her collarbone. She tracks my hand as I jump from one to another.

I haven't asked how she received them, and I told myself I never would. The origin of her wounds is not a story you can ask for; it's knowledge that needs to be given, offered because she trusts me enough to hold some of the weight for her. Because that's what these scars are—a heavy weight she's held on her own.

She scans the night sky, lost somewhere in her mind. When she returns to reality, tears line her lashes.

"I was driving home to surprise my dad for his birthday," she says, and I hold my breath, afraid if I make a rapid movement she'll close up like a sea anemone. "It was snowy, but...but I had all-wheel drive. I thought I was fine."

Her skin is pale, but she raises her chin and straightens her shoulders.

"Black ice had formed on the road," she continues, the words choppy. "I hit a patch, careened off the road, and slammed into a tree. The force of the impact shattered the windshield inward and crushed the front of the car."

She struggles to breathe, pulling in shallow, jagged breaths. I'm in awe of her, but she doesn't need to give me this—not if it hurts her.

"It's all right," I coo. "You don't have to—"

"I-I want to." She lifts a trembling hand to palm my cheek. "You're worth the fear."

I cover her hand with mine, giving her as much time as she needs. There are few words to express what it means to me that she trusts me enough to share her trauma—to take a leap of faith and believe I'll hold her confession with care.

She removes her hand to touch the scar cutting across her brow.

"When the car hit the tree and the windshield shattered, my head whipped forward from the impact. This is from a large shard of glass." Her finger lingers on the bottom of the scar, the most ragged section, before swiping away a rogue tear. "I was on a highway in the middle of nowhere, and the hospital I went to was under-staffed, so a medical resident stitched the laceration closed. That's why it's so ugly." She pauses, then almost inaudibly, she adds, "I didn't always look like this."

Charlie pulls her bottom lip between her teeth, staunch belief in her words, but she couldn't be further from the truth.

"I don't think that's true." I force her chin up. "I have never met anyone more beautiful than you, and I've never known you without the scars. They could throw a thousand people in a room, and I would look for you first, Charlie. That kind of beauty is powerful."

She gulps but rises and straightens out her dress. Her hand hovers between us, palm faced up.

"Come back to the room with me?"

She says nothing more, but I understand the suggestion in her words, and I'm flying off the ground to take her hand. Charlie giggles loudly, but I steal the sound in a frenzied, overzealous kiss.

My heart thuds, rerouting blood to other parts of my body as her breasts press against my chest. She breaks away and drags me behind her, the picnic I planned forgotten as she picks up speed, nearly running to get back to our cabin.

Our fingers are intertwined like it's the most natural thing in the world, and nerves eat at my stomach as she pushes me over the threshold and clicks the door shut.

I'm not two steps in before she's on me again, launching herself into my arms and wrapping her legs around my waist to steady herself. She claims my lips, and the desperation is palpable as we stumble.

She moves down my cheekbone, then jaw, before she works along the column of my neck. Each touch sends a spider web of tingles across my skin, and my brain is still trying to catch up with what's happening.

In a single move, I drop her onto the bed, and she bounces, releasing a surprised laugh. I drink her in: blond hair fanned out against the maroon comforter, cerulean eyes peering up beneath thick lashes, a carefree smile, and flushed cheeks. I capture the mental image, locking it away to cherish for eternity before I continue, her breasts rising and falling in time with her breath.

That dress has teased me for the last few hours, and I plan to rip it off her.

My chest buzzes with anticipation as she looks up at me with vivid desire. "Are you just going to stare?" she teases.

"I've been waiting two years for this moment, bruja. I plan to take my time." I lean over her, my hands splayed on both sides of her head, my lips hovering inches from hers. "Savor every moment, taste every inch of your skin, worship every part of you."

Her jaw falls, and she blinks as I tug at the small bow holding the top of her dress together. It falls open, leaving her breasts bare, a small pendant dangling between them.

I trail a finger down her breastbone to the iridescent stone, and her skin pebbles.

"Tell me, bruja, do you like it soft and sweet?" I ask, my dick straining in my pants as her breathing grows erratic and her pupils dilate. "Or do you want it rough and hot?"

Charlie pulls her lip between her teeth, chewing on the plush skin.

I've thought about this moment, imagined every debauched scenario, but the ones that replay the most are the ones where she's begging for more, so desperate for my cock that she's willing to *beg me* to please her.

My hand continues south until I'm hovering at the apex of her thighs, toying with the hem of her dress.

"If I slipped my hand beneath your panties, what would I find?" I hum. "Would you be wet for me?"

"I-I...uh," she stutters.

It's idiotic to find her bumbling sexy, but to know I affect her is powerful knowledge. Evens the playing field.

"Should we find out?" I ask, and she nods frantically. "Use your words."

"Yes."

"Good girl." I slip my hand beneath her sundress, dancing my fingers along the band of her white lace underwear. I dip my fingers and almost come undone from how wet she is for me.

Do not come in your pants, Mateo.

It's a genuine concern as I slide my thumb over her clit and her head falls back, a moan tumbling from her lips. My heartbeat is an erratic thing, nearly bursting from my chest as she lifts her hips, seeking pleasure.

My hand pauses as her beauty overwhelms me. It shouldn't be possible to crave someone the way I crave Charlie. I should be embarrassed by how desperately I want her. Scientists should study the effects she has on me, mind, body, and spirit.

Charlie's eyelids crack open to find me openly admiring her, and her cheeks flush a rosy hue.

"Dress off," I demand in a gravel-rough voice. She silently obeys the command, stripping the sundress over her head and leaving her bare from the waist up.

I can barely breathe, barely function with her lying on the bed, but my feet move and my knees fall until I'm kneeling on the floor, ready to seek my salvation.

Her ankles dangle off the mattress, and I wrap my hands around them and tug her to the edge. A loud, shocked squeal bounces off the walls, followed by a laugh-filled "Mateo!"

Lust strikes my cock as her giggles fill the air, and my hands move from her ankles, along her calves, up to the smooth skin of her inner thighs. She jerks when I grab the band of her panties and slide them down her legs.

My pulse races like a stampede of wildebeest barreling toward water after a long drought. I shake away the trembling in my fingers and toss her underwear over my shoulder. Charlie laughs again, but it's quickly cutoff by a moan when I dip my head and drag my tongue across her slit.

She tastes better than I could have imagined, and desire knots at the base of my dick when she releases a soft mewl. For a split second, I have to pause to pull a ragged breath of air into my lungs.

I'd do just about anything to hear more of those needy little whimpers.

Her hips lift as I swirl my tongue around her clit, and I study every moan and sigh she releases. I want to commit every inch of her to memory.

"*Fuck,*" she groans when I slide a finger inside her, her walls pulsing as I continue my work.

I'm rock solid behind my zipper, so hard it physically hurts, but the pain morphs into deep pleasure as she squirms beneath my tongue.

But it's more than her sounds that send me to the edge. It's the open adoration in her expression and how her fingers snake into my hair and possessively grip the strands.

The pressure at the base of my spine is unbearable, and when I slip another finger inside and she clenches around them, I nearly lose control.

Timing my movements with my tongue, I drive us both to the edge of madness. When I suck her clit between my teeth, her hips buck wildly and she pulls me away from the apex of her thighs.

Shame. I'm still starving.

I swipe away her pleasure coating my chin before licking my lips, and lust compounds at the base of my spine when her grip turns deadly and her chest heaves with exertion.

"Do you need something, bruja?" I purr. "I'm trying to eat." Her focus drops to my erection, which is straining against my pants, and when they reconnect with mine, they're full of hunger. "Do you want my cock?" I ask, my voice vibrating with need. She nods. "Take what's yours."

Charlie rises, her hands shaking as she undoes my belt and slips it off. My breath hitches when she grazes my shaft as she pulls down the zipper. She tugs at the band of my underwear, and my cock pops out, so hard I'm resting against my abdomen, a small bead of pre cum forming on the tip.

Fuck.

I thought I was strong enough to last, but even without her touch, I'm ready to combust.

Her fingers gently wrap around me, pumping up and down a few times, before she lets go and rises onto her knees. The kiss she offers is probing and unsure as she unbuttons my shirt and slides it off.

Sparks shoot down my arms as her hands explore while we kiss, and I can feel the small tremble in her fingers as she passes along the planes of my skin. Heart slamming against my ribcage, I traverse the gentle slope of her spine and cup her ass, lifting her into the air.

Her legs wrap around my waist, and I spin to sit on the bed with her in my lap.

Charlie breaks the kiss and cups my jaw. The reverent touch sends a wave of warmth across my limbs, and I lean into the contact, savoring how a simple touch is capable of expressing so much.

"I'm breaking my rules," she whispers.

"Rules?"

"No lights. No missionary. No sleepovers."

Her inner thigh grazes against my dick, and I hiss. Soft curves mold to my palms as I slide them up until my fingers tangle in her hair. I wrap the honey curls around my knuckles, pulling her head back to expose her neck to me.

I suck on the column of her throat, moving left, then right, leaving angry red marks that scream *mine*.

Charlie whimpers, squirming in my lap. "Mateo, *please*."

"Do you like breaking the rules, bruja?" With my free hand, I guide her palm over my cock. "Do you like knowing how badly you affect me?"

"I like breaking the rules with you," she replies, nearly snapping the tether holding me back.

Releasing her, I lie back on the bed and grab her hips, lifting her up and guiding her to hover over my face. I can smell her arousal, and my dick twitches from the sight of her thighs slick and ready for me.

"Sit," I command, digging my fingers into her skin. She gasps when I tug her down.

"Mateo..." She trails off, uncertain.

"I've dreamed of this, bruja. Make it my reality."

She gulps but lowers her hips so she's hovering right over my lips. Close, but not close enough. My hand collides with her ass, and she yelps, but her pupils enlarge with desire. *There's my girl.*

Her thighs bracket my cheeks as she sits, and I drag my tongue up her slit to circle her clit.

"Oh, *fuck*," Charlie moans, one hand falling back to rest on my upper thigh, her nails imprinting half-moons on my flesh.

Maybe I'll add a third tattoo—those small little marks to remind both of us who I belong to.

I nip and lick, chasing every breathy sound she offers me until I'm high on her, on this moment. Peering up over hooded lids, I find her lost in the pleasure, tweaking her nipple between her finger and thumb, her head tossed back. The view is fucking magnificent as she grinds her hips against my jaw.

Her breath hitches, and her thighs begin to shake. I drag her down by the globes of her ass, sucking her clit between my teeth.

"I'm gonna..." She trails off, breath shaky. "Oh, Neptune."

Charlie's grip tightens as she climaxes, grinding her hips against my five-o'clock shadow as she moans. I don't stop my assault until she's pushing off my chest and flopping onto the bed.

Her breath is erratic, but she chokes out, "Holy fucking Neptune."

"Mateo," I correct, leaning over her. "Not Neptune. Mateo."

I can feel the cocky smile tugging my cheeks upward as Charlie lies on the bed, sated and content. Her hair is splayed along the pillow, and I lean down to place a kiss on her chest. One by one, I move from scar to scar, doing what I told myself I always would if I had the opportunity: pour admiration into each wound.

As I reach the long, straight scar on her hip, Charlie mutters, "Broke my pelvis."

I move up to the curved one along her abdomen from her spleen removal. I continue my path, peppering kisses along her chest on all the small marks before I reach her face.

Starting at her temple, I offer languid kisses along the raised flesh. When I'm done, there are tears pooling on her lashes.

"You are the most beautiful person I've ever beheld," I admit. Her hands fly to cover her face, but I peel them away. "Only the truth."

"I...Thank you," she says, her face flaming.

I lean down to kiss her when she grabs my shaft, squeezing slightly. She catches my moan with a kiss as she quickens her pace, tightening her grip at the base. Charlie nibbles at my lower lip, pulling it between her teeth, and it's all it takes for the pressure at my spine to coil like a spring.

My muscles tighten as I barrel closer to completion. Is it a tad embarrassing that I'm about to come from a hand job? Maybe, but I thought I was going to come in my fancy pants. A win is a win.

Charlie kisses me, her hand picking up speed until I combust, spilling all over her chest, covering her with spurts of cum. My breath is uneven, ragged, and when I rise and realize she looks *claimed,* I lose my breath completely.

Regardless if she knows it yet or not, Charlie Bowen is mine. Mine to cherish. Mine to worship. Mine to *keep.*

CHAPTER 25

CHARLIE

Raucous chatter fills the lounge area overflowing with boat and production crew, who are enjoying the evening off as the vessel transits to a new location. Bottles of cheap beer and wine litter the bar counter in the corner, and Sofía laughs as Jett mimics a horrible Australian accent.

A dozen things happen at once, but every brain cell I possess is focused on one thing: Mateo's hand resting on my thigh, perilously close to where his face was last night.

The sexual tension has been thick all day, twisting me tighter and tighter until I'm ready to combust. Lingering touches in the lab. Longing looks across the room. Whispered words as he passes by. I'm a firecracker ready to explode.

My inner thighs ache from the beard burn he left behind—a constant reminder of him. For the first time in a long time, I wasn't self-conscious of how I looked or what scars he might see, but rather, I could experience the moment as it was. I didn't realize how badly I've trapped myself in my mind until I felt the freedom I've denied myself.

I didn't get lost in the anxious thoughts because Mateo tethered me to earth.

Speaking of the devil, Mateo swipes his thumb against my inner thigh, right atop the raw flesh, pulling a hiss. His eyebrows scrunch while he repeats the action.

"Are you hurt?" he whispers.

"I'm fine." I'll apply some cream on it tonight when I oil my joints, and by morning, I won't have to hobble when I walk. Plus, I like the sting. It's a reminder of what happened and how I felt. He doesn't look like he believes me, so I add, "It's a bit raw from your beard."

"Oh."

His face is stoic before it blooms into a pleased smile, overflowing with male pride. I try to school my features, to prevent my own, but it cracks through anyway.

He removes his hand to place a card down on the table, then glances at me, and his delight morphs into something smug from the take four Uno card sitting on top of the pile.

"Are you serious?"

"As the plague. Take eight, bruja." He pushes the pile of cards in my direction. "All is fair in love and war."

I scowl at Mateo, and Jett releases a belly laugh, banging on the table.

"This isn't war, it's freaking Uno," I yell, clutching the two dozen cards already in my grip, thanks to Mateo and Jett, who have been harassing me all evening.

"And you're losing," Jett adds. "You do know you're supposed to get rid of the cards, not collect more."

I hate them.

Sofía and Vivian stifle their laughter, and I glare daggers at them. What happened to best friends at sea? Do the sacred bonds of boat friendships mean nothing anymore?

"Traitors," I cough, fixing my glare on them.

"I'm glad it's not me," Sofía says as I begrudgingly take the eight cards.

"I would *never* betray you," Jett whispers, winking at her.

She turns away, but I see her crimson cheeks.

"Did you hear that, Mateo? Jett would *never* betray her." I lay the sarcasm on thick.

Mateo cackles. He *fucking* cackles. "If I let you win, you would force me to play again, just to prove you could win without me handing it to you."

I nearly draw blood from how hard I bite the inside of my cheek. Because he knows he's right, he winks and returns his focus to the table.

We work in a circle while everyone's cards dwindle. Well, every-one's except mine. Mateo's hand returns to sit on my thigh, his fingers playing a silent tune as they tap my skin. He places down a card with his free hand, looks me dead in my eyes, and calls out, "Uno."

The table is a chorus of "whats" and "hows" as he holds a single card in his grip.

His concentration never wavers and mirth swirls in his gaze. This was his plan all along. Have them focus on sabotaging me so they stop paying attention to him.

Evil genius.

I shake my head in disbelief.

Everyone panics, shuffling through their cards to find a skip or debating what color he has. It's futile. Mateo is many things, and brilliant is at the top of the list, right beside charming.

In the week and a half we've been on the boat, I've realized maybe I know more about him than I thought. Sure, I didn't know his favorite color or how he likes his eggs—scrambled with hot sauce—but I know *him*. I know he needs to read in special fonts on his computer, otherwise his temples throb with a headache. I can identify all of his tics. Running his fingers through his hair when he's unsettled. Humming when he's content. I can decipher each of his smiles and understand the meaning behind them.

I know him, which means I know he's holding a wild card in his hand. It doesn't matter what color they change it to or if they skip him. The only way he loses is if the person in front of him plays a take four. That person is me—thanks to Jett's reverse card—and while I have a billion options, none of them will add to his deck or delay his inevitable victory.

"How did you get rid of your cards so quickly?" Vivian questions.

He shrugs. I lay down my card, and Mateo drops his wild on top. His shoulder grazes mine, causing my skin to buzz.

"He's clever," I groan. "He lures you in with his good looks and kind smile, then *bam*! He takes the victory, and you're none the wiser that it was his plan all along."

I'm working myself up into a tizzy, but I've been strung tight all day from his touch, and now I've lost in a card game. I hate losing. Mateo's lips quiver as he fights laughter, and Vivian is outright cackling, her face red from lack of oxygen.

Add poor loser to my list of undesirable attributes.

It wouldn't have hurt as badly if I wasn't part of Mateo's grand plan for victory, using me as a pig for slaughter. I can slash any worry that the change in our relationship would alter our dynamic. He's still annoying as ever, only now I find it endearing and weirdly hot rather than the bane of my existence.

He's still a cocky asshole, but now he's *my* cocky asshole.

"If you're trying to insult me, you're doing a poor job."

Jett, Vivian, and Sofía watch us like we're prime time TV, and the urge to kiss the victory off his face is overwhelming. The only thing stopping me is the others. I don't think I'm ready for public displays of affection yet.

Mateo's hand on my thigh was anxiety-inducing enough.

"You'll pay for this, cariño," I mutter, dropping my cards into the pile.

Mateo beams the same way he always does when I call him the silly nickname, like it's the greatest word in the world.

"What? Are you going to curse me again?" The rest of the room fades away as he fake glares at me. "It went *so well* last time."

"Listen, cariño," I start, jabbing a finger at him, "I will cut your CPAP cord if you don't—"

"That's so sweet," Sofía coos, glancing between Mateo and me.

Uh...I'm not sure how sweet my threat to destroy his medical equipment is.

Mateo pales, examining the walls with immense curiosity.

"What exactly is sweet, Sofía?"

I have an idea, but I want her to confirm my hypothesis. Mateo refuses to meet my stare. I'm not sure if I want to smack him, laugh, or kiss him. A combination of all three, really.

"That you call him cariño..." Sofía trails off, confused.

"What does cariño mean?" Jett asks.

"Yeah, Mateo. What *does* cariño mean? Please, enlighten us."

He knows he's been caught, but when his glassy greens return to mine, they're full of fire and passion.

"Sweetheart. Cariño translates to sweetheart or honey."

"And would you like to tell the group what you told me it means?" I prod.

"Annoying asshole," Mateo grumbles, though his expression is victorious as the group laughs.

Vivian nearly falls over in her seat, cackling like a hyena. Jett is snorting, his worn-out beanie slipping off his head as it's tipped back in laughter. Sofía shakes her head at Mateo with a soft grin.

"Are you going to stop calling me the nickname?" he asks, his voice quiet. There's a thread of uncertainty in the question, and I pause. Does he think I'm truly upset?

I rest my palm on his thigh, above the butterfly tattoo.

"No." I squeeze his leg. "You're my cariño. Both meanings," I whisper, offering him a truth that frightens me.

He is both my annoying asshole and my sweetheart.

When Mateo exits the bathroom, I'm going to pounce on him like a cheetah attacking its prey, but slowly, because my joints ache from standing in the lab for hours and sitting crisscross in the uncomfortable chairs in the lounge.

It's always a mistake to bend my knees and ankles for long periods of time, and my hip screams in its socket.

I'm standing right outside the door, waiting like a creep.

When people would talk about the incorrigible itch they felt with someone else, I always waved them off as lovesick fools who couldn't separate physical attraction from emotional connection.

Now I've turned into one of those lovesick fools I've laughed at.

The door cracks open and he reappears, hair wet from his shower and glasses perched on the bridge of his nose. Gray sweatpants drape low on his hips, and his shoulders pull against the worn-down URI t-shirt.

"You don't have to change in the bathroom," I blurt out. "Or wear clothes. You don't need to do that, either."

Fucking cool it, Charlie.

Mateo laughs deeply, quirking a brow.

"Is that so?"

My cheeks flame, but I double down on my comment and nod, stepping toward him.

"Why are you hobbling?"

I wave him off, wrapping my arms around his waist to try to climb him like a tree. I've never been this horny in my life, and if he doesn't take his clothes off in the next thirty seconds, I may scream.

Mateo leans into the embrace, his cheek falling onto mine.

No!

This is not an emotional moment, this is a "tear each other's clothes off like horny animals" moment. Mateo needs to catch up.

"You're supposed to kiss me," I say, directing him. "That's how it goes."

His hands trail down my back, palming the globes of my ass. It ignites a fire in my veins, and lust settles in my lower stomach. Mateo's tongue darts out as his pupils dilate. I shiver, and based on his hoarse laugh, he knows the effect he has but is choosing to do nothing about it.

"Have you ever heard of buildup, bruja?"

He squeezes my ass, and I yelp.

"You've built me up. Now *tear my clothes off.*"

I pull at the hem of his shirt to get the party going, but my hip locks up and I stumble into his chest.

"*Why* are you hobbling?"

"It's my joints. I'm fine." I tug at his shirt again, but he stands firm, so I add, "I just need to oil up the ole hinges, and then we can get this party started." His eyebrows pull down in confusion. *Neptune on a cracker.* "*Sex*, Mateo. The party I'm referring to is sex."

Taking his hand, I drag him to the bed.

"Charlie." His voice is full of laughter as I push him onto the mattress.

He hauls me with him so I'm lying flush against his chest. The green of his irises is deeper in the cabin's dim light, like looking up from the forest floor before the first rays of dawn. Dozens of small freckles pepper his nose, something I've never noticed before.

I'm counting them when he trails a hand down my cheek.

"Why do your joints ache?"

"Chronic post-traumatic arthritis." I shiver as Mateo traces my scar. "The scars, pins, and spleen removal weren't enough. The universe gave me chronic pain on top of it. Really, I'm fine."

"You say that a lot." He hums. "*I'm fine*. You don't need to be 'fine.' Not with me." It's hard to look at him, but even more difficult to look away. "I'm not afraid."

He may not be, but I still am.

Every day, I'm taking another step. They're small and unsure, and more often than not, I'm freaking the fuck out, but I'm putting one foot in front of the other—for him, for myself, and for the future that's forming in my mind's eye.

"How do you really feel?" he asks.

Well, I *was* incredibly horny, which hasn't entirely disappeared, considering his erection is digging into my lower stomach, but beneath it all, I'm tired.

"My joints are on fire," I admit.

"Do you have anything that helps?"

His hands gently run over my back, up and down along my spine.

"I have a balm." I scoot off his chest to grab the Tiger Balm I keep on hand. "It's smelly."

Mateo takes the small glass container and sniffs. He jerks back, surprised, before taking a deep breath. He's smiling like he's discovered something groundbreaking.

"It smells like *you*," he says, clutching the container. "I could never figure out the scent. I only knew it smelled like *you*."

My heart is doing this odd pitter-pattering thing, and it's so strong I think the muscle might jump right out of my body.

"I got a whiff of it in a grocery store once," he admits, smiling to himself, "and I searched for you."

I slip into my pajamas so I can apply the balm, but when I try to take the jar, Mateo pulls it close to his chest.

"Can I?"

My head tilts. "Huh?"

"Can I apply it for you?"

Oh.

Words clog my throat, but I manage a nod and sit back on the bed, allowing my legs to dangle. He scoops out a small glob of the orange paste.

"Where do you need it?"

"Hip and knees."

Mateo drops to his knees, spreads mine open, and smears the balm over the aching joint. He's focused on his task, massaging my sore muscles and working the balm into the skin.

This is a different type of intimacy—one I'm not used to. His touch isn't electric or meant to lead to more. It's methodical and intentional, each stroke of his thumb meant to relieve pain and tension.

He moves from my knees to my hip, and I curl onto my side. I can't help the groan that escapes when his thumb digs into the tension in my lower back. Mateo huffs a laugh while his hand lingers on the surgical scar along my hip, then taps my ass.

"All done," he says, placing a soft kiss on my shoulder before returning the balm to my bag.

"Thank you."

He stops to admire his work, and my heart skips a beat.

I'm so fucking screwed.

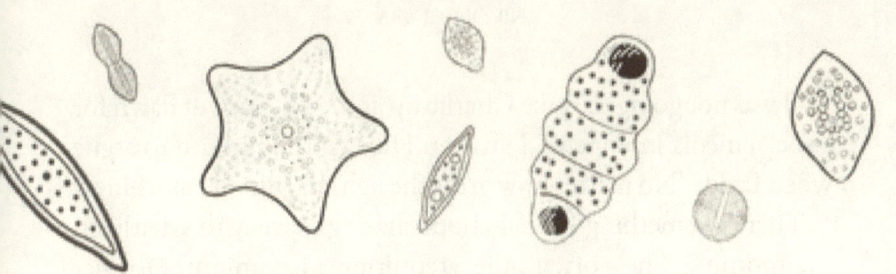

CHAPTER 26

MATEO

"Where's Blondie?" Jett asks, looking around me for Charlie.

I rub the sleep away, forcing back nausea from the early wake-up and the mild swaying of the boat.

Jett's camera gear and tripod are set up in front of two deck chairs, the ocean and the first rays of sun acting as a backdrop. Doug riffles through bags, pulling out wires and lights.

"Nice pants," he comments as he passes.

I was only told I needed to look nice from the waist up. I'm wearing my nicest button-down shirt and a pair of joggers. Business on the top. Comfortability on the bottom.

Jett hands me a mug of coffee, and steam wafts off the top as I watch them methodically set up recording equipment. I will admit, I did not realize how much work Jett put into his videos.

I assumed he turned his phone on and began recording, but based on the detailed schedule he emailed me last night—complete with interview questions to prepare—he's far more organized than he appears.

"I was not going to wake Charlie up at the ass-crack of dawn for a social media interview," I answer. He opens his mouth to argue when I add, "No matter how great the lighting is in the morning."

There's something special about sharing space with Charlie in the morning. She's often quiet, requiring a few minutes for her brain to wake up. When she's alert enough to make sounds, it's often grunts and groans as she stomps around the cabin.

My girl is not a morning person, but it's the most beautiful sight in the world when she rolls over in bed and offers me a sleepy smile. I've memorized its curve, the barely there tilt of her lips as she wakes and registers my presence.

It's exceptional—a special one, only for me.

Doug silently guides me to a deck chair and stands behind the camera, adjusting the angles.

"If she says no to these interviews," I start, "don't question her."

Jett attaches a microphone to the lapel of my shirt and gives me a knowing look.

"If I didn't know any better, I would say you're falling in love with her." He winks but adds, "I'll respect her decision. The video would be so much better with her in it, though. She's remarkable."

Remarkable.

It suits her perfectly. Beauty. Brains. Personality. Every part of her is one-of-a-kind.

Right beneath my breastbone, I feel *it* every time I think of Charlie or see her happy. When she laughs, it flares with delight, demanding to hear the sound over and over.

I know what it is—I heard my abuela talk about it and witnessed it with my parents. It's a small seed, meant to be nurtured, but it's present, growing stronger and more apparent by the day.

I'm falling in love with her.

"Mateo."

"What?"

I return to reality, where Jett is grinning at me like I'm an idiot.

"Are you ready to start?"

"Oh...um, yeah." I wince, hiding my mild embarrassment behind my coffee mug.

Doug signals he's started recording, and Jett gives me a thumbs-up.

"Hi, my name is Mateo, and I'm a PhD student at the University of Rhode Island, where I study microbial community assemblages at varying depths and environmental conditions to understand anthropogenic effects on biodiversity."

"Cut," Jett yells, a frown pulling the corners of his lips. "Mateo, man, you know I love you..."

"But?"

"Cut it with the scientific mumbo jumbo. You're going to put my viewers to sleep. And maybe breathe between sentences. What do you do in the lab?"

"Uh..." He's stunned me a bit, and it's still early. I've practiced my elevator pitch for my research so often I could do it in my sleep, but I wasn't prepared to go off-script. "Dirt."

"Dirt?" Jett rubs between his brow. "You went from science nerd to 'dirt'?"

"It's early," I mutter.

He forced me to wake up at the butt crack of dawn, destroyed my pre-planned speech, and now he wants me improvise? He's lost his—

Oh my god, Charlie's rubbing off on me.

"Let's try again."

Twelve takes later, Jett is satisfied with my introduction. I try to make my escape, but he hauls me back onto the deckchair. His exuberance is overflowing, but I have zero idea why he's giving it to me. He spent the last hour yelling at me and sighing in disappointment.

"So...you and Blondie?" He waggles his eyebrows, and the top of his beanie falls over his eyes. He shoves it back up. "Your date looked *amazeballs*."

"Uh..."

"Have you kissed her?" His voice jumps a few octaves, and my heartbeat skips, I'm so startled. "You have to tell me everything. Love is super dope."

Doug gives me a knowing look as he passes, packing up the recording equipment. He reaches down to pull the microphone off my shirt while he whispers, "Jett can't stop talking about how you two are falling in love."

I cough, hacking up half a lung at his casual words.

Is that what Charlie and I are doing? Is she falling in love?

He squeezes my shoulder, and Jett waits with anticipation. I sigh.

"You have to swear on the Brotherhood of Catan not to say anything to Charlie," I say, and Jett nods emphatically. "We kissed."

He leaps from his chair, throwing a fist into the air in celebration. "Have you told her you love her?"

"Slow your roll, man."

"You're right. I'll be more chill."

He bounces up and down. Nothing about him screams *chill*, but I drain the last of my coffee, rising from the deck chair. "I gotta go make Charlie a coffee before she wakes up."

Jett's goofy grin mirrors my own.

"She's beautifully grumpy in the morning."

I'm nearly out of sight when he screams, "Go get your girl!"

Vivian adjusts the trajectory of the ROV, shifting it to the right to scan the seafloor. It's been a quiet morning, only having reached two thousand meters a half hour ago. Charlie sits in the corner with Sofía, sipping on her iced coffee, the both of them focused on their laptops.

The camera jerks back to the right, and Vivian starts jamming buttons, increasing the zoom. A sharp inhale is the only sound in the control room, and then her hand flies up in the air, waving around frantically.

She hits me in the abdomen. Hard.

"Mateo," Vivian hisses. "Is Charlie paying attention?"

"What? No," I cough out, pain spidering out from where her punch landed.

Charlie bops her head to her music, none the wiser I'm being beat up by Vivian.

God, she's adorable as she mouths the words to her song.

"Get over here," Vivian whispers, and I step closer to the screen. The air is ripped from my lungs. *No fucking way.* Wild excitement blooms on her face as her head jerks to Charlie.

A haze of disbelief settles over us both, a momentary silence followed by surprised laughter.

"She's going to fly off the handle," I warn.

"Go get her!"

I take a few deep breaths to cool the enthusiasm thrumming in my veins, and only when I'm confident I won't blurt out the news do I tap Charlie on the shoulder.

She rips out an earbud, One Direction blasting from the small speaker.

"Hi."

She peruses my body, and I suppress a shiver.

"Could you help me identify something?" I ask, trying to hide a manic smile.

"Oh, sure." She pops up from the table, pausing to drag a hand along my bicep. She follows me to the monitor, and I step aside for her to view the screen. "I'm glad you've realized my intellect is far superior..." Charlie trails off.

Her head jerks over her shoulder, disbelief contorting her face, before she steps closer to the screen.

I plug my ears, prepared for the scream about to escape her lungs. This is her holy grail, one of the top five on her scientific bucket list tacked to the wall by her desk.

A glass-shattering squeal fills the room as Charlie leaps and cheers, her fists punching the air. She performs the world's most adorable wiggle. God, I hope someone is recording this moment so I can experience her joy over and over.

She groans, her face pinching before it returns to pure joy. Then she launches, wrapping her arms around my neck and smashing her lips to mine.

I'm so stunned that I don't move. So surprised she's kissing me in front of all these people that I don't kiss her back.

She pulls away, horror creeping over her features. "Oh my god. I didn't...do you not want—"

I cut off her rambling with a sloppy kiss of my own. People cheer in the room, either for Charlie and me, or for the once-in-a-lifetime discovery.

"This is the greatest day of my life," she screams, kissing my cheek.

Her laughter is deep and joyous as I twirl her around, basking in the happiness she radiates. I would spend every day of the rest of my life chasing her laughter, even if she's laughing at me.

"We kissed," Charlie says, her fingers touching her lips like she's in a daze.

"We did."

"In front of people. We kissed in front of other people." Her skin pales, and the slight tremor in her voice frightens me. "Is that okay?"

"Okay?" I laugh in disbelief. "Bruja, I would kiss you in front of a million people just so they know you're mine."

Her smile gradually blooms into something magnificent. I get lost in her before she jerks.

"The whale fall!" She grabs my hand, dragging me over to the screen. "Do you think there will be tissue left?" she asks, bouncing on her toes.

Jett pounds a fist against my shoulder, his focus darting to Charlie.

"How's it feel?"

"She's fucking incredible."

Jett laughs, moving to stand beside her, both of them watching the monitor with rapt attention. Vivian is locked into her work, guiding the ROV closer, and Lucas is scrambling to get clear video for the documentary.

The bottom of the ocean is vast, and stumbling upon a whale fall is rare, even in areas with large whale populations. Hell, the first one wasn't recorded until 1977.

"What is that?" Jett asks, awe and disgust creeping into his voice.

Charlie's hand flies backward, slamming against the center of my chest.

"Tell him, Mateo. I'm too excited to speak!"

Her fingers linger between my pectoral muscles, and I clear my throat. Her hand flies back to her side, a small blush creeping up her cheeks when she peers over her shoulder.

"It's a whale fall," I explain, choking down my lust. "They're pop-up ecosystems. When a whale dies, they fall through the water column, and organisms feed on the carcass. At the surface, sharks, birds, and other large pelagic species will scavenge the flesh."

"Sick," Jett mutters.

"It's insane," Charlie cheers. "Get closer. Get closer!"

"When the whale falls to the seafloor, scavengers descend on whatever remains. Sevengill sharks, octopi, crabs, and other deep-sea organisms eat the remaining tissue."

"Then the bone-eating worms appear..." Charlie says ominously, never looking away from the screen.

"Bone-eating worms?" Jett asks, and for the first time on this trip, he looks slightly uncomfortable.

"They secrete an acid that dissolves the whalebone. They don't even have a stomach," Charlie exclaims, failing to read the room. "Or a mouth!"

Confusion flickers over half the faces in the room. I can hear the silent questions.

How do they eat the bones if they don't have stomachs or mouths?

The simplest explanation is that the natural world is fucking insane, and everyone should hold a healthy amount of fear for the wild shit that's evolved.

"A symbiotic bacteria digests the organic material, and that's how the worm gets energy," I explain, but it's futile. It's only creating more confusion. "It's wack," I amend.

Doug and Jett nod, and I drop the topic. Most people don't find bone-eating worms as exciting or appealing as Charlie.

I stand back, content to watch her excitement as she chirps in Vivian's ear, asking her to circle the whale remains so she can count the number of octopus and rattail fish.

There's little flesh left, but organisms pick at what remains between the rib cage. The vertebrae are void of flesh, covered by a layer of orange-pink fuzz. Bristle stars are scattered along the seafloor, surrounded by a bed of worms, feeding on the nutrients released into the sediment.

While Vivian communicates with the captain to circle the boat so the ROV can hover over the whale, Charlie appears at my side.

"This is on my scientific bucket list," she whispers, snaking her arm around mine to hold my bicep.

"Why are you whispering, bruja?"

I have to fight my laughter as her shoulders press up to her ears and she bounces on her toes.

"I think I might faint from excitement." She presses the back of her hand to her forehead. "Catch me, Mateo."

Her body goes limp, crashing into my side as I stumble to catch her. The smell of cinnamon and menthol fills my nostrils, and I take a deeper breath. My hands dig into her waist, holding her steady as she completes her dramatics.

"Charlie, get over here," Vivian yells. "There are worms!"

"Shut the fuck up!"

She darts out of my grip, and all I can do is watch her. The way she beams and laughs. How she chatters with Jett, pointing out things on the screen. The blood rushes to my brain when she peers over her shoulder and points excitedly at the decaying flesh remaining on the bones.

Fucking remarkable.

CHAPTER 27

CHARLIE

The door slams shut, Mateo facing away from me, and I push against his back with the force of my body so he launches forward.

He releases a yelp but flies onto the bed.

Right where I want him.

I catapult myself, colliding with him and pinning him beneath my weight.

"What are you—"

I cut him off with a sloppy kiss.

It's a desperate action, one I've been waiting for all day, since the last time I kissed him. In front of everyone. In my fervor, I smooched the shit out of him, offering the crew a free show, and I've yet to regret it.

Truthfully, it was freeing, like one of the barriers holding me back crashed down.

"Seducing you," I respond, trailing my hands up his torso as I straddle him. My hip joint pops, the sound echoing, but Mateo's laugh—deep, throaty, and doing wicked things to my vagina—drowns it out.

His hands fall on the globes of my ass, pulling me down and onto his erection.

I can't stop the shuddered breath that escapes at the feel of him.

"What's the date?" Mateo asks, mid-kiss.

Who the fuck cares what day it is? He needs to take his pants off. "Why?"

"You're ovulating."

I try to scramble off his lap, but he holds me firmly in place with one hand.

"How on earth do you know that?"

He scrubs at the back of his neck, his cheeks deepening to mirror a bloody-belly comb jelly.

"Cariño."

His head snaps up at the nickname. "Well..." He gulps. "I didn't figure it out on purpose."

"I would hope not," I mutter.

"But I started to notice you would make this odd groaning sound. It's not like your normal groaning, but more...caveman-like." He mimics the sound, which is awful yet accurate. My period cramps are horrible, even with pain medication. "I connected the dots after a few months."

"And you uncovered when I'm ovulating..."

"Your cycle is very regular. Twenty-eight days. Like clockwork. I can do the math." I'm staring at him like a gaping fish. His face blanches. "I just inadvertently admitted something incredibly creepy."

"*So* creepy," I confirm, kissing him again.

I should be more bothered by his mapping of my menstrual cycle, but he's hard beneath me, and it's difficult to think about anything but *him.*

"You're obsessed with me," I tease, grinding my hips against him.

He doesn't miss a beat. "Yes." The conviction in the single word nearly topples me. But he doesn't stop. "Maybe it's creepy, but I haven't been able to keep you out of my thoughts."

He has no idea how obsessive I was with him. Well, with crushing him. But it was still incredibly concerning how much space he consumed in my mind.

"I'm going to ignore the fact you've memorized my menstrual cycle and, instead, focus on *this*."

I grab his cock over his trousers, and he twitches beneath my palm. I squeeze and he groans. It's a desperate, raw sound.

"You're playing with fire," he grits out. "Can you handle the consequences?"

Leaning down, I steal another kiss, reveling in the scrape of his scruff against my cheeks. His question opens a door in my mind I've firmly kept shut. Sex has always been a means to an end for me. A way to scratch an itch and move on. It's not the same with Mateo. With him, I want to *explore*—to try all the things I've wanted to but never trusted anyone enough.

Mateo uses my silence as his opportunity to rebalance the scales, and he flips me over, pinning my hands over my head. I buck my hips, but he presses his knee between my thighs, keeping me pinned to the bed.

My heart pounds in my throat, and the pulsing in my core matches the timing.

"Want to know what I think?" He hums, grazing his thumb against the inside of my wrist.

I can only nod.

"I think you want someone else to take control." His grip tightens, and his words strike true. The corner of his lips tips up. "Am I right?"

My core clenches in response, but words are lost on my tongue. I manage a nod, and Mateo's pupils burst.

Fuck.

He drops his head to whisper in my ear. "Safe word?"

My mind blanks, and I scramble for a word—one I won't accidentally say. The first thing that pops into my mind is "Agarose."

Mateo's face blanks for a split second before he lets out a roaring laugh, his grip loosening on my wrists. "Agarose?"

I nod as he pulls air into his lungs.

"All right, then. If you want to stop, that's the word."

He releases me and rises. Anticipation tingles my skin as I crawl to the edge of the bed and wait for him to do something. I've given him the control I've held on to for years with a white-knuckle grip. Instead, he stands and watches me, scorching a path along my skin.

He's possessive—consuming—as he assesses me.

"Strip for me." Mateo falls into the desk chair, leans back, and spreads his thighs. It's a cocky, confident move, and it's hard not to focus on how his dick begs for freedom, straining against his zipper. He drags his palm against himself, and I watch him beneath my lashes.

He wears that infuriatingly smug smile, the one that sets my blood on fire.

My chest heaves, battling to draw in a full breath, as I strip off my socks. I dangle them in my grip and toss them at Mateo.

"Actions have consequences," he purrs.

That's the idea.

My shirt is next, and I allow it to flutter to the floor before shimmying out of my pants. All that's left is the painfully boring underwear I packed for the trip.

I didn't anticipate having to strip for Mateo, so all I've got are worn-down bras and granny panties that have seen better days. I'm frowning at the small hole in my crotch—super attractive—when Mateo clears his throat.

"Everything."

All thoughts of ancient undergarments fly away with the look on his face.

With zero grace, I pull the sports bra over my head and immediately sigh in relief. Mateo chuffs as I fling it away.

Goodbye, boob prison.

I slip off my underwear, and then I'm standing bare before him.

It was not a graceful seduction or a striptease, which I realize now as I'm standing naked as the day I was born.

Whoops.

"All done," I say awkwardly, filling the silence.

I'm not sure what to do with my limbs, and I'm not used to standing naked in front of someone, so I begin to squirm. He lounges in the chair, stroking himself over his zipper. He lifts a finger and beckons me forward.

I shuffle in front of him, bouncing from one foot to the other. Not because I'm naked, which is the typical cause, but because I have no idea what's about to happen, and it sets me on edge.

An anticipatory type of edge, but the silence hangs heavily.

He draws me into his lap, exploring the curve of my waist, and the rough texture of his calluses scrapes against my skin.

"I want you to say your affirmations," he whispers, and my heart drops. "The ones you tell yourself in the mirror. I want to hear them."

His hands continue to explore as I blink at him like a deer in headlights. Those aren't things he's supposed to hear—words I whisper to myself every morning in hopes they'll stick one day.

"Did you forget them?" he asks playfully, dragging his thumb along the seam of my lips. "I'll help you. *I am smart.* What's next?"

"I am kind," I croak. He nods, urging me on. "I am beautiful. I am hard-working. I am deserving. I am not broken."

My voice cracks on the last word, and Mateo seals the affirmation with a probing kiss.

"Good. One more time."

I repeat them, but again, my voice cracks on the last one, because even though I'm saying the words, I don't fully believe them.

"Again."

He peppers soft, tender kisses along my neck and down my collarbone as I repeat the words, staring back at myself in the mirror along the wall. My skin is blotchy, and I barely recognize the woman reflected back to me. I continue the affirmations, and this time when I say the last phrase, my voice is steady.

He tips my chin.

"You are not broken, Charlie," he declares, and I try to avert my gaze, but his grip is firm. "Not to me."

I nod, words lodged in my throat. He takes my mouth in a heated embrace, his tongue trailing along the seam of my lips. A demand for entry.

I give it to him, and he guides the kiss deeper. The pressure in my core builds, and I grind my hips against him, ignoring the slight burn in my joints.

The power disparity between us right now is not something I thought I would ever offer someone. Even though he's fully clothed, I've never felt more balanced or secure with another person.

When we break apart, I'm struggling for breath.

"On your knees, bruja." I drop to the floor with zero hesitation. "Take me out," he commands, voice edged with lust. With shaky hands, I unbutton his pants and free his erection. A small bead of precum forms, and I wrap my fingers around the base, squeezing lightly. "Now suck."

I slowly work him into my mouth, adjusting to his size. His fingers tangle in my hair, loosening my braid as he guides me farther down his shaft. He's gentle yet demanding as he pushes me deeper until I'm at the base.

I force back a gag, and he swipes away the hair that's fallen around my face.

"You look so pretty with your lips wrapped around my cock."

I've never been more turned on than I am right now—him holding me with his cock down my throat. I'm fully at his mercy, but I look up at him under hooded lashes, and the truth slams into me.

There's no one I trust more than Mateo.

Not now.

It was always Amy.

She was the one person I could trust, but that's shifted, and he's taken first place.

Mateo releases my hair, and I pull in a gasp of air before taking him again and twirling my tongue around the head. He groans, and the sound spurs me onward, alternating between licking and sucking until his thighs are trembling beneath me.

"Oh, shit," Mateo mutters, pulling me off him. He's more disheveled than when we began, and victory soars through my veins. I fucking love when he looks undone. "You're very good at that." His praise causes my cheeks to burn.

Mateo doesn't miss the response, so he says it again, and my cheeks flame deeper.

In one graceful move, he rises from the chair and drops me onto the bed. He's disrobing when he says, "Let's talk logistics."

My jaw falls.

"What *logistics*?" I screech, slightly bratty. "You fuck me. Those are the logistics."

He barks a laugh, pulling his shirt over his head, and my throat dries.

"Are you on any form of birth control? Do you want to use a condom? Those logistics, bruja."

"Oh."

He stops midway through pulling his pants down. "Don't worry. I'll fuck you so thoroughly you'll forget your own name."

"Uh...I—" I'm floundering. God, I hope he's true to his word. "I have an IUD. I-I haven't been with anyone in a while..." My voice quiets. "I got tested during my last checkup."

His pants finally hit the floor, and his cock bobs against his muscled torso as he saunters to the bed.

"I want you bare, bruja. Nothing between us."

He lays out the proposition, and my stomach flutters. "A-and you've been tested recently?"

I never would have given Mateo's intimate life a second thought before this trip, but the idea of him having dated other people, *slept* with and beside other people...it makes me want to vomit and then metaphorically piss all over him to mark my territory.

It's an unhealthy urge.

"I haven't slept with anyone since the day we met," he admits, upturning my world in one sentence. "But I had the panel run at my last blood draw. I'm clear."

"Never...No one...*How?*" My brain short-circuits while trying to comprehend what he's saying. He hasn't slept with anyone in two years?

"I think the question you want to ask is *why.*" He reaches the end of the bed, a large palm landing on each of my thighs, running up and down along my skin. "Ask me why, bruja."

"Why?" I ask, my voice barely a whisper.

"Every other woman ceased to exist after I met you. You were—*are*—all I think about."

I've never met someone who so openly admits how they're feeling or can express their thoughts without shame. He's a breath of fresh air after spending time underwater.

Mateo Alvarez is by far my greatest discovery.

This time with him has made me a better person, and I don't know what more someone could ask for than that. Since I've been on this boat, I've morphed and evolved, and none of it would be possible without him—his quiet encouragement and staunch belief in me.

He spreads my legs wide, pushing up my knees to settle between my thighs. His dick grazes against my clit, and I release a small yelp.

Without warning, he plunges two fingers deep inside me, and I launch off the bed as he slides in easily. Giving him a blowjob was all the foreplay I needed. I want *him*, and I want him *now*.

I claw at his forearms, trying to pull him closer, but he tsks and pulls his fingers out.

My core hollows out as he sucks his fingers into his mouth.

"Delicious."

I've died.

I've died and this is some alternate reality. Holy fucking shitballs.

He drags his shaft against my entrance, coating himself in my arousal. Up and down until I'm delirious with need and squirming beneath him.

"*Please*," I beg.

I hate begging him. Hate it as much as the cocky grin he offers when he hears the word. Hate it so much I want to fuck him.

"Are you going to take my cock like a good girl?"

"Mateo," I growl. I'm growing impatient and hot—so fucking hot I might implode. "Fuck me. Right. Now."

He chuckles but lines himself up at my entrance and slowly presses his hips forward. The first inch burns, and my breath catches as he slides deeper, using my thighs as leverage.

Mateo groans as he moves in shallow thrusts. He's teasing me—teasing the both of us—as he takes his time.

Every stroke is too much and not enough, and I'm trying to match every one of his thrusts before the undercurrent of pleasure pulls me under.

He shifts, pushing up my knees to deepen the position, and then slams into me, hitting a part so deep inside me I see stars.

"*Oh, fuck.*" His pace is steady but deep, and pleasure coils in my abdomen.

It's not until Mateo leans down and captures my nipple between his teeth that we're in missionary. The final rule broken.

He pulls the taut bud between his teeth, and the sting of pain adds to the pleasure. I lift my hand, cupping his jaw, and he leans into the touch. A swell of tender understanding washes over him. He knows the significance of the position we're in. Understands the power he holds.

And for the first time in my life, I'm not afraid that someone else holds power over me.

Because Mateo may be the only person I trust enough not to use it against me.

"So fucking pretty," he mutters, picking up his pace.

My breasts shake with the force of his thrusts, and I'm halfway to the edge when he stops and pulls out.

I can't say I'm proud of the desperate sound that escapes my lips, but he chuckles and crouches to dig through my bag. When he rises, he's holding the vibrator I assaulted him with.

"We forgot our *friend*," he says, placing the toy against my clit and driving back into me.

The toy clicks on, and I nearly ascend to a new plane of existence. The pressure compounds until my fingers begin to tingle and my thighs start to shake from holding back.

I'm desperate to orgasm, but I want him to go with me.

"I'm close." I grab his forearms. "Come with me."

Mateo's pupils blow, and he tosses the toy to the side, pistoning in and out of me until we're both groaning with need. He pulses inside me when I clench around him.

"Do that again and I won't last," he grunts.

Obviously, I do it again.

"Fuck, Charlie. You'll be my undoing." Something about the words—spoken with such truth and desperation—incites my smile. He steals it with a kiss, nipping at my lower lip. "Where do you want me, bruja?"

I want to feel claimed by him, so I answer in away I would *never* with someone else.

"Fill me," I moan, near begging.

Mateo's response is feral as he drives into me like this moment is his last on earth. The words are all it takes for me to unravel, and the orgasm barrels into me, so strong my vision blackens. A few strokes later, he follows, pulsing as he finishes inside me.

He drags out my orgasm by stroking my clit with his thumb until I'm hypersensitive from the pleasure and push his hand away.

The silence shared between us as he pulls out is foreign, and his attention fixes on the apex of my thighs, where I can feel him leaking out. Almost in a daze, he reaches out a hand and scoops up his load before plunging it back inside me.

I lose the ability to breathe.

He stands for a moment in contemplation before he says, "*Dios,* you're fucking hot."

I choke on a laugh, my limbs heavy and brain foggy as I lift onto my forearms to watch his ass sway before he slips into the bathroom. Mateo returns with a warm towel, cleaning up the mess we made between my thighs with a tender touch.

I can't help but swipe away his unruly hair and marvel at his beauty. A sharp jawline paired with full, soft lips. Dark, wavy hair and gorgeous, stunning eyes. Thick brows that furrow in confusion when he notices my staring.

"You're handsome," I blurt out, then pull my lip between my teeth.

I want to shove the words back in my mouth when he blinks at me like I've said the craziest thing on the planet. They used to think bloodletting cured nearly every disease; my declaration that Mateo is handsome is not that insane.

We stare at each other until he launches back onto the bed and pulls me beneath the covers.

"Thank you, bruja. Another compliment I'll hold tightly to my chest."

I level him with an unamused look.

Do not say it.

"Right beside how I smell like a summer breeze."

He laughs as I whack his bicep. Annoying asshole.

"Shut it, cariño."

We settle beneath the covers, the boat swaying gently.

"Your final rule is broken," he whispers against my temple, pulling me close.

"I-I don't think I need rules anymore."

The rules were made to keep myself detached from emotion—to keep myself "safe." I don't need the safety net anymore because I have it right now in Mateo's arms.

But I don't know what to do now that I don't have any rules at all.

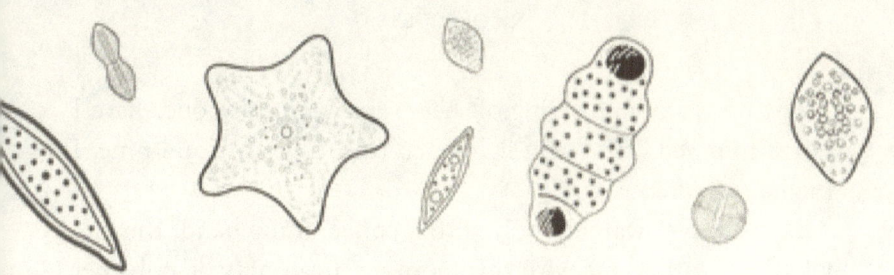

CHAPTER 28

MATEO

"My thesis work focuses on identifying genetic differences between populations of Arctic invertebrates to understand how shifts in environmental conditions may drive adaptation and evolution."

The lounge area is quiet as Charlie and Jett film on the couches in the corner, his video equipment illuminating them in blinding light. Doug adjusts the brightness, then moves the microphone to hover between them both.

Charlie pulls out every buzzword to explain her thesis, but instead of forcing her to reshoot the video two dozen times, Jett cheers her on as she explains the differences she uncovered between octopi at different sites in the Arctic.

I've read the paper she helped another PhD student with in her first year of our program. Her insight is brilliant, and though she's the fifth author, she poured her heart and soul into the work.

A kernel of warmth spreads out from my diaphragm as her hands wave wildly while she speaks, features alight with excitement as she explains the laboratory process and the results of the paper.

Jett nods along, hanging off her every word. Not once have I heard him yell "cut," and if I weren't floating on cloud nine, I might take offense.

Instead, I'm watching on with a coffee in my hand, the one Charlie surprised me with this morning. I can only describe her radiance as breathtaking as she brutally woke me up and shoved the coffee in my face.

She proceeded to spend ten minutes talking about how she woke up earlier than me—she really emphasized the point—to make me the drink. After she offered the play-by-play of her coffee-making expedition, she perched next to me and watched as I took the first sip. I smiled through the bitter, assaulting taste of burnt espresso and sipped the scalding liquid like it was the best thing I've ever tasted.

It's the same mug, but her botched attempt has been replaced with black coffee.

Charlie has been all giggles this morning, chatting with Vivian about the whale fall and talking in hushed whispers with Sofía while glancing my way. When I winked, they all fell into a fit of giggles, and Charlie's blush reached the tips of her ears.

"Come over here," Charlie beckons, waving her hand. She's holding Jett's phone with the other, giggling to herself. As I get closer, the sound comes into range, and I recognize my voice.

She's watching my interview. What I'm unsure about is what in the video is funny enough for her nose to turn a cherry hue.

"What's so funny, bruja?" I ask, leaning down to whisper in her ear.

Her lip quivers when she turns her head, trying to contain her laughter, but she loses it and chokes, waving around the phone.

"Sexy...Daddy...Bacteria."

Huh?

When I look at Jett, he's in the same boat as her, clutching his sides as they fall into a fit of laughter. I take the phone from her hand and stare at the screen, which is full of comments on my interview.

Who knew bacteria could be so sexy?

If he was my professor, I would sit front row in his class. And on his face.

Did I just fall in love with a man talking about bacteria? I think so.

Bacteria Daddy.

I choke on the final comment before I shove the phone away.

Well, at least they're kind comments, sort of. Some are a bit objectifying, and I'm unsure how I feel about *Bacteria Daddy*. Leaning toward I hate it and never want to hear it again.

"These are..."

"Amazing," Charlie cheers. "When will you post mine? I want to get more views than Mateo."

She and Jett exchange predictions on how her video will perform since her research is "way cooler than mine," according to Jett. She holds an unfair advantage. Everyone loves biodiversity and population genetics. Only the *super dope* people care about the microbial composition of deep-sea ecosystems.

It's me.

I'm a *super dope* person.

Charlie steals the frown on my lips with a kiss.

"Your video was great." She pats my bicep in as lightly patronizing way, but I'm reveling in the simple kiss she offered. "But mine will be better."

She's had a good day, and I want it to last forever for her.

Instead of pulling away, she burrows against my side, slipping her arm around my waist.

"They're going to put a movie on in the lounge. Did you want to go?"

I'm going to need thirty seconds to float backdown to earth before I can answer any question. I don't know how to express to her what these small moments of intimacy mean to me. An innocent touch in public. A chaste kiss. Shared whispers.

"Sure, bruja."

She detaches from my side but doesn't move toward the lounge. Instead, her attention darts between my hand and my face. Back and forth until she reaches out and intertwines our fingers together.

"You're being very affectionate today," I comment, keeping my voice neutral, as we walk to the lounge. "Accidentally drink a love potion?"

I don't want her to stop, but I'd like to know why.

"Isn't that what couples do?" she asks, her shoulders growing tense.

"Some." I shrug.

The last thing I want is for Charlie to pretend for my sake. To put on a face and do what she *thinks* would make me happy, or do something because it's "what couples do." What makes me happy is being with Charlie. Point blank. Period.

"Do you not like it?"

Fuck.

Her question is soft and so full of uncertainty it sends an ache through my chest.

I reroute our path, drag her into the empty lab, and flick on the fluorescent light. She releases a surprised squeal when I lift her into the air and drop her onto the countertop.

"This is against lab protocol," she says, before giggling.

Fuck, I could listen to that sound for the rest of my life, grow drunk off the way it makes me feel.

Her arms wrap around my shoulders as I step between her thighs. I'm overwhelmed by her infectious giggle and the intoxicating scent of the balm she wears, the freckles decorating her nose and how her feet dangle and softly tap my knees.

"I couldn't care less what other people do, Charlie. I care about *us*. What's right for us might not be right for someone else." At my words, she drags her bottom lip between her teeth. "If you don't want to be physical in public, that's fine. If you want to hold hands, I'm all for it. But you don't need to do something because you think it's what I want or because you think it will make me happy."

She scans the space, pausing on the different machines and pipettes, but she refuses to meet my gaze. It happens when she's lost in the maze of her thoughts. I've observed it when she's stuck trying to write parts of her dissertation or struggling to identify and express her emotions.

"I want to," she admits barely above a whisper. "With you, I think I want to."

There's this odd sensation stumbling around my chest—an unsteady beat as Charlie's fingers drag across the back of my neck to tangle in the edges of my hair.

"I'm trying," she continues. "I don't know if I'm doing anything right, but I'm giving you everything I have."

I don't think she has any idea the power she holds over me, but I think it's time she should know. She has complete control over my heart.

Fear grips my chest as I rest my hands on her hips.

There's no telling how she'll take the truth I'm going to offer her. I'm baring my soul to her—offering her the opportunity to crush me. But I'm faithful she won't.

"There is no 'right,'" I say, pushing a stray curl of blond hair from her cheek. My finger trails down her cheekbone, right along her scar. "There is only you and me. Does this feel right to you?"

Does this feel like fate to her? Like the stars she believes in guided us together?

I feel it, down to the marrow of my bones. With her, there is an inexplicable sense of comfort. She is both the raging wind before a summer storm and the first rays of sunshine at the break of dawn.

"It feels easy," she says, "and it scares me." Charlie's head tilts. "Is it supposed to feel this way?"

"I don't know," I admit, shrugging. "It feels that way for me, too, though."

Charlie's nose scrunches the way it does when she doesn't understand something or one of her undergrads asks an obvious question.

"You're supposed to know," she says defensively. "You are the 'knower' of these things."

"I have no idea what I'm doing, but I'm pretty confident 'knower' isn't a word."

She exhales a large gust of air that tickles against my skin.

"There's not enough room in this relationship for two people who know nothing about relationships. That's my role."

Her head jerks back, and her mouth pops open to form an O.

What is happening to her? I haven't seen this reaction from her before, so I can't pull out anything to combat what's happening inside her mind.

"What's going on up here?" I tap on her forehead, right between her brows. A crinkle forms beneath the pad of my finger.

"I called this a relationship," she mumbles.

Oh.

Now is probably an unideal time to tell her she's done it a handful of times, and each time I've wanted to hear it again.

Trepidation settles deep in my gut.

"And that...bothers you?"

My question is neutral, but I feel far from it. Every day with her, my feelings grow deeper—more cemented.

Her chin lifts, and her arms cross over her chest in defiance.

"I didn't say that."

"What are you saying, then?"

"I'm saying...I'm saying that's what this feels like for me." Her fingers grip my hair in a possessive way. "You feel like my partner."

I stay silent to allow Charlie the space to make her claim because it's what it feels like. I might have also lost function of my tongue.

"You make me feel alive, Mateo. More than I ever have in the last few years. I didn't think I would ever feel safe enough to desire a relationship with someone, but I want it with you."

A lopsided grin forms on my face. "Well, that's good," I say, trailing my thumb along her jaw. "Because I told my abuela about us."

"*What*?"

"Don't freak out." The look on her face tells me that's the wrong response, but I tell her everything, and she's known about Charlie since the day we met and I spent the entire dinner talking about her.

My abuela has pestered me relentlessly to tell her how I feel. She was obviously my first call post-confession.

"It's fine," I continue, "she's known about you for a long time. We talk about you a lot." Her face pales, and I scramble to back-track. "Because I like you!"

"Oh, well, okay." The apples of her cheeks blossom into a cherry shade, giving away her feelings on the matter. "She's probably cooler than you, anyway."

Her cockiness falls away when I steal it with a kiss. She melts into me, her arms dragging me closer and legs wrapping around my thighs like a boa constrictor. The energy in the air heats, crackling with electricity as Charlie's tongue drags along the seam of my lips.

A request.

I give in to her immediately.

Should we be making out in the middle of the lab? Absolutely not.

It goes against probably a million safety protocols, but I would be a liar if I said I never imagined this.

Her hands drag up my back, beneath my shirt, and I hiss from her cold fingers. Jesus, that is not normal. I release my grip from her hips to peel her hands off my body.

"Your fingers are ice cubes," I mumble between the kiss. She presses them into my skin, huffing a laugh when I jerk away.

She suppresses a yawn, but another quickly follows.

"What time did you wake up this morning?" I ask, lifting her from the benchtop.

My hands linger after she's on solid ground, my palm resting against her lower back.

"Around six," she boasts as I guide her out of the lab before anyone catches us in an unbecoming situation. "I snuck out, and you didn't even move." She pauses to stick her tongue out of her mouth and roll her eyes to the back of her head. "You were *dead*. If your CPAP machine wasn't making noise, I would have been concerned."

She yawns again, and I change course toward the room. It's time for bed or else waking her up tomorrow will be a battle. She makes no protest about skipping the movie as we slip into the cabin and wordlessly settle into our nightly routine. As she occupies the bathroom, I move all of her trinkets half an inch to the left, snickering to myself.

We may be in a relationship—saying that feels like a fever dream—but I'm not going to waste an opportunity to mess with her a little.

Charlie steps into the room, and I refuse to look at her because I'll give myself away, so I slip into the bathroom and wait by the door. I hear a quiet "God damnit, Mateo," followed by a louder "Stop messing with my shit, cariño!"

I peek my head out of the door. "You called me cariño," I sing.

"In this case, its translation is annoying asshole."

She huffs, dropping onto the bed, but a smirk breaks through when I wink.

I undress, and Charlie's gaze scorches my skin as I move around the cabin. Her adorable strawberry pajamas bunch up as she pulls her legs to her chest and rests her cheek on her knees.

"Are you ever going to tell me what it means?" she asks, gesturing at the phrase tattooed on my thigh.

I've stopped wearing anything but my boxer briefs to bed, so my tattoos are on full display. There's no reason for me to sweat to death at night in the name of chivalry any longer, and Charlie did say clothing is optional, so I'm cashing in on her offer.

Plus, I love when her eyes linger. And they do—a lot.

"It's a line from a poem I read in a college Spanish course." She raises a brow in silent question. "I thought the class would be easy," I grumble, "but we were reading thirteenth century literature, which is *barely* Spanish. I'm still pissed about the course grade I received. Only bad mark on my record."

Charlie giggles, burrowing into my side and resting her head in the crook of my neck after I settle in beside her. The scent of her joint balm wafts through the air. I could spend a lifetime of moments like this with her. Quiet whispers exchanged between two people choosing each other every day.

"What's the poem called?"

"*Canción de Pirata.*"

"Oh, that was hot. Say it again."

I repeat it for her, laying the accent on thicker than necessary. I am only a man—a weak one when it comes to Charlie—and if she finds my slight accent sexy, I am going to lean into it.

"I was struggling with the idea of going to graduate school. My family couldn't understand adding another five years of school with little pay for marine science. But one verse of the poem stuck with me. Helped me prove to myself I could chase my dream."

"Your family doesn't..." She trails off.

"They came around when they realized it's what I love. It was hard for them to wrap their heads around five years of work with a very *small* stipend."

"That's fair." She intertwines our fingers, placing our hands in her lap. "What's the verse?"

"Que es mi barco mi tesoro, que es mi dios la libertad, mi ley, la fuerza y el viento, mi única patria la mar."

"Can you translate that for us non-Spanish speakers?"

"My ship is my treasure, my god is freedom, my law, strength and the wind, my only homeland is the sea."

My only homeland is the sea.

The line that stuck with me, reverberating through my chest when I first heard the words.

I was born in a town hundreds of miles from the sea; I had never seen the ocean until I was fifteen. But it spoke to me nonetheless. As a child, I was enthralled by documentaries of ocean exploration, fascinated by the creatures that inhabit the depths.

The ocean always called to me, a beacon guiding my life, but as Charlie rests her head on the crook of my neck, I recognize that everything has shifted; my homeland is no longer the sea.

My homeland is Charlie.

CHAPTER 29

CHARLIE

There's a very large *something* resting rock fucking solid against my inner thigh.

I tilt my head over my shoulder, and Mateo buries his deeper into the crook of my neck as I move around. His CPAP mask is pressed against my skin, and the tubing runs along my spine. His arm slings over my hip, curling around my stomach to drag me closer.

Before this trip, I had never woken up beside someone else—Amy excluded—and I would have sworn on Charles Darwin's grave that I was okay with that; it was my choice. No sleepovers. Rule number one to keep things physical, and damn, it was a good rule, because right now everything is emotional.

Volatile, consuming emotions.

It's incredibly unsettling, but I want to crawl inside Mateo's skin just so I can feel a bit closer to him. I want to feel his hand in mine and inhale the soft, clean scent of his cologne. When he's on the other side of the room, he's too far away, and when he's beside me, my head grows light and bubbly.

I'm not really sure what to do with those emotions. It's like figuring out what to do with my hands during a presentation so I don't look like an idiot.

Right now, I'm a relationship idiot.

I have no idea what I'm doing, or if I'm doing it right, but now I understand what a relationship feels like—how wonderfully consuming life can be with another person—and I want it. More and more everyday.

There has to be a cooling-off period, right? Where my hormones rebalance and I stop feeling like a goblin obsessed with Mateo and his every movement.

He makes a soft sound, and warmth blooms in my chest, spreading to the tips of my fingers.

Is staring at him while he sleeps creepy? It feels like something a creep would do.

Amy would know if it's socially appropriate or not. Do the rules change if you sleep together? Like if the person you're watching is your boyfriend, does it make it okay?

When Mateo rolls, I slip out from his grip and run into the bathroom.

I perch on the toilet as the phone rings. Amy's head pops onto the screen, only the top of her forehead and eyebrows visible. Her eyebrow piercing jiggles, her brows raising.

"Hi, Charles," she cheers. "I miss you."

"Is it normal to watch someone while they sleep?" I blurt out.

Whew. That question was eating me alive.

"Uh...good morning?" She stares at me incredulously. "Why are you whispering?"

"I'm hiding in the bathroom and don't want Mateo to wake up and hear me."

"And the person you want to watch is Mateo?"

I grimace. When she says it, it sounds creepy.

"My initial response is that watching people sleep is a no-no."

"Once I asked, it became pretty obvious." She nods in agreement. "Wait," I scream a bit louder than I intend, and nerves flutter in my chest. "I had sex with Mateo." She gasps. "With the lights on." An even louder gasp. "In missionary."

"What the *fuck*?" Amy screams, and I slam the phone against my chest to muffle the sound. Mateo doesn't need to know I'm talking about him to my best friend. I'm sure he knows it's happening, but I would like him to stay ignorant. "Charles, that breaks all of your rules."

"And I think we're boyfriend and girlfriend," I whisper into the microphone.

I can't let her see the massive blush on my cheeks. I almost threw up yesterday when I called it a relationship. It feels too fast to call it that, and though I know little about being one half of a couple, it feels like that's what Mateo and I are—two halves of a whole.

"Rewind and tell me *everything*," Amy demands.

I give her the CliffNotes version of the last few days, and she responds with the appropriate *ooh*s and *aah*s as I tell the story. When I finish, she's quiet, her brow furrowed in thought.

Every time Amy goes mute, I know I'm in for a hard-hitting, emotionally devastating question that will force me to reevaluate my life. I hate it. She doesn't do it often, but when she decides to impart her infinite wisdom or ask a probing question, I'm left reeling.

"Do you think you're falling in love with him?" she asks.

The air whooshes from my lungs. *Case in point*. She just shoved me over the cliff with no parachute, tumbling toward collision with emotions I'm not ready to address yet.

I can't look at Amy in fear she will see what's written on my face, so I scan the bathroom. His toothbrush sits beside mine, next to both of our contact cases. A pair of my underwear hangs on the towel rack, like Mateo picked them off the floor and left them where I could find them. His glasses sit on the edge of the sink, ready for him to put on after he stumbles to the bathroom when he wakes up in the morning. The space is an ode to two regular people whose lives have merged, even for a short time.

She's going to let me stay silent, but she's not fooled. Not for a moment.

"When you admit it, I am the first person who gets to know." I raise a brow. "*Fine.* You can tell him first, but then I get to know."

"Deal." There's a long pause before I add, "I love you, Ames."

My voice cracks with emotion, and Amy sniffles. "I love you, too, and I'm so, so proud of you."

"Proud?"

Here come the tears. Amy's opinion holds weight, and so do her words. But I don't know why she's proud.

"You've grown so much since we met. I can see your shine." Her voice quiets. "You've always had this...armor to protect yourself—a solid shield to hide your emotions. There's something softer about you now. He brings it out in you, I think. He lets you shine, Charlie." A tear falls down her cheek, and matching those streaming down my own. "I think he understands your soul."

"I hate when you make me cry," I wail, swiping away the pesky moisture.

Her words linger, though. An arrow piercing what little is left of my shield.

"So...you have a boyfriend?" she screams through the phone, ending the emotional moment—for my sake.

"I-I think so..."

My face heats, the warmth creeping out to my ears and down my neck.

Before Amy can answer, the door to the bathroom cracks open, and I yelp. Mateo's head pops in the room, his hair unruly and sticking up at a million different angles.

"She does," he says confidently before he winces and slams his eyes shut. Amy squeals, wolf whistling, and the grating sounds echo through the small bathroom. "Hi, Amy."

"I've been waiting for this moment for my whole life." She sighs. "Greatest day ever!"

Amy rattles on about how she knew we would work together, but her words fade away when the pinched expression on Mateo's face worsens.

"We have to get to work," I say quickly, "I'll talk to you later."

I hang up and open the door wide to take a closer look at Mateo. Something is wrong. A tight, twisting sensation settles below my diaphragm. His eyelids are pinched shut as he leans against the doorframe for support.

"What's wrong?" I grab his cheeks between my palms, moving his head around. He groans and I stop. "Are you hurt? Did you fall? Are you going to vomit?"

Please don't vomit.

I don't know if I can handle that. I babysat once, and the child threw up all over me. I've never been able to shake the trauma of that experience.

"It's just a headache," he says, but he groans again.

"Sit," I demand, guiding him to the edge of the bed.

He falls unceremoniously, his lashes still fanning his cheeks.

"My CPAP didn't seal properly," he mumbles as I sit beside him, dropping my survival kit between us.

I massage the nape of his neck to relieve some of the tension. He sighs, leaning into the touch, and something inside me cracks before mending back together.

I've never taken care of somebody before. I was always the person needing the care. Weeks in the hospital. Trips to physical therapy. Years of struggling with arthritis. Someone has always offered support, even when I was too embarrassed or stubborn to want to accept.

My mother spent weeks helping me complete simple tasks after my hip surgery. Showering, moving around, *existing*, wasn't possible without someone else. The total dependence on another person morphed into hyper-independence.

I was capable of doing everything on my own. I didn't need someone to take care of me or coddle me. Amy was the first person I let help me with anything, and even now I hate asking her—I hate burdening her with my problems.

"Take this." I hand him a pain reliever and my water bottle and watch to make sure he swallows. When I'm happy he's ingested the medicine, I pull out the essential oils I use when I'm overwhelmed or have a headache from staring at my computer for too long.

I perch on my knees behind him and dab the essential oil on my fingers before pressing them to his skin behind his ears, gently massaging the oil into his skin. His head lulls to the side as a small mewl falls from his lips.

This is the first time someone has let me take care of them, and I'm not going to screw it up.

It's hard for me to verbally express how I feel about Mateo. It's there, banging around my chest, but putting words to the feeling makes it real, and I'm not ready for that. So, for now, I'm going to take care of him, the way he's taken care of me.

Adding more oil, I work the muscles in his neck and at the base of his shoulders, working out the stiff knots where the two meet. His sighs are the only sound in the room, and his muscles loosen until he becomes dead weight, shedding all the stress he carries.

The whole time, I am shoving down my giddiness.

I like taking care of Mateo, I realize as I finish. It's fulfilling, like it's something I'm meant to do. The same way I'm meant to publish a paper in *Nature* and discover a new species.

I lean down and kiss him on the temple as I wrap my arms around his shoulders like I'm a backpack. He grabs my hands and squeezes.

"Thank you, bruja," he whispers, swiping his thumb against the top of my hand. "I'm feeling a bit better."

"Yeah?" The elation in my voice is unmistakable.

He feels better because of *me*.

Fireworks erupt in my chest, and I could live off the feeling for the rest of my life—knowing that instead of being the burden, I was able to help shoulder someone else's.

CHAPTER 30

CHARLIE

The hushed whispers in the mess area raise the hair on the back of my neck. The usually loud room is eerily quiet, and when I turn the corner and step into the space, I could hear a pin drop.

What the hell?

My skin crawls as crew members offer me varying looks—sympathy, concern, *pity*.

Something is very, very wrong.

At this point, I'm sprinting to Mateo. I hear the tail end of his conversation with Jett when I reach him.

"...before Charlie sees."

The pit in my stomach grows, a deep, endless abyss of anxiety capable of drowning me.

"Before I see *what*?" I ask.

The guys turn, both wearing looks of shock and discomfort. Mateo moves first, taking a step toward me. Jett slips his phone in his pocket, but his face is frantic.

"It's nothing," Mateo rushes out.

I know every one of his smiles—cataloged every one he's ever offered me into my mental storage. This isn't one I've seen before; it's forced and uncomfortable.

"Tell me," I demand, anxiety clawing its way to the surface as they exchange a glance.

"Charlie." Mateo says my name with an air of caution, like speaking with a cornered animal. "It's not worth it. Trust me."

He exhales deeply when I shake my head. I want to know.

Silently, Mateo hands me his phone; the video I recorded for Jett plays in the background, but that's not what he was trying to hide from me.

There are thousands of comments, each one worse than the previous.

The other chick was hotter.

Scargirl is an appropriate nickname.

Some people shouldn't show their faces online.

A handful are kind, and I try to cling to them, but for every positive one, there are three that comment on my appearance. Each one slices like a knife, flaying me open.

Mateo's hand covers the screen. "They're wrong," he says, full of conviction. "None of those comments are true."

Good thing she's smart. She'll get nowhere with looks.

Keep her in a lab and away from a camera.

"I'm taking the video down," Jett says. "I'm so sorry, Blondie. If I knew—"

"Keep it up."

My voice is strong, resolute, which is surprising because I'm one moment away from crumbling to the ground.

Every self-deprecating thought in my head is on the screen, making each one real. It's been easy to forget them on the boat, but this is a bubble. This isn't the real world.

The comments—that is the real world.

And now Mateo has a taste of how the real world perceives me.

The phone is pulled from my death grip while my hand shakes. Anxiety coils in my chest like a cobra poised to strike as Mateo tips my chin with his thumb. It takes everything I have to fight the tears. I don't want to crumble, not here, but he surveys me with unease, and my lip quivers.

The room closes in, and then I'm running away, my phone ringing as I fly down the hallway, trying to escape every thought chasing me.

I'm not soft in the way Mateo deserves. I've always had hard edges, but after my accident, I became jagged, sharpened to a point. He deserves someone gentle, who makes him homemade chicken noodle soup when he's sick and can carry his burdens.

He doesn't need someone who wakes up thrashing after a nightmare, someone who *is* the burden.

I tried to be that person—the one who takes care of him.

My phone rings again, and I answer Amy's call with shaky fingers, crouched in the room's corner where it feels safe.

"Charlie, are you okay? Mateo called me. He said..."

She trails off when I peer into the camera. I shake my head, words clogged in my throat. No, I'm not okay, not when I may be falling in love with Mateo, but there's no way this will last in the real world when he realizes I'm more than he bargained for.

"Do you want to talk about it?" she asks, and for the first time since she began asking the question, I change my answer.

"Yes."

"All right."

I stare at Amy through the phone screen, focused on the pieces of hot-pink hair falling out of her bun. I can't carry this on my own, but maybe I don't have to.

"Mateo sent me the video," she murmurs. "None of what they said is true, Charles."

"It feels true," I croak, pointing to the center of my chest, where pain twists every time I breathe. "It's nothing I haven't told myself or others have said to me."

Tears stream down my cheek, and I press tighter into the corner, hoping I'll melt into the walls and escape the demons chasing me.

I don't want to be this way. Don't want to look in a mirror and wince. Don't want to hide in a crowd or dodge the stares of children who know nothing more than curiosity. I don't want to question Mateo every time he calls me beautiful or deny his words.

And I've tried so hard to battle the whispers and stares. I've fought the self-deprecating thoughts with affirmations in the mirror. I've stepped so far out of my comfort zone and let someone else see my scars, but it's done little to rebuild the confidence I lost.

The confidence that was stripped away from me with a few callous words on a screen.

It was foolish to think I could curl my hair, put on makeup and a nice outfit, and pretend everything was normal—that *I* was normal.

"I don't want to feel like this anymore," I admit, my voice cracking with the confession.

There have been slivers of time where the thoughts shut off and I was *free*. I want to feel the shine that Amy talked about, and I want to believe Mateo when he compliments me. I want to be confident enough to ignore the stares in public.

"What do you mean?"

"I don't want to look in the mirror and hate the reflection." The words are out, and the floodgates open on everything I've been holding in and allowing to grow until it consumes me. "I want to be strong and brave, but I feel weak and powerless. I wish I had thick skin and could brush the comments off, but I don't know how to let it go, because they *hurt*. Those words burrowed deep into my bones, right to the marrow like bone-eating worms, where they're devouring what self-esteem I have left. A few comments tore me apart, and I'm letting them." My voice cracks. "I'm letting strangers destroy me, but I don't know how to stop because part of me *believes them*."

"They only have the power if you give it to them," Amy says. "But you are beautiful and strong, and there are days I wish I had your confidence and intelligence, because maybe I wouldn't be a barista with a useless art history degree and a mountain of student loan debt. Everyone has something they don't like about themselves. And if they say they don't, then they're liars."

"I don't know *how* to like who I am. Or how to get back the woman I lost."

Before Amy can respond, a deep voice rattles through the room. "That's how you feel about yourself?"

Amy hangs up, and my phone slips from my grip, tumbling onto the floor as I spin to face Mateo, who stands in the doorframe. He blinks, and the sadness that flickers across his gaze is proof he heard every depressing, self-deprecating thought I shared with Amy.

He's not supposed to know that I hate my reflection and that, some days, it's easier to pretend I don't exist than face the world's icy stares.

Mateo takes a hesitant step into the room, approaching like I'm an injured animal moments away from attack. Maybe I am, because the words "Don't look at me like that" slip from my mouth, full of vitriol and fear.

"Like what?" he asks, taking another step, closing the space between us.

"Like you pity me."

I don't want his pity, nor do I want to be the recipient of the look he offers: one full of understanding.

"Come here, bruja," he demands quietly, extending a hand. When I make no effort to move, he adds, "Please, Charlie."

It's the use of my name in place of his nickname that moves me to place my hand in his, allowing him to pull me into the small bathroom. There's barely enough room for us to both stand, and Mateo's chest is pressed against my back, where the warmth of his skin burrows deep into my bones.

He stares through the mirror until the silence is thick and I'm squirming beneath the intensity of his gaze. Mateo lifts a hand, tenderly tangling his fingers through the loose strands of my hair. I hate how his touch settles the rolling in my stomach, how it only takes one look from him for me to soften into something vulnerable. And I hate how much I need him to help me calm down—that he's become the rock tethering me to reality.

"I'm not going to tell you you're pretty," he murmurs, the confession hanging heavily between us.

My stomach hollows out.

I never asked him to do that, but now he's telling me he won't...why does it hurt so much?

"I know what I look like." The crumbling foundation I've been standing on the last few years finally breaks, burying me in the rubble. "I'm mangled."

The confession is a whisper, and I choke on the rancid memories the words resurrect.

Embarrassment twists tightly in my chest. I don't know how to look in the mirror and see anything other than what I am: undesirable.

A rogue tear slips out, and I turn to flee, to escape the way my heart clenches knowing how the world views me, but his arm strap me and bracket the sides of the small wash basin.

"I'm not going to tell you you're pretty, Charlie, because that word falls so short of what you are. You are stunningly beautiful." His finger trails down the scar cutting across my brow, the touch reverent as he swipes the tear from my cheek. "I could tell you that your eyes remind me of the Caribbean Sea, or how, when you smile, the air is knocked from my lungs."

I lose the capacity to inhale as he tugs on a few blond strands, twirling them around his pointer finger.

"I could wax poetic about your hair, how I love the wispy bits that fall out of your ponytail, or how it's a beaming gold beneath the setting sun. I could tell you these things, Charlie, but they aren't a fraction of who you are."

My back faces the mirror, and I'm glad I can't see whatever's written on my face or how I react to every word.

"The things I love most about you have nothing to do with your beauty. It's *you*. Your brilliant mind. Your loyalty to your friends. The way you laugh with your whole chest until you're snorting. It's the way you devour chocolate like it's the last piece on the planet, and how you collect trinkets and knickknacks and hoard them like they're the greatest treasure you've ever found."

"I'm not soft," I admit quietly, tears streaming down my face.

I don't know why it's the first thing out of my mouth, or why the confession feels like someone is sliding a knife between my ribs. Maybe it's because I *am* soft. A hermit crab without its shell is susceptible to death. It has no armor to protect its vital organs.

With Mateo, I have no shield, and maybe that's why I'm afraid.

"You don't need to be gentle. You need someone who is gentle with you. Let me be that man. I *want* to be that man."

Clarity strikes me like a rogue lightning bolt, electricity pulsing beneath my skin as I stare at him with wonder.

I will never find a man better than Mateo, nor do I want to.

I've fallen in love with him.

He swipes away a rogue tear, cradling my face like I'm the most precious thing in the world.

My arms wrap around his neck as I barrel into him, clutching him like he's the only reason I'm still standing. I sob into the crook of his neck and drench his collar with tears as he casts soothing circles on my back.

Wrinkles form on his linen shirt from the force of my grip, and I try to smooth them out as I release him. He brushes the hair away from my face and presses a soft kiss to the center of my forehead.

Intertwining our hands, he leads me out of the bathroom and sits down in the chair at the desk, then pulls me into his lap. My skin is splotchy and red, my lower lashes rimmed red, but I offer him a watery smile through the mirror.

It's weak, but it's real.

"Can you tell me one thing you like about yourself?" he asks, grazing up and down my thigh.

Pulling my hair to the side, he peppers soft kisses down my neck to my collarbone, making it difficult to focus on anything else.

"One thing, bruja," he demands, nipping at my earlobe.

"I-I like my...hair."

His fingers tangle in the loose blond curls, wrapping the strands around his knuckles and tugging so my neck is bare to him. Goose bumps break out along my spine as his hands dip beneath my top and roam along my skin.

"For now, I'll value all the parts of yourself you're still learning to love. But every day, we're going to find something else you admire about yourself." He drops another soft kiss on my shoulder. "You're not broken, or mangled, or any of the things people on the internet have said. Give it to me, Charlie."

"Give you what?" I ask, my vocal cords raw from crying.

"Everything you don't want to carry any longer. I'll carry it for you. And when you're ready, we'll let go of it. Together."

I nod, words clogged in my throat. His lips hover over my ear, his warm breath dancing along my skin. Desire pools deep in my lower stomach as his hands roam my body. His touch is reverent and gentle, but my skin heats as the need builds.

His hand slips under my bra, and he pulls my nipple between his fingers, twisting slightly.

Fuck.

My head, clouded with pleasure, falls back to rest on his shoulder.

"Now, bruja, you're going to ride my cock and see just how beautiful you are as you take me."

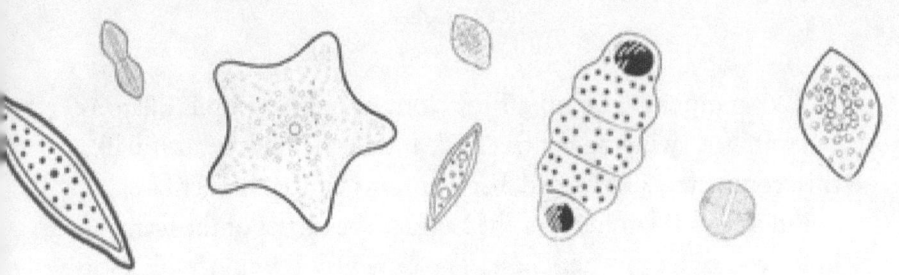

CHAPTER 31

MATEO

Charlie exhales a breathy moan when I pinch her nipple between my fingers, twisting the taut skin until she's writhing in my lap.

The discomfort lodged in my chest dissipates a fraction as her tears dry away and lust glazes over her irises, transforming them into a radiant blue.

"Hands up," I demand, before I raise her shirt over her head and toss it to the side. Her flesh pebbles as I unclasp her bra.

I'm captivated as I examine her through the mirror, her breasts heaving while she drags air into her lungs. If only she could see herself from my view—understand how deeply I admire her.

Her beauty is incomparable. In a thousand different lifetimes, it would always be her for me.

I rise from the chair and take Charlie with me, then drop her on the edge of the desk beside her trinkets. Darwin's head bobbles, and her cheeks push up as she readjusts his position.

There she is.

Taking my time, I strip off my clothes, and her pupils dilate as she watches, swinging her feet back and forth. She's beautiful like this, completely unguarded, her emotions written on her face.

I'm not afraid of her—of the baggage she carries or the fears she holds too tightly to her chest. The only way I would walk away from someone as special as Charlotte Louise Bowen is if she forced me to.

As scared as she's been, she's never truly pushed me away. She throws up the walls to protect herself, but she leaves a door wide open for anyone daring enough to walk through it and see everything she tries to hide.

Desire compounds at the base of my cock, and though she's barely touched me, I'm aching for her. I need nothing more than a weighted glance and I'd be on my knees for her. She's far more powerful than she gives herself credit.

The seed of discomfort that planted itself in my chest from her confession fades away with her touch—soft, exploratory, admiring. I stand between her thighs while her hands continue their path, working over my shoulders and across the muscles of my back to settle on my ass.

She tugs, and I stumble into her, palming my hands on the desk to stabilize myself.

The sweet sound of her giggles ricochets around my chest as she squeezes my ass.

"It's unnatural," she murmurs against my lips, "how attractive you are. There's only one explanation."

"Oh?"

She presses forward and takes my bottom lip between her teeth, nipping until the metallic tang of blood hits my tongue.

"My spell was a reverse curse. Instead of horrible hair, it made you *more* attractive. I don't know if it makes me a horrible witch or the best the world's ever seen."

A surprised laugh escapes me, lifting the somber energy lingering in the air, and she steals the sound. Her fingers tangle into the rogue strands of hair at the nape of my neck—the ones I can no longer tame thanks to Charlie's exploring hands.

Despite what she thinks, her curse *did* work. I no longer have perfect hair.

I release a shuddered breath when her fingers tug at the strands, a small pinch of pain adding to the pleasure zapping across my skin.

Kissing her is the high of a scientific discovery. Each moment we have is new and uncharted, and I could spend the rest of my life exploring with her. Learning about her. Building her up. *Loving her*.

Charlie wraps her legs around my torso and pulls me against the desk, my erection pressed to her inner thigh. She gasps and drags her fingernails down my chest until she's dangerously close to the elastic of my briefs.

Her finger trails back and forth, dipping between the waistline before retreating.

She's teasing me, and the smile brushing my skin tells me she's proud of how I twitch beneath her palm when she *finally* drags her hand along my shaft.

She's going to be my fucking undoing.

"Be careful, bruja," I whisper, and she shudders as my breath hits her skin.

"Or what?" she counters, full of defiance. Her chin tilts up in triumph but falls back when I tweak her nipple between my fingers, twisting the bud.

"*Oh, shit.*"

I take her other nipple in my mouth, leaving small red marks along her skin before lifting her from the table. She yelps when I grab the band of her shorts and tug them off, leaving her bare.

"You are stunning," I say, pushing a strand of hair from her face. She blushes, red creeping down her neck, but she doesn't look away. Her irises swirl with something I've never seen before—not from her. It rips the air from my lungs.

"Mateo, I—"

"Tell me later, bruja." If she says what I *think* she might say—what I want to say to her—then I want to hear it later, when I have the time to hear it over and over and let the words settle deep into my soul. "Sit on the desk."

She stares at me, stunned, but recovers when I drop my boxers and take myself into my palm, working my hand up and down my shaft. Perched at the edge of the desk, Charlie watches with uninhibited desire, and the lust builds at the base of my spine.

"Scoot back," I command, dropping between her legs and spreading her thighs open as she moves farther onto the desk.

She hisses as the cold cabin air hits her soaked flesh.

"Such a pretty pussy." I drag a finger up her slit, coating it in her arousal. She's fucking drenched, and I've barely touched her. "Who does this pussy belong to?"

Charlie's jaw unhinges, her chest heaving as she stares down at me. I push her knees up until she's completely splayed out. She squirms when I kiss the inside of her left calf, working my way up the soft flesh until I'm hovering between the apex of her thighs.

I graze my thumb over her clit.

"Fuck!"

"Answer the question."

"Mateo," she grits out, her hips rising to search for contact.

"Who does this pussy belong to?"

"*You*," she moans as I slip a finger inside her, curling upward to hit her G-spot.

"Good girl," I say, latching on to her clit and sucking deeply. "This pussy," I murmur against her skin, "is *mine*."

I slide another finger into her, and she clenches around me, sending a wave of pleasure through my body.

She's untethered, floating away toward her pleasure as her breathy moans fill the cabin. I chase each small sound she makes until she's squirming beneath my tongue, her hands buried in my hair for stability. A small sheen of sweat forms on her brow, her blond hair plastered to her face and neck as she climbs closer to an orgasm.

"*Mateo.*"

Do not come.

When I'm confident I'm not going to finish early, I add a third finger, increasing my pace until her legs shake and her breath grows choppy and uneven.

"Come for me," I demand, pulling her clit between my teeth.

Her hips rise off the desk as she barrels into her orgasm, her fingers tightening around my hair, forging pleasure from the pain. I continue to lap and nip until her body slackens and she releases my hair from her death grip.

"So pretty," I admit when she's recovered enough to sit up.

She blushes as I brush away the hair matted to her temple, kissing her gently, before falling into the chair and facing her. My cock stands tall and hard against my stomach.

I rub the bead of precum along the head, a small groan escaping me when she gulps, her gaze darkening to a shade of deep cerulean. She drops to the floor in front of me, her tongue darting out to wet her lips.

"And this is *mine*," she says, pushing away my hand to wrap hers around me, squeezing at the base.

Stars twinkle in my vision as Charlie leans forward and runs her tongue along my shaft, coating it in saliva. She twirls her tongue around the tip, and I briefly lose control when she pulls my cock into her mouth.

My hips lift from the chair, and I push myself down her throat. Her muscles work around me, making space for me to press farther.

She gags, gripping my thighs as her head bobs up and down, taking me deeper with each pass.

I won't last long like this, and my balls tighten when she moans, as if offering me pleasure increases her own. The vision of Charlie on her knees, sucking my cock like it's her last meal, is not only one I've fantasized about but will do me in more quickly than I want.

Her fingers release my thighs, small half-moons embedded into my skin. She takes my balls into her palm, cupping them as she takes me to the base, the head of my cock pressing against the back of her throat.

"Fuck, I'm going to come," I groan, gripping the chair's armrests as she hums against my dick, the same tune she offered in the lab. She makes it to what should be the second line in the first verse when I wrap her hair around my wrist and drag her off my cock.

She whines, saliva trailing down her chin as she sits back on her knees, breasts pushed outward.

Holy fuck.

Her position is not helping delay my orgasm. Instead, the pleasure compounds, and I have to squeeze my eyes shut.

There's only one thing that can postpone the orgasm: reciting the steps of polymerase chain reaction. I have to list the entire master mix to cool down enough to look at Charlie, who watches from her knees with thinly veiled amusement.

"Come here," I demand, helping her off the ground before I drag her into a frenzied kiss.

Before she can settle on my lap, I grab her hips and twirl her around to face the mirror. She's blocking my body from view, but she's completely exposed. I wait, expecting her to cover herself and shy away from her reflection, but she surprises me and instead offers a tentative grin.

My fingers tighten on her hips, almost enough to bruise, as I use her as a tether to reality.

It's hard to verbalize the pride banging around in my chest. Difficult to breathe as I watch her analyze herself in the mirror, starting at her face and slowly traveling south.

"I have another thing," she whispers, breaking my trance.

"What?"

I'm stuck between staring at her ass, begging for me to sink my teeth into the soft flesh, and the way her breasts rise and fall in the mirror. Both are captivating and stealing my attention.

"Another thing I like about myself," she says, "I like how I feel when you look at me." She rubs her breastbone. "I feel...seen, but not in a bad way. It's like—" She pauses, her lashes fluttering as she searches for words. "Like I'm *shining*."

"You do," I say, kissing her shoulder. "You shine like bioluminescence in the abyss."

She slips her hand beneath mine.

"Thank you for seeing me. And not being afraid."

The words are whispered, barely vocalized.

Admiration is the last thing I expect from her. It's frightening—what I feel for her. Threatens to take over my thoughts, command my actions, dictate my future.

It's unsettling, yet the most comfortable thing in the world.

Loving Charlie is easy, regardless of what she believes.

She releases my hand, and I guide her over my thighs, the soft skin of her back pressed against my chest.

With my hands on her hips, I help her stretch over my cock, inch by inch, until she's flush against me, the inside of her thighs bracketing the outside of mine. She gasps as she takes me to the hilt, and I give her a moment to adjust, nipping at the flesh of her neck.

She pulses around me, and my balls tense with pleasure, which peaks when she shifts, sinking even deeper.

"Holy shit," she moans, her hands flying to the armrests and head falling onto my shoulder. "So fucking deep."

"Eyes open." My voice shakes with the need to move, but she heeds my command. "Look how well you take me," I whisper in her ear, stroking her clit with my fingers.

She jerks, a breathy gasp escaping her as her hips lift, but I hold them steady until she's desperate to move—overcome with need.

"You *consume* me, bruja."

A soft moan tumbles out of her as I pull her hair to the side and drop my mouth to her collarbone, sucking deeply on the skin.

Am I too old to be giving Charlie a hickey? Sure, but it scratches an itch in my caveman brain, and I'll spend the next few days getting hard from the sight of it.

Her lips pop open to admonish me, but any words fall away as I lift my hips and piston into her.

"*Oh,*" she moans, grinding back and forth as she uses the chair to stabilize herself.

She rides my cock in earnest, and I sit back, allowing her to take her pleasure. I keep my hands on her waist to minimize the impact on her joints, and she clenches around me.

A groan slips out, and I catch the tail end of Charlie's smile before she does it again.

Fuck. Two can play this game.

Wrapping one arm around her waist, I tease her clit until she's pulsing around me.

"I-I'm going to come," she moans, her breath choppy as she moves.

I'm right there with her, the need to come buzzing through my veins. I know myself—I'll come the moment she does.

"Your pussy takes my cock so well. Are you going to be a good girl and take my cum?"

She nods frantically, her head banging against my shoulder as she shatters around my cock, tumbling into oblivion. I pump my hips upward, and then I'm falling with her, ecstasy barreling into my chest with such force stars flicker along my vision.

Charlie returns to earth before I do, flopping against my chest as I soften inside her. My cum leaks out and coats our thighs. I've never seen anything hotter than her splayed out on top of me, flushed from her orgasm.

I kiss her temple, and she sighs. It's soft and content, and it flares the kernel of happiness lodged beneath my diaphragm.

She rises and disappears into the bathroom while I catch my breath.

It's the moment of silence that allows the memory to slam into me.

I'm pretty sure she was going to tell me she loves me.

And I told her to tell me later.

I might be an idiot.

CHAPTER 32

CHARLIE

He fucking stopped me.

I was going to tell him I love him, and the annoying asshole stopped me.

I know why.

He wants to say it first.

If I know one thing, it's that Mateo likes to win, and there's no bigger win in a relationship than being the first one to say I love you.

Mateo is shit out of luck, though, because it's going to be me. He can't woo me out of my panties, make me feel seen and adored, *and* be the first one to say the three little words.

Nope. Not happening.

You could say I'm a woman on a mission—I am Darwin searching for his finches—as I stomp through the vessel, searching for my cariño so I can make sure I beat him to the punch. I don't know why it matters so much that I say it first, but it does.

I want Mateo to know how I feel about him—that he's worth breaking down the walls I've constructed around my heart, and with him, I'm starting to find the pieces of myself I've lost.

"Blondie!"

I halt my expedition, spinning on my heels as Jett chases me down. My stomach twists. I might have been avoiding him after my meltdown yesterday.

It's one thing for Mateo and Amy to see me crumble. For Jett to witness my breakdown is *unprofessional*, and I haven't worked up the courage to face him after how I reacted to the comments.

Being upset is an appropriate response. Running away in tears is based on trauma. It's not something I'm proud of, and after Mateo fell asleep last night, I booked an appointment with a therapist. It's not a solution for my trauma or internalized issues, but it's a step. A baby step toward becoming a person I'm confident in—of finding my shine and the woman I lost somewhere along the way.

"You're a hard woman to find," he says with a toothy grin. "I wanted to show you this."

He holds out his phone.

Last time I had his device in my hand, I was reading horrible comments about myself on a video meant to shine light on my research. Needless to say, I do not want to see what's on that screen.

"I'm good."

I've had enough with social media in this lifetime. If Darwin didn't need it, neither do I. Except nightly videos with Mateo. But if we watch on his phone, then it's not me using social media, it's him.

"Please," he presses. I make no move to take his phone, and the interaction grows awkward. When he realizes I am not going to look, he adds, "I went through them all. Every last comment. I want you to see the good."

"What?"

My brain spins in disbelief at the gesture.

The time it must have taken to go through each one...there were *thousands.*

He flips his phone around and scrolls through his camera roll where he's screenshotted each positive response and blacked out everything else. We make it through about ten—all comments about how interesting my research is, or how I'm a role model for young girls interested in science—before I begin to cry.

Fat tears stream down my cheeks as I read each one.

"I didn't take the video down," he says, "but I disabled the commenting on all of my posts and shared a video to let my viewers know how disappointed I am. I started my channel to have fun, not to tear down bright, hard-working women."

I take the phone from his hand, scrolling through, when I pause on one full of vulgar language and threats.

"I hope you choke on your tiny penis." I read it out loud and look at Jett, baffled how this is a kind comment.

First of all, they got my anatomy incorrect. Second, if I had a penis, it would not be small. It would be the biggest schlong the world has ever seen. I would win awards and sling it around.

"Oh, that's Vivian. She responded to hundreds of comments before I told her to stop."

A choked laugh escapes as I read her other responses.

Can you even legally drive, considering how blind you are?

^^^This translates to "I'm an asshole with nothing else to do than tear down incredible women who wouldn't give me the time of day."

If having a horrible personality was an Olympic sport, you would have a gold medal.

"This is..." Words fail me. "Thank you, Jett."

The tears continue to roll as I read through each one, letting the words burrow into the marrow of my bones and heal a little of what's been broken, the fissures slowly mending back together.

"You made her cry *again*?" a shrill voice screams from the end of the hallway.

Vivian barrels into me, wrapping her arms around my shoulders in a brutal yet comforting hug. Sofía joins from the other side, and after a moment of confusion, Jett completes the sandwich hug.

"I didn't make her cry. She did it on her own," Jett grumbles.

"She didn't spontaneously burst into tears," Sofía counters. "What did you do?"

Jett releases me from the hug to stare down at Sofía. She folds her arms over her chest, half a foot shorter than him, but holds her ground as they participate in a charged face-off.

"Why do you always assume I'm the cause of the chaos?" Jett asks. She levels him with a look that screams *be fucking for real*. "I showed her all the kind comments on the video. Erasing the bad with good."

"Oh." Her brow furrows, and when she looks back at Jett, there's something questioning in her gaze, like she's surprised by the gesture.

"He also showed me Vivian's responses," I add.

"Her *what*?" Sofía asks, running to my side to see the phone.

"I also posted a very heated response video, but it only got sixty views," Vivian says, leaning over my shoulder to read her replies. "Oh, that's a good one."

"We tried to come to your room yesterday," Sofía whispers, low enough so Jett doesn't hear, "after we heard about the video, but you were a bit...occupied."

"You were getting *fucked*," Vivian amends.

It takes a few seconds for the words to settle, but when they do, my face flames to a million degrees and my hands fly to cover the mortification written on my face.

We couldn't have been that loud, could we?

The looks on their faces tell me we accidentally put on a show for anyone who walked by in the hallway.

I'm going to die, right here on this ugly carpet.

Neptune, mighty ruler of the sea, take me away from this place.

"Why are you whispering?" Jett sticks his head between Sofía and me, and she whirls, her fist landing in his gut.

"Bell," I yell. "Someone needs to get you a bell. You move like an assassin."

He smiles proudly. "Thank you."

"Let's go," Vivian says, locking her arm around mine.

"B-but," I sputter, searching the hallway like my cariño will magically appear and I can get back to the purpose of my mission: telling Mateo I love him.

"We have wine," Sofía whispers. "Let's have some fun."

"Fuck, marry, or kill," Vivian says, pouring wine into the plastic cups we stole from the kitchen. "Dracula, bigfoot, and a centaur."

"Oh, easy. Kill bigfoot. Fuck Dracula. Marry the centaur," Sofía responds, draining her glass and stumbling over to the desk.

It's littered with empty bottles and snacks. After the first bottle, we devoured Sofía's stash of crackers. The second bottle of wine was followed by Vivian's pre-packaged pastries and Pringles.

The third bottle of wine—now emptied into Sofía's glass—is paired with my chocolate stash, the lemon bars Amy gave me, and the half-smashed, bulk-size bag of animal crackers I forgot about in the bottom of my duffel bag.

It's quite the spread.

"Agreed." I raise my cup. "Centaurs are the obvious choice. Great pectorals and free transportation."

Like every normal preteen, I was obsessed with mythology. Creatures with chiseled muscles in particular. They were often tall, brooding, and the owner of very squeezable pectoral muscles.

My dream man at ten years old.

Now my dream man has annoyingly perfect hair, dimples that appear when he's pleased with himself, a slightly crooked smile. And *very* squeezable pectoral muscles.

Twenty-six-year-old Charlie is still very much on that train.

"Centaurs are *fine.* Too bad they aren't real," Vivian says, falling onto the bed beside me.

Sofía flops down in the chair, popping chocolates back like they're nothing. If the bag wasn't still half full with only a few days left, I would be watching her like a hawk to make sure she's not eating it all.

But I'm too tipsy to care right now.

Plus, Mateo has a whole bag. He just refuses to tell me where it's hidden. I have a feeling it's on the top shelf in the closet where I can't reach.

"You know who else is *fine,*" Sofía says, hiding her smirk behind her cup. "Mateo."

I fall back on the bed, throw an arm over my face, and kick my feet like a schoolgirl.

He is pretty hot, isn't he?

I'm in this limbo state of smug pride and utter bafflement where sometimes it's hard to believe Mateo and I are together, and then other moments I look at him and all I can think is how he's *mine.*

"I don't even bat that way, but I will say his features are very symmetrical," Vivian says, tugging at a strand of my hair. "Your man is hot and down bad. I think you hit the dating lottery."

They don't know the half of it.

Couldn't imagine how he understands my soul—sees the scars and darkened edges and cherishes them. They'll never know how his thigh twitches when I trace his tattoos, or how his breathing changes when he falls into a deep slumber.

Vivian and Sofía will never know of the way he holds me while he sleeps, like I'm what tethers him to the real world, or how he methodically rubs balm into my joints.

Winning the lottery is statistically improbable, but discovering Mateo feels statistically impossible, like the universe played its part. He was right in front of me for two years, and I never saw him, not how I do now.

"He's magical," I say wistfully, trying to pour the rest of my wine into my mouth hole while lying down. Half of it dribbles onto my chin, and I swipe it away. "He's got a magic schlong, too."

I jerk my hips up, and the chorus of giggles that follows loosens my tongue further. I wish Vivian and Sofía lived in Rhode Island. Amy would love them. *I* love them.

"I've seen a few ding-a-lings in my day—not that many, but at least six—and his is the nicest." The room grows eerily silent. Good, they're paying attention. "Just the right size." I hold my hands up so they have an idea. "But best of all, he knows how to use it. He gives a wonderful wienering."

Once you've had a good wienering, you really can't go back. Your mind—and vagina—are open to all the possibilities, and you're ruined for life.

Mateo has ruined me for life with his perfect dick.

I need more wine to come to terms that I'm dick-whipped.

"A wonderful wienering?" a deep voice purrs, full of amusement and male pride.

"You traitors!" I fly from the bed, pointing an accusatory finger at Vivian and Sofía, who are silently laughing, beet red and wiping away tears.

I'm wobbling toward them, ready to give them a piece of my mind.

"You two let me wax poetic about his wiener while he was *in the room*?" I practically screech. Mateo snorts, and my hand whirls out to connect with his chest. It morphs into a grunt. "Is the sisterhood *dead*?"

"Please don't stop on my account," Mateo says, his cocky smile fully formed.

Screw him, and screw his infuriatingly attractive dimples that appear at the most inopportune of times, making it painstakingly difficult to focus my thoughts. I'm supposed to be annoyed with my friends, but the dimples pop and I'm a sucker, so I focus on that long enough for them to scramble toward the door.

"He snuck in," Sofía yells, collecting the wine bottles.

"It was too late. You were on a roll," Vivian says, then extends her palm for a high five. "Glad you're getting dicked down."

The alcohol tamps down my annoyance, so I slap my palm against hers.

Mateo grabs my waist, steadying me as I stumble from the force.

"See you later," Sofía screams. I don't know why. Maybe wine makes her loud?

She tries to slip out the door but slams into Jett's chest.

"Jett is going to help you back to your room," Mateo says. "Goodnight, ladies."

A chorus of goodbyes fills the air as the door clicks shut, and then it's just Mateo and me, his grip still tight on my hips.

His head dips to rest on my shoulder, his chest rumbling with laughter. "How much wine have you had?"

"At least a bottle."

I try to escape from his clutches to hide in the bathroom until I can look him in the eye after tipsily admitting he has a dick and knows how to use it.

"And would you say you've been satisfied with your *wienering*? How would you rate it on a scale from one to ten? One being 'worst wienering ever' to ten being 'his wiener makes me astral project.'"

His voice cracks, and when I glance in the mirror, his face is a fire-engine red from the strain of holding back his laughter.

I slip out of his grip but don't make it far before I'm ripped from the ground and spun around.

"'Wonderful wienering' is going right beside 'smells like a summer breeze' on the list of my favorite compliments. You really know how to stroke a man's ego, bruja."

"I hate you," I grumble, but my annoyance cracks when he spins me again, his laughter filling the cabin.

I could get drunk on the sound.

"You might hate me," he says between laughs, "but you love my dick."

He's still laughing as he carries me into the bathroom and drops me in front of the mirror. He pokes my frown, then hands me my toothbrush and wordlessly guides me through getting ready for bed.

I'm not quite drunk, and still capable of taking care of myself, but I let him help with all my tasks.

He undresses me and slips on my strawberry pajamas, but not before taking a moment to rake his gaze along my skin, igniting my veins like a wildfire. Deft hands rub balm into my skin, and I sigh from the gentle touch and the knowledge that tomorrow will hurt a bit less because of this.

When he's content I'm set for bed, he gets himself ready, fiddling with his CPAP I've mentally nicknamed Finch. I have Charles Darwin, and Mateo has Finch, an ode to Darwin's iconic finches.

I don't know how he'll feel about the nickname, so I've kept it to myself, but I did look up Etsy shops that will embroider a CPAP bag in case he's on board with the name.

My head is heavy from the alcohol, and I'm nearly asleep by the time Mateo rolls into bed and pulls me against his chest. As I fall into a blissful slumber, it strikes me that I never finished my expedition.

I'll tell Mateo I love him tomorrow.

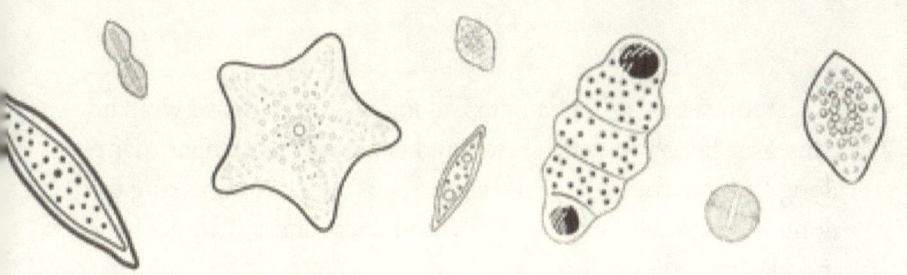

CHAPTER 33

MATEO

"I think I might cry," Jett says as the ROV sinks beneath the choppy waves, descending into the depths one last time on this voyage.

One final shot to film, and the anticipation in the room is palpable.

Charlie spent the morning whispering sweet nothings to her crystals, hoping to manifest something spectacular for the final dive. Vivian mutters to her controls like it will guide her to greatness. Jett bounces on his toes and annoys the ever-loving shit out of Sofía as he chatters in her ear.

Charlie's back is pressed against my chest as we stand behind Vivian, watching as the ROV sinks.

It was hard to look at her this morning and not laugh, the memory of her starfished on the bed, monologuing about schlongs and wieners and how nice she finds mine. It was glaringly obvious she was tipsy from the moment she said ding-a-ling, but my heart leaped from my chest witnessing her so open and free.

The soft wisps of her hair graze along my forearms as I wrap my arms over her shoulders, clutching her tightly. My fingers dance along her collarbone, and she shivers, goose bumps breaking out along her skin. She sinks deeper into the embrace, lifting a hand and placing it on my forearm.

We're intertwined with each other, subtle intimacy in every touch.

It would be difficult to believe Charlie and I made it this far in only three weeks, but I've spent the last two years slowly falling for her, uncovering her every quirk and intricacy and finding space for each in my heart.

She woke me up this morning buzzing with pent-up energy. Before I could remove my mask, she was on top of me, asking me if I had plans tonight.

We share a room and we're on a boat. Her plans are my plans.

When I told her that, her smile grew brighter and she nodded frantically, insisting we watch the stars together tonight. One last time before the light pollution ruins the view.

That's what she said out loud, but her body language and her energy told a different tale—the opening lines of a story I hope to tell for the rest of my life.

"If you start crying, make sure you do it from your good angle," Doug deadpans from across the room. He gets a few bewildered looks before adding, "Makes for good footage."

He shrugs and returns to his computer, slipping his headphones over his ears to block out the noise.

The room is quiet as the ROV hits five hundred meters, but Charlie is on edge. Every few minutes, she glances over her shoulder, peruses my body, blushes, and then returns her focus to the footage.

She does it again when we hit eight hundred meters, and another time at a thousand.

"Is there something you'd like to say?" I ask, biting back a laugh.

"N-no." Her voice cracks.

Liar.

She's never been great at keeping a secret or hiding her emotions. She's making an attempt, and I commend her valiant effort, but everything she feels is written all over her face. It's easy to read, like a children's book.

"Sure, bruja." I kiss her temple.

I'm trying to keep my cool and not behave like a lunatic, but the muscles in my face are beginning to twitch.

"You're freaking me out," she whispers. "Why does your face look like that?"

What does she expect from me?

The woman I love is going to tell me she loves me back. I would say, given the circumstances, I am handling myself wonderfully.

"No reason." I reach into my pocket. "Here. Chocolate. Eat."

She shimmies as she devours the treat, turning back to the monitor and softly humming a tune I can now identify as a One Direction song.

The video grows hazy as the sunlight fades and darkness creeps in. The floodlights flash, illuminating heavy debris in the water.

"*Oh*...Marine snow," Charlie mutters, inching closer to the screen. Jett elbows her, and she elaborates. "It's biological debris that falls from the surface. A number of deep-sea organisms rely on it as a food source, like a—"

"Holy shitballs," Jett yells as a rust-colored blob darts along the screen. "What is that *thing*?"

It hovers in the water column, tentacles fanned out as its long filament collects marine snow and zooplankton to feed. Its massive eye faces the camera, giving the illusion the creature is staring at us. It's unsettling.

"A vampire squid," Charlie yells, "but the best part is it's a faux moniker. It's not a squid at all!"

"What is it, then?" Sofía asks.

"Squids belong in the cephalopod family with octopi," I explain. "Vampire squids belong in a family of their own. They're both mollusks, though."

"And it doesn't even eat live prey. It's a detritivore," Charlie adds.

"It eats dead organic material," I translate for those in the room unfamiliar with the term, which is everyone but Charlie and me.

She's an incredible scientist, but when she's excited, she forgets other people don't understand scientific vernacular.

It hovers in the water, barely moving, and once Vivian and Lucas are happy with the footage, they leave the creature behind. Jett and Charlie chit-chat about the vampire squid, and she lists off facts. The seafloor is riddled with anemones and basket stars, and Vivian slows the ROV, capturing as much video as possible on the final dive.

I scribble down the species I recognize with the timestamps and mark anything we need to rewatch the film to identify. Charlie is lost in conversation, abandoning her duties to giggle with Sofía.

"Please," she begs, shaking Vivian's shoulders, "just for a minute. *Please*."

I'm too far away to hear Vivian's response, but I see Charlie scrunch her nose and say, "I promise not to crash."

Excitement dawns on Charlie's face as Vivian rises from her chair and lets her sit down and take control of the ROV. Her feet pitter-patter beneath the control board, and she squeals when she alters the trajectory.

"Mateo," she yells, her head swirling around until she finds me. "Get a photo."

I pull out my phone and snap a few of her guiding the ROV, then immediately make it my screensaver, selecting the one where her face is contorted with glee.

Vivian kicks her out of the chair, and Charlie returns to my side, her cinnamon and menthol scent permeating in the air.

"That was *awesome,*" she mutters, instantly wrapping her hand around my bicep like it's the most natural thing in the world.

Almost as natural as loving her.

Charlie guides me to the chairs on the far end of the deck, away from busybodies or unexpected guests. Our hands are interlaced, and I pretend not to notice her slight tremor when her grip loosens.

I could say *no need to be nervous, I've been in love with you for a long time*, but that would ruin the fun.

The corner of the deck is quiet, and Charlie's laid out blankets on a chair. When I reach the seat, she shoves me onto it with brutal force.

She's acting insane, but I don't want to ruin this for her. Anyone can see she's nervous as hell, and I know how much this moment means to her, but does she really need to catapult me into the chair?

Asking me to sit down like a good boy would work just fine.

"Enjoying the view?" I tease.

Charlie stands rigid in front of me, wringing her hands as she stares at me. She looks away momentarily, offering a side view of her face as she mumbles something to herself.

I would bet a hundred dollars she asked what Darwin would do.

Her eyes glow beneath the starlight when she turns back to face me. She unfolds a crumpled piece of paper, clearing her throat.

"I have something I would like to say, but you can't cut me off." She gives me a serious look, and the bottom edge of her scar wrinkles.

Fuck, she's hot.

This seems like an inappropriate time to sport a boner.

I know she's referring to when I cut off her last attempt at a confession, but it led to this moment, and I won't apologize for that.

"So bossy," I mutter, gnawing at my lip to fight a smile.

This is a serious moment, and no matter how adorable she looks with her crinkled paper, I'm not going to laugh.

"I used to call you Satan," she says, her voice thick with emotion. "Sometimes I'm still convinced. I mean, who wears long sleeves in the summer?" She pauses, reviewing her words, and I let her work through her thoughts. *Pot meet kettle*. "Disregard my last comment."

"Completely forgotten."

My lip twitches.

"There's something so...infuriating about the way you steal my attention, but I don't—"

"Hey, what are you guys—"

Charlie whirls, glaring at Jett, who's making his way over to us. I try to signal for him to run the fuck away, but he misses it and gains ground.

"Go away," she screams, the paper receiving the brunt force of her grip. Jett gives me a confused look but runs back down the stairs without another word. I try to cover my laugh with a cough, but it's futile.

This is the best—and worst—confession I've ever been a part of, and only weeks ago, Charlie stomped into the bathroom and told me I smell like a summer's breeze.

"This is going horribly," she grumbles.

"You're doing amazing." I reach out to smooth a hand down her thigh. Her muscles relax, and she straightens her shoulders. "Keep going."

She smooths out the paper once more.

"I would spend a lot of time thinking about you."

"That's sweet."

"Like how to assert my academic dominance and how to ensure you would have a horrible hair day." That's a lot less sweet. "I've spent *a lot* of time thinking about your hair. Big fan now."

Her confidence gains with every word, but now I have a sliver of trepidation.

"I spent a lot of time thinking about you, Mateo, but I never *saw* you. And that will always be my greatest mistake." She sniffles as she focuses on the paper. "I never knew the best thing to ever happen to me was sitting across from me every day, leaving me chocolate and humming songs."

She drops onto the edge of the chair and takes my head between her hands, tears streaming down her face. The monologue she wrote is forgotten, and the moment shifts into something tender.

Tears burn at the corners of my eyes as her thumbs trace my cheekbones.

"You are a wonderful man," she says, banishing a tear that falls. "Charming. Kind. Supportive. You make me feel seen and understood, and these last three weeks with you have been the best of my life. I am wonderfully lucky to call you mine."

Tears stream down both our cheeks. I never expected to cry, but hearing her words, feeling her touch on my skin...it's all too overwhelming.

I reach out to hold her, but she steps back.

"I have more I want to say." My heart skips a few beats at her radiance. "Being with you has made me a better person. Someone I'm proud to look at in the mirror. I'm not perfect. I'm messy and competitive, and I'm still learning to appreciate who I am, but I want to experience life with you. I want the ups and downs. I want to wake up with your CPAP hose plastered to my back and spend quiet mornings drinking coffee together.

"It's crazy, but I've never been so sure about something in my life. I'm in love with you. Amy once told me that falling in love is an act of blind faith. But you made it so easy to fall, because I knew you would be there to catch me. I could spend the next forty years as a scientist, but you will always be my greatest discovery. My most important find. My *purpose*."

I've never been overwhelmed to the point of tears, but if anyone could manage the feat, it would be my Charlie.

She squishes my face. "These are happy tears, right?"

I'm staring at her like an idiot, but what the fuck?

That was the most beautiful declaration of love I've ever heard—it brought me to tears, for fuck's sake—and now I'm expected to top it?

My "I love you" is going to sound super freaking lame compared to her "you're my greatest discovery."

She's not the only competitive one in this relationship, and the only reason I was letting her say it first was because I planned to stun her with my words of love and adoration.

Now I'm the chump who has to follow up her heartfelt, authentic admission.

How the hell am I supposed to make her feel as loved as I do right now?

Chapter 34

CHARLIE

Oh, Neptune.

I did it.

I told Mateo I love him.

And he's yet to say a single word.

If he wasn't clutching on to me like I'm the most precious thing in the world, I would feel sick to my stomach, but his gentle touch is settling any fear in taking the leap of faith.

Perched on his lap, I run my fingers through his hair. The cool sea breeze sends goose bumps along my flesh, and I burrow deeper into his chest, savoring his warmth.

Now would be a good time for him to say something. I'm pretty sure he loves me—I can feel it in my chest when he looks at me—but I'd like to hear the words, revel in the way they wash over my skin like a balm, healing everything I thought was once broken.

"You can speak now," I whisper, in case he thinks I have more to say.

I've said all I can right now. Maybe more will come to mind later, but it took me two hours to put together the small confession. I'm not a great speaker, and I am even worse at expressing emotions in a logical manner, so I'm tapped out.

His mouth opens, then closes, and his grip on my sundress tightens.

"I've spent the last two years falling in love with you," he says in a thick voice. "Only I didn't realize the depth of what I feel for you until you gave me the final piece. Like you amass trinkets, I've been collecting the small pieces of yourself you offer. An addiction to chocolate. An obsession with crystals and Charles Darwin. A brilliant mind and an even sharper tongue. The queen of trivia and proud owner of an alien dildo."

"It's a normal penis," I grumble.

His laughter strikes my solar plexus. "But when you let me see behind the wall—trusted me with your fears and worries—that's when I knew I was a goner." My hands shake from his confession, reality setting in. "Te amo, bruja. I love you. Deeply. Unconditionally. It transcends logic or reason, time and space. There is no fear you could show me, or insecurity you could whisper, that would change how I feel."

The smile on his face shines like moonlight against the water, and my heart is so full it could burst out of my chest. I pour every emotion I couldn't quite place or put words to into a gentle kiss. The sundress I borrowed from Sofía billows as I shift on his lap, straddling his hips to deepen the connection.

"I love you. I love you. I love you." I chant the declaration—full of promise and hope—until my voice is hoarse and he's cutting me off with another kiss.

There's this throbbing in my chest, a small kernel of heat lodged in my diaphragm. It flares when Mateo enters a room or calls me bruja.

I've sat on the feeling, trying to uncover every intricate layer, but I don't think it's something meant to understand, at least not fully. Love is meant to be felt. It is meant to be given and received without judgment or forced reciprocity.

Before Mateo, love was obligatory. Amy loves me because we're best friends; my family loves me because we're related. It's never felt like someone loved me simply because they could, and I had never *fallen* in love with somebody. Uncovered small pieces of a person until they became a work of patchwork art.

There's so much I still don't know, like how he celebrates holidays or if he has any superstitions. If it was possible, I would enter his mind through his nose and go on an expedition like Charles Darwin, learning and uncovering everything unknown to me. Like Osmosis Jones, minus the evil bacteria.

I'm not convinced I'm not insane for telling a man I'm in love with him after only a few weeks, but there's a fine line between love and hate, and I've walked the line for so long it was an easy push.

His fingers are in my hair, tangled in the strands, as he works down my neck, peppering kisses against my skin, pausing to nip at my small scar.

"Say it again," he demands, his grip tightening around my hair until the column of my throat is exposed.

"Won't it get old if I say it too much?" I tease, grinding my hips against his dick, which is begging for freedom.

"Never."

"I love you."

The words give meaning to the sensation in my chest. There's another living presence lodged there, right beside my heart. It's where Mateo has taken root in my soul.

He pounces the moment the words are out, and the kiss is primal—it's overflowing with emotion, with words unsaid, but I understand every one, like a secret language between only us.

"I need you," he whimpers, and *holy fuck,* I don't think I'll ever hear anything hotter than Mateo begging. His hand slips under the dress and between my thighs, dragging a finger along my soaked panties. "So wet for me."

"*Mateo.*"

He pushes the thin fabric to the side, plunging a finger inside me, and a loud moan tumbles from my lips.

"You need to be quiet, bruja, or we're going to get caught."

It's that comment that clears the haze enough to recognize that anyone could walk up the stairs to the top deck and catch us. A tingle travels down my spine, my core clenching.

"Oh, that excites you," he murmurs, adding another finger as he increases his pace.

I scramble at his belt and zipper, tugging at his belt loops so he lifts his hips. I slide his pants down just enough to free his erection.

There's no lead up as I reposition myself over his lap and guide him until his tip is pressing against me. He slips inside me easily, stretching me until I'm fully seated and have to take a moment to breathe. His hips thrust upward, and I have to bite down on his shoulder to suppress the small scream that wants to escape.

The angle is glorious, but his pace is tortuous—slow, deep thrusts, both too much and not enough.

"*More,*" I demand. His chuckle is sinful, and his movements stop. "That's the opposite of what I asked," I growl.

I'm on the precipice of a mind-blowing orgasm; this is not the time to stop.

"If you want it, take it, bruja."

He leans back on the deck chair, his arms folded behind his head and a mirthful smile on his lips. His pupils are blown, hair unruly. Mateo looks undone, and it only pushes me closer to the edge.

I sway my hips, back and forth, palms pressed against his thighs for leverage as I take what I want, and he watches like I'm the center of the universe—his point of gravity.

"You're so beautiful," he praises. "Look how you take my cock so well."

He sits forward to lift the hem of my dress, guiding my gaze to where we meet. His finger brushes against my clit, and I nearly levitate from the sudden zap of pleasure. His touch is feather soft, and I begin to unravel, my movements choppy, breath labored.

"O-oh, *fuck*."

Stars flicker across my vision as he pistons into me.

"Come for me, bruja."

The demand sends me over the edge, and I tumble into oblivion, riding the wave of ecstasy as far as I can. He continues to move inside me, his thrusts shallow and uneven as I tighten around him. He releases a shuddered breath before his head falls against my chest and he erupts into his own orgasm.

Labored breaths mix with the sounds of the waves crashing into the side of the vessel.

Mateo's erection softens, and he pulls out, cleaning the both of us up the best he can before sliding my underwear back into place and pulling me against his chest.

His heartbeat pounds beneath my ear—a heavy drum with a steady beat.

"I love you, Charlie."

His words are a declaration, but they're also a balm over un-healed wounds.

When you have days where it's hard to admire yourself, it feels impossible to believe someone else could desire what you find lacking. How could anyone love me if I don't feel that way about myself?

That's what everyone says. You need to learn to accept yourself before you can offer or accept love from someone else. While I believe there's a sliver of truth in the phrase—it's important to grow, to accept who you are, and find pride in yourself—I think they're missing one crucial piece: It's easier to believe in something when someone else also shares the belief. To have someone in your corner who says "I'll love every part you're still learning to accept, and I'll hold your hand while you work through it."

I'm not healed—far from it—but I know I wouldn't be on the deck of a research vessel confessing my feelings if it wasn't for Mateo's unwavering confidence in me. I've stood on my own for a long time, learned how to operate in a world where I felt judged and examined, but in doing so, I lost pieces of myself along the way.

Over time, I regained a few, clawed and hustled for each one, but I was far from whole. I stopped hiding inside the house, but I was still hiding from the world. Covering my scars with clothing. Avoiding social interactions. Missing two years of flirtatious cues because I struggled to believe anyone could see who I am and decide what they saw was worthy.

The things I love most about you have nothing to do with your beauty.

His words have played in my mind every time I look in the mirror and question what reflects back. It's knowing what he loves about me—wait a damn minute.

"Mateo?"

He hums, his thumb stroking against my thigh.

"When you found me crying after the comments on the video, what did you say to me?"

"That I wanted you to ride my cock?" There's both a furrow between his brow and a subtle, cocky smile on his lips, like he's confused by the question but proud of past Mateo.

"No," I say, trying to fight a blush, "the other thing."

"That the things I love most about you have nothing to do with your beauty?" I nod, and he adds, "I do think you're beautiful. Is that what you're getting at?"

Ugh. Dense man.

I wanted one thing. And it was to tell Mateo I love him first, and he still inadvertently managed to beat me to it. I want to laugh at the irony of it; I used to despise him because he always beat me, whether it was a better grade or a more prestigious paper submission, and here I am, once again beaten to the punch. It's hard to be annoyed by it this time, though.

"Say the first half of that again."

"The things I love most about you...Oh, *Dios*."

His smile slips, before it blossoms into something extraordinary—a rare thing of astonishing beauty. His laugh is like melted honey, sweet and warm, as his head tips forward and a soft kiss is placed on my temple.

"I've never been able to keep my faculties around you. Hell, the first time we met I got so flustered by you, I tripped and spilled my wine all over your dress."

I scramble to lean back so I can see his face. "What?"

He's silent—contemplative—and his finger runs along my scar. Every time he touches it with such reverence, like now, it's hard to keep the tears away. I'm not sure I'll ever get comfortable with how openly he admires it.

"You were laughing with Cheryl when I was walking over to introduce myself, but when you spun to look at me, I was so shocked by your beauty, I faltered a step, which caused me to trip and spill my wine all over you." He sighs deeply. "I felt so bad, but I couldn't get my tongue to work—didn't know what to say to you—so I panicked and ran away."

When I reminisce about the day we met, it was always clouded by my annoyance at a lost dress and the embarrassment of being in the center of a scene when I wanted so badly to stay on the outskirts of a crowd. But beyond it all, he intrigued me, too.

Instead of leaning into the pull, I ran far away and put up as many mental shields as possible.

He's stuck with me now, so I can admit the one thing I haven't said out loud, not even to Amy, and barely allowed myself to ponder since we met—in fear I would never stop thinking about it. "I thought you were *hot as fuck*."

He laughs, a confident smirk taking over his features. Can't have him get a big head, though, so I add, "And then I wanted to melt you with my laser eyes."

Mateo drags me back into him, his chest rumbling with laughter as he locks me in a tight embrace.

"Forever," he says with unquestionable conviction. "You can disintegrate me with your lasers forever, as long as I'm the only one being melted."

"How romantic," I tease, but the truth of it is, I couldn't imagine looking at anyone else.

And now I'll never be able to.

He's the one thing I never expected to uncover, but he'll forever be my greatest discovery.

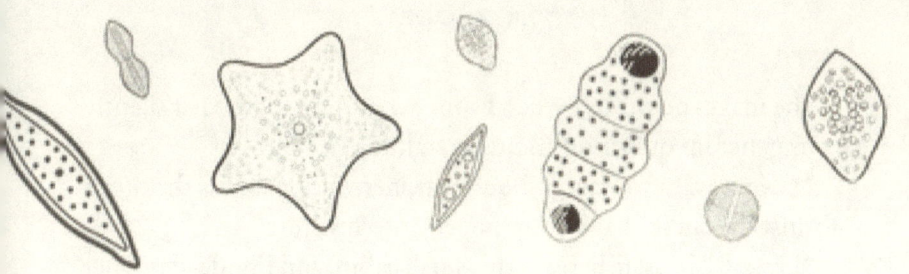

Chapter 35

MATEO

"Do you have everything?" I ask, doing one last check of the closet and bathroom of the cabin we called home for the last three weeks.

Charlie gingerly places Charles Darwin on the top of her duffel bag before protecting him with clothing. She woke up like she does most mornings—quietly. But it's a different quiet. Not a silence required to fully wake from a deep slumber, but a silence created from heavy noise inside her head.

Three weeks flew by, and for Charlie, it's a hard goodbye—to the people she met and grew to love and to the woman she was believed to be when she embarked on the vessel.

She's blossomed in this environment, one full of friendship and new memories, which makes it hard to leave.

I would be remiss to say I want to leave this small bubble, where she belongs to me alone. But this isn't reality, and as much as I've cherished every memory made, there are millions more to be made off the boat.

"Bruja?" I place a hand on her shoulder, which shakes beneath my palm.

She makes no protest when I spin her around to find her silently crying, her lip quivering and tears staining her cheeks.

"I don't want to leave," she admits, her voice shaky as she drops against my chest, digging her fingers into my shirt.

"I know." It's safe here, in this small cabin, and I understand her hesitance, but there's beauty in the unknown. "But the world is waiting."

Charlie sniffles a few times before retreating and wiping the tears from her cheeks. She finishes packing her bag, paying special attention to her bobbles, and takes a deep breath before moving to the door.

I hike her duffel bag over my shoulder before she can protest, then take in one last look at the room that changed my life.

The bathroom where Charlie confessed her feelings. The bed we slept in every night. Laughter and tears, heart-wrenching confessions and whispered secrets.

It all started right here.

The click of the lock feels like the end of a chapter.

Charlie's hand snakes down my arm from where she's holding my bicep to interlace our fingers. I give her palm a squeeze—are assuring gesture as we walk to the galley for the last breakfast before disembarking.

"I'm sad," she says as we move through the ship, "but grateful for all of it. For you, and Jett, and Sofía and Vivian." She stops and nibbles on her lip before she timidly adds, "I'll never forget this trip, because I got to fall in love with you."

Warmth flares across my body, and I steal another kiss—her lips plush against mine.

"I love sappy Charlie," I joke, kissing the frown that forms. "But it's the same for me, bruja."

"You'll never meet her again," she grumbles.

"Love you," I whisper, saying it simply because I can.

It will never grow old.

She rolls her eyes, batting my stomach, but blushes all the same, a coral hue spreading to the tips of her ears.

The chatter is loud in the galley, most of the crew eating before they finish the final work needed to dock the ship. Charlie scans the room, landing on Sofía and Vivian, and her tears begin again.

She's not the only one fighting the emotion as the three fall into an odd embrace, quiet words exchanged between them.

So much for never seeing sappy Charlie again.

I offer her privacy and drop our duffels in the corner before making us coffee. Jett appears out of nowhere, startling me as I pour a third shot into her latte.

How she's not bouncing off the walls with this amount of caffeine is truly astonishing.

"This is for you," he says, shoving a manila envelope toward me.

I gesture at the coffee in both hands, and he nods emphatically, following me to an empty table with enough space for all our friends.

Shaun nods as we pass, and I offer one of my own. A small kernel of smug pride flares knowing I got the girl.

"What is it?" I ask, picking up the folder with an air of caution.

"Open it," he prods. "Ain't nothin' gonna jump out and bite ya."

I'm not so sure, but I peel back the envelope to find a handful of papers and a USB.

"The paperwork lays out your percent of the profit from the videos I made while on the boat," he explains. "You and Blondie will each get ten percent of the revenue from each video you were in. As horrible as the comments were, Charlie's video did well."

He points out a figure, and the number of zeros beside her name is astonishing.

"This wasn't part of the contract," I say, slightly dazed as I stare at the five-figure number beside my name.

"I know, but you guys made this experience special, and you deserve pay for your work." He's more serious than I've seen him when he picks up the USB. "But this is truly special. Doug and I put it together last night."

"What is it?"

"Your love story. All caught on tape." My stomach drops. "We parsed through the B-roll, and it was right there—evidence of two people clumsily falling in love." He drops the USB into my shaking palm. "I cried when I watched the final cut. You and Charlie have a beautiful love story."

His features turn somber, contemplative, before his focus flickers to the women on the other side of the room, huddled around the pastry tray. He lingers on Sofía, before he shakes his head and plasters on a plastic smile.

"Thank you," I say, though the words don't feel like enough. "For all of it. Approving two graduate students to advise you. For pushing me to go for what I wanted. For being a good friend."

I didn't expect to grow so close to Jett on the trip, but he's surprised me with his humor, kindness, and outlook on life.

"Just invite me to the wedding, okay?" He laughs, but I nod.

He can stand right beside me as Charlie walks down the aisle if she decides to privilege me with a lifelong commitment like marriage.

We'll probably start with smaller steps, like meeting each other's families, but it's a goal—getting her in a white dress and walking down the aisle.

One day, she'll be mine forever—legally binding, of course.

Charlie lingers at the front entrance of her apartment building, her hands twitching as she glances between the building and me. She's working herself up to ask something, and I'm not going to push her.

"I was...well, I thought maybe—" She stops, adorably nervous. This is new and unexplored outside of our bubble, so I understand the nerves, but clearly she still doesn't realize how loopy I am for her. I would follow her anywhere.

"Yes, bruja?"

I take a step, closing the space between us and claiming her mouth until she's melting into me while I steal the small little moans she makes.

She's flushed and a bit disheveled when we part, but her smile illuminates her face, and joy peeks through the cracks of her earlier melancholy.

"It's weird," I admit, "returning to the real world. But we'll find a way to weave our lives together." Her cheeks flush a rosy hue. "There's no rush or timeline."

Her shoulders relax.

"Did you want to come up?" she asks, breathless. "I think my room is messy, but—"

"Yes."

There's nothing I want more than to see Charlie's cave, which is no doubt full of crystals and knickknacks. I wasn't sure how she would feel today—with the tough goodbye and plane flight home—but my girl is a champ and slept most of the flight, her hand tightly holding mine.

Charlie drags me into the apartment building, and the moment she unlocks the door, a blur of hot-pink hair tackles her, nearly taking her to the ground.

They slam into my chest instead, and it takes all my strength to remain standing as Charlie and Amy reunite, yelling over each other as they try to say everything they couldn't over the past three weeks.

A goofy grin spreads across my face as I watch Charlie wiggle and squeal, laugh and huff. We're still standing halfway in the entry, and I usher the two into the apartment.

Dozens of colorful throw pillows decorate an old couch, and the furniture is all mismatched, but it's homey—a mosaic of Amy and Charlie. Photos of them pepper the walls beside old posters of boy bands and musicians. There's a shrine to Charles Darwin—naturally—and candles everywhere, illuminating the space in soft light.

It's exactly what I pictured: slightly messy and overflowing with love.

I'm chopped liver—completely ignored—as I drop our bags in an empty corner and walk around the room, waiting for them to grace me with their attention.

The girls have migrated to the couch, and I'm waist deep in the fridge, searching for a snack, when I hear a loud gasp, followed by a squeal, and then one final gasp.

"You told him first instead of me?" There's a heavy pause. "Yeah, I heard it. That was insane."

"I kinda had to," Charlie murmurs back. My head is still deep in the fridge as I eavesdrop when Charlie adds, "It was epic, Ames. I had this whole speech, and it was under the stars."

I snort into the almond milk.

It *was* epic.

"...and then he slipped my panties—"

And that is enough sharing for the moment—at least when I'm around. I'm not stupid; I know those two share everything with each other, but I prefer not to hear it.

"Jett gave me something," I say, startling them both, and drop beside Charlie, who instantly leans into my side.

"Oh. My. God," Amy screams. "She's cuddling. Don't fucking move." She scrambles around. "Don't move," she wails, grabbing her phone and shoving it in Charlie's face like a mom at a dance recital.

She doesn't stop until Charlie is physically pushing the phone away, her iconic glare at full force. I kiss the glare—because I can—and Amy starts up again, the clicking sound filling the air alongside her laughter.

"What did Jett give you?" Charlie asks, whacking Amy as she sits back down.

I slip the hard drive from my pocket, twirling it through my fingers. I had contemplated watching it while Charlie slept since it was burning a hole in my pocket, but it felt wrong to watch it without her.

If Jett says it's our love story, it's only fair we watch it together. With Amy, too.

I fish out my laptop from my luggage and plug the USB into the computer, and Jett's face immediately pops onto the screen.

"Blondie! I miss you already." He winks on the screen, and Charlie laughs, drawing deeper against my side. "I made this special, just for you and Mateo. Love is found in the most unexpected of places, and Doug was able to capture it all on film. I'll see you guys again soon."

"Mateo..."

Charlie's nerves ruminate, and I squeeze her thigh.

Music starts to play—a slow, soft song.

It begins with a video of Charlie and I boarding the boat, her yelling at me to be careful with her bag and its precious cargo, a.k.a her bobblehead and crystals. I'm wearing a lovestruck grin the whole time. The film switches to all of us playing Catan, Charlie staring at me from across the table. The camera bobs back and forth between us before it turns around and Doug says into the lens, "I can *feel* the sexual tension."

"I told you the tension was off the charts," Amy exclaims.

The video continues, and my chest pounds as every moment between us plays out; a memory to keep forever.

Lingering glances.

Subtle touches.

Stolen kisses.

There's video footage of Charlie victory dancing after she beat me in go-fish, and quiet moments shared in the lab, working shoulder to shoulder. Mornings spent on our computers, surrounded by chocolate wrappers. Doug captured us lying beneath the stars, our makeshift picnic spread out across the deck.

By the end of it, Amy is sobbing, her arms wrapped around Charlie and me. Amy rattles on and on about how beautiful it is and how amazing love can be, and Charlie clicks her tongue.

I squeeze her thigh again, and a smile blooms, warming my chest like a steaming bowl of my abuela's pozole on a frigid night.

The video plays on—a montage of every time a piece of my heart became hers.

It's the evolution of love.

CHAPTER 36

CHARLIE

If I hadn't already told Mateo I love him, I would do it right now.

He extends me an iced latte and falls into the chair beside mine, across from Cheryl's desk. His hand lands on my thigh—a comforting touch—as our advisors watch us with hyper focus.

We're meant to debrief them about the trip, but Cheryl won't stop smiling or staring at Mateo and me like a lunatic.

She's a wonderful advisor, but she's starting to give me the creeps.

It's taking everything I have not to fidget or grab on to Mateo's hand like it's a lifeline. Dan sits back in his chair, unbothered or unaware by the odd energy in the room; I'm unsure which, but I wish I could be him.

Unbothered, sipping on his coffee, legs kicked back.

I'm teetering on the edge.

Finally—under immense pressure—I crack and dart my hand above the desk, grab Mateo's, and then rip our hands into my lap. His finger swipes against the back of my hand, and the energy buzzing in my chest immediately calms.

"*Yes*," Cheryl screams, leaping from her chair to peer over the desk and into my lap, where I'm holding on to Mateo for dear life.

I used to suffer the anxiety of these meetings alone, with only my notebook and crystals to keep me safe and guide me away from throttling Mateo. I could still throttle him if I wanted, but I'd rather hold his hand and live a princess life while he carries all my things.

That's not something I expected to enjoy, but not having to hold anything leaves my hands open to explore—pick up rocks, steal snacks from Mateo's desk, squeeze his ass when he's least expecting.

I could get used to domestic life.

"I told you, Dan," Cheryl yells, shockingly accusatory. "What did I say?"

"They're meant for each other, they only need a little shove," Dan responds in a monotone voice.

"Uh...What?" Mateo asks.

He's adorably befuddled, and while I'm usually the one behind on picking up the cues, this one is loud and clear.

I glare at my advisor, who smiles brightly, as if she submitted a paper to *Nature* and it was accepted without revisions.

"They were scheming," I explain to my confused boyfriend. "We were their test subjects." I turn to Cheryl. "How long?"

She knows exactly what I mean.

"Oh, a few months into your program. Caught you ogling him while his back was turned. Then I watched him do the same. Been trying to shove you two together since."

"Why do you think I agreed to Mateo's pestering about holding joint meetings?" Dan asks.

"Because you guys love being with each other?" Mateo offers.

Cheryl cackles like that was the most insane thing he's ever said. She's an icon.

"Oh, honey, no. I see him plenty at home." She barrels over Dan's guffaws and continues, "We did it so you two had to spend time together because it wasn't going to happen otherwise."

Now she's looking at me, giving me a knowing look. Mateo's hand is still in my lap, and he's finally caught up, which mean she's starting to laugh—loudly.

"So you two are dating, right?" Dan asks.

Mateo peers down at me, love radiating from him as his hand squeezes mine. He's giving me an option to tell them or to evade, not that our hand-holding isn't evidence enough.

If I shook my head, he would honor the decision. But I know it would kill him—the thought he isn't worthy of the declaration, or that I'm still unsure about us.

I've never been more confident about something in my life.

My features are granite as I turn to Cheryl.

"You know what they say." I shrug. "It's an easy evolution from hate to love."

"Love?" she shrieks, her face red with excitement.

"It was hard *not* to fall in love with him."

I'm staring directly at him when the words escape my lips. If I could only accomplish one thing in life, it would be loving Mateo in the way he deserves—freely, fully, without reservations.

I want him to feel as loved as I do, as cherished as I am.

He helped me find my shine again, and while there's still so much work I need to do—process my trauma and build my-self-confidence—it's easier to face those battles knowing he'll be right there, holding my hand and giving me a shove when I need it.

When I need a shoulder, he's there, but I want to be his shoulder, too. Take care of him when he has headaches in the morning and make him soup when he's sick. Cheer him on in his achievements and pick him up when he fails. I want to end the night in bed, quietly watching videos and appreciating the time we get together.

He winks, and my cheeks flush.

I'm never going to get used to how beautiful he is.

"Charlie decided hating me was a useless endeavor and fell in love with my intellect and charm," he teases.

Cheryl and Dan laugh when I knock his shoulder with mine.

They offer congratulations, which seems excessive, but we thank them anyway, before the meeting shifts toward its true purpose.

Mateo debriefs them about the trip, explaining what samples we collected, how many were processed in the lab, and how many are being shipped to the university. We give them the list of species we couldn't identify or wanted second opinions about, then show them the video footage of the whale fall I convinced Vivian to steal for me.

It's the highlight of the meeting—outside of me admitting I fell in love with Mateo—and we spend nearly an hour pausing clips to nerd out about the organisms scavenging the whale carcass. This is what I was hoping for on the boat, but everyone got weirded out by the mention of bone-eating worms, and the vibe died.

The vibe is back, baby.

We discuss less exciting things—manuscript edits and the biology labs Mateo and I run—before they send us on our way, another round of congratulations filtering through the hallway. We're halfway back to our desks when Mateo snatches my hand and changes course.

He peeks his head into his lab, looking left and right, before pulling me over the threshold and slamming the door shut behind us.

A question sits on the tip of my tongue, like *What the hell has gotten into you?* But it's silenced as Mateo lifts me off the ground and onto the lab bench.

"I've always wanted to do this," he admits.

"Sit me on the lab bench?" I ask. "This has to be against safety protocol."

"No," he responds. The curve of his mouth is sinful as he says, "Kiss the shit out of you in the lab."

His lips are on mine before I can remind him we made out on the boat, in almost this exact position. I melt into him, the world fading away as his fingers trail up the back of my neck and tangle into my hair.

The kiss is unhurried as he explores my mouth.

When he finally pulls away, I'm practically panting.

"So, did it meet your expectations?" I tease.

His tongue darts out, tracing the seam of his lips. "Exceeded expectations. But that shouldn't surprise me with you." His thumb pulls down my bottom lip. "Everything you do is remarkable."

A blush creeps onto my cheeks, and he chuckles, helping me down from the benchtop. I'm wobbly on my feet thanks to the kiss and his proximity, but if three weeks crowded in a small cabin wasn't enough to kill the butterflies every time he passes by, then I fear it's going to be a lifelong sensation.

"I'm kinda excited to get back to normal," he admits, holding my hand as we return to the PhD room.

Based on the odd looks some of the other graduate students are giving us, I wouldn't say we're back to normal. It was common knowledge I wasn't Mateo's biggest fan, and now we're holding hands and I'm smiling like a lovestruck idiot.

The urge to yell, *No, he isn't holding me hostage—unless you consider being dick-whipped a form of glorious torture. He simply convinced me to fall in love with him. Shocking, I know. Let's all move along,* is nearly overwhelming, but I'm not in the mood for a speech this morning, so I make prolonged, uncomfortable eye contact with every other person until they look away.

Mateo is blissfully unaware of the people staring, and while the instinct to shy away from them still lingers, it's not an incessant voice in my head.

It's quiet with him, and one day, I'll learn to silence it on my own.

He sits down at his desk, and it's like every other day. He starts to hum a tune—this time it's One Direction, which warms my heart. He's listening to the playlist I made him. The sound of shuffled papers and tapping on keyboards fills the space, and I should start working, but I can't stop staring at him.

Perfect chocolate-brown hair, swept back like it takes no effort at all. I've learned it takes two hair products and at least ten minutes of rearranging the strands. Coy dimples and cocky smirks. Broad shoulders and hidden tattoos.

He leans to the right to hide behind his monitor.

"I can't work if you keep staring at me," he says, laughter lacing his voice. My nose scrunches. "Stop frowning, bruja, and get to work."

"You can't even see me," I grumble, opening my laptop to work on the lab protocols.

"Don't need to." His head darts back into view, and he offers me a beaming smile and then chucks a chocolate at my head.

It hits my forehead before dropping to the desk.

I stare at him, stunned.

Guess I didn't need to spend the morning worrying about our new normal and if working across from each other would be weird. Luckily, Mateo is reestablishing the status quo: he annoys me and feeds me chocolate, and I have to pretend his smile doesn't send vibrations to my vagina.

It really is another average, pre-voyage day.

The wrapper is open and the chocolate is devoured before I respond. "You'll pay for that later."

He winks. "I hope so."

He returns to his work, and I focus on mine, but every so often, he flutters into my thoughts, even though he's a foot away. I'm still evolving—learning to admire myself, to trust in myself and others, let go of the trauma that holds me back—but he gives me faith I can tackle everything in my path.

I've always held a lot of weight in luck and the universe, in Charles Darwin and the theory of evolution. In crystals and astrology. All of these things have brought me peace when life is heavy, but they all pale in comparison to the kind I've found with him.

The research cruise gave me so many things: new friends, a revitalized sense of self, and once-in-a-lifetime memories. But most of all, it led me to Mateo.

I can visualize the life we'll build together. Completing our PhDs and starting postdoc positions. Traveling the world. Growing together, but discovering who we are individually. An intimate wedding with our friends and family. A home with a large study and two wooden desks facing each other. Children, if we both want them.

The dream is so vivid, I could reach out and hold it in my palm. It will require work and sacrifice, and the path may not be smooth, but if Mateo is by my side, I'd walk any road with him.

He hums a new song, and my heart bursts.

I'm not sure I would have ever uncovered what was right in front of me, but as Mateo peeks around his computer to wink at me, I know, beyond a shadow of a doubt, falling in love with Mateo was the greatest discovery of all time.

EPILOGUE

CHARLIE

Three year later...

"It's time to wake up, bruja."

The ornate blood-red curtains blocking the abrasive morning sunlight are ripped back, and I scramble beneath the covers, hiding like a vampire burned in the daylight.

Truthfully, I've been up for the last half hour, but I like when Mateo drags me from the bed, pats me on the butt, and tells me it's time to get ready for the day.

He's like a personal butler, with sexy hair and a sinful smile.

The covers rustle, and the edge is pulled back to expose the top of my head. I'm blessed with a glorious smile before he leans down and presses a kiss to my forehead.

I've grown greedy. I know it. Mateo knows it. Hell, I think the whole world knows it. I love when he wakes me up in the morning, and when he stopped for a few days early on in our relationship, I may not have taken it well. There may have been tears and questions whether he was upset with me.

"Good morning," I whisper.

The bright light filters into the upscale hotel room Mateo booked for our graduation trip. It's exactly what I expected for a hotel room in London. Ornate gold details and historical wooden furniture. A massive four-poster bed sits in the center of the room, with plush linen sheets and a deep-red bench in front.

The sheets are heavy and expensive—I could spend forever here—but Mateo flips back the covers and pulls me out of bed and into a chaste kiss. It deepens until I'm pressed against him, but he separates and corrals me into the bathroom.

When I'm done, he's hovering by the door, waiting to usher me back to the bed.

He's acting strange.

"You're being weird..."

"No I'm not." The left corner of his mouth twitches. It's his tell when he's lying. Over three years together, and I know everything there is to know about Mateo. How he likes his eggs. How he celebrates holidays. I even know when to avoid the bathroom.

I've shared every secret I have with him. He's held my hand in therapy as I worked through my trauma from the car accident, and carried all the things I couldn't at the time. And when I was ready, he kept his promise, and we let go of them together. On mornings my joints ache, he's there with the balm, and on nights where sleep evades me, he's ready to pull me closer.

He holds every single piece of me in the palm of his hands—the good, bad, and ugly—and he keeps them safe.

Mateo is a good, kind man, and he's continued to prove it every day.

We're staring at each other in a state of silence before he breaks it with a wobbly smile.

"I got something for you."

He pushes me onto the bench, and while he digs through his suitcase, I admire his ass. He turns around, a small box in his hands, wrapped in bright-pink wrapping paper and a white sparkly bow.

The gift has Amy's name written all over it.

He hands it over, shifting on his feet. I untie the large bow, and beneath the knot, written with Sharpie on the paper, it says, "Mateo did not wrap this. I did. Love, Amy."

I laugh softly to myself and peel away the decorative wrapping and open the box. I inhale a sharp gasp. A beautiful white sundress, covered in small tropical fish, lies within the garment box.

I'm afraid to touch the dress or dirty it in any way, but Mateo lifts it out of the box by the thin straps and displays it for me.

"Amy made sure I got the right size, but I wanted something special for you to wear today."

"Why?"

We only landed in London yesterday. I still have jet lag, and I planned on finding the first place that sold a sausage roll and gorging myself on them until he had to carry me back to the hotel for dinner with Oliver.

"After breakfast, we have a tour scheduled."

"What? Why?"

I'm still admiring the dress, the crisscrossed straps in the back and the billowy skirt. It's beautiful and exactly what I would choose for myself. The reef fish are small and cover the dress in a way that's both youthful and sophisticated.

Mateo tips up my chin. My core clenches whenever he looks at me like this—like I'm the sun and the center of his universe—but the feeling is replaced with disbelief when he says, "Today, you're going to meet your idol."

"No..." I think I'm going to faint. My heart thumps erratically as the room spins. I fall onto the bed.

"Our private tour starts at eleven. Oliver pulled some strings for us."

I finally find the nerve to look at him, and he's watching me nervously.

"You're going to see Charles Darwin's grave."

I launch myself at him, nearly taking him down to the creaky wooden floors, but he catches me right before I offer him the world's sloppiest but most-thankful kiss ever. I don't dillydally too much with him, because I'm on a time crunch.

"I get to fucking meet Darwin," I scream, kissing him one more time before taking the dress.

I have no idea how I got so lucky, but I'm not questioning the universe.

Not today.

Not when I'm hours away from meeting my idol.

The verger guides us through the airy hallways of Westminster Abbey, and as expected, the massive church is gorgeous and brimming with history. Tombs of royalty and grand minds. Stained glass windows and intricate art along the walls. Cloisters brightened by summer light.

It's beautiful and quiet, and as wonderful as the tour has been so far, I'm jumping out of my shoes as we get closer to where Darwin is entombed.

The final resting place of an incredible mind.

We round the corner, and Mateo squeezes my hand as we're guided into the north aisle of the nave. The verger stops, and his long black robe billows. On the ground, a large slab of slate-gray marble reads "Charles Robert Darwin."

Mateo's grip on my hand is firm, which is good, because my knees give out beneath me.

I've imagined this moment a million times. Wondered what I would say or if I would ask him anything. Every word in the English language is lost on my tongue as I reread his name.

He's right beneath me. Well, his bones are. I'm sure he's entirely decomposed at this point, but the idea stands.

I'm occupying the same space as one of the greatest naturalists to ever live.

"Hi, Darwin," I croak, giving the grave an odd wave. "Can I call you Darwin, or would you prefer your full title?" Mateo chokes on his laughter, and I stop my introduction to glare at him. "Please ignore my rude boyfriend," I continue, "he doesn't understand the importance of this moment."

"I'm Mateo," he says, stepping forward to greet the grave.

I can feel the odd looks from the verger and the other people in the church, but I've waited a lifetime for this moment, and I'm not wasting any mind power on people staring at me.

Yes, I'm talking to a grave. People do it all the time. Let's move along.

There's a bouquet of flowers sitting above his name, and I crouch down to place a small aquamarine stone beside them. When I pondered what crystal he would carry, the one bringing intelligence and thought was my first choice.

"I'll give you a moment," Mateo says.

Before he steps back, I kiss him. "Thank you."

All other words fall short, but he nods, hearing what I don't know how to say, and leaves me with Darwin.

I let the silence sink into my bones, mentally throwing questions into the universe in hopes they'll reach him.

Do you have any regrets?

How do you feel about the state of the world?

What are your thoughts about spray cheese?

The last one is a panic question, but it's equally as important as the others. He would definitely have something insightful to add about canned cheese.

"We can go," I say, content in the memory.

"Just one more thing," Mateo says, as he kneels down, right beside the marble inscribed with Darwin's name.

"What are you doing?" I hiss, trying to pull him off the ground. "You're denigrating a sacred space."

The verger coughs to hide his laughter, but I'm not focused on him. I'm worried about my boyfriend accidentally cursing us by disrespecting Darwin and his sanctified resting place.

Instead of rising, Mateo slips a small velvet box out of his pocket. *Oh, Neptune.*

My hands immediately begin to tremble as Mateo kneels on Darwin's grave. It's damn near impossible to pull air into my lungs as he opens the box and displays the shiny ring sitting on the plush fabric.

A pear-shaped deep-blue sapphire sits atop a gold band, bracketed by smaller sapphires in varying shades of green. It's by far the most stunning ring I've ever seen. It's unique and reminds me of the sea and the moss green of his eyes in the morning light.

"Mateo?" My voice is shaky, and I clutch my purse tightly to my chest.

He clears his throat, and with the hand not holding the gorgeous ring, he reaches out and takes my left hand.

"You have been the object of my affection from the day I spilled wine all over your dress," he starts in a gruff voice. "And once I got to know you—studied every intricate detail—I knew you were it for me. You are my homeland, Charlie. Tu eres mi patria. Loving you the last three years has been the greatest honor of my life, and I'm hoping to do so for the rest of our lives, if you'll let me."

A choked sob escapes as he pulls the ring from the box and extends it toward me.

"Charlotte Luise Bowen, mi bruja, will you give me the—"

"Hurry up," a familiar voice yells.

Another adds, "We want to celebrate!"

I spin to find Amy and Oliver not-so-patiently standing at the end of the hall.

"Yes!" I scream, turning back to Mateo. "Yes, yes, a million times yes."

"I didn't get to fully ask," he mumbles as I launch at the ring. He pulls it away. "Will you marry me?"

"Yes, now put it on!" I shove my hand in his face as he rises.

The ring slips onto my finger perfectly, and I admire the jewels and how they shine in the light against the backdrop of Darwin's grave. I only have a moment before Amy collides into my back, wrapping me into a tight hug, the aroma of vanilla cupcakes perfuming the air.

"Congratulations, Charles," she says, weeping into the back of my dress.

I spin around to hug her fully, and she pulls Mateo into our embrace and cries happy tears into his shirt as well.

Mateo offers me a warm smile, and I return it, my heart thumping in my ears.

Amy releases me, and her smile falters as Oliver walks over, pulling Mateo into a hug of their own. She and Oliver exchange a look I can only describe as intense longing, mixed with sadness and resolve. I don't like the look on her face one bit.

It can't be easy for her to be here with him. *I think he'll always be my what-if.* It's all she would say after I returned from the research trip, and I never pressed. They've been cordial over the years, but the shared melancholy between them is hard to ignore.

"Will you be my maid of honor?" I ask.

Her expression instantly shifts, and the Amy I know and love returns. "I've already been planning," she admits. "I have a whole vision board hidden beneath my bed."

"So...yes?"

"Yes!"

Strong arms wrap around my shoulders, and I sink into Mateo's chest. "Let me see the ring," he whispers, goose bumps breaking out along my skin.

I lift my hand up so the ring sparkles in the light, backdropped by intricate ribbed vaulted ceilings.

"It's beautiful," I admit. "And I'm honored, too—to get to love you every day, I mean."

His lips press against my temple, and we bask in the sunlight filtering through the stained glass windows.

I always believed meeting Charles Darwin would be the greatest thing to ever happen in my life, but Mateo does love to prove me wrong.

And now he gets to do so for the remainder of our lives.

Acknowledgements

Since I could remember, I've always loved the ocean. But, perhaps "love" isn't the right word— beguiled maybe. I suppose it was only right to write a love story centered around the ocean. The deep-sea is not something I actively study, but the "alienness" of the more elusive parts of the ocean has always fascinated me. How could something on this planet seem so extraterrestrial? Obviously, those creatures are perfect for a romance novel, especially for Charlie and Mateo.

This book wouldn't exist without my parents and their unwavering support of me in the pursuit of my dreams. My staunch interest was nurtured by my family, who centered family vacations around picking up shells at the beach and snorkeling. They walked through the same aquariums dozens of time, simply because I wanted to be there. It was no surprise to them when I told them I wanted to become a marine biologist. The average salary for a marine biologist, however, was a shock. I also have to thank my grandma, who bought countless snorkels and masks after I continued to lose them in the ocean waves, and my grandmother, who cheers me on in everything I do, including moving across the world to study marine science.

There are so many other people I need to thank, so buckle up and get comfy.

Brooklyn, you saw the bones of my manuscript and helped me build something incredible. I'm extremely proud of this book, and you played a significant role in helping me get it to that point. Whether it was my overuse of commas (you can pry them from my cold dead hands) or encouraging me when I was unsure, you were pivotal. I couldn't have found a more knowledgable, kind or funny editor than you. You're stuck with me. And to immortalize it, just in case: Mateo is yours. You licked him first.

I would be remiss not to mention my incredible cover artist, Summer, who took my scribbles and insane powerpoint and turned it into a masterpiece. The cover is more than I could have ever imagined. Hell, we got the font right on the first try. That never happens, and it will likely never happen again.

Another massive thank to Sydney for the scientific illustrations in the book. Your talent continues to blow me away.

To my friends: Taylor, Darcy, Aliah, Christian, Sabrina, Emily, Jaxi, Katya, Nicole, and everyone else I've forgotten to list. You're all awesome and whether you know it or not, you helped me at some stage of writing this book. To my beta readers, thank you for taking the time to offer feedback to make sure the story is the best it can be.

I owe a humungous, ginormous, extravagant thank you to my emotional support post-doc, Emma, and the greatest hype-woman alive, Casey. From letting me pick your brain about your experience in graduate school to teaching me all about Rhode Island and URI, this book is better, and more accurate, because of you two.

To scientists everywhere, regardless of discipline, who continue to do the work despite cuts in funding, lack of government support, and the dismissal of research. Science saves lives. Full stop. Everyday, I am inspired by other scientists. Most people who pursue research do not do it for the money (spoiler alert: there isn't much) but because they love what they do, and they believe in what they're studying. While this is a romance novel, it's also a love letter to scientific discovery and how mesmerizing the natural world can be.

Finally, a special thank you to you, the reader, who picked up this STEM romance. I wouldn't be anywhere without you, and everyday I'm grateful. I hope you love Charlie and Mateo as much as I do.

ABOUT THE AUTHOR

Nicole Cubba writes romance with the belief that every person deserves a happily-ever-after and her favorite stories are ones that reflect that sentiment. Nicole works as a marine biologist and has a deep passion for the ocean and the planet. When she isn't in the lab, you can find her searching for new coffee shops, wandering in tidepools, and watching sports. She was born and raised in Michigan, but now lives in Massachusetts with her cat, Beefcake the Mighty, close to the ocean.

www.ingramcontent.com/pod-product-compliance
Lightning Source LLC
Chambersburg PA
CBHW030235120726
47903CB00005B/1490